A
Bachelor's
Travels

a novel by

F. M. Cipriano

FMC Press

A Bachelor's Travels

[ISBN 978-0-9941743-0-7]
First published 2015 by FMC Press
PO Box 13179
Law Courts VIC 8010
Australia
Copyright © F. M. Cipriano 2015
Book Cover Design: Mohit Goswami
Editor: Amanda J. Spedding
Publishing Consultant: Julie Postance

National Library of Australia Cataloguing-in-Publication entry:
Cipriano, F. M., author.
A bachelor's travels / F. M. Cipriano
ISBN: 9780994174307 (paperback)
Australian Fiction.
International Travel--Fiction.
A823.4

Disclaimer
This book is a fact based fiction.
All names used in this publication are fictitious, other than those in the public domain. All care has been taken in the preparation of the information herein, but no responsibility can be accepted by the publisher or author for any damages resulting from the misinterpretation of this work. All contact details given in this book were current at the time of publication, but are subject to change.

Published by FMC Press

www.fmcpress.com

DEDICATION

I dedicate this book to my dearly departed parents, Porzia and Giuseppe, whose dedication, responsibility and love instilled in me many things, including the perseverance to stick to a task, which greatly assisted me over the years that it took to complete this project.

TABLE OF CONTENTS

ACKNOWLEDGMENTS

I extend my appreciation to all the people from around the world who I had the pleasure in meeting and travelling with over the course of the 15 years that formed the basis for this book.

Thank you to my family and friends whose words of encouragement meant a great deal to me, particularly in my times of doubt.

Thanks to Ross Coniglione who was the first person to read and the last person to proofread my manuscript and who provided me with useful and positive feedback.

Finally, thanks in advance to the people who read this book. I hope it provides you with as much of a rewarding journey in its reading as it gave me in its writing.

ABOUT THE AUTHOR

F. M. Cipriano (Frank) was born in Melbourne, Australia. He has a Bachelor of Business, a Graduate Diploma in Accounting, and a Master of Taxation.

Frank was a career public servant where the flexibility of his work conditions allowed him to embark on extensive overseas travels, which inspired the writing of this, his first book, entitled *A Bachelor's Travels*.

Frank's greatest pleasures and life experiences emanated from his lifelong travels, and in putting these experiences in words he discovered the joy of creative writing.

Chapter 1 – Let the Travels Begin

Roland is a 27-year-old bachelor who lives with his parents. He had a carefree existence with an active social life that revolved around his mates; mates he had made over the years from school, university and work. However, his life quickly changed when, one by one, his mates got married.

With his single friends reduced to a mere few, Roland wondered whether he too should be considering marriage. Although it didn't take long to conclude that the bond of holy matrimony was not for him, and he gained solace from the comment of a workmate who often exclaimed as he got off the phone to his wife. "Don't get married and don't have kids!"

Travelling around Australia with his few remaining single friends was Roland's favourite pursuit, but this came to an abrupt end when his best friend became smitten with an attractive, young lady and was soon married.

Even though Roland had no wedding plans of his own, marriages seemed to be creating havoc with his life.

Roland gave his predicament a lot of thought and one day he pulled his parents aside. "I'll be taking eight months off work to embark on a working holiday in Europe!" he exclaimed.

His parents looked at each other with mutual expressions of consternation and after a moment his dad uttered his usual reassuring words. "Do as you wish son; it's your life."

Roland trawled through a myriad of brochures, catalogues and travel books, meticulously planning his detailed travel schedule, including setting aside a few days to meet the relatives in his parents' home country.

It wasn't long before the big day of his departure drew near.

"Do you want a lift to the airport, son?"

"No thanks, Dad; there's no need to go through all that trouble. I'd prefer to catch a taxi."

"Don't forget to set your alarm," Roland's father suggested, even though his dad always proved to be the most effective wake-up call.

In the morning, the two alarms sounded – Roland's dad followed by the alarm clock.

Roland finished packing his canvas suitcase and was ready ahead of schedule. As his departure time neared, he and his parents were perched on the side of the bed in the front room, looking out for the taxi in silence.

When the taxi arrived, Roland's mum and dad gave him a huge hug. There was a quiet moment, which was broken by Roland dad's yelling,

"Hurry up before you miss your plane!" And Roland was off.

It was midday on Sunday, 13 March 1988 when Roland set foot in the Melbourne International Airport terminal, and his mind unwittingly clicked into automatic. *Very well, let's check in. Through immigration, no hassles, that's good; they have no concerns about me leaving the country. In excess of one hour before boarding...hmm...let's do some pre-flight window shopping.*

Roland took a flurried tour of the shops, examining merchandise that took his eye, without having any intention to buy.

It was time to board and Roland joined the last remaining passengers in the queue for his 14:15 CX100 Singapore Airlines flight to Hong Kong. He took his seat and shut out the surrounding noises of rustling, idle chatter and crying babies.

The pilot started the engines and Roland took in the loud rumble reverberating around the cabin. He felt invigorated, and on take-off, he was euphoric. These sensations were very rare for this public servant and a big smile emerged that almost covered his entire face.

Roland slept comfortably, assisted by the complimentary cognac and wine, although he made sure he was awake for all the meals. He was reasonably happy with the flight, other than the mishap of having missed out on a bread roll, which peeved him off for some time.

A stopover in Hong Kong allowed for sightseeing and the obligatory shopping. After six days, Singapore Airlines flight CX201 provided his onward journey to London.

Soon after the plane touched down at London Heathrow, Roland's mind again clicked into automatic. *What are these aisles? British, European and Other; so much for being part of the Commonwealth; oh well, I'll just join the long line.*

"Next! What are you here for?" asked an official sounding, male customs agent.

"A working holiday," Roland responded automatically.

"You are on an Australian passport?"

"Yes."

The custom agent's gaze flicked robotically from the passport to Roland then back to the passport. "Do you have a Working Holiday Visa?"

"Yes."

"Do you have details of accommodation here in London?"

"Yes."

"Do you have a return ticket?"

"Yes."

"Do you have proof of funds available to you over the period of your stay in England?"

"Yes."

The passport was stamped and returned. "Go on."

Roland caught the train to Victoria Station then weaved his way through the crowd to the taxi rank. He was thrilled to take a back seat in a classic London black cab.

The cab ride through central London was clustered with historic landmarks and red double-decker buses. The city was bustling and intense, with sounds amplified to levels Roland had never previously experienced. He was so unprepared for the onslaught of attractions that he was gobsmacked.

Roland checked in at the Tavistock Hotel and he couldn't wait to go exploring. He wasn't good with his bearings so it took him a couple of attempts before he headed in the right direction for the city.

It was late Friday afternoon when Roland walked down Tottenham Court Road and along Oxford Street. The city was overflowing with people: workers on their way home, shoppers on their way in, and droves of school kids appearing everywhere. He was soon being buffeted from all directions. Overwhelmed, he decided to retreat to his hotel for some much needed repose.

Early Saturday morning, Roland set off armed with his camera and his list of attractions. Over the weekend he travelled the length and breadth of central London; from Kensington Palace to Buckingham Palace; from Big Ben to the Tower of London. He was ticking off the numerous attractions from his list as he went along.

Fatigued by his weekend activities, Roland hauled himself out of bed on Monday morning and headed off to seek longer term accommodation for the balance of his three month's stint in London.

Earl's Court was where he concentrated his efforts, as it was a popular haunt for Australians; however, he was unsuccessful in finding anything suitable so he placed his name on hostel waiting lists in the central London area.

Roland returned to Tavistock, changed into a business suit and set off to go job hunting. He visited a number of professional job agencies where they spent some time going over standard questions, although they appeared to leave out the more obvious checks.

"Don't you want to see any of my references?" Roland queried one agency.

"No, that won't be necessary at this stage," a casually-dressed young woman said in a blasé fashion.

"What about my working holiday visa?" Roland asked.

"Oh okay, I wouldn't mind having a look at that; I've not seen one of those before."

Other agencies were slightly more professional, but they were also not too encouraging. "So you're a civil servant with no experience in finance, budgeting or year-end accounts?" a recruitment agent asked.

"Well no," Roland admitted, "but I'm a qualified accountant and I'm sure I'd have no trouble undertaking those tasks."

"Yes, but you don't have any practical experience. We can place your name on our lists, although we can't promise you anything."

After a disappointing day on the job-front, Roland decided to contact a friend from university who was working in London.

"Hey Sean, it's Roland."

"Hi Rollo, how's it going?"

"I'm in London."

"London, whereabouts?"

"I'm in a hotel in central London at the moment, but I hope to get some longer term accommodation," Roland advised.

"If you have any trouble getting accommodation, you're welcome at my apartment," Sean offered.

"That's great, I'll see how I go and let you know. I'm also looking around for some accounting work, but I'm having some difficulty," Roland explained.

"To score a good job in London, you have to be prepared to bullshit."

"I can't do that, Sean."

"That doesn't surprise me, Rollo. I'll give you details of an accountancy personnel firm. You probably won't find a top-of-the-line job there, but they should be able to get you some accounting work."

"Cool, thanks. We'll have to catch up soon for a drink, eh Sean?"

"Is the Pope catholic?"

A quick visit to the accountancy personnel firm, and they seemed marginally optimistic; however, they couldn't promise anything and placed Roland's name on their list.

Roland was feeling a little down when his day was topped off with a phone call from one of the more sought-after hostels – The Court.

"I thought The Court was the hostel in most demand," Roland said.

"I guess you've been lucky," the hostel receptionist replied. "We have a place for you, as long as you are willing to share."

"Share; no problem!"

Chapter 2 – Enter The Court

There was a flurry of activity at The Court's reception. "Hi, I'm Roland and I understand you have a placement for me."

"Oh yes, you're the guy who's sharing with Tom. Fill out this form," a young lady receptionist instructed. "Here's your key. Tom's not in at the moment, but you can move into the room."

The twin-share was a very basic, small room on the second level with a communal bathroom at the end of the floor. The room was furnished with two dark oak, single beds, each with a matching cupboard. Roland's single bed was distanced from the wall, away from the double hung, cream painted, timber window and the cream coloured, cast iron heating radiator.

Returning to reception, Roland used the public phone to ring the accountancy personnel firm to advise them of his change of address.

"Fortunate you rang Roland, we have a placement for you," the recruitment agent advised. "If you can make it to our office sometime today, you should be able to start first thing Monday."

"Sure thing; thanks!" Roland replied excitedly. With long term accommodation and now a job, everything was finally falling into place.

When Roland returned to his room, he found a young man lying on the other bed. The man had light brown hair, green eyes, a cracked front tooth, and was sporting a goofy smile.

"Hi, you must be Tom," said Roland.

"Yeah and you must be Roland."

"Yeah."

"Have you heard anything about me Roland?"

Roland winced. "No why?"

"Oh, nuffin. You're Australian, aren't you?"

"Yes I am."

"There are a couple of other Australians in The Court; I can introduce you if you like?"

"Sure. That'd be great."

A young man walked past the door.

"Mike!" Tom called out.

"Yeah Tom?"

"This is a new guy at The Court. Like you, he's Australian."

"Hi Mike, I'm Roland."

"Hey Mike," said Tom, interrupting the two. "Where's Shirley?"

"Dunno, but she might be in the TV room," Mike responded.

"Come on Roland, let's check it out," cried Tom, leaping from the bed.

Tom, Mike and Roland scurried down the stairs to the basement television room where Mike introduced Roland to Shirley, a young lady from Brisbane with blue eyes and red hair.

"By the way Roland, this is Jill," said Tom.

Blonde hair, green-eyed Jill smiled at Roland. "We're going for dinner, you should join us," she said with a broad Irish accent.

Shirley, Jill, Mike and Roland headed off for dinner while Tom went to pick up his girlfriend, promising to meet the group at Chinatown.

Arriving at the Wong Key Restaurant, they climbed the stairs before they came to a halt ahead of a queue lined up between the second and third floors.

"What's the hold up?" Roland asked.

"This is the Wong Key," Mike replied. "It's got four levels of seating and it's usually packed. It must be the most popular restaurant in London."

"Gee, the food must be good," said Roland.

"No, the food's pretty average," Mike responded.

"But it's damn cheap," Shirley added.

They had advanced slightly in the queue by the time Tom arrived with his girlfriend, Suzie, a young, attractive Chinese lady. "We've got a bit of a wait," exclaimed Tom, who continued to banter with whoever was close enough and at all responsive. Suzie was also sociable, and she didn't stop smiling and laughing.

It took another half an hour before they were seated. The place was very noisy and chaotic. "Where are the bleedin' menus?" Tom shouted and the menus appeared out of nowhere. After a short respite, the waitresses were calling for orders and it wasn't too long before the food was being served.

The eating was voracious and the discussion lively. After they downed their last morsels of food, the waitresses presented the bill and were wiping down the table. They paid the bill and Tom proclaimed, "Okay, it's time for a drink!"

It was a short walk to the pub and, after a number of ales and more lively conversation, the group called it a night.

"Where are you going Roland?" Jill asked.

"To the Underground."

"We don't take the Tube at this time," informed Jill. "We take the bus."

They arrived back at The Court at around 2.00 am. Roland was exhausted and welcomed his newly acquainted bed for a good night's sleep.

Breakfast at The Court was a cafeteria-style buffet with a reasonable selection. Roland enjoyed his meal, as he did the beaming smiles of the lady servers who were from various parts of Britain and Continental Europe.

After breakfast, Shirley, Jill, Mike and Roland enjoyed a wonderful spring Sunday morning at Kensington Gardens before checking out the shopping stalls down Portobello Road. As Roland had his thoughts on his first day of work, he returned to his hotel room in the early evening to organise himself and get some shut-eye.

The following morning, Roland dressed in his conservative grey business suit and grabbed the brolley he purchased from Portobello Road – it was the first umbrella he had ever owned – and set off for the heart of the business district.

Roland had little trouble finding the quaint building that housed the stock broking firm: England Investment Group.

"G'day, I'm Roland and I was sent by the accountancy personnel firm to report to Mr Grant Scott."

"Oh yes," said the fair-haired, lady receptionist. "Grant's not in as yet, but I can show you to your desk."

Roland followed the woman through the doors of the reception area, past a number of desks lined up in a row and stopped at the last desk.

"This is Glenn, our resident accountant," said the receptionist.

"Hi Glenn, I'm Roland," they shook hands.

"Roland eh, so you'll be working for the great Scott. Settle in and I can fill you in about the place," said Glenn.

"You've come into this humble abode at an interesting period. The establishment is a product of a merger between two stock broking firms. Both were medium sized firms thriving during the bull market. Record-keeping was an afterthought and the accounting records were a shambles. People were simply too busy making money. However, as all good things come to an end, the 1987 stock market crash hit and both firms were exposed. They were laden with debts that they should never have accumulated. They have since been subjected to a merger, restructure, rationalisation and any other business process you could care to mention."

"This must load you with enormous responsibilities," Roland commented.

"No, thankfully not me," Glenn replied. "I do the business-as-usual work. They've contracted out the fun jobs. In fact, Grant is the primary contractor who's in control of the ongoing review and he reports directly to management. You're the contracted assistant accountant working for him."

"Good morning, gentlemen."

Roland turned to the deep voice of a man in his mid 30s with brushed-back, blond hair and deep blue eyes. He was immaculately dressed in a grey, pinstriped suit, pink shirt and blue tie.

"Good Lord, speaking of the devil," Glenn remarked.

"You must be the new starter," Grant said. "If you would care to follow me into my office, we can have a chat."

"Yes, sir."

"Take a seat Roland."

"Thank you, sir."

"You may call me Grant."

"Thanks, Grant."

"I expect Glenn has already given you a run-down about the place and there's no denying the task here is a difficult one. The merger assisted the two firms to stay afloat, but we're not out of the woods yet. The records and reporting systems have been improved substantially; however, the financials are loaded with far too much debt; debt that should never have found a home with the organisation. We must rid ourselves of the debt while improving the business and you will be assisting me with this process."

Roland enjoyed accounting as he liked all things symmetrical, which included the double-entry accounting system. He got absorbed in his tasks and was happy to work back as he was paid by the hour.

Returning to The Court, Roland changed before meeting up with his new found friends, looking forward to go to the pub. *It's been a long day and I could do with a drink.*

Jill, Shirley, Mike and Roland went to the local pub where there were a number of the other residents from The Court. Jill filled Roland in with the gossip and the various cliques within The Court. She also gave him a rundown about Tom.

"Tom was expelled from University and kicked out of a hostel in Yorkshire. He's had a run-in with his former roommate at The Court; apparently Tom's roommate didn't appreciate Suzie's sleepovers. But you don't have to worry about the sleepovers anymore – they go elsewhere – and Tom has been warned; he's on his last life at The Court."

After another long session at the pub, the gang called it a night.

The first few days at The Court set the tone for the next few months. Roland soon realised the exhaustive extra-curricula activities were to be the norm and the pub scene was to be a daily event. It was a routine he didn't mind in the least.

Roland developed a close relationship with Jill, Shirley and Mike – the four of them spent every day together and, on weekends, they would either go on day excursions around London or take long weekends travelling around different parts of England and Wales.

After almost three months in London, Roland decided to leave and squeeze in an organised tour around the Republic of Ireland. He bid his friends at The Court goodbye and promised to catch up with them on his return. An uncertain future awaited, but there was a definite feeling this was the end of an era.

Chapter 3 – An Irish Tour

Even though the Irish tour was organised, Roland had little time to plan ahead and this made him feel uneasy.

Now where does this tour start? …Say what? Holyhead, where the hell's that? Holyhead, okay that's miles away. It says using British Rail. Shite, what's the time? 11.30 pm. No time to pack, I'll do that tonight. I'll rush to Paddington Station and buy a ticket for tomorrow. Pack tonight and travel tomorrow; beautiful.

Roland rushed to Paddington Station, running most of the way and scampering through red lights. As he approached the station, things didn't look promising. *It's pretty quiet, what's the time? Midnight. Okay, what's the timetable for Holyhead? Last train 23:40, not a problem. Tomorrow, Saturday, leaves from Euston Station, 05:31, 06:59, 08:04 bada bing, bada boom, bada take your pick. Fine, I'll just go to Euston Station tomorrow and grab the first train available.*

Returning to The Court, Roland had a spring in his step. Tom was staying at Suzie's so he could pack with the room to himself. He whistled along to the tunes on the radio until he was all done and, with great relief, he fell asleep.

Roland slowly awoke and sang to the tune playing on the radio. *"Holyhead, Holyhead, HOLYFUCKINGHEAD!"* he cried as he realised he'd slept in. "Bloody terrific, what's the time? Shit, it's almost 10.00 am." He grabbed his gear and raced out.

On arrival at Euston Station, Roland lined up at the British Rail queue and waited impatiently until he was called up. "I need to get to Holyhead before 5.15 pm," he explained.

"We have an 11.00 am train that arrives at Crewe at 1.48 pm, Chester at 2.27 pm and on to Holyhead, arriving 4.29 pm," the teller advised. "There's a large group from the United States travelling to Chester, although we do have some spare tickets."

Roland purchased a one-way ticket for that day – 4th June 1988 – and in order to avoid any more dramas, he also purchased a return ticket to London on the last day of the Irish tour. It was a half hour before departure. "I'm not sitting down and I'm not falling to sleep again," he mumbled. "I'll get a coffee and something to eat. I can relax on the train."

The horn tooted for people to board and the station staff assisted. "Sir, you may place your luggage in the baggage compartment."

"Thank you," Roland replied. *That's one less thing to worry about.*

Weaving through a large group of American tourists, Roland found a secluded cabin for himself, kicked up his heels and snuggled up against his daypack.

Roland slept most of the way to Chester and was woken by the loud American tourists as they disembarked. "Bloody Americans," he grumbled. "Why do they have to be so loud?"

It was another two hours before the train arrived at Holyhead. *It's 16:30, jolly good show chaps, you're bang on time.* Roland had forty-five minutes before the ferry sailed. *I'm not taking any risks; I'll scoot straight over to the port once I grab my bag.* "My bag! Where's my friggin' bag?"

The baggage compartment was empty, but this didn't stop Roland scouring it a number of times before he resigned to the fact that his bag wasn't there and he made his way to the stationmaster. "Excuse me, I stored my bag in the baggage compartment in London, but it's no longer there," Roland complained.

"Yes sir, I know."

"You know?"

"Yes, the American tourists mistakenly took the entire luggage off in Chester, believing them all to belong to their group," the stationmaster explained. "But that's no problem sir, we can place your luggage on the next available train and it should arrive here at 6.28 pm."

"That's no good, I'm due to sail for Dublin at 5.15 pm," Roland said, trying to contain his frustration.

"Oh. Let me look into it sir."

After a little time, the stationmaster emerged with a smile. "Sir, once your luggage arrives we can store it here and then place it on the early morning ferry to Dun Laoghaire."

"Dun what?"

"Dun Laoghaire, it's just out of Dublin and it should arrive there by 6.00 am."

"Oh, okay, that should work, thank you."

Rushing for the ferry, Roland was greeted by a middle-aged gentleman, Roger, who was the tour guide as well as the driver. Roland was introduced to the rest of the tour group and they exchanged pleasantries, although his mind couldn't stray from his bag.

They arrived at Dun Laoghaire and the group was assembled. "We'll be soon boarding the bus for Bray," advised Roger.

"Where now? Excuse me, sir, Bray, where's that?" Roland asked.

"It's only about 12 miles south of here and we should be there within half an hour, arriving around 9.30 pm."

The group disembarked at their hotel. "Where's your luggage?" Roger asked Roland.

"It's a long story, but I hope to pick it up tomorrow morning," Roland replied dispiritedly. "What time are we scheduled to depart tomorrow?"

"Breakfast is from 6.00 am until 10.00 am and we need to depart shortly after," explained Roger. "It's a leisurely start on our first day. However, I can't promise that sort of luxury for the rest of the trip."

After booking a cab for the next morning, Roland retired to his room. He was running facts, times and distances in his head, cursing the fact that he had not planned properly, the fact that he slept in and everything else that pervaded his mind.

Not getting much sleep, Roland couldn't wait for the alarm to sound. He shaved, showered and was downstairs before time. The cabbie was punctual and they immediately headed off.

Roland was very quiet and downtrodden on the way to the port with the only meaningful communication being his destination of Dun Laoghaire and return to Bray.

They arrived at Dun Laoghaire and Roland had to be coaxed from the cab. "The port's just over there," the driver indicated.

Roland reluctantly extricated himself from the vehicle and meandered towards the port shed. He squinted away from the dawn light and placed his hands deep inside his pockets as he felt the biting, early morning wind.

"Sir, are you Roland?" the port worker enquired.

"Yes," Roland responded as he looked up in hope.

"I have something for you." The port worker disappeared momentarily and then reappeared with a large item.

"Is it? Yes, it is. It's my bag!" Roland exclaimed. "Thank you, sir. Do I owe you anything?"

"No sir, it was our pleasure and we apologise for the inconvenience."

Roland frolicked with his bag towards the cab and the driver assisted him with his prized possession. Ecstatic, Roland released all the tension that had been bottled up inside of him over the past two days by commencing to chatter.

The driver looked over to Roland. *I think I prefer the quieter person.*

"That'll be eighteen punts, sir," the driver stated as they arrived at Bray.

Roland slapped thirty punts in his hand. "You can keep the change," he gleefully advised.

Returning to his room, Roland freshened up and had breakfast. He then collected his things, ensuring nothing was left behind, and was the first to board the coach.

"Top of the morning to ya," was Roger's cue.

"And the rest of the day to yaself," was the chorus reply.

"We're heading west through County Westmeath into the heart of Ireland," Roger informed. "Athlone is our first destination, on the mighty River Shannon and a lovely location for our lunch break."

They hit a sizeable bump in the road. "Oh, sorry ladies," Roger remarked; it seemed to tickle the evergreen lasses.

After lunch, there was a visit to the ancient Christian settlement of Clonmacnois before moving on to Galway for two nights.

The group witnessed the beautiful area of Connemara in the western region of County Galway. The majestic Twelve Bens Mountain Range dominated the views, which were sprinkled with lakes and lapped by the ocean waves of the Atlantic coastline.

The tour passed through Outerard to Maam's Cross then north through the heart of Joyce County to Leenane. There was a stop at Kylemore Abbey – a magnificent gothic chapel ornamented with Connemara marble. It was then on through Letterfrack to Clifden and through Roundstone, Spiddal and Salthill along the shores of Galway Bay.

Leaving Galway they journeyed south through Ennis in County Clare before reaching Limerick on the River Shannon for a lunch stop. Then it was southward-bound through Newcastle West and Castleisland to the town of Killarney. There was a free day and Roland joined the younger two members of the group – Mary and Tim – for a ride on a jaunting car and a cruise on a waterbus on Lough Lean.

The next day involved a full-day tour around the Ring of Kerry. It covered a hundred miles of lovely scenery through Killorglin, Glenbeig, Cahirciveen and Waterville. It was a wonderful blend of majestic mountains and rugged Atlantic coastline.

Mary, Tim and Roland got into the habit of enjoying the local stout as a nightcap. Roland found the Irish brew to be an ultimate drinking pleasure and vowed to make the most of it during his stay on the Emerald Isle.

It was Thursday morning and the group was off through Kenmare and Macroom for Blarney and Cork City. The lunchtime stop in Blarney provided the opportunity to climb the tower and kiss the Blarney Stone.

Tim and Roland walked towards Blarney Castle. "Are you going to kiss the Blarney Stone?" Tim asked.

"I don't think so; it's just a tourist gimmick," Roland replied.

"Well, whether it's a gimmick or not, you may only ever be here once in your life. What have you got to lose?"

"What have I got to gain?" Roland countered.

"There's lots to gain," Tim persisted. "You can get it out the way, you can say you did it and you may gain the gift of eloquence."

"Tim, you should have been a salesman," said Roland with a smile.

"I am a salesman," said Tim, grinning. "A used-car salesman, no joke. Oh, and by the way, you can also get a certificate."

"A certificate? Like an official record?"

"Yes, exactly."

"What the hell; I'll do it."

They made their way up the castle and stood in line.

"Sir, if you can lie down, hold on to the two bars in front, reach down and kiss the stone," instructed a guide, a big, burly man with a gruff accent.

"Bloody hell," Roland cursed as he struggled and finally managed to kiss the stone.

"Now where do we get our certificates?" Roland asked Tim once they were both done.

"I think it's in that building over there," Tim guessed.

"This is a gift shop," Roland observed.

"Excuse me, where can we collect our certificates for kissing the Blarney Stone?" Roland asked the shop assistant.

"Right over here, sir. How many certificates would you like to buy?"

"How many would I like to buy?" Roland exclaimed. "So you just buy the certificates and you don't even have to kiss that slimy, saliva-saturated, sacrosanct stone!"

"There you go Roland," Tim remarked. "Sounds like you've been bestowed with the gift of eloquence."

The group spent the night at the seaside resort of Tramore ahead of a short drive the next day to Waterford City where the group visited a crystal factory. They travelled on to Kilkenny City with a visit to the castle. After lunch, it was on to Emo near Portlaoise where they spent their last night.

On the morning of the last day of the tour, the group heard the standard spiel for the last time. "Top of the morning to ya," Roger jovially announced.

"And the rest of the day to yaself," was the hearty reply.

Most of the group had a few nights' stay in Dublin, but as Roland had purchased his return ticket, he was committed to move on. He downed his last pint of stout before he said his goodbyes and headed back to London.

Roland arranged to stay with Sean for a few nights. He arrived at Ealing Common Station and scrambled the few blocks from the station to his friend's apartment.

Sean rented a three-bedroom apartment where he usually sub-let two of the bedrooms. Someone named Beth was staying in one of the rooms and the other spare room was available for Roland.

Roland decided to return to The Court for a visit and he had an odd feeling as he arrived. He stood outside the front door for a few minutes before a resident who was unfamiliar to him allowed him entry. He knocked on Shirley's door, which was situated on the ground floor, but there was no response.

"She's not in," shouted the receptionist.

"Oh, thanks. You wouldn't happen to know where Jill, Mike and Tom are?"

"Tom doesn't live here anymore and I don't know where the others are, but you might want to try the television room."

Saddened by the news about Tom, Roland's spirit was slightly lifted with the hope the others may be around. He made his way towards the stairs, which took him back to his first day when he flew down the stairs with Tom and Mike to meet Shirley and Jill for the first time. He now went down the same stairs; however, this time he was slower and pensive.

As he entered the television room, Roland saw there were few people and no one he recognised. He was about to leave when he heard Jill's voice. "Hello, Roland."

Roland looked around to see Jill and Mike in a corner together holding hands. "Oh, hi Jill. Hi Mike, I didn't see you there."

"So how was your trip to Ireland?" Jill asked.

"Oh, it was great," Roland responded and chatted with them about his trip.

"I guess you know about Jill and me?" said Mike.

"No, I didn't know," Roland replied. "But that's terrific; I think you make a great couple," he added unconvincingly.

There was a little more small talk before Roland stated that he'd better be off. "Goodbye, guys, and say hi to Shirley for me."

Chapter 4 – The Scandi-Russian Tour

It was Thursday morning of 16th June 1988 – the date Roland was to commence his tour of Scandinavia and Russia. Sean said farewell as he left for work. Beth was still sleeping so Roland left her a goodbye note before heading to the Royal National Hotel, which was the meeting place for the tour's departure.

There were people milling around the tour bus. "All right people, if you can board the bus as soon as you've loaded your bags," the tour guide yelled out.

As the bus edged away, *Take a Chance on Me* by ABBA blared from the speakers, and it drew a mixed reaction. The tour guide then addressed the group.

"Good morning everyone. My name is Gerome and our capable driver is Paul. There's nothing like the famous Swedish band to get us in the mood for the start of our Scandi-Russian tour. Pity if you don't like the song as it's going to be our morning theme song for the next twenty-two days. I need to go over a few rules and then I'll come around to check on the remainder of everyone's paperwork. In the meantime, as we will be a family for the next three weeks, it would be good if each one of you could come up and tell the rest of the group a little about yourself."

"Terrific," Roland gasped. He couldn't see the sense of everyone going through the trouble of telling their story.

"Oi, you're next mate!" A heckler barked out to Roland.

"Hello everyone, my name's Roland."

"Could you speak up mate," someone cried from the back. Many of the others weren't paying attention or were engaged in their own discussion.

"Sorry, is that better? Okay. My name is Roland."

Roland was most put off by the situation and the audience's lack of courtesy so he thought he would treat the experience with the trivialness it deserved.

"I come from Melbourne, although I grew up on a farm up in the Snowy Mountains. My early years are all a bit of a blur, but as I understand it there was a radical group of lesbians who decided to break off from society and set up their own sect, known as the Amazonian Sycophants, or Sycos for short."

As Roland continued with his story, more and more of the group seemed to be paying attention.

"They had no time for men, but every so often the Sycos went to various towns and cities to be serviced by the men there and I'm a product of a servicing. The Sycos were Right–to-Lifers and didn't want to give me up so they decided to raise me as a communal baby, without divulging who my Syco mum was. It is because of this strange upbringing that I have certain issues so apologies in advance if I mistakenly use the ladies' toilets."

By this time, everyone was paying attention and clinging onto his every word.

"The Sycos felt guilty about the secrecy and deception of my beginnings and they eventually told me which Syco was my mother. They also advised that around the period when I was conceived there were likely to be four men who could be my father. The Sycos assisted me in trying to track down my father, but without success. I'm still not sure who my father is, but I suspect he's either the trapeze artist from Uzbekistan or the bullshit artist from Never Never Land. Thank you."

Initially, Roland had a rush of people asking him questions; however, once they learnt about his real story, his novelty value soon evaporated and his popularity waned.

Roland's seating companion was a fellow Melbournian named Stephen who barracked for the Carlton football club, as did Roland, so they immediately hit it off.

The tour group was made up of 29 women and 20 men. *Not too bad,* Roland thought. *You need to have a balance and the ratio of men to women seems to be a reasonable balance.*

The bus travelled to the port at Harwich where the group took the Dania Anglia ferry to Esbjerg, Denmark. It was an overnight crossing and the accommodation was in four berth cabins. Roland shared with Stephen, Gary from Canada and Ken from New Zealand.

The ferry had good facilities with a pool, sauna, disco and movie theatre; however, the guys preferred to settle in the bar. They didn't get too much sleep before it was time to disembark and the group continued on their bus journey.

They arrived at the campsite just outside of Copenhagen and the guys were still feeling a little seedy.

"Okay, this is your crash course in erecting your two-man tents," said Gerome.

Roland was not keen on camping and wasn't too impressed to learn he had to put up his own tent. Nevertheless, he accepted the situation by adopting the tour philosophy of going with the flow, although he was quick to confirm he wasn't required to do any cooking.

Day three of the tour was a full day of exploring Copenhagen where they visited the Royal Palace, the Little Mermaid Statue and Thorvaldsen's Museum.

In the evening, the group enjoyed an excursion to the Tivoli Gardens and Amusement Park. It capped off a wonderful day, although the beer buffs were disappointed none of the Danish breweries were available for visitation.

Travelling north to the tip of Denmark, they boarded a ferry that carried them to Sweden. There was a special playing of the ABBA theme song, which was sung with a little more gusto. They passed Hamlet's Castle at Elsinore before reaching Stockholm where they spent a relaxing evening.

Day five and it was another ferry trip to experience the old city and the changing of the guard at the Royal Palace. Further sightseeing and shopping was the order of the afternoon and the following day.

Leaving Stockholm, the group was required to take the Viking Line ferry crossing the Baltic Sea to Finland before heading to their campsite in Helsinki. Roland was thankful it was the last ferry crossing for a while and confessed he could never have been a Viking.

The tour of Helsinki included a visit to Sibelius Park that incorporated the Sibelius Monument and a visit to the Olympic Stadium, the stage for the 1952 Olympic Games.

After one full day in Helsinki, they were on the move again. The tour was heading for the USSR where Mikhail Gorbachev was the leader of the Communist Party. "It is the time of glasnost, it is the time of perestroika, we have a box full of vodka, we have a tank full of gas and we're on a mission from God!" Roland declared.

The cavalier attitude quickly evaporated when the group met the hard-nut customs and immigration officials where it took hours to complete the formalities. The passengers changed the recommended minimum currency at the official exchange as the word was that the balance of their currency exchange could be transacted on the black market.

Arriving at the campsite outside of Leningrad, Gerome announced there would be a party after dinner to celebrate their safe arrival into the USSR. "So could this party be officially classified as a Communist party?" Roland quipped.

Early the next morning, the group was feeling the effects of their party drinking. Gerome called the group together to introduce the official Intourist guide who was a very rounded and solid lady. "Yes, I will be your guide throughout the next eight days, over the entire period of your stay in Russia and my name is Irene Bendová."

Roland looked at Stephen and then at Gary before he commented. "I'm not cracking any jokes about that."

The group was escorted on a tour around Leningrad that included the St. Peter and Paul Fortress, the Admiralty, St. Isaac's Cathedral and, scene of the Russian Revolution in 1905, the Winter Palace.

The following morning, the group visited the Hermitage Museum where they were spoiled and overwhelmed by the exceptional artwork, numismatic objects, archaeological artefacts, arms and armoury.

In the afternoon, they took a hydrofoil ride to Petrodvorets where they took great pleasure in viewing the splendid former Summer Palace, the lovely gardens and the wonderful fountains. There were also female and male models displaying the garments of the former Czars and Czarinas.

The group packed up the next day and left Leningrad. They passed through Novorod where they wandered through the Fortress and War Memorial. They then continued to their next campsite stopover in Kalinin.

It was on the move again the next day to enter the capital city of Moscow. Everyone cheered as they arrived at their accommodation with a surprise change to cabins from the dreaded tents. Not having to wrestle around with tents allowed more free time to rest and prepare for the evening events, which promised to be a traditional dinner and show.

There was a buzz around the place as they assembled for their big night out.

"All right everyone, just a quick word before we depart," Gerome said, waiting for them all to be quiet. "Tonight is a special night where you will have an opportunity to taste some Russian cuisine and to witness a traditional Russian show. It is also a chance for everyone to let their hair down and have a good time. However, having said that, just bear in mind that you are in a country with a vastly different culture and values to your own so try to respect that. Now let's go and enjoy ourselves!"

It was a spirited ride into central Moscow with non-stop talking, joking and singing.

On arrival, the group proceeded into an ornate building, which housed a large hall made up of a stage, a dance floor and seating on two levels. They were escorted up a marble staircase covered with an elaborate runner held down by decorative brass bars.

"Let's sit over here," Gary called out to Roland.

"Hey, I want to sit over there, too," yelled Barbara, an Australian lady on the tour.

"Gee, this is a great vantage point; we have a fantastic view down onto the stage and dance floor!" Roland exclaimed.

As they got settled, a procession of waiters brought out assorted food and drinks. It was a festive mood and everyone was gorging themselves on the delicacies. A band took their positions on the stage and commenced playing soft, slow music before it picked up in volume and tempo. Dancers appeared next, wearing an array of colourful costumes and they were soon joined by a female singer and an acoustic guitarist. The lady dancers were wearing flowing dresses and their dance routines accentuated the visual effect.

"This is really cool and look, they're doing Cossack dancing, how impressive is that?" Barbara commented with excitement.

The audience joined in with the locals singing and everyone else clapping and cheering. The group continued eating and drinking in time with the music.

"Hey Roland, pass over the vodka," said Stephen.

"You've got to try this fish, it's delicious," said Gary as he popped some more into his mouth.

"Oh, I don't know about these anchovies, they smell off," Barbara said, turning up her nose.

"Where's your sense of adventure Barbara?" Roland asked. "Pass the anchovies over here."

Roland grabbed a few of the anchovies and, one by one, held them by the tail and scoffed them down. A few moments later he started to perspire. He loosened his collar and sipped on water.

"Are you all right?" Barbara asked.

"I don't know... oh shit!" Roland suddenly jumped from his seat and rushed towards the staircase in an effort to get to the toilet; however, his effort was in vain. As he was scurrying down the magnificent staircase, he could not contain the eruption from deep within his bowels and he left a distinctive trail of vomit all the way down the previously pristine stairs and the once impressive plush runner.

Roland managed to find the toilet, although by this time most of the putrid matter had been discharged. He leant on the side of the vanity, splashing cold water over his face and rhythmically moaning. He caught a glimpse of a cleaner with a mop in one hand and a bucket in the other, shaking her head. He couldn't utter a word, but managed to eke out a smile and shrug his shoulders.

The group enjoyed the bus ride back to their cabins, except for Roland, who was in a very sad state. Barbara was less than sympathetic. "So much for being adventurous," she stated.

Roland was bunking with Stephen, Gary and Ken who expressed their support.

"Don't worry mate, you'll be right," Stephen said.

"Get a good night's sleep and we'll hit the town tomorrow," reassured Gary.

"Yep, much to look forward to in Moscow tomorrow," Ken added.

The following morning, the group got up for an early start to make the most of what had the potential to be one of the most eventful days on the itinerary.

"How are you feeling Roland?" Stephen asked.

Roland didn't immediately reply as he was unsure so he first tried to resurrect himself from bed. He was a bit wobbly and light headed, but he was able to get up. "I'm good," he replied, although he didn't sound too convincing.

"We'll have breakfast then hit the road," Ken suggested.

"I don't know about breakfast, but I could do with some water," Roland said.

Roland was not the only person feeling under the weather, so the bus ride back into central Moscow was a much more subdued affair than the previous evening.

When they arrived, Gerome set out the ground rules: "All right everyone, listen closely. Today, each one of you has the option to see a number of attractions; however, that number depends on how much ground you cover and how well you organise yourselves. Make sure you get to see your main attractions first, as there's no way you can see it all."

Gerome's last words echoed in Roland's head. *No way you can see it all?* Roland was sure there should be enough time to see all the main attractions as well as other attractions he had on his personal list.

Gerome commenced outlining the options for the group whilst Roland considered how he could best fit these into his plans. "We'll start off with a morning tour that takes us to the Kremlin, Red Square, and Lenin's Tomb..."

As Gerome explained, Roland mentally itinerised: *Kremlin, okay. Red Square, okay. Lenin's Mausoleum, okay. Lenin's Tomb, I don't think so. Looking at the queue building up, it could take upwards of an hour to view the body. Lenin's Tomb is not a viable option.*

"You are free to have lunch where you desire, but after lunch we have an excursion of the Moscow Underground and then onto the Park of Economic Achievements," Gerome added.

Lunch would have to be at a Mu-Mu or Drova restaurants. They are popular self-service eateries offering a huge choice of Russian-style food and are usually frequented by your average Russian student or office worker. The Moscow Underground should be a must and the Park of Economic Achievements should also be worth a visit.

Roland mentally listed the attractions that Gerome mentioned with his own attractions and then tried to process the information in terms geographic sectors, travel times and duration of the stay. He came up with a plan that had him back by 2.30 pm.

"Oh Gerome, what time do we need to be here for the Metro tour?" Roland asked.

"You obviously weren't listening Roland," Gerome stated. "You need to be ready by 3.00 pm."

During the tour of the Kremlin, Roland felt tired and started to become slightly hot and bothered.

"Are you all right Roland?" Stephen asked.

"Yeah, I'm fine; I just need some water."

The group eventually departed the Kremlin and Roland took a few photos of Red Square and the Lenin Mausoleum. He then headed for St. Basel's Cathedral.

After visiting St. Basel's Cathedral, Roland started off for Gorky Park. He was 30 minutes behind schedule so he rushed off. He didn't have a map; however, he was confident of finding the park by following the river.

Feeling hot, light headed and starting to perspire, Roland was becoming distressed. He found that in order to continue along the road he was forced to depart from the river. He was not good with his bearings at the best of times and his condition was not helping matters. He was becoming frustrated and he felt like he was going around in circles. It was now almost midday so he decided to abort the Park of Arts and Gorky Park.

Roland turned his attention to the Russian Government and Parliament buildings; however, in order to find these he was relying on finding the Golden Ring – the ring road that circled central Moscow. From what he could remember, the Golden Ring went through Gorky Park and without being able to locate Gorky Park it made finding the Golden Ring unlikely.

Structuring his plan around geographic sectors and, given that the Arbat Mall was in the same sector as the Government and Parliaments buildings, Roland decided to abort the Arbat Mall as well.

Roland's only concern now was to get back to Red Square, but he couldn't figure out the way he'd come, and he couldn't find the river. He was very confused, hot and distressed. He reached in his bag and discovered he'd forgotten to pack his cap and he only had a little water left.

Appalled by how badly he had organised himself, Roland was now so desperate he considered doing something he would normally never do – asking someone for assistance.

Looking around, Roland could see no one in sight so he continued walking until the hazy vision of a man approached. "Excuse me sir, can you direct me to Red Square?" Roland asked. The man looked at him expressionless so he rephrased his question. "Where is Red Square?" The man's expression did not change.

It dawned on Roland that the man didn't speak English and had no idea what he was on about. He then tried to convey his enquiry phonetically. After some deliberation, he thought he had it. "Kremlin? Krem-lin? K-rem-lin?"

The man just looked at Roland, gave him a hint of a smile and shook his head. Roland considered it pointless and lowered his head in despair. When he looked up, the man was gone.

Roland headed in the direction he guessed, or more realistically hoped, would lead him to the river. "What's that?" he said to himself as he noticed the sunlight reflecting off water and he hurried along. He had found the river.

Roland marched alongside the river, although he wasn't convinced he was going the right way. *I didn't cross the river, I'm sure I didn't. Is it the same river? It has to be. There's only one river this large in central Moscow. I've been walking for a long time; surely I should have arrived back to Red Square by now.*

At about the stage of giving up, Roland rounded a bend in the river when the red-brick walls of the Kremlin came into view, but he was totally unmoved by the find. As though in a trance, he just kept walking.

Roland entered Red Square and the sound of an empty vodka bottle rattling along the cobbled stones made him turn. A scruffy, old man with a grey beard, wearing in a soiled, old suit sat leaning against a wall. The two looked at each other; the man's stare was so piercing and intense, Roland looked away. When he glanced back, the man was gone.

Red Square was quiet with only a few Muscovites who were wearing drab, grey clothes. Roland heard a whirring sound that was getting louder. A group of elite cyclists wearing colourful riding silks flashed past the square, soon vanished and everything was quiet again.

The silence was soon disrupted by the sound of motor vehicles. Three black limousines flying miniature Russian and diplomatic flags entered the square. As the motorcade passed, men wearing expensive black suits stared at Roland expressionless. The motorcade made its way into the Kremlin and the gates closed shut.

Roland made his way across Red Square and entered a store that was very hot and stuffy. It was crowded with people all wearing drab, grey clothes. The shop assistants and cashiers were wearing drab, dark uniforms. All the people were expressionless, had glazed eyes and moved like robots.

In the glass cabinets were basic products with no variety, no advertising, no colours and no information of any kind.

Customers lined up in different queues: one to order goods, one to pay the cashiers, and one to collect goods.

There was a beautiful, young lady with blonde hair and deep, blue eyes. Roland couldn't take his eyes off her. Without warning, the lady collapsed and a number of people rushed to her aid.

Everything seemed to happen in slow motion and, as the crowd circled the lady, she became hidden from Roland's view and his vision grew very fuzzy.

Chapter 5 – Meeting Muscovites

Roland was drowsy as he seemed to come out of a dream and he found himself sitting on steps at the entrance of a shop.

"Hey Roland, what are you doing here?" Gary asked.

Roland turned towards him. "Hi Gary; not much."

"Where have you been?"

"Oh, around."

"What's up with you Roland, you don't seem yourself?"

"I'm okay. Do you have any water?"

"Sure, I've got an extra bottle," Gary said and continued talking as Roland drank. "I still haven't had lunch yet, do you want to get a bite to eat?"

"Yeah lunch, I wanted to go to Drova," Roland said.

"Drova it is then."

They walked a short distance to arrive at the Drova restaurant. "Here it is," Gary said. "Gee Roland, look at the food selection."

"Gary, you get some lunch whilst I try and grab us a seat." Roland looked around, saw a spare table along the window and settled in. He was still recovering from the events of the day and trying to figure out what had happened to him when a lady approached.

"Do you mind if I sit?" an attractive, middle-aged lady asked as she hovered close, holding a tray.

"I'm here with a friend, but you are welcome to join us," Roland replied.

"My name is Ivana."

"Hello, my name is Roland."

"Pleased to meet you, Roland."

When Gary approached with his tray, Roland introduced them.

"Hello, Ivana," said Gary, placing his tray on the table.

"Pleased to meet you Gary."

"Excuse me while I get some lunch," Roland stated and headed for the food counter. He perused the offerings and decided on something he thought looked the most appetising and collected a couple of bottles of water before returning to the table.

"Roland," Ivana said. "Gary has told me about himself, now you must tell me about yourself."

"What would you like to know?" Roland asked.

"What are you doing here in Russia?"

"Same as Gary," Roland quickly replied.

"Yes, and that was?" Ivana persisted.

Gary attempted to assist when Ivana intervened. "Yes, I know what you told me Gary, but I was interested in what Roland had to say."

Gary and Roland glanced at each other. Gary had a concerned look on his face. Roland changed his facial expression to one of seriousness. He looked one way and then the other, as if to make sure no one else was listening. Ivana also looked one way and the other before leaning forward in eager anticipation.

"Do you have any idea where I come from and who I work for?" Roland asked.

"No, no I don't," Ivana said, her eyes widening.

"I come from *Australia*," Roland said, drawing out the pronunciation.

"*Australia?*" Ivana repeated.

"Yes and I work for the Government," Roland stated.

"The Government?"

"Yes. Now, do you have any idea what I am doing here?" Roland asked provokingly.

"No," Ivana shook her head, "I don't. What are you doing here?"

"I am on a mission," Roland said as he leant back in his chair.

Gary's mouth was hanging open as Roland spun his tale.

"Mission, what mission?" Ivana asked.

Roland leant forward. "It is the time of glasnost, it is the time of perestroika, we have a box full of vodka, we have a tank full of gas and we're on a mission from God!"

Ivana had obviously not seen *The Blues Brothers* movie, and was totally nonplussed. She soon packed up her lunch and departed.

"What the heck are you playing at Roland?" Gary said in a stern voice.

"I was just having some fun," Roland said in a nonchalant tone, trying to diffuse Gary's obvious concern.

"Who knows where that lady is from. She could be KGB."

"I don't think so Gary, but I guess we may as well be off as we need to get back to the bus by 3.00 pm."

The group was still waiting on a couple of tour members so Roland began roaming the car park.

"Hey Roland, where are you going?" Stephen asked.

"Just over there to talk to those guys," Roland advised as he headed towards a group of young men hovering around some cars.

"Wait I'll come too," Stephen said.

"Ok, but hurry up," Roland told Stephen.

"Roland, you're always in a hurry."

"Hello, my name is Roland and I'm from Australia."

After some discussion about their respective backgrounds, Sergei commented on how he liked Roland's jeans.

"Oh thanks, but I've got a better pair of jeans in my pack."

"They are okay."

"Okay? They're Levi's, they're good. I've also got an American T-shirt."

"Yes I like T-shirt," said Viktor.

"I might be willing to part with the jeans and the T-shirt, if you have anything I might like," Roland suggested.

The Russians took two bags from the boot of their car and revealed Russian dolls from one bag and Russian fur hats from the other. Roland was interested in both and as he considered what deal he could drum up, there was a shout from the group. "Come on guys, were going!"

"Okay, we'll be there in a minute," Roland shouted back.

"All right gentlemen, I don't have much time so I will make a suggestion. How about I give you these pair of Levi jeans and the T-shirt for this set of seven nestling Babushka Dolls and this Ushanka?"

"Come on, Roland we're going!"

"Yes, I'm coming!"

"I do not want Levi jeans, I want those jeans," said Sergei.

"These jeans? The one's I'm wearing? But the Levi jeans are better."

"Yes, but Versace jeans are more expensive."

"Versace? Oh Versace. Okay, the jeans I'm wearing and the T-shirt for the set of dolls and the Ushanka. Is it a deal?"

"No."

"No, why?"

"T-shirt is for friend, he has nothing to trade," said Sergei.

"Why not you get T-shirt for me?" asked Viktor.

The Russians then got embroiled in an argument.

"Roland the group is taking off, we've gotta go now," said Stephen as he turned and took off.

"Oh blast," Roland muttered as he followed.

"I didn't want to say anything at the time," Stephen confessed, "but you're lucky you didn't go ahead with the deal – you'd surely have been ripped off."

"What do you mean?" Roland asked.

"Well, I mean trading a pair of Versace jeans for that junk?"

"Junk? I wouldn't call it junk," Roland replied. "The Babushka dolls may not have been handmade, but the set of seven nestled dolls looked very impressive. The Ushanka probably wasn't top quality fur, but it seemed reasonable quality and well made. As for these Versace jeans, they cost me all of five dollars!"

"What?"

"During my stopover in Hong Kong, I bought two pairs of jeans for five bucks each. The vendor asked me whether I wanted tags stitched on for no extra charge and I said, 'whatever.' He slapped on a 'Pepe' tag on one pair of jeans and a 'Versace' tag on the other. In terms of that potential deal, I could have traded some cheap clothes for some pretty impressive souvenirs."

"Gee Roland, I don't know what to say."

"How about, what a bummer?"

The group boarded the bus and was shown through parts of the impressive Moscow Underground, and then travelled to the Park of Economic Achievements where they viewed a collection of exhibits including aircraft and rockets.

Day 14 of the tour involved travel to Smolensk where a local guide provided a tour of the city, including the beautiful Kutuzou Cathedral. After dinner, the group met local students and engaged in active conversation mainly comparing their respective ways of life.

The next day, the group was on the move again. This time it was on the way to Minsk, the capital of White Russia and famous for its Victory Mound and Monument. The mound was created from soil taken from World War II Hero Cities.

The group was accommodated in campsite cabins for their last night in Russia.

Dinner was at a traditional Russian restaurant and the highlight of the evening was a visit to the circus where Roland made an enquiry. "Excuse me, but would the trapeze artist happen to be from Uzbekistan?" The group was in uproar as they burst into laughter.

Chapter 6 – Poland

The morning travel included a stop in Brest, which had the unenviable record of being the first Russian city to be destroyed during World War II.

The group traversed the border and travelled onward to Warsaw. They reverted back to campsite accommodation and had another wrestle with their tents. Their treat was dinner in the Old Quarter of the city.

The following day, they visited the museum at the Jewish ghetto and strolled through Lazienki Park that boasted the Chopin Monument and Lazienski Palace, also called the Palace on the Water.

The history of the city of Warsaw was depicted in a documentary that vividly showed its destruction and reconstruction.

There was time for shopping and Roland joined Stephen in visiting a crystal store. "Wow, some of this crystal is really intricate," Stephen commented.

"And it's very cheap, unbelievably cheap," Roland said. "It's a pity I don't have much local currency or I'd definitely be interested in purchasing that decanter."

"Hey Roland, why don't we try to suss out one of those black market currency exchange guys?" Stephen asked.

"I don't know, Gerome didn't mention anything about currency dealers in Poland."

"Well we used them in Russia and he didn't warn us not to use them here."

"Okay, Stephen. What the hell; let's do it."

Roland and Stephen hung out around the square in the old city in central Warsaw when they were approached by a man who had been loitering nearby.

The man was tall and thin with wavy, grey-brown hair and a five o'clock shadow. He was wearing black pants, a dark blue shirt and a trench coat that was unbuttoned with the lapels flapping in the breeze. "Money, you want money?" asked the man.

Stephen turned to the man and nodded.

The man wandered closer. "You have US dollars?"

"Yes we have," Stephen replied.

"How much you want to change?" the man asked.

"Fifty US dollars," Stephen blurted out.

"I give you very good rate, don't you want more?"

"No, we only have fifty dollars," Roland confirmed.

They settled on the exchange rate. "Okay, I get zlotys and you have your money ready," said the man before he left.

Stephen and Roland put their fifty US dollars together and tried to work out how they would transact the deal.

"Okay Stephen, why don't I hold the US dollars and you count the zlotys? Once you've confirmed the zlotys are all there, I'll hand over the US dollars."

"Sounds like a plan, Roland."

The man reappeared and Stephen explained the desired procedure for the transaction. After some initial hesitation, the man agreed. They were about to commence when the man appeared to get very nervous. "Gentlemen, if we are going to do this deal it is better if we go into the alley."

"I don't think so," Roland replied.

"It is not wise to do the deal in the square as there may be undercover police; we only have to go just inside this alley," the man said reassuringly.

Stephen and Roland glanced at each other then nodded and the three men walked into the alleyway.

"Where are the zlotys?" Stephen asked.

The man revealed what appeared to be a roll of zlotys and was just about to hand them over. "I need to be sure that you have the US dollars; show me the money," the man said.

Stephen and Roland glanced at each other again and nodded. Roland took out the US dollars and held them in front of the man.

The man proceeded to hand over the zlotys and, in an instant, he looked towards the square and shouted. "Police!" The man snatched the US dollars from Roland's hand and was off.

"After him! He's got the money!" Roland shouted.

They gave chase down the alley and through a side street until they came to a juncture with many connecting paths where they both came to a whirling stop.

Stephen opened the roll he was clenching and it revealed an outer, single zloty note and the rest was newspaper. "Shit!"

"We're idiots," Roland cursed. "That guy was so suspicious we should have picked him as a con-artist right away. We knew something was wrong and we just fell for it."

Roland marched off.

"Where are you going now Roland?" Stephen asked as he set off in pursuit.

"I'm going to change some money!"

"What? After what's just happened? You want to go through all that again?"

"Yep, I've got twenty bucks left and I'm looking to change the lot. What about you Stephen?"

"Well, I think I've got ten bucks."

"That's good, depending on the black market rate, it should be enough for each of us to buy a nice piece of crystal. What do you think?"

"What the heck, let's do it."

They entered the square and surveyed the area. They noticed a bit of activity in a corner of the square and proceeded in that direction. There seemed to be some men doing exchanges and they approached the central figure. "Do you know where we can change money?" Roland asked.

"I can change money," said one man.

"So can I," another man said.

"What would you give for thirty US dollars?" Roland asked the first man. The man gave them what they thought was a reasonably competitive exchange rate; however, they were uncertain. The man then pulled down a signboard that showed his set rates being worse than the rate he was offering. They then noticed that there were other dealers with boards with the same advertised rates, openly doing deals. It was a virtual trade fair.

Roland casually took out the thirty US dollars, the dealer counted out the zlotys and they exchanged currencies. Stephen and Roland looked at each other, rolled their eyes and returned to the store where they purchased their crystal.

Chapter 7 – The Two Germanys

The group enjoyed dinner in town then viewed the city of Warsaw by night. They retired to bed early, ahead of a long drive to the Polish/East German border.

From the autobahns, they passed checkpoint Bravo and through a gate of the Berlin Wall into West Berlin. They were pleasantly surprised to find a pre-prepared dinner at their campsite where they spent a relaxing evening.

Day 19 of the tour and the group had a full day of sightseeing in West Berlin. They were taken to the Olympic Complex where the 1936 Olympic Games was staged. They then visited the Russian War Memorial, the Reichstag and observed the Brandenburg Gate.

In the afternoon, they inspected the Charlottenburg Palace and visited the Egyptian Museum. The group let loose in the evening as they became re-acquainted with some Western nightlife.

Day 20 was the chance to explore East Berlin. The group walked to Checkpoint Charlie and was shown through the museum, which contained exhibits of escapes from East Berlin to West Berlin.

They obtained day passes and proceeded to convert some Deutsche Marks for East German Marks. "Excuse me, do you give a good exchange of Mark for Mark?" Roland asked one of the checkpoint guards. He appreciated that it wasn't much of a joke; however, the stern stare from the guard reminded him to where he was returning.

Roland didn't have any great plans for the day. He had a basic map of East Berlin and was happy to join Barbara, Stephen and Gary in a stroll through the unique city. It was quiet and they spent a comfortable day roaming the streets and grabbing a bite to eat along the way.

After twenty days of touring and with the group members becoming comfortable with each other, they were soon to part. They were a bit sombre as they had a relaxing dinner at the camp, a quiet evening over a few drinks and an early night.

In the morning, the group sluggishly packed up the tents for the last time. They exited West Berlin into East Germany and crossed the Corridor to West Germany. It was then a direct drive into the bustling Hanseatic city of Hamburg.

The group boarded the ferry bound for Harwich, England. "The ferry ride will be your last chance to party," Gerome said; however, no one needed any motivation as it was an uninhibited and carefree all-night party of drinking, singing and dancing.

Arriving at Harwich, they completed the immigration formalities, which seemed hassle-free relative to their experiences in the Eastern Bloc. They then took the bus for their last ride.

The bus speakers made a few crackling noises before sound blared out with ABBA's *Take a Chance on Me*. Whereas the theme song was greeted with a mixed reaction on the first day of the tour, this time everyone was singing at the top of their voices.

Chapter 8 – Bonnie Holiday

It was early evening by the time the group arrived at the Royal National Hotel in London. Roland booked that night's accommodation, but had an additional ten days before he commenced his next organised tour of Europe.

Shall I hang out in London? I could check with Sean to see if I could stay at his place. I could visit the gang at The Court. What about Dublin? I could spend a week in Dublin, see the sights and enjoy some more of that excellent Irish stout. It then dawned on him. *McRoland you idiot, you haven't been to Scotland!*

The next morning Roland visited a number of travel agents and amassed material on Scotland. He made himself comfortable in Regent's Park where he panned through the information.

I'd like to visit Glasgow, Edinburgh and Inverness. The tours take around a week so I'd need to leave in the next day or two. I've been to Stonehenge in England so it would be interesting to visit the Ring of Brodgar Stone Circle and Henge in Scotland. I've been to the southernmost point of mainland Britain at Land's End so I must see the northernmost point of mainland Britain – John O'Groates.

After much deliberation, Roland compromised on a tour that commenced in Edinburgh, went to John O'Groates and finished in Edinburgh. It didn't go to the Ring of Brodgar, but none of the tours he examined did. It also didn't go to Glasgow, but he had enough time to squeeze in a return trip to Glasgow from Edinburgh.

Roland slept on the bus most the way from London to Edinburgh. He arrived at Andrew Square in the early morning, a couple of hours before his Scottish tour commenced.

The tour guide, who was also the driver, allowed Roland to load his bag and take a seat on the coach. The other travellers, all elderly passengers, trickled in at regular intervals. It was a group of about a dozen people, or, as the tour guide described: "tis a wee group."

The first day was a fairly long drive where they passed much scenery and had a few stopovers, including stopovers at Glencoe and Loch Ness. "Oh, I hope I see the monster," an elderly spinster stated as they approached Loch Ness.

"You do mean the Loch Ness monster?" Roland asked.

After an overnight stay at a hotel in Strathpeffer, the group travelled further north to Dornoch and on to John O'Groates. It was a fine, clear day and a signpost showed the distance from John O'Groates to Land's End of

874 miles. Visitors were allowed to place their own town on the sign with the day's date. Roland asked for Melbourne and the landmark of the M.C.G. was placed on the sign with the date of 10th July 1988 and the distance of 12,009 miles.

Roland was just about to take the photo when he stopped. *The closest distance to Melbourne, I expect, would be around 22 thousand kilometres, or around 14,000 miles, towards the southeast over the Indian Ocean; however, the sign is pointing southwest traversing the North Atlantic and South Pacific Oceans, which means from John O'Groates to Melbourne would be around 30 thousand kilometres, or around 19,000 miles. I wonder how they get the 12,000 miles?*

After much arduous deliberation, Roland was sufficiently confused that he decided to just take the photo.

The group visited the St Peter's and St Andrew's Church of Scotland in Thurso and was then driven a short way to their hotel.

The next day, they headed south with the highlight of the day being the Million Dollar View and panoramic views of the Dornoch Firth and Sutherlandshire.

The group travelled on to Inverness, which would be their base for the next three nights. They were spoilt with beautiful scenery every day, including Glen Docherty, Inverewe Gardens, Corrieshallock Gorge, the Falls of Measach, Inverness Castle and Loch Maree, which was reported to have its own loch monster, *Muc-sheilch.*

"Are you going to try your luck with this monster?" Roland asked the spinster.

"I've given up on ever finding a monster," she replied with resignation.

After three nights in Inverness, they travelled on to Aberdeen, passing the Culloden Battlefield & Cottage and Cowdor Castle.

On the last day, they witnessed Balmoral Castle, travelled through the city of Braemar and enjoyed views of Glen Shee. They had a stopover for a photo shoot of the Queensferry Railway Bridge, also known as the Forth Bridge. As they proceeded across the Forth Bridge, the driver explained. "We're now passing the firth on Forth."

This prompted Roland to query. "Firth on Forth? Who's on first?"

The group was given a tour of the sights around Edinburgh before checking into a bed and breakfast for their last night. After dinner and quite a few drinks, the elderly passengers made a special effort for a party. They put on some music and had a dance, although it wasn't too long before they ran out of puff.

Roland arose early for his bus trip to Glasgow. He stored his baggage and took his daypack with him.

Arriving in Glasgow, Roland whipped out his map of the central city and roamed the streets.

Roland took his time walking around George Square and examined the various sculptures, including the majestic 80-foot monument mounted with a statue of Sir Walter Scott. The foreground of the square was draped in many flags with the Glasgow City Chambers in the background. He took a moment to admire the view before he captured the scene with a photo.

Chapter 9 – Into Continental Europe

Roland spent most of the day watching television in his room at the Royal National Hotel and in the late afternoon made his way for the tour pre-departure meeting. He entered a room and was taken aback by the sight of a dozen or so strikingly beautiful, young women. "Hi, can we help you?" asked a delightful-sounding lady with an American accent.

"Sorry, but is this the place for the pre-departure meeting for the European tour that starts tomorrow?" Roland asked.

A number of the ladies responded in unison to the effect that they thought it was in the next room and that they had just completed the previous European tour. Roland waited until the choired reply faded.

That'd be right. Roland thought as he lingered in their presence. "I'd better try the next room then."

Roland ventured next door and took a seat at the table as a man stood.

"All right everyone, my name is Martin, your tour guide. If you could all take a seat and make yourselves comfortable. We've got a bit of stuff to cover, but we'll wait a little longer for any stragglers to arrive and then we'll start."

After the last stragglers were seated Martin outlined instructions and provided information about the tour. Roland counted the ratio of women to men in the group: 41 women and only nine men. *This couldn't be right,* he thought, *because if it is, this imbalance of women to men could be a problem.*

After the formalities, Martin offered the only option for them to have dinner together that night. "It was difficult to arrange dinner anywhere other than at the hotel as it's such a large group. There's a set menu of either meat or fish with fries, followed by dessert."

The four vegetarians politely declined, as did a number of others, which left about half of the group who took up the dinner offer.

It was mid-evening by the time the diners sat for their meal and they wasted no time with the introductions and gossip. From what they could work out, there were 50 passengers comprising two couples, 39 single women and seven single men.

"Gee guys, you'd better look out with this many women after you," one of the ladies joked. The others laughed, except for Roland as he again reflected on the imbalance of the number of women to men.

After dinner, they wished each other goodnight and looked forward to an early start to the tour the following day.

The bus departed just as dawn broke and Martin allowed the driver to introduce himself. "Good morning everyone, my name is Scott, but most people call me Lanky." This was understandable as Lanky was tall, lean and gangly. Martin, on the other hand, was short and pixie looking. As soon as Lanky finished his address, music started playing. Roland suspected it may be the tour theme song.

Roland was right; Monty Python's *Always Look on the Bright Side of Life*, which was an instant hit.

The group drove to the port at Dover with lively chatter all the way. They then jumped on a ferry to cross the English Channel bound for Calais. Numerous photos were taken with the white cliffs of Dover in the background.

Once the group reached French soil, they re-boarded the bus and continued with their socialising until Martin interrupted. "I'm sure you are enjoying your banter, but I know you all haven't met each other so to assist with this process we will all have a chance to come up and introduce ourselves."

"Terrific," Roland gasped.

Fred and Roland were seated together towards the back of the bus and they were the last to be summoned. "You can go first Fred," Roland said.

Fred was a genuinely happy, good-natured and positive person who, after his introduction, encouraged Roland to get on with it. Roland slowly made his way to the front, took the microphone and contemplated what he would say.

"Hello everyone, my name's Roland and I come from Melbourne, although I grew up on a farm in the Snowy Mountains. My early years are all a bit of a blur, but as I understand it there was a radical group of lesbians who decided to break off from society and set up their own sect, known as the Amazonian Sycophants, or Sycos for short."

As many of the tour members had met Roland and already knew a bit about him, they were aware that it was a wind up and they started to smile and giggle. Roland continued with a straight face.

"They had no time for men, but every so often the Sycos went to various towns and cities to be serviced by the men there and I'm a product of a servicing. The Sycos were Right-to-Lifers and didn't want to give me up so they decided to raise me as a communal baby, without divulging who my Syco mum was. Eventually, the Sycos felt guilty about keeping my life story a secret so they told me which Syco was my mother."

By this time there were laughs at the end of just about every statement.

"They also advised that around the period when I was likely to have been conceived there were four men who could be my father. The Sycos assisted me in trying to track down my father, but without success. I'm still not sure who my father is, but I suspect he's either the trapeze artist from

Uzbekistan or the bullshit artist from Never Never Land. Thank you."

As Roland took his seat, there was rapturous applause.

Chapter 10 – Paris, France

The group continued through the French countryside and arrived at Joinville Le Pont for their three-night stay. After dinner, they were treated to a night tour of the Paris illuminations.

The next day was a full day to enjoy the sights of Paris. Roland thought he had found his ultimate city as, not only was the city beautiful, it was well planned and symmetrical. The Avenue des Champs-Elysees, La Grande Arche de la Defense, the Arc de Triomphe and the Place de la Concorde all seemed to line up so perfectly.

Roland was so enthralled with the city that when the time came for the group to return to camp, he elected to stay behind and further explore the city, making his own way back to camp via the Metro.

"Where have you been Roland? You've only got 15 minutes before we're supposed to be heading into town," urged Fred.

Roland quickly showered and changed, but was still ten minutes late. "Hurry up, you Syco," said Joe with a grin.

The group was given the freedom for a fast food dinner before they headed to the Latin Quarter for a cabaret show in an old theatre. "This is great," Roland said. "I could picture Toulouse-Lautrec sitting in a place like this!"

The group took their seats whilst champagne was being poured. It was a carnival atmosphere and the noise levels erupted when the dancing girls, wearing frilly dresses, made the stage.

The performers exhibited their prowess at the cancan, which had everyone jumping.

"Hey Roland! Could you pass me over more of that champagne?" Fred called out.

Roland shouted back. "Yes I can can!"

The group spent the next morning visiting the spectacular Palace of Versailles with its breathtaking gardens. The afternoon allowed for more exploring around central Paris, which included a saunter down the avenues and lounging in the café's and bars. After their evening meal, the group had a relaxing time at camp.

It was an early morning start to pack up, leave Paris and head through the wonderful wine region of Burgundy en route to their next stop at a chateau in the heart of the Beaujolais. The group was able to slip in some wine tasting before their evening meal and finished off at a lively disco.

The next day offered an optional excursion exploring the scenery around the chateau, cycling around the picturesque local villages and enjoying a typical French fare, picnic lunch. It was a glorious day and the select picnic spot was on the hill referred to as the 'Top of the World'.

They were on the move again the following day. This time they were heading southward with a stop at the majestic Roman aqueduct, Pont du Gard.

The tour members were given some time to walk around the area and, if they chose, to walk along the walls of the three levelled structure. Fred, Joe and Roland raced up to walk the highest wall and they took a breather as they reached the top.

They started to walk along the wall, which Roland thought was fairly precarious. They were approached by people coming from the opposite direction and it was about half-way across the aqueduct where they met. The other people did not give much leeway even though they were walking along the inside of the wall.

"I've had enough," Roland commented and started heading back.

"Why, what's up?" Fred asked.

"There are quite a few people up here and this wall must be around 50 metres high and only three metres wide. I don't know about you guys, but I'm not keen on falling to my death today."

"You're a chicken," Joe teased.

"I might be a chicken, but at least I won't be adding to the average 15 fatalities they have here every year."

Joe and Fred made no further comment and closely followed Roland back to the bus.

"Gosh Roland, I had no idea there were that many deaths from that wall," Fred commented.

"Neither did I," Roland said. "I just made that up."

Chapter 11 – Spain

The group progressed through France, into Spain and arrived at their campsite in Barcelona. The camp was well equipped with a games room, bar, swimming pools and a water slide. It was located some way out of central Barcelona so the group had a local dinner and spent the evening enjoying the camp facilities.

Early morning and Barcelona was beckoning. The group was driven to the Gothic Quarter of the port city. It was a sunny day and they paraded up and down *La Rambla*. They commenced from the Colom Monument, in memory of Christopher Columbus, and proceeded to the square, *Placa de Catalunya*. They then walked to Gaudi's cathedral, *La Sagrada Familia*.

Roland was stunned with the artwork. "To think it was commenced over 100 years ago," he said with awe.

"I believe they still plan to have it finished," Fred remarked.

"Not that it matters," Roland said. "It's already a masterpiece."

After a panoramic view from *Mont-Juic*, the group returned to camp to prepare for the evening, which was described to be a night of Spanish cuisine, music and dancing.

The restaurant was a cellar-style cantina with a small stage that jutted from one of the side walls. The seating consisted of rows of benches placed either side of long wooden tables.

Roland joined the two couples, as well as Susannah, Sally, Val, Fred, Joe and Shane. Shane was a happy chappy who loved his booze and, as Roland didn't mind a drink either, they enthusiastically pursued their common interest. To their delight, the tables were lined with carafes of sangria.

The group was served a typical Spanish meal that included gazpacho, tapas and a huge paella to share. They were entertained with Spanish music, which highlighted flamenco dancing and singing.

"This flamenco singing is really sung with feeling," commented Sally.

"Yes it is sung with feeling," Roland agreed, "and I think that feeling is pain."

"Hey Sippy Sippy, a toast," declared Shane.

"Why do you call Roland Sippy Sippy?" asked Sally.

"I think Roland should explain," Shane said.

Roland took a decent gulp of sangria and got to his feet. "Okay, I'll explain. My surname is Cipillone, which Shane pronounces 'Sipillone' and hence emerged the prefix *Sipi* and where *Sippy* derived. Shane then took the liberty of naming me twice."

Roland took another few gulps of sangria. "However, I must clarify that I am of Italian heritage and, although my name is spelt *Cipillone*, the Italian pronunciation is 'Chipillone' as *ci* is pronounced 'chi' in Italian."

Roland took more gulps of sangria before he continued. "It's also worth noting that in Portuguese and Spanish, *ci* is indeed pronounced 'si', in which case, 'Sipillone' would, in fact, be the way they pronounce my surname."

Roland's glass was being continually filled and he took another couple of gulps of sangria before he rounded off his explanation. "Finally, it would be remiss of me if I didn't conclude, particularly as we are in the fair city of Barthelona, that whereas the Spanish may say 'Sipillone', I expect the Barthelonians would proudly state 'Thipillone' as my name."

Roland sat to a round of applause; well and truly smashed.

The night seemed to go on and on. Martin pointed out that Lanky had to drive into France tomorrow and they should leave earlier rather than later. The group started to make a move and there was a professional photographer allowing the tourists to have their photo taken whilst wearing a montero.

The bullfighting hat was slapped on Roland's head as he sat in his drunken stupor. He poked out his tongue and a photograph was taken. Inspection of the photograph drew many laughs as Roland looked more like a member of the Mouseketeers than a bullfighter.

"Do you take this photograph," asked the photographer.

Roland responded. "I do."

The next day, they headed back to France through Antibes on the famous *Cote D'Azur*. They stopped off to check out a Mediterranean beach before they travelled the additional short distance to their campsite.

The next morning, the group was driven along the *Cote D'azur* where they stopped to visit a perfumery and had a stroll around the promenades and marinas. They returned to camp for dinner before venturing into the principality of Monaco where they viewed the royal palace and visited the casino.

Chapter 12 – Italian Stallions

Italy was the next country on the itinerary and the bus headed southward to the charming ancient city of Pisa with its beautiful Romanesque architecture.

Roland joined Fred and Joe in a race up the stairs to the top of the leaning tower. "This is fantastic!" Fred said as he looked out over Pisa.

"Look at the views," said Joe, an eager look on his face.

"Just as well for this railing, as you can really feel the gravitation pull," Roland said.

"Hey, let's go down to the next level," Fred suggested.

Joe and Fred proceeded down the staircase and, after an extra couple of moments taking in the scenery, Roland followed.

"Shoot, this level doesn't have any railing," Joe stated with some trepidation.

"The stone and marble flooring is pretty slippery too," Fred added.

After a few minutes of shuffling around, they decided to head down.

The group moved on to Florence where their accommodation was in a villa with magnificent views of the beautiful renaissance city. They dined at the villa and then headed into town to check out a local disco where there were quite a few local men.

"This doesn't look too promising," Fred said with a frown.

"I don't know about that," Roland said.

"What do you mean?" asked Joe.

"Well, we've been fortunate to have the company of the couples and several of the friendlier women; however, the other women have generally been unsociable and bitchy. Tonight might be an opportunity for them to feel comfortable in their own element."

"By in their own element, do you mean with all these sleaze buckets?" Fred asked.

"Precisely," Roland said with a nod.

It didn't take too long before the local guys approached a number of the women from the tour who seemed to lap up the attention.

Fred, Joe, Shane and Roland were content to drink at the bar.

Fred noticed Sally dancing with one of the local men. "Look at that guy. Can you believe Sally's dancing with that creep?"

"Sally's just a naturally friendly person," Roland suggested.

"Look now, he's starting to get a bit fresh," Joe pointed out.

"I must admit, I didn't expect that Sally would be that friendly," Roland said with surprise.

Sally soon left the man and approached the bar. "That bastard tried to pick me up and then he tried to grope me."

"What did you expect?" Roland said.

"What do you mean?" asked Sally.

"Well this club is obviously a popular tourist spot, and I'd expect the local opportunistic gentlemen come here to pick up," Roland explained.

"Gentlemen you say," Sally said wryly. "They're not gentlemen; they're animals."

The following day was a full day in Florence with the highlight expected to be Michelangelo's sculpture of *David*. The group was initially brought to a leather factory before they wandered through central Florence to admire many attractions and sights. They had an exceptionally knowledgeable guide, who walked them through the Duomo and provided an excellent historical, artistic and engineering account of the works.

The guide then gave the group some unexpected news. "We will not be able to view the statue of *David* due the closure of the Galleria dell'Accademia as a result of a workers' strike. Nevertheless, we will take you to the Piazza della Signoria, which is where the replica of the statue of *David* is on display, being the original location for the statue before it was moved to the Galleria. So at least you can witness the replica in the statue's originally designated location."

"At least that's something," Joe said with a shrug.

"But it's not the original," Roland said. "It's not the same."

The group returned to the villa and dressed for a meal out on the town. The dinner was at a *casa rustica*, which served homestyle Italian cooking. The diners comprised a broad mix of people from various countries. It was a lively atmosphere with the group being placed on a few benches. The food was basic, but very good with a plentiful quantity of beer and wine consumed.

Fred, Joe and Roland were socialising with a group of American ladies, and Roland found himself outside chatting with Karen from Florida who was studying at a university in Florence. She was an attractive lady in her mid-twenties with brown eyes, blonde-brown hair, full lips and a curvaceous body.

"So what do you think about coming back to my place tonight?" Karen suggested.

"I'm not sure. I'd certainly like to, but we're leaving for Rome early tomorrow morning," Roland said.

"Tomorrow morning is a long time away and where's your sense of adventure?" Karen queried, running her fingers along Roland's arm.

Roland threw caution to the wind and headed off with Karen.

"Over here Roland; we'll catch a bus," Karen instructed.

The moment Roland made it to the bus stop, Karen's tongue was down his throat and they commenced to tongue wrestle. He was conscious of a multitude of people lined up at the bus stop, and was saved by the arrival of the bus.

"Where can I purchase a ticket?" asked Roland.

"I've been living in Florence for nine months and have never purchased a bus ticket," Karen admitted.

The bus took off and, in true Italian tradition, the driver floored it. As the driver was rounding the bends, Roland had to hang on to something for dear life, and that something happened to be Karen's rump. This brought a large smile to her face and another bout of tongue wrestling commenced.

Before Roland could steady himself, Karen hit the buzzer, the bus slammed to a stop and she dragged him off.

The minute Karen closed the door to her apartment, she jumped him. There was a mad scramble to undress as Karen guided him to her bedroom and onto the bed. It was a whirlwind of emotion and sensuality that came to its natural climax.

"Wow Roland, it's a pity that you're leaving tomorrow," Karen sighed.

They rested a while when they started to become playful again. They were building up their intensity when they heard a noise from inside the apartment.

"What's that?" Roland asked.

"Oh it's probably my roommate," said Karen. "But don't worry, he's cool."

A male roommate? "I'd better be going as we're leaving early," Roland said as he collected his belongings.

A quick exchange of details, and he was off.

It was indeed an early morning start and Roland was greeted with Fred's grinning inquisition. "Well Casanova, how was it?"

Roland wasn't one to kiss and tell. "It was okay."

"Come on Roland, give us the details," Joe urged.

"There's nothing much to say. Karen's nice and we had a good time together… Oh shit! I forgot my watch."

The group headed south to the eternal city of Rome. Roland was upset for having left his watch at Karen's place, and kept to himself.

They settled into their tents and had lunch before heading for central Rome. They visited the Roman Forum, Circus Maximus, the Trevi Fountain, Piazza Venezia and the Colosseum. They then went on to visit the Vatican City.

It was a very hot 40 degrees at the time they reached St. Peter's Square and there were quite a number of people lined up. Roland decided to explore the Vatican the following day and excused himself.

Roland set off on his own and viewed the Spanish steps, Piazza Navonna and the Pantheon. He was so blown away by the Colosseum that he returned for an encore visit. He then walked down Via Fori Imperiali, imagining what it would have been like to have been a Roman soldier marching down the main thoroughfare.

Entering Piazza Venezia, Roland circled the Victor Emmanuel II Monument and the Palazzo Venezia. He could visualize Mussolini on the balcony belting out one of his trademark, gesticulated and animated speeches.

Making his way back to the campsite, Roland freshened up and joined the others for a restaurant meal in town.

Doing his own thing the next morning, Roland made his way to the Vatican. He roamed St. Peter's Square and was highly impressed with the dimensions, angles and symmetrical formation of the columns. He entered the basilica and took his time to appreciate the various chapels, tombs and dome before proceeding to the Sistine Chapel to marvel the works of Michelangelo.

In the afternoon, Roland joined the others in an expedition to the Catacombs. They were instructed to catch the No.118 bus and it wasn't too long before the bus hurled around the bend and came to an abrupt stop.

Looking at the glint in the bus driver's eye, Roland thought he had a fairly good idea as to what the passengers had in store. After all had boarded, he held on for dear life and the driver was off. The ride was even worse than he expected as some of the roads were unsealed, but this didn't deter the driver from exhibiting his rallying skills.

It was hard to tell whether the dramatic expression on the faces of the passengers was one of horror or excitement; however, when the ride was over, the uniform expressions of relief were unmistakable. They disembarked and walked to the catacombs like zombies.

The network of subterranean burial chambers and galleries was fascinating, although some of the group thought it all a bit too gory. It was time for the return bus ride and, as they stood at the bus stop, there was a sense that some of the passengers envied the corpses who had found their peace, unlike the terror bus trip that was to come.

The bus came hurtling towards the stop where the driver slammed on the brakes. As the dust settled, the passengers looked at each other, took a deep breath and boarded.

On day 14 of the tour, the group headed south towards Mount Vesuvius. They were on the motorway when the bus came to a sudden stop. Lanky inspected the engine and attempted to continue the journey, but the bus slowed to another stop.

Lanky had another attempt to ascertain the cause of the problem whilst a couple of highway policemen pulled up on their motorbikes, which gave the ladies something to get excited about. The police questioned Martin and Lanky before Martin reported back to the group.

"Well, it appears we have serious mechanical problems. We will need to get someone out to take a look, which may take some time. We're also contacting the company to have a replacement bus on standby. Unfortunately, either way, we won't be able to visit Pompeii."

Huge sighs of disappointment filled the bus.

The mechanic arrived but to no avail, and a tow truck was called as the group waited for a replacement bus. Four hours later they were on their way again.

Lanky made a sterling effort to traverse the southern Italian roads to arrive at Brindisi in time for the group to grab a bite to eat before boarding the ferry bound for Greece. They were noticeably disappointed with the events of the day, but made it known to Martin and Lanky that they appreciated their efforts.

The port at Brindisi was very busy with loads of tourists, which heightened the atmosphere of sheer chaos and commercial exploitation. The group grabbed a bite from a restaurant offering a tourist menu. They then returned to the bus to collect their luggage before boarding the Poseidon ferry for the crossing to Patras.

Chapter 13 – Mediterranean Odyssey

The group travelled by bus along the Peloponnese coast and across the Corinth Canal to Athens. They stayed in a pensione located in Glyfada, a beach on the outer fringes of the city.

They went to a restaurant in the Plaka area where they enjoyed traditional Greek food and music. It was a fairly early night as the group prepared for the next day and their destination of the Greek island of Mykonos.

The ferry departed from the port of Piraeus. The group was looking forward to the island stint of the holiday – it was the halfway mark of their European adventure and gave them the opportunity to have a relaxing base for six days.

Mykonos was a beautiful island with whitewashed houses, windmills and boutique stores. It was paved with cobbled streets and surrounded by pristine, sandy beaches.

Accommodation was in a comfortable hotel with a swimming pool. Fred, Joe and Roland shared a room and they took little time making themselves at home. They lined the ceiling with makeshift clothes lines, and before long their room looked like a disaster zone.

The group quickly got into the island routine. They had late morning starts with a light brunch while relaxing by the pool. The afternoon would be time for buggie rides, shopping or swimming at the beach. This was followed by a siesta before dinner and their attack on the nightlife. It was hard for them to know what to look forward to the most, as each part of the day had its own rewards.

The six days on Mykonos elapsed quickly and the group took the ferry back to the mainland where they returned to the hotel at Glyfada in Athens.

The following day, the group had a guided tour of Athens that took in the Acropolis, the Parthenon and the Parliament building. They travelled westward back to Patras for their return ferry ride to Brindisi. They were then driven up the east coast of Italy, arriving at their overnight stay in Casalbordino.

The group proceeded through the Republic of San Marino and on to Venice. They had twin-share accommodation on the island of Lido in a grand building that was formerly a monastery. There was an option to take a gondola ride just before sunset that included being serenaded. Roland thought the experience could only be truly enjoyed if he was to sit alongside a lady he liked so for him it had to be either Susannah or Sally.

Sally was already paired off with another woman so Roland asked Susannah and she agreed. The gondolier wove his craft along the waterways and serenaded part of the way. It was a pleasant ride and Roland was just getting comfortable when the ride abruptly came to an end.

Saturday was a beautiful, sunny day and the group ventured via waterbus from the Lido to Piazza San Marco. They were brought to see some leatherwear and demonstrations of glass blowing before being permitted some free time.

Roland joined several group members to visit Doge's Palace, St Mark's Basilica, the Bridge of Sighs and various other bridges and canals. They had time to sit down at one of the many canal side cafés and sip on cappuccinos.

The group took off the next day through the Dolomite Mountain Range and into Austria where they set up at a campsite in Vienna.

The splendours of the Schonbrunn Palace and the Hofburg Palace were the highlights of the following day with the evening meal at a restaurant in the Vienna Woods.

Chapter 14 – Schnapped Up

Leaving Vienna, the group travelled on to the fairytale city of Salzburg. They admired the fine examples of baroque-style architecture as well as the birthplace of Mozart and the parks that contained a statue of Mozart.

The group had a photo stop at the house from the movie *Sound of Music*. They then moved through to Germany and, the capital of the famous beer state of Bavaria, Munich.

They visited Deutsches Museum, St Peter's Tower and the Olympic Complex, stage for the 1972 Olympic Games. Roland was so obsessed with the Glockenspiel in the Marienplatz that he hung around for two hours to enjoy a repeat sounding. Later, they visited the Dachau Concentration Camp.

The group had some time to rest before they left their camp for dinner in town. They went to a typical Bavarian beer hall where they got stuck into the beers.

A band appeared – a form of Umpapa band – which people cringed about at first, but got into the swing of things after consuming more of the amber ale.

"It's the chicken song, the chicken song," Roland would shout out at the start of each new song. To his surprise, as he shouted it out once more, the chicken song actually started playing.

Everyone was having a fabulous time and even Sally, who normally wouldn't drink much, seemed happily intoxicated. There were only a handful of people remaining at the end of the night with Sally and Roland catching a cab together.

Roland advised the taxi driver of their destination and he relaxed into the back seat next to Sally. They initially got cosy and progressed to fondling and kissing for the rest of the drive.

When they arrived back at camp, they were walking back to their tents, hand in hand, when they started to become friendly again. Sally soon pulled away. "I'd better get back to my tent as Susannah may be concerned about my whereabouts."

As Sally walked off, Roland sat on a swing and spent a moment to contemplate what could have been.

The following morning, the group left Germany through the Bavarian Alps. They re-entered Austria and stopped off for a break to go white water rafting. They had a decent tussle with the river rapids before they were back on the bus. They travelled through Innsbruck to the gorgeous village of Hopfgarten and their accommodation at a delightful gasthof.

After the heavy night before and a tiring long day, the group appreciated a relaxing evening with dinner at the gasthof. This was followed by quiet drinks at the bar, at least that's the way it started.

Glen, Shane and Roland got socialising with the barman and discussion found itself on the topic of the schnapps challenge. It was described as an informal tradition where the guests would see who could down the greatest number of schnapps shots. The record for one night was claimed to be 51 shots held by an American female tourist.

"I'm up for the challenge!" Shane declared.

Roland wasn't really interested; however, in the spirit of the schnapps tradition he stated, "I'll drink to that!"

Shane commenced the proceedings. "So what do we have here bartender?"

"We have a reasonable selection of a variety of schnapps flavours," the bartender explained.

"How many flavours exactly?" Glen asked and the barman pointed to a list on the wall.

<u>Schnapps Flavours</u>

Apfel/Apple
Apricot
Banana
Blackberry
Blueberry
Butterscotch
Cherry
Cinnamon
Chocolate
Doornkaat
Herb
Kiwi
Lemon
Orange
Pear
Peppermint
Plum
Raspberry
Spearmint
Strawberry
Vanilla
Watermelon

Stroh

Stroh Rum

"Well, we'll have to try them all," Shane decreed.

"Why don't we take it from the top so it makes it easier to keep track of what we've had?" Glen suggested.

"What a great way to start, with apple," Shane said.

"I really like the banana one," commented Glen.

"I prefer the apricot," Shane said. "And this butterscotch is out of this world."

"I don't know about the Chocolate one," said Roland.

"Hey Glen, the next one's a Kiwi; it will give me great pleasure downing this one," Shane said.

"Spearmint, haven't we had the spearmint?" Glen asked.

"No that was the peppermint," Roland replied.

Roland was heavily intoxicated when he indicated that he may call it quits.

"Come on Sippy Sippy," Shane urged. "You can't desert us now."

"What's this Stroh thing?" Glen interrupted.

"Yeah bartender, what's Stroh?" Shane pried further.

"Stroh Obstschnapps is natural and fruity schnapps that has been handed down through generations of the Stroh family," the bartender explained.

"Okay then, we'll have to drink it in honour of the Stroh family. To the Stroh family!" Roland proposed.

"To the Stroh family!" came the universal reply.

"Hey bartender, what about that Stroh rum?" Glen queried.

"You have completed the schnapps list so you may wish go to bed," the bartender suggested.

"But what's this Stroh rum?" Glen persisted.

Glen took the bottle and started reading out loud. "STROH Original is the best aromatic expression of the Austrian way of life." Glen then decreed. "All right! We'll have to taste the aromatic expression of the Austrian way of life!"

"It's also technically on the schnapps list," Shane added.

Glen and Shane then looked over to Roland and there was a moment of silence as they waited for Roland to reply. "What the hell; I'll drink to that!"

Roland was the first to knock back the Stroh rum. "Bloody hell," he cried in disgust. "This is bloomin' rocket fuel!"

"All right," Shane cheered and he also knocked back a Stroh rum. "Yikes, you're not kidding, this stuff's lethal."

"What's this big number 80 on the front of the bottle?" Glen queried.

"That's 80% alcohol by volume," replied the bartender.

"Holy shit!" Glen cried as he downed his shot.

"Well, I think that should definitely do," said the bartender.

"You're got to be joking," Roland stated. "I can't go to bed with this rough taste in my mouth; now which was the schnapps I liked the most..."

In the morning, Roland was woken by his roommates.

"Could you keep it down please fellas," Roland pleaded.

"Come on Roland, get up," encouraged Joe.

"Leave me alone," Roland grumbled. "I feel horrible."

"Today will be our only chance to explore the village so if you want to join us cycling to town, best you get up," Fred explained.

Grumbling, Roland crawled out of bed and dressed.

"You can hire the bicycles from over there," Joe said, pointing.

"I don't even have any money," Roland mumbled.

"That's okay; I'll pay for you," Sally said.

"Thank's Sally, I'll pay you back later," Roland said, mounting the bike.

"Oi Roland, you're going the wrong way!" Fred shouted out.

Roland completed a U-turn and headed back towards the others. He was still under the influence of alcohol, tired and dehydrated. Riding on the wrong side of the road for Europe, he followed the road around the bend and sought to mount the footpath, but there was a road barrier. He looked up and a car was coming straight for him.

Chapter 15 – A Near Death Experience

Roland's sight was blurry, but he could make out the vision of a beautiful, blonde lady. He couldn't discern who she was or how far away she was, but he tried to reach for her.

The lady initially tried to veer away, but as she noticed him continuing to reach for her, she took his arm and placed it under the blankets.

A nurse and I'm in hospital, Roland realised. *The car must have collected me.*

As Roland's vision cleared, he noticed a number of tubes inserted in various parts of his anatomy. One was inserted up a nostril, there were a couple of tubes coming out of his arm, a tube emanating from his belly and, upon lifting the blankets, another one hanging off his willy.

The nurse left Roland alone in the room as he wondered over the state of his condition. He was having trouble breathing, so he fiddled with the nasal tube and slid it out. *That's better,* he thought. *I can breathe a lot easier now.*

Another nurse entered the ward. "How are you feeling?" she asked.

"I'm feeling much better now that nasal tube is out," Roland said.

The nurse gasped and quickly exited the room. When she returned, she had a doctor in tow. "Hello, my name is Dr. Lehmann, how are you feeling?"

"Oh, I'm feeling fine, thanks Doctor."

"You had quite a collision."

"Yes, I guess I came off second best," Roland said. "Was anyone else hurt?"

"Apart from some very concerned people, you were the only person who sustained any physical injuries," the doctor said. "Fortunately, the worst is over, but we still have a few things that we need to attend to. We will leave you to your dinner, and provide you with a proper diagnosis tomorrow morning. How does that sound?"

"That sounds fine, thanks Doctor."

The next morning, an attractive, young nurse, named Jane, entered the room. "Good morning Roland."

"Good morning, Jane."

"Did you enjoy your breakfast?"

"It was great thanks; the food in this hospital is very good."

"The doctor should be here in an hour or so. Did you want to have your sponge bath before he arrives?"

"I think the doctor would appreciate that," Roland said. "Will you be giving me the bath today, Jane?" he asked hopefully.

"No Roland, you know we have special staff for that."

"Oh yeah, that's right; the older female staff that train in Greco-Roman wrestling."

After Roland's bath, Dr. Lehmann entered the room. "Good morning, Roland. I will provide your diagnosis now," he advised. "You had a fairly solid impact and when you arrived at the hospital you were critical. However, after we operated, we were able to stabilise your condition. You were in shock, in fact, you may still have some mild shock and it may take a little more time to get over. Our greatest concern was your spleen, which had ruptured, so we removed it. You also have a bruised left kidney, a series of broken ribs on your left side, a fracture of your left shoulder blade and a temporary skull fracture, also on the left hand side. That's basically it; so do you have any questions?"

"What do you mean by a temporary skull fracture?" asked Roland.

"It is a hairline fracture that will mend itself over time," Dr. Lehmann replied.

"What about the other fractures and broken ribs?"

"They should also heal naturally, over time. You should be well enough to commence mobilisation in a day or two and, after a week, we can commence further movement, physiotherapy and exercise. How does that sound Roland?"

"Sounds good, Doctor," Roland said, trying to take it all in.

Soon after the doctor left, a nurse entered. "Excuse me Roland, you have a telephone call, it's your parents."

"Oh no, they know about the accident?"

"I'm afraid they do and they seem very concerned."

Roland picked up the handset. "Hello?"

"Hello. Roland, how are you?" asked Roland's father in his usual strong voice.

"I'm fine, Dad, everything is fine."

"How can you be fine? From what the hospital told us, we thought you were going to die!"

"I had a bit of an accident, that's all. They're taking really good care of me and I'll be okay."

"Hang on Roland, your mother wants to hear your voice."

"Hello Roland." Roland's mother spoke as she cried.

"Hi Mum, I'm fine there's no need to cry."

Roland's mother continued to cry and he heard his father. "Give me back the phone; you heard his voice so you know he's alive."

"Roland."

"Yes, Dad."

"Do we need to send someone to bring you home? I can arrange to send someone."

"Dad, that's not necessary, believe me, I'm well and getting better. I'll be perfectly all right and when I leave here, I'll be visiting our relatives – they're bound to take good care of me."

"Hmmm, all right, but if you need anything, you call us," Roland's father instructed.

"No problem, Dad. The people here in Austria are fantastic and they're taking really good care of me. In fact, another patient told me that I was lucky to have had my accident here rather than in Italy. Apparently the hospitals here in the Austrian Tyrolean Mountains are amongst the best, while the hospital care in Italy is said to be rubbish."

"Now that I can believe," Roland's father said.

After five days of hospitalisation, a young lady entered Roland's ward. "Hello, are you Roland?"

"Yes I am."

"My name is Hanna. I am the daughter of the people in the car that collided with you."

"Oh, hello Hanna, I hope everyone is all right."

"Yes they are well, although they were worried about you. They asked me to visit you and give you these chocolates."

"Oh, that's very kind of you. I caused so much trouble for them and they want to give me something, I don't know what to say."

"They were sorry about what happened and they wanted to know whether you were all right."

"Yes," Roland said, accepting the chocolates. "I'm very well and they shouldn't feel sorry as it was entirely my fault."

Hanna stayed a little longer before she suggested that she should be going.

"Thank you, Hanna, I really appreciate your visit and the chocolates. I'd like to thank you and your parents very much."

Later that day a young man visited Roland. "Hello Roland, my name is Josh and I work for the tour company; I hope you're feeling better?"

"Hello Josh, I'm feeling much better, thanks."

"I was asked to let you know that we have organised everything with your insurance company, they have confirmed your cover and are dealing directly with the hospital to pay your bills. The only bill they won't cover is this charge from the police," Josh explained.

"The police?" Roland queried. "What do they charge for?"

"I understand it's a traffic fine," Josh replied. "Apparently whenever there is an accident someone has to pay a fine and, in this case, you're the one. Anyway, there are a bunch of guys that you might know who would like to speak to you. I'll telephone them for you now... here you go Roland."

"Hello," Roland said.

"Howdy Roland, it's Martin."

"Hi Martin, how's everything going?"

"Things are going well, but more to the point, how are you?"

"I'm fine, how's the tour going?"

"It's been good, but there's a bunch of people that miss you. Hang on…"

"Sippy, Sippy, g'day mate."

"Shane! G'day to you too. I hope you've been making up for the booze I've missed out on."

"No fear about that Roland."

"Hello, Duckie."

"Fred, you idiot, how's it going mate?"

"I'm fine, but I'm really sorry I left you in Hopfgarten."

"Sorry, what for? I was the dunce who played chicken with a car. You just make sure you enjoy yourself for the both of us."

"Hi Roland."

"Sally, hi. I'm really sorry, Sally; I owe you the money from the bike hire."

"Roland, you're unbelievable, don't worry about that, I just wish you were here."

"So do I, Sally."

"It's Martin again, both Susannah and Joe, as well as all the rest of the gang say hi and wish you all the best. Also, everyone was signing and adding things to our tour book. Well everyone unanimously voted to send it to you. And we have a T-shirt everyone has signed and we'll send you that as well."

"Gee," Roland said, "I'm really touched."

"Is that all you've got to say, Duckie?" Fred said.

"Well, I was also thinking; the things a guy has to go through just to get a free T-shirt."

Roland was in hospital for almost two weeks and had improved markedly. "When might I be able to leave the hospital?" Roland asked the doctor.

"Given your progress with the physiotherapy and your improved condition, you should be able to leave whenever you want," Dr. Lehmann replied.

Whenever I want, Roland wondered. *It seems odd that the decision to leave is left up to me.* "Okay, what about if I leave the day after tomorrow."

"The day after tomorrow," repeated Dr. Lehmann. "I shall commence arrangements to see whether we can discharge you on Saturday morning, 3rd September. We shall let you know tomorrow morning, Roland."

"Thank you, Doctor."

The next morning Dr. Lehmann visited Roland with a nurse and a physiotherapist. "Good morning, Roland. We have good news. Your discharge for tomorrow has been approved; however, it is subject to conditions. Firstly, discharge is on the basis that you are released to home care, which means that you are required to stay with someone for a further week."

"But…I don't know anyone with whom I can stay," Roland stated.

"That's fine," Dr. Lehmann said. "The tour company has made enquiries and there is a family that has a farm near the gasthof where you can stay if you are agreeable."

"That's great; of course I'm agreeable."

"Good then. The only additional things you need to know are the physiotherapy exercises, which the physiotherapist will go over with you, and the medication you will need to take, which will be administered by the nurse. Well Roland, that's it and all the best."

"Thank you Dr. Lehmann; you saved my life."

The doctor smiled. "No problem; I was just doing my job."

It was Saturday morning and the time for Roland's discharge. He gathered his things and thanked the staff who took care of him.

"The taxi is waiting outside for you Roland," Jane advised.

"Thank you Jane and goodbye."

"Goodbye Roland."

The taxi took Roland by a timber yard and he immediately recalled the familiar scent of pine. It was the same scent he smelled on that fateful day. The taxi arrived at the farm and made its way up the drive where a woman, a man, a girl and a boy waited to greet him.

"Hello, it is Roland ya?" said the woman.

"Yes I am Roland."

"This is my husband Marcus, my daughter Isabelle, my son Helmut and I am Ingrid."

"Hello everyone."

"Wait," Ingrid said. "Marcus will take your bags; it must be difficult for you with that sling."

"Thank you Ingrid and Marcus."

"We will show you to your room, you can settle in and we can then have some lunch," Ingrid said.

"That sounds wonderful," Roland replied.

After visiting his room, Roland descended the timber staircase to the kitchen. "Is everything in order, Roland?" asked Ingrid.

"Yes, thank you, Ingrid. This is a lovely home, I like it very much."

"Children, lunch is ready! Marcus is tending to the cows, but he should be back shortly. You may sit here Roland, at the head of the table. Marcus is at the other end. Children sit on that side and I will sit on this side,"

Ingrid instructed.

Marcus returned and took his seat at the table, which was the cue for dinner to be served.

"Excuse me, Mother, is it all right if Helmut and I take Roland to the village for a walk?" Isabelle asked.

"That is a nice thought, but Roland may not yet be ready to go to the village," Ingrid said. "You can take him another time, if he wishes."

"Thank you, Isabelle," Roland stated. "Your mother is right. I don't feel strong enough to go to the village; however, I would like to go for a walk around the farm after lunch, if that's all right."

"Yes, Mother, we can show Roland the farm!" Helmut said with exuberance not usually accustomed at the dinner table, and which he realised as the words passed his lips. "Sorry mother."

"That's all right, Helmut," Ingrid said. "I think that would be good."

"Thank you Ingrid, lunch was delicious," Roland said.

"I'm glad you liked it Roland. Now children, you may take Roland for a walk."

Marcus immediately followed. "I can show you a few things around the farm," he said.

Roland sensed that Marcus had a hint of pride in his voice. "That would be great, thanks Marcus," Roland said. "I really like farms."

The children burst out of the house, ran around with what seemed to be limitless energy and began playing with their two dogs. The dogs then paid their respects to the stranger by approaching him, sniffing around and wagging their tails.

"Hello, you guys," Roland said as he patted the dogs alternately with his right hand, having his left arm in the sling.

"Children, take the dogs and lead the way," directed Marcus and the children happily obeyed.

"We have a few hectares of land where we run dairy cows and some sheep. It is not a huge commercial concern, but we make a little money, as we do with renting some rooms. I retired from an engineering job and I thought I would pursue my love of farming. Ingrid is happy and the children seem to enjoy it," Marcus modestly explained.

"Yes, your children definitely seem happy and this scenery is beautiful," Roland said as he took in the rolling, green hills.

"Yes it is," agreed Marcus with contentment. "Let me know when you are ready to return to the house."

Marcus showed Roland his animals, sheds and pointed out the extent of his land. Roland waited until he sensed that Marcus had shown him the main attractions. "I think I might be ready to return to the house," Roland advised.

"Children, we are heading back now," Marcus shouted.

Roland settled in well with the family, largely due to the fact that they were all perfect hosts. Ingrid was the most talkative and Marcus was friendly, but more reserved. The children were quiet and respectful in the common areas of the house, but opened up into happy, playful children in their own rooms and the outdoors. Roland concluded that it must be due to a good upbringing. He thoroughly enjoyed his time with the family and his walks with the children to the village were a highlight.

After six days at the farmhouse, Roland felt that he was just about strong enough to move on. He took the opportunity to visit the gasthof and found Josh. "Hi Josh, I'm about to move on now. I really want to thank you, Martin, Lanky and the tour company for everything you have done for me. I really appreciate it."

"It was no problem Roland. I was going to come over to the farmhouse to give you these small items. You may already know what they are," Josh said, handing Roland a package.

"Yes, I think I do; thanks Josh."

Roland returned to the farmhouse to thank and say goodbye to the family.

The taxi made its way through to Hopfgarten's neighbouring town of Worgl and Roland was dropped off at the train station. His first rail journey was from Worgl to Innsbruck with an interconnecting train from Innsbruck to Lucerne.

Checking into his accommodation in central Lucerne, Roland rested and was contemplating the incidences of the last month and many thoughts entered his mind. *Did I leave Hopfgarten too early? I'm still thin and feel weak. I've never met my Italian relatives before; it will be awkward to meet them for the first time, especially in my condition. What a pity the accident occurred – I missed out on the last week of the tour.*

Roland found Lucerne to be a perfect stopover to convalesce. The town was situated on the northwest extremity of the Lake of Lucerne with the Reuss River flowing through.

The old town featured the original gate, the town wall, watchtowers and narrow, cobbled stoned streets. Roland was impressed by the distinctive architecture of the city and the Chapel Bridge with its water tower. He was also moved by the Lion of Lucerne, a sculpture carved in 1821 out of solid rock, being a monument to the Swiss Guards who were slaughtered defending Paris in 1792 during the French Revolution.

Chapter 16 – Meeting the Relos

The train ride from Lucerne Station to Genoa took just over six hours. Roland needed to ring his relatives, and while he'd not really envisaged this moment, his Italian was limited and his nerves took hold.

Roland's movements were almost in slow motion as he subconsciously delayed the inevitable. "Where are those silly gettoni?" he complained as he searched for his Italian phone tokens before he made the call. He spoke to Alba, one of his mother's cousins. They went through some preliminary introductions and he was instructed that he had the option of taking a taxi or the No.18 bus.

Catching the bus, Roland asked the driver to be notified of his stop. He was relieved to find the bus driver was a lot more restrained than the bus drivers he had experienced in Rome and Florence. He was alerted of the stop and climbed up the hill.

Locating the address, Roland rang the bell and spoke to Alba via the intercom. She arranged for another one of his mother's cousins, Nina, to escort him up to the apartment via a small, rickety elevator they had to squeeze into. They reached the apartment on the top floor with views towards central Genoa.

Roland was introduced to his mother's other cousins and two teenage children. He settled in and freshened up before dinner. They were all fussing over him and he didn't mind it in the least.

Dinner was served on the balcony – the usual practice during summer. It was a plentiful and scrumptious meal, which they rounded off with percolated coffee and homemade limoncello.

During Roland's stay in Genoa, his relatives escorted him to many attractions, including the port area and the Italian Riviera. It was a beautiful and proud city that highlighted the contribution of its most famous former citizen – Christopher Columbus. Roland had a happy time during his stay in Genoa and his relatives were disappointed with the news of his leaving.

The relatives left early on the day of Roland's departure and he spent the day making his final preparations. At mid-afternoon, he made his way down the apartment block via the rickety elevator and caught the bus to Genoa Station.

Roland took the overnight train to the city of Bari on the Adriatic coast in southern Italy. The train arrived at six o'clock in the morning and he was then required to take a small train to the country town of his mother's birthplace.

Arriving at midday, Roland found a public phone booth and made the call. His aunt, Clara, lived close by and he made his way along narrow streets through the small town before knocking on the door of a small, old brick house.

There was an excited welcome as Roland was invited in and introduced to his grandmother, Maria, who cried at the sight of him as he closely resembled his mother.

As emotions calmed, spirits lifted and happiness took over. They discussed many things over the course of the day and, as the day progressed, more and more of the relatives arrived.

Staying only a few days, Roland's departure dampened the happy mood. He was escorted to the train where the relatives waved him farewell as the train pulled away.

Roland took the train from Bari to Foggia, then a bus up the mountain range to his father's birthplace.

It was overcast and gloomy as the creaky, old bus reached the mountains. Roland was exhausted with his arm and ribs causing him pain as the bus tugged up the mountains and slowly weaved its way through the valleys.

On arrival, Roland was again in search of a public phone and he made yet another call. Again, it was fortuitous that the house was very close, and he walked the narrow, cobbled stoned streets and quickly found the address. In a flash, Angela opened the door and greeted him then introduced him to Rita who took his bags and sat him down.

Roland's father had few surviving relatives, comprising a few cousins and their families. Rita was his father's cousin, and Angela her daughter. They chatted with him for a little while before they led him to a room that they had set aside for him. They gave him time to settle in before dinner.

Roland was introduced to Rita's husband Antonio and their son Vito. They had an enjoyable dinner and he was made to feel at home. The relatives sensed that he was tired and encouraged him to get some rest.

In the morning, Roland was feeling much better, and Angela took him to the town centre where a crowd had gathered. His father was a popular character and, even though his father had left the town some forty years earlier, the townsfolk remembered or had heard of him and were enthusiastic to meet his son.

Many of the townsfolk shook Roland's hand. A booming voice then echoed from the midst of the crowd and a solid, old man approached and hugged Roland. The man soon introduced himself as Pepe, a close friend of Roland's father. Pepe insisted on taking Roland on a tour of the town to check out some of his father's old haunts.

In every place they entered, whether it was a café, a bar or a shop, there were people who knew or had heard about Roland's father, which made Roland feel tremendously proud.

Roland spent the next few days visiting his father's family and friends. Every meeting was a grand affair and an eating extravaganza. He enjoyed the continued tradition of the passeggiata where the townsfolk socialised during their daily promenade along the streets after dinner.

The news of Roland's impending departure was met with sadness, and many of the townsfolk gathered to see him off.

Roland's return bus trip through the mountains was not the overcast and gloomy experience of his arrival. The sun was breaking through, he felt uplifted and was eager to hear his parents' voices again.

Arriving at Foggia, Roland was checking the timetable for Rome when he came across the timetable for Naples. *Naples! That's near Pompeii and not far from here. It's closer than Rome in fact it's virtually on the way to Rome in a roundabout way. Why didn't I ever think of this before, it's perfect.*

Regretting having missed out on Pompeii on the European tour, Roland purchased a ticket for Naples.

The train eventually arrived in Naples and Roland couldn't wait to call his parents. He rushed to the telephones at the station, dialled the number and the phone rang and rang and then rang out. *Why didn't they answer? What day is it? It's Saturday here so it's Sunday morning there. Dad must have taken mum to church.*

Roland found hotel accommodation, and after he checked in, he tried to ring his parents again. The phone rang for some time, and worry settled in. *It's almost 9.50 pm here, which would make it almost midday there; they should be home now.* Just as Roland was expecting the phone to ring out again, his mother answered.

"Hello, Ma!"

"Roland, how are you?"

"I'm fine, Ma. How are you?"

"I am good."

"I've met your family Ma and they all send you their love," Roland said excitedly.

"That's good," she whispered, and Roland could hear her fighting back tears.

"Who is it?" Roland's father's voice sounded in the background.

"It's Roland," his mother said.

"What's wrong now?"

"There's nothing wrong; he met the family; here talk to him."

"Hey."

"Hi, Pa. I met your family and friends, they all say hello and send you their love. I had no idea how many friends you have and how popular you are," Roland said with admiration.

"Ah yeah, I know," was his father's matter-of-fact reaction.

"Anyway, I'm in Naples now and I'm going to visit Pompeii," Roland declared.

"Oh, Naples," his father stated. "I remember Naples from when I was in the navy."

Roland thought he would interrupt just in case his father was going to recite one of his never-ending monologues. "Hey, Pa?"

"What son?"

"I love you, Pa."

Roland's father was not one to show emotion. "Yeah, yeah, you just take care of yourself and come home safely."

"Okay, Pa. Can I speak to Mum again?"

"Here, your son wants to speak to you."

"Roland?"

"I love you, Ma."

"I love you too, son."

Roland booked a tour of Pompeii and the Amalfi Coast for the following day. He used the remainder of the day to enjoy some of the attractions in Naples, including the Castel Nuovo, Castel Sant'Elmo and the Piazza Municipio.

The tour bus was only half full with about a dozen, mainly middle-aged travellers. When they arrived at Pompeii, they were escorted through the site by a guide.

Roland was overcome with an eerie feeling as he walked along the excavated streets and looked into the rooms, buildings and areas with the various exhibits and archaeological finds. Pompeii was badly damaged by an earthquake in 62AD, which was followed by the eruption of Mount Vesuvius in 79AD.

Pompeii lay undisturbed beneath ashes for over 1,500 years, with the excavation commencing in 1748 and new discoveries extending throughout the 19th and 20th centuries. There were even new excavations continuing to that day. In fact, more than a quarter of the city still remained to be excavated.

Roland viewed the exhibits in the museum erected near the Porta Marina, one of the eight gates of the city. He strolled down the streets, including Via dell' Abbondanza that once contained an amphitheatre and several houses. He had to take a few back streets to track down the popular attraction of Lupanare, the once famed brothel of Pompeii where phalluses engraved on rocks of roads and stones of buildings pointed the way to its location.

The group left Pompeii around midday and drove along the Amalfi Coast where they stopped at a café for a spot of lunch. Continuing along the coast, the passengers were treated to views out to the Gulf of Naples and the Gulf of Salerno. They also enjoyed views of the towns of Sorrento, Amalfi and, the place of the rich and famous, Positano.

Returning to Naples, Roland had a small dinner, walked around the local streets near the railway station and then retired to his hotel room.

Taking the first train to Rome, Roland arrived around midday. Even though he'd had a hearty breakfast he was still hungry so he had a snack at the railway station before finding a reasonable hotel at a modest rate.

Roland wanted a few days to rest before his first plane flight after his traffic accident. His condition had improved, although he was still weak and was having headaches. With two weeks left of his travels, he decided to split the time equally between Rome and London.

Chapter 17 – Home Time

During the first couple of days in Rome, Roland took it easy with his first priority being to purchase a flight from Rome to London. The first travel agent he stumbled on had a bargain flight on Air India. He couldn't think of airline disasters with Air India so he accepted.

Roland visited a number of attractions in Rome that included Campidolio, Piazza Della Republica, Piazza Del Popolo, Castel San Angelo, Piazza Colonna and Porta San Paolo with the nearby Pyramid of Cestius.

Making his way to the airport, Roland was confronted with confusion. His Air India flight had been changed. "Why?" he enquired of the staff.

"Mechanical problems," was the reply.

"So what plane am I flying on now?"

"Iran Air," was the unexpected answer.

You get what you pay for, Roland thought as he waited along with the other passengers.

The passengers were notified to board, at least that's what Roland suspected was the message from the muffled public announcement. He boarded and showed his boarding pass to a steward. "Where's my seat?" Roland asked.

"You can sit anywhere you like," was the apathetic response.

There was a mess in some areas and people socialising around the plane in groups. Roland just plonked himself down on the first available seat and proceeded to put on his seat belt, but it was broken. By this time most the other seats were taken so he stayed put.

The flight was a complete shambles with children throwing food around and people disregarding the seat belt signs. Roland was so relieved when the plane landed safely in London that when the passengers commenced the customary applause, he enthusiastically joined in.

Roland settled into a bed and breakfast in central London. He took it easy over the week, enjoying the parks and gardens. He even managed to watch the Changing of the Guard, something he never got around to see during his previous stays. He caught up with Sean and anguished over whether he should return to see the gang at The Court. He finally decided to visit and procrastinated until Sunday afternoon to make the walk.

There were many unfamiliar faces and Roland struggled to find anyone he knew. After seeking information from a number of people, he discovered that just about every person he knew had either permanently left or were away. Jill and Mike had broken up and left The Court and Shirley had returned to Australia. Roland felt a sense of loss as he walked away from The Court, which he felt would be for the last time.

It was Tuesday morning on 18th October 1988 when Roland left London and caught his Singapore Airlines flight bound for Melbourne.

Flying into Tullamarine Airport on Thursday morning, Roland gazed over Australia's wide open spaces. It was a smooth passage through immigration and customs, and he was unfazed having to wait for his luggage. As the automatic sliding doors opened, he was preparing to make a turn for the taxi rank when his mother and father came into view.

They hurried toward each other and hugged. Roland's mother was crying and his father, who often boasted that he had never shed a tear in his life, was slightly emotional.

"Come on, let's hurry up and go home!" Roland's father stated in an authoritative voice.

"Yeah, let's go home," Roland said. "I need to start organizing my next trip!"

Chapter 18 – The Holy Land

The plan for the second trip was to seek out new destinations and at the top of his list was the USA. Roland could take up to three months leave from work and was determined to make the most of that time. His previous trip focused on the West and the history that founded it – the home of the Greeks and the Romans. He now wanted to explore other ancient civilizations and Egypt readily came to mind.

Once he decided to incorporate Egypt, it seemed natural to tack on a visit to Israel, which made him wonder whether a visit to the Holy Land may re-ignite his faith. He also desired to visit destinations in Europe that had eluded him on his first trip.

Roland finalised his itinerary, which comprised a week tour of Israel, a week tour of Egypt, backpacking around Europe for four weeks, a four-week tour of the East Coast of the USA and a two-week tour of the West Coast.

Satisfied with his broad plans, Roland then got to work on his micro plans. He constructed a travel schedule that set out specific dates and times, which he cross referenced to a more detailed page summary for each city, highlighting the main attractions and the gourmet delights.

Roland purchased his Eurail ticket, booked all his flights and arranged his tours. He then patiently played the waiting game for 18:05 on Saturday, 15th July 1989, which was his scheduled flight to Tel Aviv via Athens on Olympic Airways flight OA472.

"The taxi's here, hurry up before you miss your flight!" came Roland's reminder call from his dad and the routine was in motion.

The drive down the Tullamarine freeway to Melbourne International Airport. Airline check-in followed by window shopping with no intention to buy. Board the plane and sit down with the engine noise reverberating around the cabin. The plane moves onto the tarmac and commences take off, at which time, a big smile emerges that almost covers Roland's entire face.

There was absolute chaos on the Olympic Airlines flight and a huge round of applause on landing in Athens. Roland checked in at the hotel, quickly freshened up then walked to the city centre where he spent the day re-acquainting himself with the area around the Athens market, Constitution Square and the Royal Palace.

Roland caught his onward Olympic Airways flight and it was only a couple of hours to the first of his new destinations: Israel. On landing in Tel Aviv, there was another round of applause.

The immigration and custom checks had tight security, which Roland didn't mind as it was handled quickly and professionally. He saw a sign displaying his name and he identified himself. After a few more people appeared, they were taken for their hotel drop off.

"Shalom and welcome to Israel," the tour guide announced. "My name is Steve. I know a number of you have had long journeys so I will let you get some well-earned rest tonight ahead of our tour of Tel Aviv and Jaffa tomorrow."

Roland made his way to his room where he was told his roommate had already settled in. He knocked on the room door and it was promptly opened by a tall, lean gentleman with ginger hair and light brown eyes.

"Hello, I'm Roland."

"Hi Roland, I'm Morris; come in."

Morris was from New York and was into computer software. He loved to travel, although most of his travel had previously been restricted to America. They chatted until midnight before going to sleep.

Morris and Roland had an early breakfast and were the first to the bus where they were heartily greeted by Steve. The group was soon off for their orientation drive, which took in the vibrant promenade of Dizengoff Street. They then drove to an elevated point that provided an excellent panoramic view of Tel Aviv.

They proceeded to the artist's colony of Jaffa where the travellers viewed the old town's sites, including the old monastery and archaeological diggings. They were given some free time and enjoyed the sunny day at the beach. At night, they were entertained with drinks at their hotel, which gave them a good opportunity to get better acquainted.

The group members were from various parts of the world. Roland sensed that they were generally mature, intellectual and spiritual people, which he thought made a count of the ratio of women to men unnecessary.

The next day, the group travelled to view the Roman ruins at Caesarea. They went on to Haifa where they enjoyed a panoramic view of the city from the Carmel Hills. They then visited the beautiful Bahai Persian Gardens, the golden Bahai Dome and the site of Baha Allah's tomb.

They proceeded to visit Nazareth via Acre and were accommodated in a Kibbutz in Galilee. They were welcomed by some of the Kibbutzniks and were provided with some details about the Kibbutz way of life.

The Kibbutz was a purist form of communal living where the food was Kosher with some of the produce grown on the Kibbutz itself. The accommodation was basic and there were certain restrictions, such as lights out by 11.00 pm.

Leaving the Kibbutz, the group visited the Golan Heights, the Mount of

Beatitudes and Capernaum. The travellers enjoyed a swim at the Sea of Galilee, which was like a gigantic, natural swimming pool with resort facilities. They spent the night at Tiberius.

The group crossed the Jordan River and passed through the Christian baptismal site of Yardenite, the Jordan Valley and an Arab refugee camp. They explored Jericho, the excavations of Jericho and the Mount of Temptation Oasis. They were then moved by the eerie location of Masada.

Masada was the scene of the last stand made by the remaining Jewish rebels of about 1,000 men, women and children who withdrew to the remote mountaintop in their revolt against Roman rule. They withstood a two year siege, killing themselves rather than surrendering when the Romans finally captured the fortress in 73AD. The mountaintop ancient ruins situated in the desert were transformed from a fortress to a shrine in honour of those who had sacrificed their lives.

Later that day, the tour group visited the Dead Sea and some of them elected to have a dip. "Could you take a photo while I float in the waters?" Roland asked Morris as he handed over his camera then waded into the sea.

"Will I take the shot now?" Morris asked as he waited patiently.

"No hang on a tick," Roland said as he was really having trouble stabilising himself in the waters. "Bloody hell, it's hard to float evenly, I'm bobbing around like a cork. Hang on, okay, no, jeepers and they say you can't drown in the Dead Sea, I think I'll be the first. Okay, now...no...yes...yes now. Blast! Okay Morris, just keep on taking shots until I say stop. Keep going. Okay, stop. That will do. Thank you."

In Jerusalem the next day, the group ascended the Mount of Olives. They then visited David's Tomb and the room of the Last Supper, which was followed by visits to Yad Vashem, Israel's Holocaust Museum, Bethlehem, Mary Magdalene Church and the Church of the Nativity.

The next day was another in Jerusalem where the group viewed a number of historically significant sites, including the Jewish quarter, the Garden of Gethsemane, the Stations of the Cross and walked the steps to the church located at Calvary.

The group was given some free time to explore the area around the Wailing Wall. It was the western wall of a temple built by Herod in early BC and a special site of Jewish prayer. Roland was curious why people were placing little rolled up pieces of paper in the cracks of the wall so he searched for Morris.

"So what's with the pieces of paper?" Roland asked.

"They're probably written prayers," Morris replied.

Roland noticed a middle-aged man with a beard and wearing a skull cap looking at them. The man approached and greeted them. The man then looked to Morris. "Are you Jewish?" the man asked.

"Yes I am," Morris responded.

The man proceeded to introduce himself and talked a little about himself and his family then invited Morris for dinner. Morris was indifferent to the invitation. "You are welcome at my house if you wish to visit," the man said as he handed Morris his address and left.

"Morris, that's wonderful," Roland remarked excitedly. "This is a great opportunity to dine with a Jewish family; you are so fortunate."

"I don't know Roland," Morris said. "It could be okay, but I don't think I'll go."

"Not go? Why not?"

"I'm sure they are Orthodox Jews and they have probably invited me to put the hard word on me about being true to my religion," Morris explained. "I love my heritage and my religion and I respect those who live in the traditional orthodox manner, but I simply do not choose to live in that way."

"Oh well, at least you have the rest of the day to think about it," Roland suggested.

Later in the day, Morris confirmed that he would not be taking up the dinner invitation and went off with Roland to enjoy their last dinner in Israel with the rest of the group.

Roland was moved by the pilgrimage to the Holy Land and he gained a sense of what life may have been like some 2,000 years earlier. It would not be the miraculous enlightenment that he craved, but it was an experience he would value.

Chapter 19 – Land of the Pharaohs

On the seventh day of the tour, the group said goodbye to Steve and left Israel. They crossed the Sinai and the Suez Canal into Egypt; travelling to the metropolis of Cairo.

They checked into their hotel and were astonished by the tri-level condominiums with balconies overlooking the Nile. It placed them in good spirits and they enjoyed an extravagant Egyptian feast with copious amounts of alcohol.

It was a bright and early start the next day with scheduled sightseeing in and around Cairo. They met their Egyptian tour guide, named Masud, and took the bus to Memphis. They examined the Great Statue of Ramesses II and proceeded on to Sakkara where they witnessed the site of the world's oldest pyramid and the Sakkara Step Pyramid.

The group visited the Egyptian Museum where they viewed some astonishingly spectacular excavated antiquities, such as golden busts, animals and caskets. They were also treated to the Abdin Presidential Palace and the Citadel. As they crossed the congested El-Tahrir Bridge in Cairo over the River Nile, a dead horse was observed floating on the side of the river bank.

The group went for an excursion to Giza where they walked around and savoured the views of the great Pyramids and the Sphinx. Tourists were then given the option to take a camel ride.

A friendly camel driver led Roland into the desert and, after a while, Roland asked to return. The camel driver seemed hard of hearing so he repeated his request, this time a little louder. The camel driver looked across with a smile. "Oh sir, we can go faster and further into the desert."

"No, I don't want to go faster or further; I wish to go back," Roland said.

The camel driver went into an elongated story of his life hardships and family responsibilities before he requested more money. Roland reminded him of their agreed price and repeated his request to return. The camel driver was unmoved, became angry and insisted on more money.

Having heard of stories where people had been left in the desert for some time until they relented and paid over money, Roland didn't desire an Egyptian standoff so he pleaded. "Sir, I implore you, we have agreed on a price for this ride and I very much want to give you your money, but I left my wallet with a lady on my tour." He then turned his empty side pockets inside out and waved them about.

The man tilted his head and thought for a moment before turning the animal around and giving Roland an extremely rough ride back. Roland's backside was sore by the time they returned and he complained about it to the camel driver; however, the camel driver seemed unsympathetic.

Roland dismounted and was greeted by Betty, the lady on the tour who was minding his wallet and she returned it to him. He took out some notes from the wallet and handed over to the man the originally agreed price.

After dinner, the group returned to Giza. They had endured a long day of impressive sightseeing, which was topped off at night with the sound and light show at the Pyramids and the Sphinx.

Masud encouraged the group to make the most of a free day to explore the hidden delights of Cairo as it was their last day in the city before they took the overnight train to Luxor.

Morris wasn't feeling well and suggested that he would meet up with Roland in the afternoon. Betty didn't feel like exploring the city, preferring to check out the local shops, but suggested that she may join him later for lunch.

Roland set off and his immediate impression of Cairo was that it was a noisy, anarchic madhouse; however, he also found it intriguing. He dodged through traffic as he tried to cross one of the main streets. He eventually managed to get across and struggled to settle himself with his daypack, map and camera.

Going down one of the many roads, Roland found himself in a complex web of interconnecting streets. He knew that going down any one of them would make it difficult to navigate his way back so he decided to take some photos before heading back to the main roads.

As Roland raised his camera to take a shot, a number of men began remonstrating. He didn't think there was anything of cultural or religious significance so he tried to take a photo once again. The men reactivated their protestations and he sensed that they may have been putting it on. He then proceeded to take a couple of photos without any repercussions.

Walking back to the hotel, Roland was approached by a number of men. "Hello sir, where are you from?" asked one of the men.

"I'm from Australia," Roland replied.

"Ah, Sydney, Melbourne, Brisbane?"

"I'm from Melbourne."

"Ah Melbourne, I have a cousin in Melbourne. Do you wish to come to my place for mint tea?"

"That would be nice; however, I'm on the way back to my hotel, but thank you."

Roland moved on, but one man persisted. "Sir, you offend me. I invite you to my place and you say no. I am Moslem, I am not like others. I ask you to be a guest in my house and you refuse."

Sensing that the man was sincere, Roland didn't want to offend him so he finally agreed. The man was elated and led him down an alley, turned into a street and down another alley. Roland began thinking. *Where in the hell is this guy taking me?*

The man climbed up an external flight of rusty, metal stairs and led Roland into a small residence that resembled a cluttered shop with a myriad of items. The man pulled up two wooden stools to a wooden table and invited his guest to sit. He then momentarily left the room and returned holding a tray with a brass tea set.

"This is my place and here is the tea," declared the man as he poured the tea.

"Thank you sir," Roland said as he felt that the faith he placed in the man was justified.

The man then started talking about a number of items that he had in store and walked about before he produced a box of perfumes. "Yes I have perfumes, you want perfumes?"

"No, I don't want perfumes," Roland answered as he sipped the tea.

"They are very cheap."

"No, I don't want any."

"You must buy some for your wife."

"I don't have a wife."

"Your girlfriend."

"I don't have one."

"Your mother."

"My mother wouldn't want it."

The man walked about again and this time he produced a box of incense. "Okay, I have incense."

After a similar offering to the perfume with the incense, the guy was about to commence with teas and that's when Roland lost his patience. "Enough, I am going!"

The interjection did not seem to deter the man. "You should buy something from my place," the man insisted.

Roland looked at the man before he responded. "I am not Moslem, but I am not like the others, I buy nothing! But thanks for the tea."

Roland retraced his steps to track his way back to his hotel. Other men approached him with their standard spiel; however, after his previous experience, he declined all offers and just walked on.

Returning to the hotel, Roland checked on Morris who was feeling better. They bumped into Betty as she returned from shopping with a couple of other ladies from the tour and they all set off for lunch.

Later that day, the group met up for a light dinner before they returned to their rooms and packed for their overnight train journey to Luxor. It was a rough, but fun train ride where they managed a little sleep. They settled into their Luxor accommodation before going to the Valley of the Kings and the Valley of the Queens. Unsurprisingly, the highlight was a visit to the Tomb of Tutankhamen.

The group visited the Temple at Luxor and Roland was left wondering how on earth the Egyptians could have assembled such enormous columns and statues. Masud had to return to the temple to collect him. In the evening, the group attended the sound and light show at the Karnak Temple.

The following day, the group was driven along the Nile Valley, passing Nubian villages and getting a flavour of Egyptian rural life. They visited the Temple at Edfu, considered to be the best preserved Egyptian temple, and Kom Ombo, being the Crocodile God Temple.

They travelled to Aswan where they inspected the enormous construction of the Aswan Old Dam and High Dam. They then visited the Philae Temple on the River Nile and granite quarries where the ancient obelisks were once cut.

The next day, there was an optional excursion to visit Abu Simbel. The temples had been relocated due to the threatened submersion in Lake Nasser by the construction of the Aswan High Dam. It was a massive engineering feat to relocate the temple up the sandstone cliff.

The 3,000-year-old temples of Ramesses II and his wife Nefertari were reassembled in the same, precise relationship to each other and the sun. Roland was in awe as they travelled up the cliff and guided into the artificial mountain that supported the construction. Once inside, Roland's awe was converted to a verbal, "err."

"What's up?" Morris asked.

"It's a huge modern concrete dome," Roland replied with disappointment.

"That's right; we were told about the reconstruction," Morris said.

"I know," said Roland, "but actually seeing the modern internal construction detracts from the original ancient works. I would have preferred not seeing the inside."

"Yeah, I know what you mean," agreed Morris.

The tour members caught their flight from Abu Simbel and Roland, who had been a little sombre, seemed to perk up when he looked back to take in the aerial view of the construction.

"Hey Morris, the temple looks fantastic, doesn't it?"

"It certainly does," Morris agreed. "It's as if there's an intertwining of the old and the new to preserve a masterpiece."

"Yeah, I know what you mean," agreed Roland.

The group took the overnight train back to Cairo and was delighted to return to the luxury of their condos. They visited the Khan El Khalili

Bazaar and then did some shopping before going for a swim.

It was the last day of the tour and the group was determined to make the most of the evening events. They enjoyed a special Egyptian dinner with an abundance of food, drink, entertainment, music, belly dancers and a big bong.

Chapter 20 – Return to Europe

Roland had an early morning flight to London. He said his goodbyes and exchanged contact details with the other tour members before catching his British Airways flight to London Gatwick. He checked into a bed and breakfast and then booked a ferry departing the following day before he retired for the night.

After catching the train from Victoria Station, Roland caught the ferry from Dover to Oostende and was back on the train that arrived in Brussels late afternoon. He sat back on his hotel bed, relaxed and gloated. "Ah Europe, the organisation, don't you just love it?"

Roland left the hotel to hunt for some dinner. He walked into a bar and took a seat at a table.

"Would you like to see a menu?" asked the barman who doubled as the waiter.

"Do you have Moules Hollandes?" Roland asked.

"Yes, it's our specialty."

"I'll have that and a beer."

"What beer would you like?"

"What beer do you recommend?"

"What about a Leffé Blu?"

"That sounds perfect."

The mussels and vegetables casserole was to take twenty minutes to prepare. Roland sipped on his beer as he waited for his food, and listened into the casual conversation between the barman and a couple of patrons, which he joined in from time to time.

"Here is your Moules Hollandes; would you like another beer?"

"Oh yes please."

"Enjoy your meal."

Roland did enjoy his meal and then went for a pleasant walk before returning to the hotel to plan for his hectic day ahead. He only allowed one full day for his sightseeing and activities in Brussels and at the end of the day he was reasonably content with his scorecard.

<u>BRUSSELS</u>

	<u>Ate That?</u>
<u>Eats:</u>	
* Moules Hollandes (Mussel Casserole)	✓
* Belgian Waffle & Cherry Beer	✓

	<u>Done That?</u>
<u>Attractions:</u>	
* Brewers' Museum (Musei de la Brasserie) Maison des Brasseurs on the Grand Palace Monday to Friday 10-12; 14-17; Sat 10-12	✓
* Mannekin Pis: Statue corner of Rue de L'Etuve & Rue du Chine	✓
* Jeanneke – Pis. Statue end of Impasse de la Fidelité which branches off Beenhouwersstraat two blocks from the Grand Palace (Female counterpart – urinating statue)	✗
* 15th Century Notre Dame des Victoires Church	✓
* 17th Century Flemish Houses nearby Place du Grand Sablon	✓
* Place Parc du Bruxelles Gardens & Lakes At one end – The Royal Palace	✓
At the other end – The Belgian Parliament.	✓
* Grand Place – Surrounded by 17th Century guilded houses & Town Hall (climb the 420 steps & enjoy the view)	✓

Roland was keen to move on to Amsterdam, being one of the highlights of the European holiday he'd missed the previous year due to his traffic accident.

Wanting to take advantage of the last hours of daylight, Roland set off and visited Vondel and Rembrandt's Park, Ann Frank's House, the Royal Palace, Rembrandt's House and the Sailors' Quarter. He also visited the Red Light District where he entered a café and purchased hash brown cookies. "You should not eat them all at once," warned the vendor as Roland was leaving.

Returning to his room, Roland couldn't stop thinking about the cookies. He had heard of one group member on the tour the previous year who ate some cookies and was so spaced out he ended up being mugged in the streets of Amsterdam.

Roland considered it wouldn't hurt if he ate a couple and had the rest when he returned. He devoured one and waited a few minutes, but felt nothing. He then consumed another and waited another few minutes. Again, he felt nothing.

There were originally six cookies. Roland decided to eat one more and have the remaining three when he returned. He consumed a third cookie and prepared to go out. As he was about to leave, he was still feeling no different and he looked back at the bag of leftover cookies. "Stuff it," he said, "I'll eat them all now."

Taking the tram from his hotel to central Amsterdam, Roland was feeling happy as he walked around Central Station and down the main thoroughfares. He was strolling down Damrak when he stumbled upon the Sex Museum (Venus Temple) and recalled that it was on his list of attractions.

Entering the museum, Roland completed a quick lap. He found the establishment uninspiring and was about to leave when he bumped into two young ladies in conversation. "Oh, I'm not used to such open exhibition of sex," one of the ladies complained.

Roland shook his head as he thought. *Yeah right lady, you might want to look at yourself in the mirror with that low-cut brassiere, micro mini skirt and fishnet stockings. You'd fit right in with some of the more objectionable displays in this establishment!*

Moving on, Roland checked out the Chinese restaurants close to the Red Light District and settled into one. He enjoyed his meal whilst chatting with a few tourists.

Intent on seeing a show in the Red Light District, Roland wandered around the area, but he was being put off by a number of guys touting for business. He ended up patronising a couple of bars where he had a few drinks before returning to his hotel.

Roland was disappointed with the evening, particularly due to the fact that the space cookies were ineffective and he cast his mind back to what the vendor stated. *Don't eat them all at once the guy said; yeah right!*

The following day, Roland returned to Rembrandt's Park and visited the National Monument and Rijkmuseum. He enjoyed a canal cruise and then rushed to the Heineken Brewery to take the popular tour. He was pleased to have arrived in time and asked for a ticket. "Sorry sir, we're sold out."

Returning to his hotel, Roland switched on the television and the Australian Rules Football game between Carlton and Melbourne was showing. He started watching the game and then switched off the TV set as he didn't want any more disappointments that day.

Roland caught the train from Amsterdam to Copenhagen then another train to Oslo, arriving early the next day.

Allowing two nights in Oslo, Roland took up accommodation in the suburbs. He soon set off and visited Karl Johans Gate, Oslo Cathedral, the Norway Parliament, the Royal Palace, the Town Hall, Akershus Castle, Frogner Park and Vigeland Sculpture Park.

The next day, Roland set off to complete his planned attractions. He visited Bygdoy with the Norwegian Folk Museum and took some short term refuge in the Stieve Church. He then moved on to the Viking Ship Museum and the Kontiki Museum.

Roland spent some time around the Oslo Harbour and the rest of the day on a fjord cruise. The cruise commenced peacefully and he thought it was the perfect way to finish off the day. However, the atmosphere was soon ruined when a rowdy group of tourists found their singing voices.

The Oslo to Bergen rail trip was reputed to be one of the most scenic rail journeys in the world. Roland found a carriage with two empty bench seats facing each other and settled in. He was so looking forward to take some great scenic shots that he had his camera at the ready. Before the train set off, a young lady sat across the aisle and they exchanged smiles.

Sitting with his camera on his lap, Roland noticed a few nice scenery views, but was unmoved as he was sure there would be better scenery to come. Time was elapsing and he started to get a little impatient. He raised his camera a few times, but the train was moving too fast. He then became frustrated and held his camera up to his face.

The unpredictable motion of the train caused Roland to knock the camera against his head a couple of times, which further annoyed him. He then became so determined that he fixed the camera's viewfinder to his eye and placed his finger on the trigger; however, he soon became tired and decided to take a rest.

The lady sitting across had been observing Roland and they exchanged smiles once again. "Do you like the scenery?" asked the lady.

"I think it's beautiful," Roland responded. "Although I find it very hard to capture."

The lady joined Roland and they began chatting. Heidi was in her mid-twenties, had flowing blonde hair, big blue eyes and was from Norway. He was fascinated by her, being a Jehovah Witness who did volunteer work around the world for the underprivileged.

Heidi pointed out a number of attractions along the way.

The train arrived in Bergen on time. Heidi and Roland exchanged addresses and said goodbye. She was about to disembark when she stopped and turned to him. "You didn't take any photos," she remarked.

"No, not one," Roland acknowledged. "However, I enjoyed sharing the scenery with you and I know what photos to take on my return trip."

They exchanged smiles for a final time.

Roland settled on accommodation at a house in the suburbs of Bergen. He didn't spend much time at the house as he was scheduled to leave early the next day and wanted to get in his sightseeing.

Taking the funicular ride to Mt Floyen, Roland took some wonderful panoramic photos of the picturesque town. He then visited the Bergenhus Fortress and Hakon Hall before he strolled along the quiet streets where the colourful, evening lights reflected mesmerisingly off the waters. He had dinner before returning to the house and went straight to bed.

Waking early in the morning, Roland agonised over the option of heading further north to a small town with a population of a few hundred, named Hell. *Is it worth travelling an extra couple of hundred kilometres and losing a couple of days just for the sake of being able to boast that I've been to Hell and back?* In the end, he aborted the idea and settled on purchasing a postcard of Hell.

Catching the early train back to Oslo, Roland sat down with his camera next to him. He was looking at the scenery he had viewed the day before, remembering all the attractions Heidi had pointed out. He could almost anticipate the views moments before they emerged and was taking shots on cue with every one of them being a gem.

After arriving in Oslo, Roland caught the train for Koblenz. He had to catch interconnecting trains in Copenhagen and Hamburg before arrival at Koblenz Station from where he booked a youth hostel. "You will need to catch the bus," the station assistant advised. "When you reach the stop, don't worry about the chair lift, just walk up the hill."

Roland caught the bus and the driver alerted him of the stop. As he was disembarking, the driver pointed in the direction of the youth hostel and his finger was pointing straight up. His eyes followed the driver's finger and he got a crick in his neck. He loaded up his backpack and started climbing up.

Making it up the hill, Roland had to catch his breath before proceeding to reception. "Hello, I'm Roland."

"Yes, we have your dormitory accommodation and please be aware that all your belongings are kept here at your own risk."

Roland settled into his dorm where he was required to take the top bunk. He found the hostel to be fairly comfortable with a great location that provided stunning panoramic views of Koblenz. He soon set off to town, and wasted no time to take one of the river cruises, opting for the Lorelei Rock/Rhine River cruise.

The boat was not too crowded so he could relax under the sun, take in the views and listen to the English commentary. They cruised by vineyards, landscapes, fortresses, castles and palaces before they reached the main attraction of the Lorelei Rock.

One description was that the Lorelei rock sculpture was named after one of the beautiful Rhine maidens whose song was said to have lured navigators to their doom. When they reached the Rhine maiden, Roland observed a small statue perched on the bank of the river and took an obligatory photo.

After the cruise, Roland made his way back up the hill to the hostel and freshened up. He started chatting to a few tourists and ended up joining them for dinner and a few drinks. He excused himself as he had a big day of sightseeing ahead and departed for yet another climb back up the dreaded hill to the hostel.

In the early morning, Roland made tracks for town and visited many sites that included the Old Town Hall, St Castor's Church, Stolzenfel's Castle, Prince Elector's Palace, Ehrenbreitstein Fortress, Old Castle, Mint Master's House, Old Mint & Square, Baroque Franconian Royal Palace, the Romanesque Church of Our Lady, Altes Kaufhaus and Schoffenhaus.

Roland's last attraction was Deutches Eck, being where the Rhine River and Moselle River met. He was impressed with Koblenz and he took some time to relax in the town centre. He had dinner and a couple of drinks before making his last trek up the hill to the hostel.

Sleeping in, Roland missed his planned train, but it gave him the opportunity to have short stopovers in Cochem and Luxemburg. He then proceeded by train to Manheim on route to Heidelberg.

Chapter 21 – Missed Misses

The train carriages were reasonably crowded, but everyone managed to find a seat. Roland was seated across from a very attractive lady in her thirties who kept on glancing at him.

After a while, Roland felt like stretching his legs and noticed that the lady was now almost incessantly looking at him. He stared back until they both broke out into a smile. He then looked towards the door, looked back at the lady and left the cabin.

Roland waited in the corridor and the lady soon emerged. She was Yugoslavian and did not speak any English; however, this did not stop them from having lively conversation. He pulled out whatever he could to aid their communication, such as maps, pictures, notes, travel information and timetables.

From what Roland could decipher, the lady was going to Frankfurt and seemed to be asking whether he was going there too. He indicated that he was travelling to Heidelberg, although the idea of going to Frankfurt was growing on him. He was pondering the situation and gazing at the lady with the beautiful smile when all hell broke loose.

The public announcements were muffled, which everyone was questioning and no one could explain. There was a hive of activity with people moving in all directions. The train was approaching Manheim and the passengers were unsure whether they had to get off the train or what to do next.

Roland led the lady back to their cabin and they collected their belongings. In all the commotion, he was still toying with the idea of going to Frankfurt.

The consensus was that everyone should get off. Roland had to change at Manheim in any case so he followed the crowd off the train. As the people descended onto the platform, it was sheer chaos and Roland lost touch with the lady.

Roland made some attempts to find her, even checking the trains to Frankfurt, but it was hopeless. He noticed the platform for his connecting train to Heidelberg and made his way there. He looked around every now and then, just in case he came across the lady.

Arriving at the platform, Roland waited for his train, wondering what potential experiences had escaped him.

The Heidelberg bound train arrived and Roland found a quiet cabin and succumbed to rest. He arrived in Heidelberg in the evening and there were a few people gathered around the hotel phone dialling service.

Roland waited his turn and he was last in line with another backpacker. The backpacker did not speak English and Roland indicated that he could go next. The backpacker indicated no, bowed and allowed Roland to go first.

Trying a number of hotels, Roland discovered that there was only one accommodation left and it was twin share. He asked the operator to hang on and turned to the backpacker. "Do you wish to share the room?" Roland asked the backpacker.

"Hai," the backpacker said a number of times so Roland took this to be yes.

After booking the room, Roland introduced himself to the backpacker, Shouhei, who was from Japan and travelling around the world on his own. Shouhei managed to say a few words in English, which seemed to be growing as he gained confidence.

Roland tried to locate the street on his map, but he was having trouble and Shouhei seemed to be equally unsure. He tried to ask a few of the locals, but they couldn't help.

It was puzzling that he couldn't find the street and it started to drizzle, which was not helping matters. He was about to cross the street to try a couple of other off streets when an attractive, young lady approached them. "Can I help?" she asked.

"We're trying to find this street, but we can't seem to locate it," Roland explained.

"I know this address," she said. "I can take you in my car."

"I don't want to cause you any inconvenience," Roland said. "If you could direct us to the street, we could walk there."

"If I was concerned about any inconvenience, I would not have made the offer," she said in slightly offended tone.

"We would be very grateful if you could take us," Roland said apologetically.

The lady smiled and pointed to her car. "You can place your bags in the boot."

They squeezed into her Volkswagen Beetle and were off. The lady was named Gabrielle and she was from Heidelberg where she attended university.

The ride to the hotel was very short and Roland was in no hurry to leave the vehicle. "Well this is the hotel," Gabrielle said. "You just need to press the buzzer over there."

They got out of the car and Gabrielle assisted them with their bags. "Thank you very much for your assistance," Roland said with a smile. "I wish there was some way I could repay you."

"It was nothing," Gabrielle said. "I'm glad I could be of help."

Roland spent a moment gazing at her lovely face, blue eyes and her frizzy, blonde hair that melded into the drizzle and the street lights. It was like admiring an Impressionist painting and he suspected that Shouhei was admiring the same vision.

"We'd better sound the buzzer, I guess," Roland eventually said.

Gabrielle got into her car and started the engine. There was no immediate response to the buzzer and, after a minute or two, he pressed it again.

Gabrielle wound down the window and called out. "If you can't get accommodation there, you can come and stay with me."

Roland almost fell over in an effort to grab his bag when a response came from the intercom.

"Oh well," Gabrielle said on hearing the response from the intercom and she drove off. Roland almost collapsed on his bag with disappointment.

"Are you coming in or not?" a voice on the intercom asked in a strong voice.

"Yeah, we're coming in," Roland replied in an equally strong, but disconsolate voice.

Shouhei and Roland were buzzed into the hotel, they proceeded through the security doors and appeared before the receptionist. The hotel did not accept credit cards or US dollar travellers' cheques, they only accepted Deutschmarks. Roland was embarrassed that he had insufficient Deutschmarks to pay his share. He checked with Shouhei, who was happy to assist and promptly presented the money.

They settled into the room and communicated for some time, assisted by hand signals. They seemed to be on a similar wave length with many nods, bows, smiles and laughter.

It was some time before Roland fell asleep, as he had much on his mind. The lovely Yugoslav lady, the need to repay Shouhei first thing in the morning and, most of all, the beautiful lady that he dubbed Angel Gabrielle.

Shouhei was first to rise the next morning and Roland was up soon after. Roland led Shouhei to the bank, exchanged money and repaid him. Cashed up, they set off for some breakfast.

Roland proceeded with his sightseeing and Shouhei was happy to tag along. They rode the funicular where they gained some fantastic views of Heidelberg. They then visited the Heidelberg Castle and Germany's oldest university dating back to the 13th century. They also visited the Kurpfalzisches and the Palatinate Museum that featured the wood carved altar of Christ with the 12 Apostles.

Shouhei and Roland had two long and exhaustive days on the move, which they capped off with two celebratory dinners. However, they were soon to be going their separate ways; an occupational hazard for itinerant travellers.

Roland woke late Sunday morning and caught the train to Basel. The train travelled through the Black Forest and arrived in Basel late afternoon where he booked into a youth hostel.

Allocating only one day for Basel, Roland soon set off to visit Dreilandereck, being the three nation's corner splitting Switzerland, Germany and France. He checked out the view of the city from the Wettstein Bridge and visited the Munster, Munsterplatz, Rathaus and Marktplatz. He intended to explore St Jacob's Park, but as it was late he decided to do this early the next morning.

Waking up a little later than intended, Roland quickly set off. He completed the St Jacob's Park walk and then concentrated his search for the Dinosaur. It was supposed to be life size so he expected that it shouldn't be too hard to find.

Time was dragging on and Roland still couldn't locate the Dinosaur so he aborted his search. He rushed back to the youth hostel and gathered his things. A couple of the guys in his dormitory held him up and by the time he made it down to reception the check-out time had expired.

"You're too late," the receptionist stated.

"Yes I know I'm late," Roland conceded. "I got held up and it's only a few minutes."

"If you are late to check out you have to pay accommodation for the night."

"Yes I know; I will pay for the night."

"You will also have to wait."

Roland waited an eternity before he was summoned to be checked out. "Five hours to be checked out, was that really necessary?" he queried.

"Well you'll know better next time," the receptionist remarked.

"Don't worry," Roland assured the receptionist as he was handed his passport, "there will not be a next time."

Most unhappy with the day's events, Roland hurried for a train to Geneva and on arrival checked into a youth hostel. He was in no mood for sightseeing so he just spent the rest of the day walking around Lake Geneva before having a bite to eat and retiring for the day.

It was a brand new day and Roland felt recharged. He skipped down to the railway station and organised a scenic rail journey looping around the lakes and mountains of Switzerland. He travelled from Geneva to Lausanne, Brig, Spiez, Bern, back to Lausanne and finally returned to Geneva. He enjoyed the cities, towns and scenery, snapping many photographs throughout.

After exploring Jardine Anglais, Roland walked to Lake Geneva and gazed at the fountain, Jet d'Eau. As he approached the fountain, it abruptly stopped operation. "It was just working," he cursed, "and now that I was about to take a photo, it stopped!"

Roland dedicated the next day to sightseeing around Geneva and his priority was to take a photograph of the fountain. He woke early, had breakfast and went directly to Lake Geneva. The fountain was spraying high above the lake. *Thank goodness*, he thought. *Now I'd better hurry up and take a photo, just in case it turns off again.*

Getting on with the rest of his sightseeing, Roland visited St Peter's Cathedral with the pulpit from which Calvin preached. He also visited Promenade de Bastions Park with its giant chess boards, Place Neuve and Palais des Nations.

Roland went to the train station and purchased an overnight rail sleeper to Madrid. He returned to the hostel to pack and reflected on the cost of the train fare, which he considered to be expensive.

Whilst packing, Roland kept thinking about the rail tickets and he sensed that something was amiss. He examined the tickets again and noticed that they had printed, *x 2*. He then considered that they may have charged him for a double sleeper.

Returning to the station, Roland confirmed that they had indeed charged him for two sleeper fares and they corrected the situation, providing a partial refund. *How fortunate am I to have made the enquiry*, he thought.

Roland made sure he checked out of the Geneva youth hostel in time and made his way to the station with plenty of time to spare. He grabbed a bite to eat as well as packing food and drinks for his long train ride. He caught his train and made himself comfortable on a few empty seats.

The train was nearing Barcelona Station and a lady approached Roland. "Do you know whether I need to get off here for Madrid?" asked the lady.

"I think you may need to get off here. I'm also going to Madrid and I need to get off here," Roland said. "In any case, I think it is the last stop for this train so I think everyone will need to disembark."

"You seem very knowledgeable," the lady commented.

"Yes, I am indeed very knowledgeable," Roland said, and they both laughed.

Claudia and Roland sat together on the platform. She was from Germany and on her way to meet up with her brother who was working in Madrid. They talked for some time and Roland pulled out his food and drinks, which he offered to share.

"I couldn't take your food," Claudia stated.

"I insist," Roland replied. "You'll also be doing me a favour as I always buy too much and it would save me having to carry it."

They both enjoyed the feast, using a large plastic bag as a table cloth and their backpacks as seats. "We'd better start getting ready for the train," Roland suggested.

"Why should we get ready so early?" Claudia asked.

"The train is due to depart at 11 pm," Roland replied.

"No, the train doesn't leave until midnight," Claudia corrected.

Roland was certain of his times. "Do you mind if I see your ticket?" he asked, and Claudia handed over her ticket. "Oh," he sighed. "You're on the next train while I'm on the express train that leaves earlier."

Claudia also sighed. "What a pity, I would have loved to be on the express train with you."

Now totally demoralised, Roland thought back to the double sleeper ticket he held in his hot little hands, looked at the pretty, young lady with flowing blonde hair and big brown eyes and thought, *what a bummer*.

Roland said goodbye to Claudia and she thanked him for sharing his food. He boarded his train and turned to face her, waving to her as she waved back. His mind was in gaga land and it took him a while before he managed to find his sleeper cabin.

There was a large, middle-aged man in trousers and a tank top lying on the bottom bunk. Roland thought that he may have made an error, but he confirmed that it was indeed his cabin. He introduced himself and the man made a half-hearted effort to acknowledge his existence, seemingly annoyed by the intrusion.

Placing his backpack out of the way, Roland scrambled onto the top bunk with his daypack. He then shuffled out of his clothes that he folded and placed around him.

The train started kangaroo hopping and edging away from the platform. The man rose and leant up against the door jam. Roland looked over to the obese, unattractive man with dishevelled hair and hairy armpits and thought back to the German bombshell. He then looked up to the heavens, shook his head and turned over to face the wall in an attempt to get some sleep.

The train made it to Madrid by mid-morning and Roland checked into a hotel for three nights. He followed his list of attractions, and visited Puerta del Sol, Palacio Real, Templo Debod, Plaza de Espana with the stone monument to Cervantes, Parque del Retiro with the monument to the fallen angel Lucifer, Paseo de la Castellana, Plaza de Colon, Plaza de la Cibeles, Plaza Mayor, Plaza de la Independencia, San Miguel Basilica, San Isidor Cathedral and the Prado Museum.

Roland wanted to re-acquaint himself with some of the Spanish delicacies he enjoyed when he was on tour in Barcelona the year before. He selected his restaurant and ordered gazpacho for entree, paella for mains and sangria for the accompanying beverage.

"Sir, would you like a carafe or half carafe of sangria?" the waiter queried.

Based on his previous experience with the alcoholic concoction, Roland opted for the full carafe.

The gazpacho was not like the one he remembered in Barcelona, but

Roland considered it to be just as appetising. He thought the paella was excellent and the sangria strong and fruity.

"Is everything all right sir?" asked the waiter.

"Excellent," was Roland's spirited reply. "The sangria is particularly good and it seems to be stronger than the one I've had before with a tour group."

"Oh sir, they normally make a watered down version of sangria for tour groups as they have to consider the passengers' different tolerance levels. Would you like anything else, sir?" the waiter asked.

"Yes, I would like coffee and the bill."

Having finished his coffee, Roland paid the bill and polished off the remainder of the sangria. He rose to exit and had to steady himself against the table. He then staggered out of the restaurant, smiling at the waiter as he departed. He started off for a stroll when he noticed that he was pretty well smashed so he did an about face, returned to the hotel and went to sleep.

Roland's final day in Madrid was a Sunday and he reserved it for a casual day of walking. He checked out the famous football ground of Real Madrid and the Estadio Santiago Bernabeu before making his way to Las Ventas, Plaza de Toros.

The Corrida de Toros, or Run of Bulls, commenced at 7.00 pm. Roland purchased a ticket for the bullfight and returned to the hotel to freshen up and have a bite to eat before returning to Plaza de Toros.

It was a large bullring and arena with the stadium's capacity being 25,000. Roland estimated that the stadium was about 20% full or about 5,000 people. There wasn't much of an atmosphere, but it seemed to pick up a little when a trumpet started to sound. The program was to be a typical Spanish-style bullfight of six bulls and three matadors, with each matador fighting two bulls.

The participants entered the arena in parade form, which was accompanied by a band. Shortly after, the ring was vacated and a bull entered the ring sporting colourful ribbons. Roland was most impressed with the size and strength of the beast.

The bull showed stern ferocity as it pranced around the ring, showing acute alertness to any sign of movement. A few banderilleros entered the ring and thrust their capes at the bull, which the bull obligingly attacked.

The banderilleros exited, making way for two picadors, each armed with a long spear and mounted on heavily padded, blindfolded horses. The bull was intimidated to attack the horses and the picadors stabbed the bull in the shoulder with their spears.

Roland found this deplorable and felt sorry for the animal as it commenced to bleed from its initial wounds. The bull kept charging and tried to lift the picador's horse as it was being speared.

After the picadors had inflicted their torture, three banderilleros positioned themselves and, when it suited them, they ran at the bull at an angle. Passing by the bull, they thrust spikes into the bull's flanks, which caused more loss of blood and caused the bull to further weaken.

A matador entered the ring holding a small, red cape in one hand and a sword in the other. The matador used his cape to attract the bull in a series of passes. He then tried to manoeuvre and steady the bull into position. By this time, the bull had lost so much blood and was so exhausted that it could hardly stand. The crowd picked up on this and, as the matador was taking so much time, some of the crowd began to boo.

Eventually, the matador struck by stabbing the bull between the shoulders and it dropped. The crowd stood and applauded while the matador paraded like a victorious hero. As a final insult, the bull's carcass was dragged away by mules.

Sickened by the spectacle and, knowing that the same process was to be repeated five times over, Roland left the arena in disgust. *Those bullfights aren't fights at all; they're a form of ceremonial slaughter in a glorified abattoir.*

Roland left Madrid and had whirlwind tours of Granada, Seville and Lisbon, spending one night in each city.

In Granada, Roland was blown away by the Alhambra complex with the elaborate gardens, the Royal Palace and Alcazaba Watchtower Fortress. He was also impressed by Generalife with the Summer Palace and water gardens.

In Seville, Roland was equally blown away by the Alcazar Palace and the Plaza de Espana. He enjoyed the Maria Luisa Park and the gothic style Corpus Christie Cathedral where he took a photo of Columbus Tomb. He found it curious that one of the pall-bearer statues had a striking resemblance to himself.

In Lisbon, Roland visited Jeronimo's Monastery and Church, the Basilica de Estrela, the Torre de Belem, the Monument to Portugal's Sailors, the Golden Gate 25 de Abril Bridge, Praca de Comercio, Black Horse Square, St Georges Castle and the old quarter of Alfama.

Arriving at the railway station in Lisbon, Roland booked a train for Friday 25th August bound for Paris. The train was two hours late and further long train delays resulted in the arrival in Paris at midnight on Sunday 27th August.

Roland had thoughts of visiting Mont St. Michel; however, the train debacle put paid to that idea and he spent the time in Paris instead. He enjoyed panoramic views of Paris from the Maine-Montparnasse Tower and then visited the Pompidou Centre.

Taking the train from Paris to Amsterdam, Roland slept most of the way. He checked into a cheap hotel in central Amsterdam and went for a walk, passing by the Heineken Brewery. To his surprise, a tour was available and he purchased a ticket.

There was a good turnout and they were shown through the brewery with its various pieces of equipment. Most of the group seemed restless and uninterested until they were guided into a bar area and seated around tables.

Roland sat next to a man and they started chatting. After a few beers, the people relaxed and it turned into a very pleasant social gathering. "This tour is pretty good value," Roland said to the man.

"Sure is," the man replied. "This is the fourth time I've taken it."

The group was ushered out, although a few of the people had to be subjected to added efforts of persuasion as they showed a strong reluctance to depart.

Roland returned to his hotel where he reconsidered viewing a sex show. *It's Amsterdam and, regardless of the touts, it had to be done.*

Visiting the Red Light District again, Roland encountered touts and they started to get to him again. He was almost about to abort the idea, when he forced himself to walk straight into one. He paid his entrance money and took a seat in the theatre-style establishment.

It was an unruly crowd and the stage was soon occupied by a man in a doctor's uniform and a couple of women in nurses' uniforms. There was a revolving bed and the trio didn't do much more than take off their clothes and have sex on stage.

The next performance was pretty much like the previous act, but this time the performers were in school uniforms. *School uniforms*, Roland thought. *What else?* He soon tired of the show and left the establishment to return to his hotel.

The next day Roland was off to The Hague. He had some free time so he visited the Dutch Parliament of Binnenhof, the miniature town of Madurodam, Vredespaleis and Scheveningen Beach.

Returning to the station, Roland still had a couple of hours to spare and the only attraction in the immediate area was a sex shop so he wandered in.

Roland looked at a number of the movie covers and was pretty unimpressed. He then stumbled upon the bestiality section and, as he had never seen anything like it before, he grabbed one of the video cases and approached the counter.

"I'd like to see this one," Roland stated.

The man behind the counter looked at him strangely. "I just need to know the number; you didn't have to take the video case off the shelf," the man advised.

"Oh, sorry," Roland replied. "Here's the number."

Roland was directed to a booth, which was a small, dark, dingy room and he took a seat. There was a medium sized screen in front of him, a vanity basin on the side and a box of tissues.

The screen came to life and it was a very low grade movie with actors who appeared to be drugged out of their minds. There was a guy having it on with a chicken, a lady with a horse, another lady with a dog and yet another lady with a pig. The movie was about half way through when Roland decided to pull the plug.

Roland was glad to be on the train to Hoek van Holland and he then caught a ferry to England. He had three nights in London where he did some laundry, had a haircut and visited some of his favourite places.

Chapter 22 – Going to America

On 2nd September 1989, Roland caught the 10.00 am Continental flight to Miami. Settling into a resort hotel in the warm Florida climate was not too tough an assignment.

The tour was scheduled to commence the next day; however, the hotel staff had no knowledge of the tour. Roland was unimpressed with the lack of organisation, but was somewhat relieved when he stumbled across other people in the same predicament.

The passengers consisted of two Austrian ladies, three Dutch ladies, an English lady, four Dutchmen and a German guy.

The tour guide, Chris, turned up and he didn't endear himself to the tour members with the statement he made from the outset: "I've been touring for nine months, I'm sick of travelling and I'll be glad to see the end of this tour as it's my last."

The group left Miami and drove to Panama City Beach, arriving some 12 hours later. They quickly set up their tents and went to a local disco. The Dutch guys and Roland soon hit it off as they were all keen drinkers. The Budweiser took a bit of getting used to, but once they acquired the taste they were knocking back the cans.

Roland didn't remember too much of the previous evening as he woke up with his head poking out of his tent. The passengers were packing up and making a racket, which caused him to roll out of his tent and haul his things together.

The group had breakfast and moved on with a six-hour drive to New Orleans. They enjoyed a Mississippi River paddle steamer cruise and sightseeing around the city.

Roland and one of the Dutch guys, named Jorg, checked out Jackson Square. They were admiring St Louis Cathedral when a man approached. "Hey man, I bet I can tell you where you got your sneakers," the man said to Roland.

"No thanks," Roland replied as he started walking off with Jorg following. The man pursued them and repeated his challenge. "No thanks," Roland repeated and he kept on walking with Jorg. The man followed for a few blocks before giving up.

Jorg hadn't interfered, but as soon as the man stopped following them he spoke up. "Why didn't you take the bet; what were the odds of the man knowing where you bought your sneakers?"

"I expect the guy was probably trying a stunt I once saw in a movie. The guy claimed he knew where I got my sneakers, not where I bought them. Where do you think I've got my sneakers?" Roland asked.

"On your feet," Jorg guessed.

"Exactly," Roland said. "Even you know where I got my sneakers."

The group took a day tour of the Louisiana Superdome and later visited Bourbon Street. They appreciated the yesteryear character of Bourbon Street and the fact they could just about walk in any bar and hear a live jazz band playing.

After two nights' stay in New Orleans, the group proceeded along to Memphis where they visited Graceland.

"May we visit Beale Street while we are in Memphis?" Monique, one of the Dutch ladies, asked Chris.

"We need to get a move along so we can't," Chris replied.

Roland was unfamiliar with Beale Street so he asked Monique about it.

"Beale Street is significant in the history of the Blues. It is lined with clubs and restaurants and is reported to be one of the major tourist attractions in Memphis," Monique explained.

After hearing this, Roland approached Chris. "I think it's more than reasonable to visit Beale Street, particularly since it's nearby and shouldn't take long."

Chris glared as he responded. "Beale Street isn't such a big deal and we need to move on."

The tour members looked at each other before they solemnly boarded the van.

The group pushed on from Memphis to Nashville where they spent an easy day at the camp. At night, they dined at a bar where Country & Western music was playing and where patrons wearing cowboy and cowgirl outfits were performing impressive line dancing.

The following day, the group visited Mammoth Cave National Park. They also enjoyed a step back in time to the colonial days at Elizabethtown where they played ping pong, pool and old style pin bowling.

"I'm keen to pass by Fort Knox; can we do that?" Jorg asked Chris.

"There's really nothing to see there," Chris replied.

Roland happened to pick up a brochure and showed Chris. "Look, this brochure features a picture of the Fort Knox US Bullion Depository and a map showing that it's only a minor detour. Fort Knox is on the way so we could easily pass by without wasting much time and have a photo stop."

Chris looked annoyed as he stared at Jorg and Roland. "Leave it with me," Chris stated. Chris spent most the night entertaining the two Austrian ladies in his tent with alcohol, which the others suspected was purchased with the tour's petty cash.

The group was up early the next morning and was keen to move on.

Chris on the other hand was lethargic and grumpy. As they drove towards Chicago, Roland thought it might be wise to remind Chris about the Fort Knox detour. "I've thought about it," Chris replied, "but I've decided against it."

Chris's negative attitude angered Roland, and he wasn't impressed with Chris's antics so he challenged Chris about the administration of the petty cash. "My understanding is that the funds were collected for camp meals and other camp expenses. We've missed out on a number of camp meals as we've gone to restaurants or grabbed takeaway and you seem to be using the funds for other purposes. I would like to inspect the records of the expenditure."

"You needn't worry about the funds," Chris said. "It will all work out in the end and I'm not prepared to discuss it any further."

Roland started to keep a log of everything Chris did that he considered to be improper or inappropriate and the list started to mount. He told the Dutchmen of what he was doing and they were excited with the prospect of someone taking a stand against the little dictator, although they wondered what Roland hoped to achieve.

The group was scheduled to spend three nights in Chicago and two nights in Toronto. Chris confided in one of the Austrian ladies that he lived in Toronto and wanted to get back there a day earlier.

The tour operated in a loop spanning four weeks with two weeks from Miami to New York and two weeks from New York back to Miami. Chris was only scheduled to do the first two weeks that finished in New York. Roland also ascertained that the tour company's office was in Toronto.

As the group only had two days in Chicago, they were fortunate to have two days of fine weather. On the first day, they visited Sear's Tower and viewed Buckingham Fountain. They also walked the streets in the city centre and around Lake Michigan.

The next day, Roland headed off to visit the Museum of Science & Industry. As the hotel was only a few kilometres from the museum and it was a beautiful day, he decided to walk. He was walking through the suburbs and noticed that all the people he passed appeared African American and he seemed to be getting a few stares. He didn't feel unsafe, more out of place.

Roland spent a few hours at the museum examining the exhibits and displays. He then decided to walk back to the hotel, taking a different route. He had walked about half way when a man of Hispanic appearance approached him. "Why are you walking around this area by yourself?" the man asked.

"I'm a visitor," Roland explained. "I've just visited the museum and I'm walking back to my hotel."

"This isn't a good idea, as it may not be safe," the man suggested.

"Thanks for the advice," Roland said, and continued on his way.

What the man said was starting to play on Roland's mind, particularly as the man's advice seemed to be given in good faith. However, as he had planned to walk, that's what he was going to do.

Roland started to feel a bit uneasy as he was passing a number of African American men and one of the men was walking straight towards him. The man neared, walked by Roland and gave him a broad smile. "Good day to you, sir," the man said.

"Good day to you too thank you sir," Roland replied.

Arriving back at the hotel, Roland decided what he would do regarding Chris. He drafted a letter of complaint explaining what had occurred in order to draw the matters to the company's attention in the interests of people who travelled with them in the future. He sought to have the letter countersigned by the other passengers and all the other passengers were happy to countersign the letter, except for the two Austrian ladies.

When the tour reached Toronto, the group enjoyed the main attractions, including CN Tower, Toronto Skydome, the Parliament Buildings, Toronto University College and the University of Toronto.

On the third day, Roland took a walk up Yonge Street, supposedly the longest street in the world. He located the tour company's office and personally dropped off the letter of complaint.

The ride from Toronto to Niagara Falls was subdued. The group admired the falls and thoroughly enjoyed the spectacular views. There was an eerie silence during their night stay at the campsite at Beaver Valley in upstate New York.

The next day, the group was driven to New York City. Chris parked the van in a busy street and Roland wondered where they were. As he looked up, he saw a large street sign, which read, *BROADWAY*.

Chris welcomed the group to New York. "I suggest we disembark with two guys unloading the baggage, two more guys moving them into the hotel and two guys standing guard. We are now in New York, situated in the sunny side of Harlem and it's crucial that you stay alert. I'll give you further instructions after we've checked in."

Chris addressed the group and gave them a few words of advice whilst in New York. He thanked them for the trip and refunded an amount from the petty cash for each passenger, except for the Dutch guys and Roland.

The group said goodbye to Chris and proceeded to leave. "I'd like for the Dutch gentlemen and Roland to stay behind," Chris requested and the others vacated the room. "I'm very disappointed with you guys and I can't understand, if you had a problem, why you couldn't just talk to me about it."

The Dutch guys and Roland were amazed how, after everything that happened, Chris could articulate such meaningless words. As Chris wound up his talk and noticed that there was no response, he handed them their refunds and walked out.

The Dutch guys and Roland looked at each other and shook their heads. Roland then raised his refund and announced, "the drinks are on me!"

The group had three days for themselves in New York before they continued on the second half of the four week tour. They had a great Chris-free time where they enjoyed the sights and sounds of the city.

They packed in a lot, including the Empire State Building, the Statue of Liberty, Rockefeller Center, the World Trade Center, Times Square, 42nd Street, Central Park, Columbus Circle, Madison Square Gardens, Greenwich Village, Washington Square, Little Italy, Chinatown, the New York Stock Exchange on Wall Street and a bay cruise.

Roland was keen to check out the nightlife; however, the group reminded him of the warning not to go out at night and only going out in groups at other times. "I know there's some risk," Roland acknowledged, "but if we travel in a group and only visit the safer Downtown area we should be fine."

The consensus from the ladies on tour was a decisive no. Roland then turned to the Dutch guys, but they gave him the reply he was not seeking, which was a firm, "ah no, we don't go."

After dinner, Roland set off to check out a few of the stores. As the daylight diminished, there were fewer people on the streets. He was around 110th Street, a few blocks from the hotel, when he sensed that someone was following him.

Roland walked a little faster and the person seemed to move faster. He picked up the pace and it was matched by the person following. He had enough and darted into a brightly lit store with the man continuing down the road, giving a menacing stare as he passed.

Lost as to what to do in the women's lingerie shop, Roland glanced at the merchandise at a distance and gave staff the odd smile. He noticed a lady with a pram who had left the shop and was going in the direction of his hotel. He poked his head out of the shop to make sure the coast was clear, caught up to the lady and walked alongside her. The lady was an attractive woman of Hispanic appearance who seemed totally unperturbed by the stranger.

Arriving back at the hotel, Roland was still toying with the idea of going out. He freshened up and approached the hotel reception. "Is it a problem if I wish to go out and can a taxi be arranged?" he asked.

"Taxi drivers don't generally drive to this area, but I have a friend who might be willing to drive you," the male receptionist said.

"I'll think about it," Roland replied.

Roland went over to the balcony overlooking Broadway to ponder the situation. *It's our last night in New York, I haven't been out at night and my only*

Looking down onto the dark and dimly lit street, Roland noticed that as it got darker and the shadows loomed larger a number of suspicious characters began loitering around, which got him thinking. *It's a jungle out there; no way am I going to go out there alone; I'm going to bed.*

The group reassembled on the morning of Wednesday, 20 September 1989. They had lost two members, being the English lady and the German guy. In their place were two lively Australian ladies, named Ava and Amy.

The group was introduced to their new tour guide and driver, named Trudy. She was a very friendly and bubbly person who went to extra lengths to individually meet every member of the tour. She allowed them to take turns to sit next to her while she drove. They found Trudy to be a breath of fresh air after their Chris experience.

They drove from New York to Washington and the weather became cloudy, dark and gloomy. They went out to a pub where they enjoyed a night of peanuts and beer. Trudy hit it off with Jorg and Amy hit it off with one of the other Dutch guys.

The next day, the group had a full day admiring all the monuments and buildings that Washington had to offer. These included the White House, the Smithsonian Institute, the Capitol, Jefferson Memorial and, the venue where Abraham Lincoln met his fate, Ford's Theatre.

After a campsite meal, the group was scheduled to go on a night city tour; however, the weather took a turn for the worse and it was raining heavily. "Are you still interested in travelling into the city?" Trudy asked.

No one appeared to be interested, but Roland was keen. He appreciated how people may prefer to give it a miss and how unpleasant the drive would be, but nevertheless he spoke up. "I'd be interested in going if anyone else was interested."

Trudy didn't have to wait for anyone else to express an interest. "Let's go then!" she shouted. This sparked a ripple effect. "Yeah let's go." "We have to get our raincoats." "Hang on, I'm coming too."

Trudy drove the group to the city and around various monuments. Roland took photos of the illuminated Lincoln Statue, Lincoln Memorial, the US Capitol, the Washington Memorial and the Reflecting Pool.

"Has everyone seen enough?" Trudy asked.

"Would we be able to get a view of the White House?" asked Jorg.

"I don't know whether there would be a suitable viewing point," Trudy replied.

By this time, it was pelting down rain and some of the roads were flooding. "Maybe if you parked nearby, we may be able to go on foot to view the White House," Roland suggested.

"You're crazy; you'll get drenched," Monique said.

"So?" Jorg replied.

Jorg and Roland jumped out of the van, ran along the street and over parklands. They ran for some distance and Roland totally lost his bearings. "I have no idea where to go," Roland shouted.

"Neither do I," Jorg yelled back and they simultaneously turned back the way they came.

They started to yell and cheer as they jumped through puddles and torrents of gushing water. Their frolicking seemed to attract a number of rats that were scampering around. As they approached the van, they thought their eyes were playing tricks on them.

Ava, Amy and Trudy were outside the van, dancing around and kicking up water at each other. The others were in the van laughing and cheering. "Hey, they're coming back!" those in the van cried out.

Trudy and Ava scrambled back into the front seats. Amy jumped into the back of the van and slammed the door shut. As Jorg and Roland neared the van, the door slid open, they jumped in and the door was slammed shut again.

All the drenched crew were back in the van where there was laughing and shouting. "Did you see the White House?" Ava asked as the noise subsided.

"What White House?" Jorg said with a grin.

The next day, the group travelled to Winston Salem. They settled into their campsite and the weather was getting worse. Trudy picked up news reports about hurricane Hugo. It had developed in the Atlantic Ocean and had hit South Carolina. The winds were picking up in North Carolina when the group settled into their campsite tents.

Trudy decided the tents were probably not the safest place to be and recommended they take refuge in the toilet block, which was constructed of solid brick and concrete. Everyone was more than willing to move, except for Monique. Trudy gave the group a reasoned recommendation as a tour representative, but was in no position to force anyone to move.

"We're all going to move and you should join us," Roland said, but Monique dug in and refused to move.

Roland resigned to the fact that it was her decision; however, Jorg had other ideas. Jorg expressed a number of choice words in Dutch, grabbed some of her belongings and dragged her into the toilet block.

It wasn't long after they had settled into the toilet block that the winds kicked up and items could be heard being hurled around the campsite. Most of the group members were up all night and there were times when they thought the roof was going to come off the toilet block, but it held firm.

In the early morning of 22nd September 1989, the group slowly got up to examine what had happened to the campsite. A number of the tents had been disassembled and ripped apart. Monique's tent had a large trunk from an overhanging tree crash square on top of it.

Stunned at the sight, Monique's eyes widened and her jaw dropped before she turned to Jorg. "Thank you," she whispered.

The group moved on to Cherokee country and hiked in the beautiful misty Smokey Mountains. They visited the Cherokee Indian Museum before travelling to the old charm town of Savannah.

They were impressed with the quintessential southern town that featured wonderful town squares with moss-hung trees lining the streets. They took photographs of the Waving Girl Statue, River Street, Lafayette Square, Madison Square with the statue of Sgt. William Jasper, Savannah City Hall and Jones Street.

The group continued south along swamplands and lakes to arrive at the city of St Augustine, USA's oldest town. They enjoyed viewing the St Augustine Memorial Presbyterian Church, Flagler College, St Augustine Museum of Weapons & Early American History, Zorayda Castle, City Hall, the cathedral, Castillo de San Marcos in the Spanish Quarter and the oldest house in the oldest town.

After one night in Augustine, the group travelled to NASA's John F. Kennedy Space Center. They were given a tour of the facilities and free time to explore the many exhibits.

They were on the move again to Orlando where they had a choice of visiting Disneyland or the Epcot Center. Roland had planned to go to Disneyland in California so he chose Epcot, being the Experimental Prototype Community of Tomorrow.

The group was then off to the Florida Keys where they had a ride in a glass-bottom boat, which Roland discovered was not the best experience with a hangover. He was almost sick as the boat's engines stopped, the air-conditioning malfunctioned and the boat was left rocking for ages to view the coral and swaying seaweed.

The next stop was Florida's Everglades where the group could enjoy the enormous wetlands with its diversity of vegetation, birdlife and wildlife. They were offered an optional hovercraft ride, which was promoted as being the best way to see the interior of the Everglades.

The quiet of the area was all of a sudden disturbed by the loud motors of the crafts as they sped off. The drivers seemed to be the only people who were really enjoying the ride. When the adventure eventually came to an end, Roland thanked the driver for stopping.

The group set off on their final drive from Key Largo to Miami, which signalled the end of the tour. Roland said goodbye to the other travellers and they exchanged addresses. He caught his flight from Miami to Houston and then on to Los Angeles, arriving just before 3 pm on 2nd October 1989.

Roland checked into his hotel, which was where his tour of the West Coast was to commence in three days time.

Over the three days, Roland visited the Dorothy Chandler Pavilion, City

Hall, the original Spanish settlement in Olvera Street, the Hollywood Hills, the Hollywood Bowl, Hollywood Boulevard, the Old Grauman's Chinese Theatre, Sunset Boulevard, Disneyland, Burbank Studios and Universal Studios.

The group assembled on the first day of the tour. Their guide, Jesse, ensured the passengers had their necessary documentation before he organised them into their hotel rooms.

The travellers were made up of 24 males, 16 females and two couples. They were from Australia, New Zealand and Germany. Among the Australians were six young farmers who had been working in the US on a farm exchange program.

The group departed Los Angeles later that morning and headed for the beautiful Santa Barbara Beach. They then moved on to the Danish community of Solvang and San Simeon. They spent a night in San Simeon, which allowed them time to visit the Hearst Castle before moving on to San Francisco.

They had three nights in San Francisco, during which time they experienced many attractions, including the Golden Gate Bridge, Alcatraz, Fisherman's Wharf, Lombard Street and Washington Square. They also enjoyed rides on San Francisco's characteristic streetcars.

A few of the group ventured into the suburbs to watch a college football game between San Francisco and St Mary's. Roland was not that familiar with American football, but he was reasonably content watching the cheerleaders. The small crowd seemed unimpressed when he periodically called out. "Bring on the dancing girls!"

After their stint in San Francisco, they headed to Bass Lake and Yosemite National Park. They enjoyed the natural beauty of the Californian Redwoods, the lakes, the waterfalls and the mountain scenery.

The group travelled through the Sierra National Park and visited Calico Ghost Town. Continuing along the road, Roland was getting stuck into some jerky and beer when the bus blew the radiator hose. They had a two hour wait before they continued on.

Arriving in Las Vegas, they checked into their hotel and feasted on a plentiful dinner before going on a limousine ride. Las Vegas transformed itself at night from a desert town to an amazing, illuminated city. They explored a couple of the casinos and the monstrous scale of the edifices blew them away.

Roland took a coin from his pocket and played a slot machine. He was not interested in casinos, but he considered that with that single play at least he could say that he gambled in Vegas.

Las Vegas provided the group with many highlights. The accommodation, food and drinks were of good standard and of exceptionally good value. The entertainment was world class and relatively inexpensive, which made even Roland a Las Vegas convert. "Gambling aside," he said, "you can't lose."

They left Las Vegas and visited the Hoover Dam before travelling to the Grand Canyon. They had an optional helicopter ride to the South Rim, Indian Village Falls and the North Rim, and were astonished by the canyon's size and the captivating views. They topped off the day with a hike down the Grand Canyon's Bright Angel Trail to Indian Gardens.

The group travelled to Sedona where they took a jeep ride around the Coconino National Forest. They ventured a little into the desert to have a photo taken alongside 20 foot high Saguaro cactus.

The next stops were at Scottsdale and Phoenix before travelling to San Diego. They took a San Diego Bay cruise on the sailing ship *Invader* and visited Sea World, the Museum of Man and Balboa Park.

In the evening, the group crossed the Mexican border into Tijuana. They had dinner in the lively tourist town, consuming a variety of beers and tequila. They ventured through the streets where they mingled with the locals and haggled at the markets. Roland had no intention of purchasing anything, but ended up with a sombrero and a poncho. The Australian farmers proved hard to track down before the group made their way back across the border.

It was on the morning of Wednesday, 18th October 1989 – the last day of the tour – when they heard news reports that a 7.1 magnitude earthquake had hit the San Francisco Bay area the day before. The tremor collapsed a section of the San Francisco-Oakland Bay Bridge and knocked out power.

The reports were of tens of people killed, thousands injured and hundreds of thousands left homeless. The news moved the group as they reflected on the fact that they were hosts of the city just days before. They headed back to Los Angeles where they spent a quiet time for the remainder of the last day of the tour.

Roland caught Continental flight CO001 that arrived in Australia at midday on 21st October 1989. He had told his parents not to bother to pick him up at the airport. He went through the airport formalities and quickly proceeded to grab a cab. The taxi stopped in front of the family home where his father was waiting at the front gate.

"Hi, Dad," Roland said.

"Hello, son. Your mother was pestering me about when you were going to return and that's why I'm waiting here at the front gate."

"Sure, Pa," Roland replied as his mother came outside. "Hi Ma!"

Chapter 23 – Parental Support

Circumstances had changed dramatically while Roland was overseas. His tenant left his rental property and caused a great deal of damage. As a result, he was without rental income and up for a hefty repair bill. He was also burdened with high interest rates, rising to over 20% per annum for his investment loan.

Roland was encouraged by his real estate agent to sell the property the previous year, which would have fetched a handsome price. Since then, during the course of 1989, the Australian economy was heading into recession and the bottom had fallen out of the property market. After assessing his financial position, Roland decided to sell his property and cut his losses.

It took a year to get the property presentable and was posted for auction at 12 noon on 15th December 1990. The forecast was for a fine morning, but with afternoon rain, which made Roland believe that things should work out all right.

Driving to the property, Roland had a few butterflies in his stomach. The skies became cloudy, but he still sensed that things should be okay. Then the skies became very, very dark. *Hold off rain*, Roland wished, but his wish would not be granted. The rain came and it was a deluge.

Roland could hardly see the road in front of him as he cursed for the rest of the drive. When he finally arrived at the property, he could not believe his eyes. It was such a downpour that one of the storm water downpipes burst and the whole front yard was flooded.

There were a number of people in attendance and they were all running for cover into the house, trampling over his new carpet.

"How do you feel?" the real estate agent asked Roland.

"I feel like crying and going home," Roland replied.

The auctioneer commenced proceedings in the front room while Roland retreated to the back room. After a torturous effort, there was little interest from the crowd. "For the last and final time, do I have any advance on $120,000?" the auctioneer cried out. There was dead silence. "Well, I'll have to confer with the vendor," the auctioneer advised.

The auctioneer headed for the back room to seek instructions whilst Roland was reconsidering his position. He had initially set a reserve of $130,000, but he now considered that in the present depressed market $120,000 may be more realistic. The auctioneer entered the room and

Roland was about to declare to sell, but the auctioneer beat him to it. "Well, there isn't much we can do," stated the auctioneer.

"Not much we can do? What do you mean? Don't we have a bid for $120,000?" Roland asked.

"Well technically we do," the auctioneer explained, "but unfortunately that was the only bid and it happens to be our own vendor bid."

Arriving back home, Roland didn't have to say anything as his parents sensed his mood.

"Bad luck son, never mind," said his father.

"Thanks, but it's okay; I'm sure everything will work out," Roland said, acknowledging his parents support.

Roland estimated that it would take four to five years to get back on his feet financially. He accepted this fact and was determined to get back to a position where he could travel again.

To keep his mind off his dire situation, Roland threw himself into his work and commenced a master's degree. He spent most of the following four years working and studying, hardly ever going out and spending his spare time with his folks and friends.

Roland was often falling ill to a series of viruses and infections. The pressure of his work, studies and sicknesses were all weighing on his physical and mental state; however, he was determined to continue with his regimented routine. Crunch time came when he fainted one day at home and his dad rushed to his aid.

Roland soon came to and tried to get up.

"Are you all right?" his father asked.

Roland was in the course of replying when he collapsed again.

When Roland came around, he was able to visit the family doctor. He explained what had happened and complained about chest pains. The doctor sent him for chest X-rays, which showed an abnormally enlarged heart and he was referred to a cardiologist.

The cardiologist undertook nuclear magnetic resonance imaging that involved injecting small amounts of radioactive material into his body to obtain images and information on his heart and heart function.

"It appears that you have a build-up of fluid around your heart, a condition referred to as pericardial effusion," the cardiologist advised and he admitted Roland to hospital.

The casualty department quickly went to work, inserting a couple of injections into Roland's chest. "We've given you a local anaesthetic," the doctor explained. "However, if you feel any pain when we insert the tube, let us know."

The doctor inserted a tube to drain the fluid and suggested that the procedure could be viewed via the ultrasound. Roland watched the screen with intrigue as the tube made its way through his chest and precariously close to his beating heart.

Roland's condition was stabilised and he was advised that he could soon be transferred to a ward. He was exceptionally relieved when they removed the tube from his chest and his fever subsided.

The diagnosis was that the splenectomy performed after Roland's traffic accident during his first overseas trip had made him prone to illness and it was recommended that he take oral antibiotics for life.

Roland's circumstances caused him to struggle during that semester's studies. He had completed his research papers prior to his hospitalisation; however, he only had a couple of weeks before his exams and he was grossly under-prepared. Nevertheless, he struggled on and managed to get through.

Roland felt that he had accomplished a great deal in the last four years, and that it may be time for a change. It didn't come as a complete shock to his parents when he told them of his decision to leave home. The issue had been raised in conversation a number of times and it was now simply a matter of when.

The day of Roland's departure came around, which he seemed to put off by the week and then by the day. He couldn't think of any more excuses to delay his departure and he prepared for his goodbye. He took his remaining bag of possessions and made his way to the lounge room. His parents were both seated and one of the neighbours had popped in. "Oh well, I'm off now," Roland stated.

The neighbour was in the middle of explaining something so Roland waited some time before trying again. "I'm leaving now." The neighbour looked at Roland with an annoyed expression as if he was unnecessarily interrupting her. "I'm leaving home now," Roland confirmed.

"Oh, goodbye Roland," the neighbour replied.

Roland's mum and dad gave him a kiss and they said goodbye. The neighbour continued with her gossiping and Roland remained stationary for a moment before making his exit.

It was a lonely drive to Roland's property and after he entered the house, he walked in and out of every soulless room. He had an overwhelming hollow feeling and a wave of sorrow came over him. He had thoughts of returning to the family home, but he knew his sense of emptiness was one he had to endure.

The departure from the family home was made that much harder because the Cipillone family were a very close-knit unit.

Roland's mother, Paola, and father, John, raised him with strong family values. They nurtured him with the greatest care and instructed him with the best intentions. Their love for their son was such that they would be prepared to sacrifice everything for him, something he recognised and respected.

Paola met John at a dance in Melbourne and, after a short courtship, they were married. "I asked your mother for our first dance and she never let me go," John once explained.

It wasn't long after Roland had left the family home that his mother's health deteriorated. Paola found it extremely frustrating when her condition meant she could no longer serve her family. The situation was accentuated with her unusual condition – something they could not give a specific name.

The neurologist explained that Paola had progressive neurological deterioration due to white matter ischaemia, which was in addition to her hypertension and diabetes. The neurologist confirmed Paola's condition in a letter that also noted she was sufficiently disabled to require high-level nursing home care.

John dedicated himself to his wife and took care of her up to the point when he could no longer physically manage. Attempts to assist him were met with his standard reply. "No, it's my job, it's my responsibility. I must do my duty. I must fulfil all my commitments."

Roland had heard this all before and for a long time he couldn't understand why his father felt obligated to help everyone and shoulder so much responsibility.

John was an only son, whose mother died when he was 17 months old. He was cared for by his grandparents up to the time his grandmother died. He was then sent to an orphanage in another city at the age of five. At 18, he joined the Italian navy and was sent to navy school in Venice. After World War II, he gained a plum position with the civil service in Rome. He worked there for five years when, in 1951, due to a number of convoluted circumstances and a rush of blood, he immigrated to Australia.

What is it about being from a small Italian town, having a military education, serving during the war and working for the civil service in Rome? Roland wondered so he decided to do some research.

It was from the inception of Rome that the concept of Citizen/Soldier/Farmer evolved. A tribe referred to as the Latins settled on the banks of the River Tiber where the city of Rome developed. However, the city was surrounded by hostile tribes. The Romans conquered these tribes and went on to build their empire.

At around 500 BC, the Roman soldiers were mainly farmers and hunters who took up the sword when called upon. This changed from around 100 BC when Consul Marius created a professional army, which took over from the citizen's army. Even so, the citizens looked back to the days of the patriotic yeomen with pride and admiration.

The cornerstone of Roman society was the virtues of gravitas, pietas and dignitas. Gravitas signified a person of substance and depth of personality. Pietas was duty and devotion to the gods, family and the state. Dignitas referred to the social standing earned by the male citizens of Rome.

John seemed to be the epitome of the ideal Roman, being that of Citizen/Soldier/Farmer and his character reflected the perfect embodiment of the ancient Roman virtues of gravitas, pietas and dignitas. Roland sensed that he now understood his father and his habit of questioning him was replaced with an overwhelming desire to support him.

During 1997, John eventually succumbed and placed Paola into a nursing home where he visited her every day. Roland visited his mother when he could. They re-united at the family home every weekend; something they knew Paola cherished.

Matters had settled down into a routine and it wasn't long before Roland's mind turned to thoughts of travel. It had been over eight years since he had a holiday and he was longing to continue his adventures.

Roland asked his father for his thoughts on taking another overseas holiday.

"Son, you should live your life when you are young."

The more Roland thought about overseas, the more enlivened he became. He started collecting brochures and the wheels were truly back in motion. In past trips, he concentrated on Western civilizations so his attention was now turning to the East.

The Cipillone family had their usual Sunday lunch together.

Roland returned Paola to the nursing home and they enjoyed the afternoon together. He fed Paola her dinner and spent time with her watching the television in the community area. He saw her to bed, explained he would be going on a holiday and said goodbye.

Paola was motionless, although her gaze made him sense that she understood.

Roland visited his father and they had dinner together. He then returned to his house to complete his packing and waited patiently for the taxi.

Chapter 24 – A Manila Stopover

The taxi pickup was on time and Roland was transported to Melbourne International Airport where he bordered his 23:45 Philippine Airlines flight to Manila. His mood was reflective during take-off; his thoughts still with his parents.

Arriving in Manila, Roland was transferred to his hotel and after checking in he went for a walk. He had his list of attractions in hand, but he just wandered the streets.

A young man approached, introduced himself as Junior and offered his services as a guide. Roland thanked Junior for his offer, but declined.

"Can I walk with you?" Junior asked.

"I prefer to walk alone," Roland replied.

"I would appreciate it if I could walk with you so that I could practice my English," Junior persisted.

Roland wasn't in the mood to argue. "You can walk with me, but I will not give you any money."

If nothing else, Junior focused Roland's mind onto his sightseeing. Roland enjoyed walking through Rizal Park and admired the statues, particularly the statue of La Madre Filipina. They inspected the Spanish styled Intramuros that incorporated Fort Santiago. They also visited the Manila Cathedral and passed by a shanty town on the banks of the Pasig River.

Roland paid for Junior's lunch, but refused to be drawn into financially sponsoring his education.

The lack of dining venues in the immediate area of Roland's accommodation influenced his decision to spend the rest of the day at the hotel. He arranged a relaxing massage, had a modest dinner at the hotel restaurant and retired to his room.

The next day, Roland set off on a canoe ride to the Pagsanjan Falls. The two canoeists assigned to lug him were of diminutive physiques. Roland marvelled at the skill of the canoeists as they hopped in and out of the canoe and manoeuvred around the rocks and rapids.

Roland was inspired by the beautiful scenery as they made their way to the falls. When they arrived, there were loads of noisy tourists. Roland allowed himself to get drenched under the waterfalls and the canoeists obligingly took his photo.

After dining at the hotel restaurant, Roland was determined to check out the nightlife on his last night in Manila. As he was exiting the hotel he was confronted by a taxi driver. "You need taxi?" the taxi driver immediately asked.

Roland didn't even reply and jumped into the back seat.

"Where you want to go?" asked the driver.

"Take me to see a girlie show," Roland replied.

"Oh, you want woman?" the driver asked. "I know a good place where you can take woman."

"No, I'm not interested in taking a woman, I just want to go to a bar where they have a girlie show," Roland clarified.

The driver seemed unsure. "I take you to good place, if you no like, we go to bar."

The man introduced himself as Angelito and he seemed to be driving for ages, which raised Roland's concern. *We've agreed on a fixed fare so where in the hell is he taking me?*

Angelito eventually drove down a small, dark street and came to a stop.

"Here?" asked Roland.

"Yes, over there," Angelito pointed. "It's a good place, I take you."

Angelito escorted Roland to a door and knocked. A bolted lock was released and the door opened allowing very bright lights to shine through. Roland needed a few moments for his eyes to adjust and, as he was being led into a large room, he could make out a hoard of women who were grabbing at him. "Me, me, pick me," the ladies pleaded.

Roland was seated in the centre of the table, two men sat on either side of him and twenty or so women sat on chairs circling the large room. "You pick girl or two," one man suggested.

Looking around the room, Roland witnessed a multitude of staring eyes, all seemingly conveying a different message. He was feeling embarrassed and eventually replied. "Girls all very nice, but none for me thank you."

The men seemed bemused and looked to Angelito. Angelito then turned to Roland. "What wrong with you?" Angelito asked. "Pick girl and you have lots of fun tonight."

Roland took another look around and wasn't able to pick anyone. *To select one would be to reject all the rest and I wonder who would be the happier.* He eventually repeated his original verse. "All very nice girls, but none for me thank you."

The men were not impressed, but allowed Roland and Angelito to depart.

Angelito drove Roland to a bar and proceeded to escort him inside. The entrance price was not cheap and he was also asked to pay for Angelito. "Do you need to enter with me?" Roland asked.

"It may be safer," Angelito suggested.

Roland paid for two entrances, he was frisked and allowed entry.

"You want two beers?" asked a waiter.

"Okay," Roland replied.

"You want a girl to talk with you?" asked a man.

"No thanks," Roland replied.

After a long delay, a female performer came out on stage. She looked totally uninterested and just moved to the music. The performer hinted at taking off an item of clothing, but then seemed to lose her concentration and left the stage.

Eventually, a second female performer came out on stage and she looked as unenthused as the first. She seemed to be moving marginally more; however, she also wasn't taking anything off until she finally removed a shawl. Roland was tempted to clap and cheer, but refrained.

"Do the ladies actually take off their clothes?" Roland asked. Angelito looked a little confused. Roland tried to clarify by motioning. "Clothes, take off?"

"Yes, take off," Angelito replied as he pointed to the shawl on the floor.

"I think we can go back to the hotel now," Roland said.

Chapter 25 – Short Stay Japan

The Philippine Airlines flight for Tokyo touched down at Narita Airport at 21:30. Roland was frisked and questioned by a jovial, uniformed, Japanese gentleman.

A tour guide greeted Roland and there was lots of bowing. The tour guide handed him 2,800 yen for a cab and a bus voucher valued at 2,900 yen. He was then given instructions on how to get to the hotel.

The cab ride was fairly short, but the bus ride seemed to go on forever. Roland eventually arrived at the Shiba Park Hotel and checked into his room, which he considered to be more like a cubby-hole. As he had sufficient food on the plane and was very tired, he went straight to bed.

In the morning, Roland was greeted by another tour guide and there was more bowing. He was then escorted onto a bus to partake in a tour of Tokyo.

The group was handed an observation ticket for Tokyo Tower where they took in the Tokyo skyline. They then visited the Imperial Palace where Roland took photos of the Nijubashi Bridge and Moat.

Roland was intrigued by the Asakusa Kannon Temple and took many photographs of numerous shrines and buildings, including the Buddhist Temple, the Nakamise shops and the Shinto Shrine.

The group was given the remainder of the afternoon to themselves. Roland visited Shiba Park, the National Diet Building, the song and dance venue of the Kabuki-za Theatre and the lively and colourful thoroughfare of the Ginza.

At night, Roland opted for a Tokyo Wondernight tour. He was looking forward to the evening as, going by the promotional material, it promised to be a lively evening of events.

The bus picked up a small group, consisting of a couple and three single guys. They started proceedings by visiting a food court where they purchased vouchers that they exchanged for food and drinks.

The next attraction was in a high-rise building that featured the history and design of Tokyo.

The group then visited a bar that had drinks at extraordinarily exorbitant prices. After they took advantage of their complimentary drink, the passengers were given the option to stay or depart. The vote was unanimous and they left.

Roland thought that the Tokyo Wondernight was aptly named as it definitely left him wondering.

Leaving the modern capital of Tokyo, Roland headed for Mt Fuji. The views of Mt Fuji were covered by the fog and cloud, nevertheless he enjoyed the journey through the lovely natural forest.

The group visited the Shinto Shrine and Buddhist Temple before stopping for lunch where they were distributed a lunch box. After lunch, they proceeded to the Peace Park at Hakone and visited the Peace Pagoda, being the resting place of the Buddha's ashes.

The tour passengers were then treated to a cruise on Lake Asahi. The weather had improved and it was now sunny and mild, although Mt Fuji was still hiding behind the clouds. They took the aerial tramway of the Hakone Komagatake Ropeway and visited the volcanic cone of Mt Komagatake. Mt Fuji was normally visible from there; however, the cloud cover persisted.

Roland was escorted to the destination of his bullet train at Odawara Station. He was handed a ticket and was pointed to a spot where he assumed he should stand. His mind was wandering when, in a flash, the bullet train appeared. The train arrived bang on time and the door opened directly in front of him.

As Roland found his seat, he couldn't stop admiring the colourful and cute rail tickets, which made him think. *I could live here, if I could speak Japanese.*

The bullet train sped to Nagoya and, after a short stop, sped on to the former Imperial capital of Kyoto. Roland was greeted by another guide and they did the customary bowing. The guide escorted him to a taxi that took him to his hotel.

The next day, yet another guide greeted passengers for their day tour and, needless to say, everyone was bowing. They visited the Golden Pavillion, Ninomaru Palace, Nijo Castle, Kyoto Imperial Palace and Higashi Honganji Temple. Roland was touched by the words of a sign from one of the temples and noted them in his diary. *Let us discover the significance of birth and the joy of living.*

The passengers lunched at the Kyoto Handicraft Centre and, in the afternoon, were taken to Nara for a tour of Todaiji Temple, Kasuga Shrine and Deer Park.

Roland enjoyed a light dinner before he returned to his room and prepared for his early morning departure.

Making his way to Kyoto Station, Roland was amazed that there was no guide to greet him. He caught the 06:45 Hanuka train to Kansai International Airport where he boarded his 09:55 Japan Airlines flight from Osaka to Beijing.

Chapter 26 – A Chinese Adventure

Roland was greeted in Beijing by a couple who transported him to his hotel. The tour group had already left to visit the Summer Palace and there was some confusion about Roland's room key. Eventually, a porter was arranged to open the door to his room.

Reception could not provide Roland with a room key card and he was unable to engineer a substitute card so he was left without electricity. The room was extremely hot, humid and stuffy. There was no lighting, no air-conditioning and no television. He settled into the oppressive environment and fell asleep.

After a couple of hours, Roland was woken by a knock on the door. It was the tour guide – an Australian named Jeremy. Jeremy gave Roland some information about the tour group, which was made up of 18 passengers ranging from 24 to 78 years of age. There were six ladies, six men and three couples. Jeremy ran through the itinerary for the 21-day tour and advised that the group would be attending a Chinese Opera in the afternoon.

Roland thought the Chinese Opera was interesting, although he was relieved when the high pitched singing came to an end. The group was driven back to the hotel and they had a free evening.

Exploring the market area close to the hotel, Roland checked out a few street restaurants and a pleasant, middle-aged lady invited him to take a seat. The lady handed Roland a menu, which was written in Mandarin; however, it included cute little pictures that graphically depicted what was on offer. He pointed to one of the items with a fish and the lady smiled.

Roland was content to sit, sip on coconut milk and watch the world go by. After a little while, he was served a large, whole fish whose beady eye was gawking at him. He liberated the fish of its head before he devoured the rest of it.

The following day, the group was taken to a vase-making factory. They then moved on to the Sacred Way where they followed the Divine Road and were given time to meander down the paths to admire the buildings, parks and gardens.

The next stop was an inspection of the Ming Tombs and then on to the Great Wall of China. They made their way to the entrance of the Great Wall at the Badaling section and Jeremy handed each person a ticket.

Roland noticed that his camera was almost out of film so he dashed off to buy another roll. By the time he returned to the entrance, the group had moved on and he was left to explore the wall on his own.

It was a fine and sunny day that allowed views into the distance. The wall weaved its way through the mountainous terrain to the point where it disappeared into the horizon. Roland took numerous photographs and a stranger happily obliged to take a couple of photos of him on the wall. He then took a ride on the Beijing Badaling Cable Car.

When the group reunited, there was much discussion about the events of the day.

In the evening, the group enjoyed Peking duck in the city that used to be called Peking.

Roland joined three of the tour group, Diana, Steve and William for an early morning walk to Tian Tan Park. They observed the locals with some conducting tai chi exercises, some performing martial arts with swords, others flying kites and yet others engaging in group aerobics.

The group took their time to explore Tiannamen Square, the Forbidden City that featured a large portrait of Mao Zedong and the Temple of Heaven. In the evening, they left Beijing and caught a China Northwest Airlines flight to Xian.

The next day, the group visited the Banpo Neolithic Museum with pits 1, 2 and 3 that featured the famous Terracotta Warriors. It was a glimpse of some of the 8,000 pieces covering more than 20,000 square metres.

The history of the warriors was put into perspective when the group was shown a short movie that summarized the story of the warriors and the significance of the archaeological find. They then toured the Museum of Terracotta Warriors and Horses of Qin Shihuang.

After learning about the life size, terracotta warriors, bronze chariots and horses, Roland felt compelled to purchase a small set of three terracotta statuettes, comprising an emperor and two guards.

The group was taken to see the Xian Great Mosque, being a famed Islamic mosque in China built during the Tang Dynasty at around 742AD.

After breakfast, the group walked through the streets of Xian. They proceeded to the South Gate, along the South Wall, on to the Bell Tower, South St and East St. The streets were lined with well maintained, traditional, oriental buildings.

The group caught the overnight train to Jinan where Roland shared a cabin with a Chinese couple and their small baby so he expected that he wouldn't be getting much sleep that night. But on the contrary, the parents were exceptionally loving and the baby responded with remarkably good behaviour.

The train arrived in Jinan mid-morning and the group was driven to their hotel. They freshened up and went to a modest restaurant where they enjoyed a tasty and plentiful serving of assorted dumplings. They then visited the Divine Rock Temple, the Thousand Buddha Temple and the Four Gate Pagoda, which was surrounded by lovely gardens.

The group enjoyed an exotic dinner in the town where beetles tested a few appetites.

The following day, the group was driven to the farming village of Shi Jia where they inspected a cultural display. The tour members were then allocated into farm houses in twos and threes. They had time to settle into the modest homes constructed of bricks and mortar, which were set in quiet, tree lined streets.

Jeremy, William and Roland were guests of the Wu family, comprising the husband, his wife and two young sons. The family treated their three visitors to a plentiful dinner of a variety of dumplings, cooked dishes and rice.

Mr Wu was keen to share his beer with his guests; however, Jeremy drank very little and William was sick, which left Roland to accompany Mr Wu in knocking back the beers.

"Come on Roland, you can't offend our host," Jeremy said. "You should match Mr Wu's drinking."

"I really don't feel like drinking too much," Roland said.

"Go on Roland," William urged. "I'd be scoffing down the beers if I was well enough."

Roland felt obliged to represent the guys and not offend his host. He sculled every glass in time with Mr Wu who didn't seem too interested in eating. Roland hardly had a chance to take a bite of his food as Mr Wu would regularly refill their glasses.

"Gan bei!" Mr Wu cried out, then waited until Roland lifted his glass, return the cry of gan bei and they drank together. Roland was required to match every gan bei.

"I think I've just about had enough," Roland said as politely as he could.

Mr. Wu was making loud, snapping noises with his mouth.

"Hang in there," Jeremy urged. "You've just about got his measure."

In the end, they ran out of beer – to Mr. Wu's disappointment, but to Roland's great relief.

After dinner, the group visited a school where they were entertained by the school children. It was a pleasant outdoor show where the cute, little kids conducted singing and dancing routines.

The guests were then called upon to perform something. After considerable deliberation by the group members, who came from various countries, they finally settled on singing *Old McDonald had a Farm*.

The school children thoroughly enjoyed the performance and joined in with the animal sounds. There was great amusement with the various sounding animal noises and everyone was left wondering why Chinese animals sounded so different to their English equivalents.

Departing the Shi Jia Village, the group had a tour of a ginger factory and made a visit to a school where they had an interesting interactive question and answer session with one of the classes.

The group moved on to Weifang where they visited a kite museum, Shi Hu Gardens Museum, the Yangjiabu Block Printing Shop and a kite factory.

Roland was looking forward to a visit to a kite factory and, after considerable deliberation, he purchased one of their impressive dragon kites. Not only were the dragon kites extremely decorative and colourful, they were also reputed to ward off evil spirits.

The group caught a morning train bound for Tai'an where lunch was had with a mini buffet of dumplings, bread, sausages, pastries and cakes. On arrival in Tai'an, they checked into their hotel and freshened up before visiting the Di Temple Rock.

The next day, they visited the impressive Mount Taishan, one of the five sacred Taoist mountains in China. Unlike some of the pilgrims who climbed up the 7,200 stone steps, the group took a bus and the cable car to the Jade Emperor Peak. They visited the Jade Emperor Temple and viewed the magnificent mountain scenery.

The group moved on to the quaint town of Qufu with its lovely, tree lined streets and gardens. Qufu was also the birthplace of Kong Fuzi, also known as Master Kong and more popularly known as Confucius.

In the evening, Jane, Susan, William and Roland went out to dinner. The foursome enjoyed each other's company and their friendships were starting to grow.

The following day, the group explored the Kong Family Forest, which was the Kong family cemetery for over 2,000 years. They visited the Kong Family Mansion with its rockery, Confucius Tomb and the Confucius Temple where there was a ceremonial re-enactment taking place.

The group was shown the tomb of Shao Hao, a legendary leader of China some 4,000 years ago. The tomb was also called the Hill of Ten Thousand Stones and was the only pyramidal tomb in China. The group enjoyed a performance of music and dance at their hotel. After dinner, they caught an overnight train to Nanjing.

It was a pretty rough train ride and by the time they managed to fall asleep they soon had to wake and quickly gather their belongings to disembark. They were driven to their hotel where they enjoyed breakfast. They then hired bicycles and rode to the mausoleum of the revolutionary leader, Dr SunYat Sen. After lunch, they rode to Lake Xuanwu and the Yangtse River Bridge.

The next day, the group visited the Fusi Miao (Confucius) Temple and explored the streets and markets of Nanjing. The markets had a variety of foods and pets, although it was sometimes difficult to work out which was which. That afternoon, they boarded another train, this time bound for Suzhou, referred to as the Venice of the East.

In Suzhou the following day, the group visited Fisherman's Gardens and a silk factory. The highlight of the day was a cruise around the canals, including the Grand Canal. That evening, they boarded yet another train, this time bound for the mighty city of Shanghai.

Arriving in the evening, the group had a light dinner and then grabbed some cabs for a night ride through the bustling, city streets. They checked out a couple of trendy bars before retiring.

The following morning, they ventured into central Shanghai again and were just as impressed with the city by day. They visited the Mandarin Gardens before taking the elevator to the 42nd floor of the Blue Heaven Revolving Restaurant in Jin Jiang Tower. They moved on to the Jade Buddha Temple before being dropped off for some free time at the Bund. It was abuzz with people enjoying the sunny day with some of them flying small, balloon shaped kites.

Having a fetish for architecture, Roland was surprised by the variation in style and types of buildings. He could appreciate how Shanghai was referred to as a living museum of world architecture and considered that some of the buildings along the Bund wouldn't be out of place in London.

The foursome of Jane, Susan, William and Roland caught a bus to the People's Square where they popped into a department store, purchased some beverages and drank them as they relaxed in the square.

In the evening, the group was treated to a gravity defying Shanghai acrobatics production and dined at an Italian restaurant. They then went to the Hard Rock Café where they downed many drinks before returning to the hotel for nightcaps. Roland realised that he may have drunk too much as he ended up sleeping with Jane and there was little he could remember.

The group caught their Eastern China Airlines flight from Shanghai to Guilin and, after checking into their hotel, they visited the Reed Flute Caves.

They then had a tour of a hospital and a demonstration of electronic acupuncture. "Are there any people who have an ailment that they wish to have treated?" asked the doctor. A few of the group members volunteered with Jane describing her problem as a pain in the neck.

Walking about the quaint town of Guilin, the group ventured into a shop that sold many regional items including highly decorative, hanging silk balls. The lady shopkeeper noticed them admiring the silk balls.

"The balls are actually made of silk and have a history of over a thousand years," the shopkeeper explained. "The girls of Zhuang would throw the silk ball to a person they wanted to express their sincere love. If the ball was caught by the intended person, it would bring them luck. The balls are also referred to happy balls and sometimes lucky balls."

Roland thought that he could do with some lucky balls so he bought himself a pair.

The group checked out of their hotel the following morning, drove to the Li River and embarked on a cruise from Guilin to Yangshuo. It was here that the travellers gained an appreciation of how Guilin attained the reputation as the most beautiful sight under heaven.

Arriving at their hotel in Yangshuo, they had a rest before going for a walk about town. They inspected the markets and were a little put off by the various animals in cages. Their stomachs were further tested by the exotic array of food and drink available, which included snails and wine bottled with snakes.

The group had some free time the next day where they explored the town on bicycles. They rode their bikes to the river and caught a ferry to Fulin. They explored the town before they got back on their bikes and headed back to Yangshuo.

The group had an early Southern China Airlines flight to Canton and then boarded a boat bound for Hong Kong. It was on the boat that William revealed to Roland that he had become fond of Susan and her of him. The revelation got Roland thinking and he came up with the idea of swapping rooms so that William could be with Susan and he could share with Jane. Roland put the idea to William and he was keen.

William didn't take long before he darted off and returned to find Roland. "Hey Roland, Susan's sweet on the idea, what about Jane?"

"I don't know, I haven't asked her yet."

"She's over there," said William, pointing. "Why don't you ask her now?"

Roland went over and asked Jane whilst William looked on. Roland then gave William thumbs up; a broad smile emerged on William's face and he returned the gesture.

Steve, another guy on the tour, mentioned that he was going for a day excursion to Macau and Roland expressed his interest to join him. After they had breakfast, they took the hotel bus to the harbour. They then caught the East Jet ferry from Hong Kong to Macau.

It was an exceptionally hot and humid day. They had only been walking a short while when they started to feel the heat and decided to seek some respite in the cool of a hotel's air-conditioning.

They entered a hotel, found immediate relief and enjoyed a refreshing drink. They noticed a few women walking around the hotel shops who were dressed rather risqué. They were curious about the women, but left the hotel to continue with their sightseeing.

It wasn't too much further that Steve felt distressed and they again sought the cool of another hotel. They didn't find the same curiosity as the first hotel and this raised their suspicions.

They were off again and enjoyed the sights of Macau, visiting Senado Square, Government House and the ruins of St Paul. Steve and Roland were both happy with the sights they had witnessed so they decided to return to the harbour to catch the ferry back to Hong Kong. As they had some time to spare, they swung by the first hotel in order to satisfy their curiosity.

Steve and Roland entered the hotel and they couldn't believe their eyes. There was a large swarm of women dressed in slinky outfits. The guys walked around, but the women seemed preoccupied window shopping and uninterested in the two gentlemen.

"Let's split up and see what happens," Roland suggested.

Roland glanced and smiled at a couple of the young ladies and they wasted little time in approaching him. "You want to go up there?" asked one of the ladies.

"What's up there?" Roland asked.

"Our room," was the reply.

"And what's in your room?" Roland asked, to which the ladies giggled.

"We will be up there," the same lady said.

"I'm not interested today," Roland told them, "but I am curious about the cost."

"The charge is $200US for a girl for one hour, including the room," the other lady explained.

Roland then caught up with Steve. "We can leave now that the mystery has been solved."

"What mystery?" Stephen asked.

"The women mystery," Roland clarified.

"What about them?"

"I'll fill you in on the way back."

It was officially the last day of the tour and most of the travellers said their goodbyes. The foursome enjoyed their last evening together before Susan and William said goodbye to Jane and Roland and the two couples parted.

Jane and Roland spent a long night of talking and play fighting. At the time of Roland's departure, Jane was slightly emotional and Roland promised to keep in touch.

Roland caught his 17:45 Royal Nepal Airlines flight to Kathmandu where he hailed a bomb of a taxi and a man stepped up to grab his bag. Roland pulled his bag away and the man reached out for a tip. "Give him nothing," the taxi driver stated as Roland placed his bag in the boot. After being dropped off at his hotel, Roland fell asleep the moment his head touched the pillow.

Chapter 27 – Mountains and Moguls

Roland enjoyed the spicy hotel breakfast where he met Carol, a Swiss lady who was on the same tour as him. They explored the municipality of Bhaktapur, referred to as the city of culture where there were festivities that featured costumed dancers and traditional music.

A young boy, named Dip, approached them and hung around for most of the day. Dip was a pleasant boy who explained to them about the life in his small town. The three of them enjoyed lunch together and explored Durbar Square with its many ornately decorated buildings. At mid-afternoon, they bid Dip goodbye and returned to their hotel.

The pre-departure meeting was held at 4.00 pm. The tour leader, Linda, commenced with introductions. The group was made up of 16 travellers with six women, six men and two couples. After some administrative matters, they went into central Nepal for a restaurant dinner. This was followed by a pub crawl before the passengers chose their own time to retire.

A young lad – Mark from Scotland – and Roland were the last at the pub. Roland indicated that he was going, but Mark wanted to stay. Roland wasn't comfortable leaving the kid on his own, particularly as there were some men who were offering hashish. They had another drink and Roland suggested they should leave. Mark, who was now very drunk, finally agreed.

Roland proceeded down the road in the direction he thought led back to the hotel; however, his ever unreliable bearings and a confusing fork in the road made him uncertain. "We'd be better off taking a rickshaw," he suggested.

"I know the way back," Mark stated confidently as he made his way down one of the interconnecting roads. However, he soon freaked out when he realised he was lost.

Roland got him to calm down. "We just need to retrace our steps back to town and grab a rickshaw."

When they found a rickshaw, Roland mentioned the name of the hotel a few times, but the driver was uncertain. Mark's attempt to pronounce the name of the hotel a number of times with a strong, slurred Scottish accent didn't seem to help.

After a few more attempts, the driver finally said, "Oh yes, no problem."

They seemed to be going in an unfamiliar direction and the driver came to a stop in a dark street. "Hotel is up the pathway," the driver explained. "I cannot go up the pathway as it is too narrow and I cannot go to the front of the hotel as the street is too steep."

Roland thought this odd, as he couldn't recall any steep streets near their hotel. Mark dismounted the rickshaw and headed up the path, eager to get to the hotel. Roland paid the rickshaw driver and was heading up the path when he heard Mark shouting out. "This isn't our hotel!"

Mark came charging towards Roland who dragged him to a stop. "The driver has left," Roland told him. "We can go to the hotel reception and order a taxi from there."

Once they arrived at the hotel, Roland asked the hotel receptionist to order a taxi for them. When the taxi arrived, the receptionist pronounced the name of their hotel completely differently to the way they had said it. Mark and Roland looked at each other and rolled their eyes.

Early the next morning, the group had the option for a scenic flight of the Himalayas, which included a view of Mt Everest. Roland didn't feel great, but the opportunity was one he wasn't going to miss.

There were three passengers plus the pilot on the Necon airplane and Roland was fortunate to get the front passenger seat. When they arrived at the area where Mt Everest was visible, the pilot pointed in a general direction of the mountain range. "That's Mt Everest over there."

Looking in the direction of the pilot's pointed finger, Roland was uncertain. "Where?" he asked.

The pilot repeated the direction and Roland looked again. He thought that he may have been looking at the right peak, but he was still uncertain.

Roland considered the fact that the Himalayas was a series of mountain peaks and, even though Mt Everest was over 29,000 feet, more than one thousand feet higher than any other peak, from their distance and depending on the elevation and angle of the aircraft, it may have been difficult to identify.

In the end, Roland zoomed into what appeared to be the highest peak and took a few photos. He resolved to place a photo with the most majestic peak into his photo album and annotate it as Mt Everest. *No one will ever know.*

The group explored the Kathmandu Valley before visiting the Monkey Temple at Swayambhunath, the largest Buddhist Stupa in Nepal at Bodnath and the most important Hindu Temple in Nepal at Pashupatinath. They then feasted on a huge lunch with as much rice wine as one desired.

Returning to central Nepal for dinner, the group had an early night and, on this occasion, Mark and Roland joined the others for the walk back to the hotel. As they realized the simple mistake they made the previous night, they looked at each other and rolled their eyes.

It was an early start the next day where they endured a four hour drive from Kathmandu to a lakeside stop and then a further four hour drive to their overnight stay at Pokhara.

The group was entertained by Nepalese dancers whilst they enjoyed their meal. After dinner, Roland joined Carol for a few drinks at a nearby café before they retired.

It was an extra early morning start the next day where they took a taxi ride to the base of the Annapurna Mountain Range. They endured a testing hike to see some magnificent views at sunrise. On their return, they had breakfast before they went on a relaxing boat ride.

The group went on a bike ride to Devi Falls and took advantage of the happy hour before dinner followed by a few drinks at a Tibetan tea garden.

Roland was not enjoying the early morning starts and he had to put up with yet another one. This time they were leaving Pokhara and heading for Chitwan via Mugling.

They arrived at Royal Chitwan National Park where they had the opportunity to take an elephant safari ride. Roland didn't really fancy an elephant ride and queried why anyone would ever want to ride an elephant; however, he accepted it as one of those things that one should experience at least once in their life.

There were four passengers allocated to each elephant, with each person placed in a corner of an open, box-like seat. The rider sat behind the ears of the elephant and, as the elephant was slightly restless, the young rider gave the elephant a right royal crack over the skull with an iron bar. The passengers gasped in fright. "Don't worry, the elephant has a very hard head," the rider stated.

"He'd wanna have," Roland commented.

The elephants paraded out and proceeded to trample their way through the thick undergrowth. They were sure footed, large and strong enough to plough through the most inhospitable vegetation and ward off the most intimidating predators. It wasn't long before Roland could appreciate why the locals developed the art of riding the elephants and he grew an admiration for the beasts.

As they crossed a river and went further into the scrub, there seemed to be some activity. There were huge bellows and trumpeting from the elephants as the riders mobilised their gigantic beasts into a mini stampede.

The passengers had no idea what was happening and their excitement reached fever pitch. The riders then steered their elephants towards each other and pulled them up to an abrupt stop. Four of the elephants and their riders were facing each other. The riders were chattering and yelling with fervent animation, their eyes bulging.

It was hard to decipher exactly what had occurred; however, from what the passengers could make out, the riders had spotted a rhinoceros and, for some reason, were trying to chase it. The rest of the ride was a relatively calm affair.

It was another early morning start and, after breakfast, they went on a canoe ride through the mist to a crocodile farm. On the return leg, they visited a Tharu village.

Back at the Chitwan National Park, Linda rolled up on a motorbike with a young lady on the back. Linda introduced her as Pamela, a friend of hers who would be helping out for the rest of the tour. They dismounted the bike in unison, both dressed in tight, black, leather gear and they stood up straight in an open stance.

Linda removed her helmet and shook her head from side to side, allowing her long, blonde hair to sway loose. She was tall, of medium build and reasonably attractive; however, at that point in time, she looked hot.

Pamela then removed her helmet and went through a similar routine. She was a petite, young lady with shoulder length, black hair and simply stunning.

Once the guys had snapped out of their momentary trance, they were nudged along and proceeded inside where the group had dinner before retiring.

The tour moved on from Chitwan to the city of Bhairahawa. They had a roadside lunch before they drove on, but were stopped due to a road accident. Apparently a truck driver collided with three cyclists and sped off. The locals were protesting and not allowing traffic through.

"How heartless it was for the truck driver to drive off," Carol remarked.

"I expect the truck driver may have feared what the locals might do to him if he did stop," a local man suggested.

In order to continue, they were required to walk through the protesters' roadblock and catch a local, public bus. When they arrived at the border they hired rickshaws to get across, proceeded to Nepalese immigration and then to Indian immigration.

Making it into India, the group checked into a very poor-quality hotel. Roland was settling into his room when he thought he would check out the balcony. He looked out at the view and then turned around to re-enter the room. To his horror, a huge bee hive was embedded in the air-conditioning unit.

Roland rushed back into the room and slammed the door shut. He then marched down to reception and demanded another room.

"What is the problem, sir?" asked a middle-aged, male receptionist

"There's a huge bee hive on the air-conditioning unit."

"Oh sir, I cannot give you another room, but it is no problem, no problem. If you keep the door closed, the bees cannot get into the room."

"Okay, I'll stay in the room as long as I don't see any bee inside. However, if I see just *one* bee inside, I'll expect another room."

"Yes sir, no problem, no problem."

Returning to his room, Roland carefully looked around and there was no sign of any bee. He tried to rest, but found it impossible so he decided to go for a walk. When he rose from the bed, he felt something underfoot. A squashed bee. "That does it!" he yelled as he stormed down to reception and demanded another room.

"No problem, no problem," the receptionist said.

The replacement room was in a worse state and had mosquitoes, but as there were no bees, Roland was content. He joined the group for dinner and, after quite a few drinks, he went to bed. To his amazement, he actually managed to get some sleep.

Roland departed without a shower, without breakfast and with a hangover. Nevertheless, he was happy to be leaving the hotel from hell. They had a roadside stop where he freshened up and got a bite to eat. He managed to get a little more sleep and, after a roadside lunch stop, he slept some more.

The group visited Sarnath, the place where Buddha preached his first sermon. They also witnessed the Dhamekh Stupa before moving on to the Archaeological Museum and Deer Park. They arrived at their next hotel, which was in Varanasi, India's most sacred city and the place where Buddha first received enlightenment some 2,500 years before.

After dinner, a small number of the group went to a nearby luxury hotel. Roland ordered a round of drinks and paid the waiter with a large denominated note. The drinks were served and he noticed that the barman was going about his business.

"Excuse me sir, what about my change?" Roland asked.

"Your change?" The barman seemed surprised that this man expected change.

"Yes, my change," Roland repeated.

The barman peered in the till. "I don't have enough money; I will have to send someone to the other bar to get it."

"I would appreciate my change as soon as possible."

Roland noticed that his cocktail was rather weak. "How do you find your drinks?" he asked the others. The common reaction was that they seemed to lack alcohol. Unimpressed, Roland noticed that the barman didn't seem to be acting on his change. He wasn't prepared to give the bartender a 300% tip for bad service and poorly mixed drinks so he persisted in his efforts to obtain his change.

"Excuse me, bartender, when exactly do you think you will arrange to get my change?"

The bartender seemed to be put out by the insistence for the change, but expected that this Roland man would not relent so he made a telephone call.

The group finished up their drinks and Roland approached the bar. The barman handed money over, which Roland counted and noticed that he was still a bit short. He looked at the barman, who was preparing himself for further remonstrations, and skulled the remainder of his mocktail. "Unbelievable," he stated and walked out.

It was another early morning start and the group was off on rickshaws to the banks of the River Ganges. They boarded row boats and floated down the river just before sunrise. As the day slowly lit up and the mist dissipated, the activity along the banks and on the water came to life.

The experience was almost magical with what started as a peaceful sunrise on calm waters was turning into a symphony of sights, sounds and visions. It all culminated to a crescendo that did not relent.

The Ghats showed off some colourful buildings of breathtaking design and architecture. There were local people on the bank of the river going about their daily routines, from bathing, to washing clothes and even brushing their teeth. There were also areas where cremated corpse ashes were dumped into the river. The surreal experience continued as the group witnessed a dead dog floating by.

After an unforgettable time on the Ganges, the group returned to the hotel and, for those that could muster an appetite, they had breakfast. They then set off and visited the Monkey Temple dedicated to the Goddess Durga, the Tulsi Manas Temple dedicated to Lord Rama, the Moslem area and the Bazaar.

At sunset, the group returned to the banks of the Ganges where they released lighted candles by floating them on the water and making a wish for family and friends.

As the morning of the following day was free, Roland slept in before he joined Linda for a leisurely breakfast. They then enjoyed the pool at a nearby hotel.

The group was bound for Lucknow and there was a mad scramble to catch the train. Once on board, they had to cramp in wherever they could and endured the oppressive conditions for the duration of the journey. At the end of the ride, there was an equally mad scramble in the exodus from the train. They checked into their hotel and had a light dinner with a few drinks before having an early night.

After breakfast, the group went off to explore Lucknow. They visited the British Residency, the Great Imamabara and the Baby Imamabara. They then took taxis for a ride around the old and new cities of Lucknow. Lunch was on the lawn of the hotel where the group was content to remain to enjoy a lazy afternoon.

The evening was spent on another part of the hotel lawn where they had dinner. The surroundings featured a turreted wall, lighted torches and a colourful fountain. It was an ideal setting for a scrumptious buffet dinner whilst listening to relaxing background music. They were very comfortable in their idyllic setting when they had to check out of the hotel and catch their overnight train to Agra.

The group was stuck on the train platform for 1½ hours, although they kept themselves entertained. They had witnessed many cows roaming around the streets in India; however, cows loitering on the platform of the train station was something they did not expect. Cows were not the only beings occupying the platform; there were also mice, rats and dogs. The people and animals all cohabitated the platform in harmony.

Roland shared a cabin with Martin, Carol, Jackie and the couple of Mary and Bob. He was finding the train journey excruciating until the lovely Pamela joined them. In the morning, he was pleased to wake up to the sight of the sleeping beauty.

There was the usual chaos in disembarking the train at Agra. As there were no buses, taxis were arranged to drive them to their hotel where they wasted little time dropping off their belongings and setting off for the Taj Mahal.

The Taj Mahal provided an amazing sunrise view and it proved to be a work of art that appropriately expressed the love of an emperor for his queen. They found the intricate and detailed workmanship of the edifice as impressive as the grandeur of the overall construction.

Roland had the obligatory photograph taken of him sitting on the bench at the foreground of the majestic marble tomb and, as they were leaving the site, he recited the words on his guest card: "So perfect are the proportions of the Taj so exquisite its workmanship that it has been described as having been designed by giants and finished by jewellers."

The group left the Taj Mahal for breakfast and then continued their cultural pilgrimage with a visit to the Agra Fort, also referred to as the Red Fort of Akbar. They took some time to explore the colossal site and were surprised by what the mighty sandstone walls enclosed. There were palaces, halls, courtyards, fountains and the impressive Pearl Mosque.

They returned to the hotel for a proper check-in and then had time for lunch and a refreshing swim in the pool. Later that afternoon, they took a taxi convoy through the madcap streets of Agra where they visited Sikandra and the Baby Taj, being the marble tomb named Itimadu'd-Daula. They then proceeded back to the Taj Mahal for a sunset view.

Dinner was at the hotel and Roland opted for the Thalie Emperor's meal, which he devoured like he thought a true emperor should.

The group left Agra with a stopover to view the Fatehpur Sikri, which comprised administrative, residential and religious buildings. Continuing along the road, the bus came to another stop. Apparently there had been another road block protest due to another road accident. They were expecting a long hold up, but the protesters allowed their tourist vehicle through.

It was a three-hour drive to Jaipur and along the way they stopped at a bottle shop where the group took advantage by stocking up. They checked into their hotel and freshened up before going out for dinner.

After dinner, the group returned to the hotel by rickshaws and migrated to the open rooftop for drinks. Hotel reception gave a subtle message for the consumption of alcohol to cease, which was adhered to by most of the travellers, although Linda and Roland were determined to polish off their wine glasses.

Linda and Roland got on famously over the course of the trip and they found themselves sitting side by side. They were having an enjoyable conversation when they stumbled upon a silent pause and were gazing into each other's eyes.

Roland wasn't sure what to do, but as he liked Linda he thought he may as well kiss her. As he slowly advanced towards her and started to pucker up, she turned her head away and his lips met the side of her head and were lost in her long, flowing, blonde hair.

"Sorry Roland, I can't."

Roland felt like he was a character in a *Mills & Boon* novel and he tried to play his part. "That's all right Linda, it's no problem."

"Why Roland, why did you try to kiss me?"

"Oh, I don't know; I guess it was just for something to do."

Breakfast was followed by an extensive talk by a guide. The group eventually proceeded to visit the Observatory and the City Palace with its impressive Peacock Gate.

The group was escorted to a carpet factory where lunch was provided. It was then off to a jewellery store before heading back to the hotel. The complimentary lunch didn't agree with Roland and he spent the remainder of the afternoon getting acquainted with the toilet bowl.

On the penultimate night of the tour, a special dinner was planned. There were pre-dinner cocktails and Roland was happy to accept Carol's invitation to sit next to her at dinner.

Before leaving Jaipur the next day, the group stopped off to witness the Hawa Mahal, more popularly known as the Palace of the Winds. Snake charmers were an added attraction. They visited the Amber Palace and Fortress where they toured the site, partly on elephants. After lunch, they continued on their long drive to Delhi.

Roland washed up and packed his belongings before joining the group for their last dinner together. He considered it appropriate to end his Indian adventure with a curry, which fortunately agreed with him.

As Roland was the first one to part the tour, everyone bid him goodbye and they exchanged contact details. He proceeded to shake all the guys' hands and to kiss all the ladies. When he got to Linda, she smiled and he returned a smile. She then swung him around, gave him a decent kiss square on the mouth and lifted him up again. The stunt gained laughs and applause from the group.

Roland grabbed his backpack, was ushered into a taxi and whisked straight to the airport. Before he knew it, he was on the 00:05 Thai Airlines flight to Bangkok.

Chapter 28 – Returning Home Again

Arrival in Bangkok was on schedule at 5.40 am. Roland was feeling drained and he sluggishly went through the airport procedures. There was a pleasant welcome by the reception staff at the hotel, which slightly lifted his spirits.

Accommodation was available immediately and Roland was swiftly guided to his room. Allowing a two day stopover to explore the city, he pulled out his map and itinerary before he headed out.

Roland planned to start off with the Grand Palace and Wat Pho; however, they were closed due to a holiday. He was unaware of a holiday on 11th November, but he guessed that it may have been for Loy Krathong Day where thanks were offered to the goddess of the water. People lit candles, made a wish and launched their Krathongs on the waters where it was believed that sins, bad luck and suffering floated away.

Re-jigging his itinerary, Roland headed for the National Assembly. He took a photo that captured the National Assembly Building, the Royal Plaza and the statue of King Chulalongkorn. His next stop was the Victory Monument followed by Lumpini Park that featured the statue of King Monkut and a small fountain.

Roland walked a long distance over the course of the day and returned to his hotel for a rest. A few hours later, he freshened up and hit the town. As his hotel was close to the infamous Patpong Road, he thought it was a good enough reason to justify its exploration.

Whilst inspecting the shops and stalls, Roland was approached by a young man named Antonio. Antonio didn't speak English, but he did speak Italian and once he learnt that Roland spoke a little Italian he wasn't going to let him go.

Antonio spoke in Italian. "Do you want beautiful lady?"

"No thank you, I'm just looking at the shops," Roland replied.

"Shops here all rubbish," Antonio stated. "I show you beautiful woman."

Roland thought Antonio was right about the shops, but was not interested in Antonio's beautiful woman. "I just wish to look around," Roland said.

"That's all right," Antonio responded. "I will look with you."

Roland was fed up with the shops and told Antonio that he was going.

"Where you going?" Antonio was quick with the follow-up.

"I'm going to get something to eat," Roland told him.

"I know a good restaurant," Antonio claimed.

It was more of a cafeteria than a restaurant, but as Roland had not eaten all day and hadn't noticed anything better, he went in.

On entering the restaurant, Roland turned around and Antonio was right behind him. "I prefer to eat alone," Roland advised.

Antonio was again quick with the reply. "Okay, no problem, you eat, I look."

Roland wasn't in the mood to argue so he grabbed a seat and Antonio sat at the same table. Roland ordered and, as he looked up, he saw Antonio staring at him. "Would you like something Antonio?"

"No thanks, I'll just grab some tap water."

Roland left the restaurant with Antonio following close behind. Antonio soon started up again. "You now want beautiful woman? I take you to a place with beautiful woman."

"I don't want a woman tonight," Roland replied and it then dawned on him that he hadn't seen a girlie show. "However, I would be interested to see a girlie show."

"Shows here on streets no good, full of Lady Boy," Antonio immediately responded. "Patpong is a tourist area and there are no good shows here, although I know a place that is close and safe."

"Okay, Antonio," Roland said. "Let's go."

Antonio took Roland down a couple of streets and up a set of stairs. There was bar, a stage with dance poles and a handful of patrons. They each pulled up a stool and Roland bought a couple of beers.

An act had just commenced when Roland started to feel hot and sweaty. Antonio noticed that Roland was acting uneasy. "Are you all right?" asked Antonio.

"I feel sick," Roland responded as he rushed out of the bar, down the stairs and had just made it onto the street when he threw up in the gutter.

Antonio arrived at Roland's side. "Maybe food no good," Antonio stated.

Roland looked up at Antonio. "Yeah, maybe food no good."

Pulling himself together, Roland started to make his way back to the hotel. "Tomorrow, I can show you beautiful woman tomorrow!" Antonio called out.

"Yeah," Roland replied. "Maybe tomorrow."

Roland had a very rough night where he consumed a lot of water and slept in until 11.30 am. He confirmed his flight back home, stocked up on more water and made the effort to conclude his sightseeing. He returned to the Grand Palace and was relieved to find it open.

After joining a tour of the Grand Palace and the Emerald Buddha, Roland visited Wat Pho and the Reclining Buddha before returning to the hotel for a rest. He went out for dinner and arrived back at the hotel at around 11.00 pm. He wasn't tired and, as it was the last night of the trip, he decided to hit Patpong.

It wasn't long after Roland reached Patpong that Antonio appeared. "You want beautiful woman?" Antonio asked.

"Yes, I want beautiful woman," Roland responded.

Antonio hailed a taxi and they both jumped in. The taxi drove for ages and Roland began to feel uneasy. Eventually, the vehicle slowed and made its way up a dark driveway.

"This is it," exclaimed Antonio.

Roland paid the driver and followed Antonio inside. The establishment featured a long line of windows that looked like shop-fronts. There were different sections with signs on them, including *Stars* and *Superstars*.

Walking up and down the area, Roland observed the ladies either standing or sitting, all carrying numbers clipped to their dresses. He thought it degrading, but could not deny their beauty. He saw a lady that, for some reason, he liked. He confirmed the price and asked for her.

Number 99 led him upstairs and introduced herself as Moon, which he thought ironic as she was in the *Stars* section.

It was the first time that Roland had involved himself with a prostitute in such an establishment. He had no idea what to do and little idea what to expect. Fortunately, Moon went into her standard routine and politely gave him instructions. "You can take off your clothes and relax on the bed."

Moon proceeded with her preparations where she filled a large bath tub with warm water, hosed down an inflatable bed and covered it with soap suds. When the bath water reached the required level, she asked Roland to hop in. He did as she instructed and, after he had settled in the bath, she joined him and commenced to wash him.

Roland was admiring Moon's taut body, her silky skin and her flowing, black hair. She asked him to stand up and she hosed him down. She then led him out of the bath and asked him to lie face up on the inflatable bed.

Moon hosed down the inflatable bed and created more soap suds by splashing foamy water out of a bucket. She then commenced to massage him, initially with her hands and then with her whole body. She was rubbing, sliding and weaving her full body all over him. The tussle went on for some time and he thoroughly enjoyed it.

Moon then asked Roland to get up. She hosed him down, dried him and asked him to get on the bed. He lay down and watched Moon as she cleaned up and dried herself off. She then joined him on the bed and they consummated the arrangement.

Roland was happy to relax and talk to Moon. She stated that she was 26 years old from Chiang Dao in Northern Thailand. Whatever money she could save she would send home to support her family. She wasn't sure whether her family knew what she did for a job, but no one back home tended to ask too many questions.

"My job sometimes good, sometimes bad, sometimes happy and sometimes sad," Moon stated. Her words echoed in Roland's head and, as they lay in silence, he was hoping that her job, at that point in time, was sometime happy.

Leisurely getting up the next morning, Roland went down for breakfast. His flight was late in the evening and he had the use of the hotel room for the day. He didn't feel like spending too much time in his room so he went walkabout. He arrived at the Shangri-La Hotel where he stopped for a relaxing beer at the bar. He then checked out Chinatown and took a photo.

Roland slowly made his way back to his hotel and lazed by the pool. He spent his last Thai money purchasing a Buddha sculpture for his father and a silk scarf for his mother. The shopping exercise made him excited about seeing his parents again.

The Thai Airlines flight went smoothly and Roland arrived back in Melbourne at 12.30 pm on Wednesday, 12th November 1997. He dropped off his backpack at his place, visited his dad, visited his mum at the nursing home in time for her dinner and saw her to bed. He returned to John's house where they enjoyed dinner. After six weeks away, Roland was glad to be back home.

Chapter 29 – Bound for South America

Roland didn't have too much planning for his fourth overseas trip and he didn't have too long to wait. It was 3rd February 1998 and his flight was scheduled to depart Melbourne at 10.00 am destined for Buenos Aires via Sydney and Auckland.

It was raining in Buenos Aires on touchdown. Roland took a bus to his hotel, arriving mid-afternoon, three days before the commencement of his organized Road to Rio tour. He was greeted by the tour guide – Allen – who had just completed a tour. Allen's group was going to dinner and she invited him to join them.

Rain was persisting as the small group made their way to a nearby steak place, which was a basic, no frills restaurant. Roland consumed his first mouthful of Argentine steak and was highly impressed with how succulent and tender it was. "This is one of the best steaks I've ever tasted," he commented; however, what he considered to be a major statement received little reaction from the other diners.

It was still raining the next morning when Roland went to the port to book a hydrofoil to Montevideo. He required a visa from the Uruguayan consulate and was advised that it would take some time to process so he went back to the port and changed his hydrofoil booking from the afternoon to the early evening.

After a couple of hours of sightseeing around the main thoroughfares of Avenida 9 de Julio and Avenida de Mayo, Roland picked up his visa from the consulate, strolled to the port and caught the Buquebus hydrofoil. He took a few snaps of the River Plate before going to sleep for most of the duration of the crossing.

Arriving in Montevideo, Roland checked out a couple of the hotels located close to the port. He settled on the second one he visited, mainly due to the pleasant nature of the lady who greeted him.

It was late in the evening when Roland walked around in search of a place to eat. He found a quaint restaurant and ordered Pollo Neron. He enjoyed his chicken and, after a short walk, returned to the hotel.

Getting up early, Roland checked out of the hotel and went sightseeing. He visited the Plaza Independencia, Avenida 18 de Julio, Palacio Legislativo, Avenida Libertador General Lavelleja and Mercado del Puerta.

Roland was booked for his return to Buenos Aires in the evening. However, as he had seen his noted attractions and was tired, he arranged to take an earlier hydrofoil. He was waiting at the port when he noticed a very attractive lady. He didn't know which vessel she was destined, but he got excited when he saw her walk the plank of the vessel he too was to board.

Noticing that she had descended the stairs to the lower level seating area, Roland descended the same stairs. There were few people downstairs so he settled into the row of seats coincidentally situated just behind the row where the lady was seated.

The lady soon got up and, in Spanish, communicated to Roland. "Could you keep an eye on my bag?"

Roland didn't really think too hard about the question before he instinctively replied. "Si, no problema."

The lady was gone for some time and Roland became extremely restless. He was tossing and turning, but he couldn't get comfortable. He would have appreciated a walk, but he felt obligated to stay and mind the bag. He considered taking the bag with him for a walk, but he didn't want to handle the bag. "With my luck, I'd probably be accused of stealing," he brooded.

It was another while before the lady finally made her reappearance and she thanked him as the hydrofoil was slowing down for the approach to the port at Buenos Aires.

Roland was keen to see her again so he quickly grabbed his Spanish translation dictionary and tried to ask her out for dinner. He pointed to her and then himself. "Possibile nos vamos para comer in juntos esta noche?" He doubted whether he made much sense, but the lady accepted.

They exchanged names and arranged to meet at the Obelisk at 8.00 pm. Anna gave Roland a peck on the cheek and was off. He just sat back and admired her curvaceous rump swaying from side to side as she strode away.

Roland had a siesta at his hotel and, true to form, he overslept. He quickly freshened up and ran off for the Obelisk. Even though he rushed there, he was still 15 minutes late. He looked around, but Anna was nowhere to be found. *What if she came and went,* he feared.

I'll give her another fifteen minutes and then I'll leave, Roland thought as he waited in hope for Anna to show up. His watch clicked over his deadline and she still hadn't shown. By this time there were quite a few people so he walked around for a last effort to find her. She still hadn't shown so he guessed she was a no show and he hesitantly started walking off when he was grabbed by the arm. "Anna!"

Anna and Roland walked around for some time chatting in a mixture of Latin tongues before they settled on a restaurant. They ordered a variety of meats, salads, a cheese platter and wine, which they shared.

"Would you like to spend some time together?" asked Roland. Anna was interested and suggested his hotel, but he wasn't comfortable going there as the tour was to commence the next morning. "Can we try a hotel nearby?" he asked.

"We could try," Anna replied.

Roland tried a few hotels and the consistent reply was that they were booked out. He found this odd, but was undeterred. They eventually found a hotel where they scored a room. They settled in and made themselves comfortable in bed.

Anna had a fantastic body with well rounded, full breasts, a curvaceous bottom and an ultra thin waist. Roland tried to get fresh and she reciprocated, but in a most unusual way. Tongue kissing was out of the question and she would thrust and gyrate in a most unpredictable fashion.

Anna was a powerful woman and they were at it, whatever it was, for some time. Roland became exhausted and lost interest. Anna was content to roll over and go to sleep.

It was six o'clock in the morning when Roland decided to leave and he tried to wake up Anna. "I'm leaving," he advised. She seemed to take in the information, but just rolled over and went back to sleep.

Chapter 30 – Road to Rio

Roland returned to his hotel, had a shower and went to breakfast. It was raining very heavily and there was a major seepage of water gushing into the breakfast café. The staff managed to contain the flow and breakfast was eventually served.

The tour group comprised Allen, as tour guide, her assistant named Dawn, two American sisters in their sixties – Irma and Emma; a middle-aged lady from England, Rhonda; Donald, a single American man in his sixties; a 21-year-old man from Wales, named Simon, and Roland.

They departed a little behind schedule and there were further delays due to roadway flooding. They had a stopover at El Palmar National Park near the Uruguayan border under another downpour. El Palmar was known for its Yatay palms and little rodents called vizcacha.

The group proceeded on to their hotel in Concordia and dined at a parilla restaurant near Plaza 25 de Mayo.

The next morning, Roland had breakfast and set out sightseeing. He went for a walk about town and visited Plaza 25 de Mayo, San Martin, San Antonio de Padua, Plaza Urquiza and Museo Regionale de Concordia.

The group departed for their long drive to an estancia in the marshy wilderness of Esteros de Ibera. The tour truck had to stop as the heavy rain caused the collapse of the bridge on the farm property. They were transported by tractor to the lodge where they enjoyed afternoon tea.

Dinner was followed by the showing of a National Geographic documentary of the surrounding area. They then retired to their beds where they had to contend with frogs, ants and mosquitoes.

The group had a relaxing morning on the farm. After lunch, they were hauled back on the tractor and taken on a canoe excursion. They had dinner before they set out to spotlight for wildlife in the swamps where they saw rabbits, caiman, armadillos and capybara. Roland retired to bed after tending to his numerous mosquito bites.

It was still raining the next day and the group lazed around, played indoor games and chatted. In the afternoon, they said goodbye to their farmhouse hosts and headed off for their next stopover in the city of Posadas.

Roland woke early the next day and walked around Posadas, visiting Plaza San Martin, Plaza 9 de Julio and the cathedral. He joined the group as they set off for a visit to the Jesuit Mission Ruins. Later that day they crossed the Argentine/Brazilian border, changed money and moved on to their next hotel.

It was a pleasant change in Brazil, both in terms of slightly improved weather and better standard of accommodation. The hotel had a large pool so Rhonda and Roland took advantage with a refreshing swim before dinner.

The following day, the group moved on to Iguassu where they opted for a helicopter ride over the falls. The helicopter turned and weaved to accommodate the amateur photographers. They then viewed the falls from the Brazilian side. They were advised to take raincoats or ponchos as cover from the strong sprays, not that they proved very effective against the wind and water.

The Brazilian and Paraguayan Itaipu Hydroelectric Power Plant was the next stop. They visited the Dam Centre for lunch, watched a movie and took a tour. After a short excursion on the Paraguayan side, they returned to the hotel for a swim at the pool, pre-dinner drinks, dinner, post-dinner drinks and bed.

In the morning, the group headed for the Iguassu Falls on the Argentine side. They took a boat ride and then checked out the paths referred to as Paseos Inferior and Paseos Superior. Iguassu Falls were the widest waterfalls in the world and the group enjoyed the views from the various vantage points, including a lookout from the tower.

The group had a full day on the road where they passed Ponta Grossa and explored Vila Velha National Park with its unusual rock structures formed by weathered sandstone.

Their next stopover was in the city of Curitiba. Roland spent the day sightseeing where he visited Largo de Ordem, Praca Garibaldi, Praca Tiradentes and Rua Barao do Cerro Azui. Later, he freshened up and joined the others for happy hour drinks at the hotel prior to dinner at a pizzeria.

It was an early departure the next day for the train station where they had to endure a four-hour train journey to the small port town of Paranagua. Roland went exploring through the streets of the town and ended up in the main plaza.

The streets were quiet before a Carnivale bloco street party took over. There was a pick-up truck with three young samba dancing girls on the back and a large number of followers. Amongst the followers was a small group of musicians blending their sounds with amplified recorded music. The party rolled on and it wasn't long before the convoy disappeared and life in the small town returned to normal.

Roland proceeded to check out the Mercado Municipal do Café and visited the Archaeological Museum before heading back to the hotel for a siesta. The group went for a seafood dinner at the port overlooking the boats bobbing about on the waters.

The weather was still cool and rainy, which put a dampener on the boat ride to Doel Island. Roland developed a cold so he didn't join the others for a walk to the lighthouse, opting to take a photo from a distance. The group made their way back to Paranagua and it rained all the way.

Arriving at the hotel, Roland had a rest to try to get over his miserable cold. It was still raining in the evening as the group made their way to a nearby seafood restaurant for dinner.

The group left Paranagua the next day and travelled to the seaside resort of Peruibe. As soon as they checked into their hotel rooms, Roland had a snooze. He met up with the others for dinner before going alone for a short walk and retiring early for the night.

The group had magnificent views of the bay on route to Parati. They checked into the hotel and went for a walk around town before dinner. They enjoyed the street music and checked out a couple of bars before retiring to bed.

The group had an early morning start to join a boat trip to the islands. They experienced some fine and warm weather, which embellished the spectacular views out to the ocean that was dotted with alluring islands. They enjoyed the island beaches and swimming the waters off the side of the boat.

In the evening, Simon and Roland joined a camp party with travellers from a few other camping tours. Roland chatted to a Danish lady, Donna, while Simon struck up a conversation with an attractive Icelandic lady. Roland arranged to go for a walk with the Donna and went over to Simon to let him know.

Donna and Roland strolled to a bar where they had a friendly chat. After a while, they exchanged addresses and said goodnight. Returning to camp, Roland noticed that Simon was sitting by himself and that the Icelandic lady was with another guy.

After little sleep, Roland arose for a quick breakfast and joined the others to depart for the city described as one of the most exciting cities in the world. They arrived in Rio de Janeiro soon after lunch and checked into their hotel located near Flamengo Beach.

Roland took the bus to Copacabana, eager to visit the renowned beach. As he set foot onto Avenida Atlantica, his eyes widened. The beach was wide and clean, with large numbers of people enjoying every grain of white sand. The islands off the shore gave the area an almost mystical and surreal atmosphere.

The street-side cafés and restaurants provided the desired refreshments and delicacies for the active crowds. Roland crossed the busy avenida and walked along the footpath, taking in deep breaths to inhale the combined smells of food, perfumes, sun lotions and sea air.

Roland returned to his hotel and freshened up in time to meet up with the others for dinner. Later in the evening, Dawn, Simon and Roland set off to attend the Black and Red Ball. They had no idea about the theme of the ball, but they expected that it would have to be more conservative than the Gay Ball.

They took the bus to Leblon and it was around midnight when they ventured into the venue. The place was packed and it was very hot and humid. One could hardly make their way through the crowd and getting a drink was near impossible.

Most of the people were wearing red and black, which seemed logical. They soon learned that the red and black colours represented the colours worn by the Flamengo Football Club.

The crowds were overwhelming and Roland soon lost touch with both Dawn and Simon. He walked around the establishment a few times, but couldn't locate them. He was in awe of the impressive, rapid-fire samba dance routines of the attractive ladies wearing glittering, G-string outfits.

After a couple of hours, Roland tired of the event and decided to head back to the hotel where he found Simon.

The next day, Roland had breakfast and enquired about the Sugar Loaf Mountain tour. The tours were booked out so he joined Dawn for an outing to Copacabana Beach. They had a swim and bumped into the girls from the camp party. Roland had a chat with Donna and they arranged to meet later at the Sambadrome.

The group had dinner at the hotel before Allen, Dawn, Simon and Roland grabbed a taxi for the Sambadrome. Simon and Roland were dropped off in the Lapa area to pick up Donna and her friend Lucy. The plan was to re-unite with Allen and Dawn in the vicinity of Sambadrome Sector 5, which was said to be a free entrance area.

After picking up Donna and Lucy, they tried to find Allen and Dawn outside Sector 5; however, they couldn't locate them and the free area was not free. Instead, they took in the atmosphere near the entrance for the Sambadrome parade.

The assembly area around the entrance of the Sambadrome was like being at the back stage of a theatre. The participants of the floats were preparing their costumes, make-up and musical instruments.

The Carnivale was the final of a national samba competition where the samba schools were judged on a variety of categories, including choreography, music, lyrics, costumes, themes and floats.

After absorbing the incredible atmosphere, they went to a bar for a few drinks before retiring.

Roland woke early the following day; however, he decided to stay in bed. When he eventually got up, he joined Dawn, Rhonda and Simon to visit Corcovado. They admired the views of the Christ the Redeemer statue and the panoramic views over Rio. Even though the day was a little hazy, they found the views spectacular.

On the second night of Sambadrome, Dawn, Allen, Rhonda, Simon and Roland had tickets for the Carnivale, which had an official starting time of 9.00 pm. They decided to go slightly later when they expected the event would be properly underway. They took the Metro from Catete Station and got off at Central Station.

By the time they arrived at the Sambadrome, the crowds were enormous. They squeezed into Sector 4 and tried to locate their seats; however, there weren't any seats. Places were captured on a first in best dressed basis and, as they had arrived late, they had to try and find a place way up the back of the bleaches.

A parade started to make its way up the colossal Sambadrome, reputed to be the world's largest parade stadium. A samba school was commencing to make its way from the far end to where they were situated.

As the school slowly made its way up the parade thoroughfare, the visuals became clearer, the sounds became louder and the colours became more vivid. There were hundreds of dancers surrounding the samba queen dancing infectiously in their bright, colourful outfits.

The dancers were followed by the drum section, or *bateria,* which comprised hundreds of drummers, beating their drums in unison. The beating started as a buzz and, as they neared the crowds, grew into a gigantic, reverberating beat.

The drummers were followed by the enormous floats, encapsulating the samba school's theme of costumes, characters and effects. The crowd was totally enwrapped in the whole experience as they felt the melding of the African and Latin cultures.

Each samba school parade took about 80 minutes. With the delay between parades, it was almost midnight by the time the second school had finished. At this point, Allen, Dawn and Rhonda had reached their limits and decided to call it quits. However, Roland was determined to see out the night and Simon was happy to stay with him.

After another two schools paraded, it was around 2.00 am. Simon and Roland had been in the same spot for over four hours and were starting to find the event testing. Simon then noticed that members of the crowd were departing, which left some spaces at the front.

Simon managed to find a couple of select spots one row away from the front of Sector 4. Simon was in raptures and the find gave Roland his second wind. "We're just up from the expensive VIP camarote seating!" Simon boasted.

The next samba school started their parade. Simon and Roland joined in with the crowd, bopping to the beat. The views, close-up, provided an accentuated experience so Roland pulled out his camera and started snapping away.

By 4.00 am the guys felt like zombies. "What do you say Roland, do you think we should leave?" Simon asked.

Roland tried to sum up the situation. "Well, I'd like to say that I saw a whole night of samba schools. The parades can go from 9.00 pm to 8.00 am and I think there can be as many as seven samba schools parading in one night. I thought we saw six of them, but that doesn't work out, unless we thought they were separate schools, but they were part of the one school. They say a single school can have as many as 10 floats. Anyhow, if we say that we saw six schools and we may have missed out on one because we arrived late, then we can say that we saw as many schools as we could have seen on the night."

"That sounds reasonable," Simon said.

"Okay then," Roland stated, "how about we get out of here before another parade starts up."

They departed the Sambadrome and made their way to the railway station. It was still dark when they descended the stairs at the Central Station, but when they ascended the stairs at Catete Station, the sun was rising.

It was becoming light when they arrived at the hotel and they freshened up before they had breakfast.

"I'm shot," Simon said.

"I feel the same," Roland admitted. "I might go to bed."

Roland woke up at midday and, as the weather was fine and sunny, he headed off for Sugar Loaf Mountain. He enjoyed the scenery and took numerous photos. When he made it back to the hotel he recalled that there was a bloco street party scheduled at Copacabana.

Arriving at Copacabana, Roland couldn't find any activity even though it had past the scheduled time for the party. It was his last night with the group and they had arranged to have dinner together so he thought he'd better leave.

As Roland was heading off, he heard samba music from a distance. Before he knew it, a parade turned the corner and was making its way towards him. There was a band, a pick-up truck transporting a few samba dancing girls and a crowd of people dancing in tow.

Roland was transfixed, as though in a dream. A lady pushing a pram was walking from the adjacent street and into the path of the parade. As soon as she met up with the parade, she commenced dancing with the rest of the crowd. This continued for a block, when she turned down another off street and reverted back to her usual gait, pushing her pram as if nothing had happened. Roland took a moment for the experience to register and, as the parade drifted away, he snapped out of his trance and made his way back to the hotel.

Dinner was enjoyable and entertaining with Donald and Rhonda reciting poems about their experiences on the trip. Simon and Roland said goodbye to those who were departing and set off to meet up with Donna and Lucy.

They walked around the Lapa area and had a few drinks at a couple of the Bohemian bars before they joined in a couple of street parties. Donna and Lucy had early morning departures so they said their goodbyes.

The following day, Roland joined Dawn and Simon to set off for a bloco party. They took the No.464 bus to Ipanema and soon found the street party where they had a few beers. They continued along Ipanema Beach and stopped off at a pizzeria for a meal. They then found another street party and joined in.

It was late evening before the threesome had enough and headed off to catch their bus. They milled around the bus stop with a gregarious group of people, including a number of transvestites. The bus arrived and the mixed crowd hopped on board.

Dawn, Simon and Roland squeezed into a small space and Roland found himself facing a transvestite who was inches away.

The bus took off and reached a fast travelling speed at high velocity. The bus seemed to be airborne most of the way as the driver maximized the effect of every pothole, curve and ramp.

The transvestite looked like a space traveller with heavy make-up and a glittering outfit. Roland felt like he was on a star ship with Wonder Woman. He found her strangely attractive and he couldn't take his eyes off her. Arriving at their stop, Simon had to nudge Roland for him to snap out of his daze and get off the bus.

Chapter 31 – The Carnival is Over

Roland slept in, which caused him to miss saying goodbye to Dawn and Allen. He had breakfast and headed for Rio Sul Shopping; however, the shopping complex was closed. He returned to the hotel and said goodbye to Simon who was heading home.

The group numbers were dwindling, but there was still Rhonda and Donald. Roland joined them for dinner followed by an early night.

The next day, Rhonda joined Roland for breakfast and they set off for the Santa Teresa Street Car. They joined a number of tourists at the terminal to purchase tickets and hopped on board.

The tram made its way over the aqueduct and weaved its way up the hill to the suburb of Santa Teresa. Travel for the locals was free, which explained its popularity with people jumping on and off the tram with free abandon.

After the tram ride, Rhonda and Roland visited Itamaraty Palace, the Candelaria Church, Paco Imperial and San Sebastion Cathedral. On the way back to the hotel, they stopped to take a photo of the World War II Monument and had a short visit to the Republic Museum.

The pace seemed to be coming off the tour and the exodus of tourists resulted in a reduced intensity to the city. It was Roland's last full day in Rio and he was at a loss as to what to do so he spent the afternoon at his favourite place, Copacabana Beach.

Rhonda, Donald and Roland caught up for their last dinner together. After dinner, Rhonda and Donald elected to have an early night, whilst Roland decided to go back to his favourite place. He took the bus to Copacabana and walked around before he entered a bar and had a drink. It was a Friday night, but the area seemed quiet and uneventful.

Deciding to go on a pub crawl, Roland came across a strip joint and entered. He settled into a seat, ordered a beer and, on cue, a stripper came out on stage. She didn't spend much time on the stage, before she approached him and sat on his lap.

Even though there were few patrons, Roland felt very uncomfortable. "Are you interested in getting together?" asked the stripper.

"I'm not interested," Roland replied. "I'm just having a beer."

The lady introduced herself as Dana, nestled deeper into Roland's lap and asked him again. By this time he was reasonably excited, but tried to resist the advances. However, it didn't take too much more tempting for him to change his attitude and only a little more persuasion before he was enquiring where they could go.

"We can go behind the curtains," Dana suggested.

"Behind the curtains, that's no good," Roland replied.

"There are rooms upstairs," she suggested.

"No, that's no good either," he said.

"We could go back to your hotel," she then suggested.

Roland thought about this for a moment before he agreed.

Dana and Roland caught a cab to his hotel where they talked for a while and she made him feel very comfortable.

Dana was a young, mulata woman from Rio. *A mulata woman and a carioca.* Roland thought he had hit the jackpot. They had sex and then slept the rest of the night.

Dana woke Roland in the morning. "It's time for me to leave," she advised.

Moments after Dana left, reception rang and a man asked Roland whether everything was all right. "Everything is very all right," he responded.

Going back to sleep, Roland got up around midday to pack and leave for the airport. When he arrived, he was advised that his plane had been delayed by four hours. He placed his backpack in a locker and found the club lounge where he relaxed. As the day wore on, he learned that the flight had been further delayed.

Eventually boarding at 21:20, the flight arrived in Buenos Aires around midnight. Roland was making his way for his connecting flight when a man greeted him and urged him to move along. They both walked at speed with the public address calling out Roland's name.

Roland made it to his connecting Aerolineas Argentinas flight to Lima and the plane jetted off straight away, which made him wonder. *How could my backpack have possibly made the flight?*

Arriving in Lima at 3.00 am, Roland's luggage was a no show. He checked at the enquiries counter and his bag was indeed left behind. "Your baggage will be on the next plane at 3.30 am," they stated.

"That's good as I only need to wait 30 minutes," Roland said.

"Sorry, that's 3.30 am tomorrow," they clarified.

"Blast!" Roland cursed as he would be without his luggage for two nights. He filled out a Property Irregularity Report and proceeded to seek out some local currency. He was advised that he couldn't exchange travellers' cheques at the bank until 8.00 am. He was exacerbated with the prospect of another long delay when he spotted the ATMs. Cashed up, he purchased a taxi voucher from one of the airport prepay counters and was driven to his hotel in the suburb of Miraflores.

Chapter 32 – Cradle of the Incas

Roland arrived in Lima two days prior to the commencement of the tour and, given the problems in having to wait a couple of days for his backpack, his early arrival turned out to be a blessing.

Wandering the streets, Roland sampled two of the local delicacies, chicha and churros. Chicha was a beverage commonly made from maize, although the word was also used in the Andes for any homemade fermented drink. Churros, sometimes referred to as Spanish or Mexican doughnuts, were dough pastries that were sold by street vendors who fried them fresh and served them hot.

Roland made his way to the city centre where he visited Plaza San Martin, Plaza de Armas, Rio Rimac, Plaza Bolivar, Plaza Bolognese, Plaza 2 De Mayo and Plaza Castilla. He had lunch in the Hatuchay area where he grabbed a pizza and a refresca orange juice.

An elderly gentleman warned Roland that the area may not be safe for him, particularly with his camera and other belongings. Roland felt a little uneasy even prior to the warning and, as he had seen the main attractions, he decided to move on.

It was early evening when Roland caught the bus back to his hotel. Dozing off, he missed his stop at Miraflores so he decided to stay on the bus and get off on the return leg.

The bus was travelling for miles and started to make its way up the mountain areas where the scenes started to dramatically change. The paved roads turned into dirt tracks, the pleasant suburbs transformed into slums and the street lights changed to camp fires.

Roland was feeling nervous as the bus finally came to a stop at a location that he assumed was the bus terminus. All the other passengers and the driver had disembarked and he was left on the bus on his own. He looked out the windows where he witnessed strange and unruly human figures roaming around the dark, eerie community.

Looking down at his SLR zoom camera, Roland felt his wallet in his pocket. *You idiot,* he thought, *you don't belong here and it wouldn't be a surprise if you were mugged or even worse.*

A man approached the bus, ascended a few of the steps, poked his head up and communicated something in Spanish. Roland couldn't make out what the man said and simply responded, with a questioning inflexion, "Miraflores?"

The man pointed to the bus about 50 metres up the road and uttered something else. Roland didn't understand what the man said, but he suspected that he wasn't going anywhere on the bus he was on and that he needed to catch the bus up the road.

Roland wasn't keen setting foot on the dirt track and meander up the potentially dangerous path; however, he didn't see that he had much choice. He swallowed his spit, took a deep breath and ventured into the night.

With the bus in his sights, Roland periodically peered to his left and right. He wasn't sure whether to move fast or slow so he just moved steadily as he tried to make his camera less conspicuous.

Reaching the bus, Roland looked up to the driver and stated the now routine word with the questioning inflexion, "Miraflores?"

"Si," the driver replied and Roland hopped on board.

They waited around ten minutes before they took off and, this time, Roland kept wide eyed and alert the whole way. He jumped up when the driver shouted out the magic word, "Miraflores."

Roland woke the next morning for an early breakfast. He then went walking around the trendy suburb of Miraflores taking a photograph of Playa Costa Verde.

Returning to the hotel, Roland was advised that his luggage was available for pickup. He was elated as he caught the Santa Rosa bus to the airport, collected his backpack and caught a Tica Taxi back to the hotel.

Roland did some shopping and laundry before having a siesta. As he was leaving his room to go out for the evening, he bumped into a guy, named Fred, who happened to be on the same tour. They set off to find a place for dinner and walked around Miraflores where they settled on a Chinese restaurant. After dinner, they headed for the San Miguel area.

The advertised nightclubs and bars were not exactly what they expected, as they happened to be pick-up joints. Two girls latched onto the two tourists, which wasn't surprising as they were the only male patrons in the bar.

The girls were keen to get the tourists dancing and the tourists eventually gave in. Roland indicated to Melissa that he had an injured knee; however, this did not deter her from completing her elaborate dance routine.

As the night wore on, Fred stated that he was heading back to the hotel. His companion was devastated by the news and pleaded for him to go with her. "I have a fiancé in America," he explained. "I'm not interested in having relations with any other woman."

On the other hand, Roland was keen on Melissa and they were off. She was a shapely, 21-year-old lady with long, dark, curly hair. She led Roland to a dingy, little room where they engaged in rapid-fire sex. He rushed back to the hotel just in time to hear his early morning wakeup call.

Fred and Roland left for the airport and caught their 03:30 flight to Cusco. On their arrival at the hotel, they were greeted by their two tour guides – Barbara and Malcolm. They were provided with a welcoming cup of warm mate de coca, being cocoa tea. Roland then went to bed to catch up on some sleep.

Roland was woken by Fred and they met the rest of the group. The other travellers comprised: a couple from New Zealand – Rhonda and Jim; a lady from Canada, named Gema; and two men travelling separately from the Netherlands – Theo and Paul.

They made their way to the main plaza in Cusco for lunch where they all opted for the special menu. After lunch, they went for a walk about town and ended up at the Plaza de Armas.

The group was feeling the effects of the altitude as Cusco had an elevation of around 3,300 metres above sea level, which made it an ideal place to acclimatize before tackling the Machu Picchu trek.

Roland couldn't wait to get back to the hotel for another nap. He was soon woken again, this time to meet the main trek guide, named Jaymen. Jaymen gave the group a talk about the trail, what they could expect on the trek and what they would need.

Malcolm was to accompany the group, which would be his first Machu Picchu experience. Barbara had completed the trek once before and that was enough for her. She was going to wait for them in Cusco.

After breakfast, the group went shopping for supplies. The main purchases were water, trail mix, health bars, chocolate bars and whatever other form of sustenance that took their fancy.

The group visited the nearby Sun Temple, named *Sacsahuaman*. The name was made easy to remember as it was phonetically pronounced, "sexy woman." They then witnessed the renowned and, to this day, unexplained process of Inca stone cutting. The buildings featured limestone blocks of rounded corners and a variety of interlocking shapes with the walls leaning inward. These buildings had not only lasted the test of time, but also survived earthquakes.

They proceeded to the town of Pisac where they saw the ruins and hiked back to town. There was a quaint little town square with small shopping stalls. Roland was in need of a hat for the trip and Jaymen noticed him trying one on. "That is a typical Peruvian hat and it seems to suit you," Jaymen commented. Roland didn't need any more convincing and he purchased it.

The group moved on and stopped along the way for lunch before arriving at Ollantaytambo. They explored the ruins and the surrounding farming area, which featured the ingenious techniques of terraced agriculture. They checked into their albergue and enjoyed the hotel dinner and drinks. An Eskimo dog took to Roland's boot laces and played with them throughout his meal.

Gema, Fred and Roland went for a stroll into the Ollantaytambo town plaza and stopped for a few drinks at an anachronistic pub that featured a mirror ball and Western style music.

After breakfast, the group was driven in a van as far as the Rio Urubamba. They had to hop off to cross the railway bridge as the road bridge had been put out by heavy rains. They hitched a ride on the back of a utility where Roland found himself holding on for dear life. He was required to dodge overhanging branches, twigs and leaves, not always too successfully.

They finally came to a grinding halt near Patallacta at the place named Camino Inca, being the start of their Inca trail.

There were three main routes on the Inca trail that joined up near Inti-Pata, being the Sun Gate that led to Machu Picchu. The route that the group was to experience was the Classic Trail, a four-day trek starting from km 82.

The weather was fine on the first day of the trek and Roland felt comfortable. The group passed the Inca ruins of Llaqtapata, a well preserved site used for crop production, and camped for the night at Huayllabamba.

Whilst the group set off on their daily trek, the porters would pack up the tents and equipment, which they carried. A little while into the trek, the group was passed by the porters, who would grind their way up and glide their way down the mountain ranges with apparent ease.

The porters were so quick that they had lunch, dinner and the overnight camp all set up prior to the group catching up to them. The meals served by the porters were amazing feasts with dinner consisting of three plentiful courses.

The group headed off on day two a little later than planned. The day included the ascent towards Warmiwañusca, being Dead Woman's Pass. It was the highest point on the trail at over 4,200 metres above sea level.

The trek was extremely difficult as they had to contend with continuous undulations. Roland found the Inca steps very hard to negotiate and they were taking a toll on his injured knee. He tried to compensate by taking most of the downward steps on his other leg, but even his sound knee was starting to cause him pain.

By the end of day two, it began to drizzle. The group hung around the ruins at Runquraqay admiring the views whilst getting wet. They eventually made their way to the campsite, which had developed into a bog.

The porters greeted them with popcorn and mate de coca. This was followed by the usual dinner extravaganza. Roland had a reasonable night's sleep and was looking forward to an expected easier day of hiking.

Day three started with Jaymen giving a bit of advice. "In order to better appreciate the scenery, you may wish to distance yourselves from each other." Roland didn't think too much about what Jaymen said, but heeded the suggestion for a number of stretches.

Taking his time to appreciate the lovely mountain scenery in peaceful silence, Roland felt richly rewarded by following what Jaymen said as he sensed that he was part of nature and felt uplifted.

Roland was in a very good mood when he arrived at the Winay Wayna camp. When other members of the group arrived, he greeted them. "Today was fantastic, wasn't it? I found it a real buzz."

Jaymen noticed Roland's upbeat mood and approached him with a smile. "I have walked the Inca trail so many times that I have lost count. People often ask me whether I ever get bored or tired of it. I tell them that every time I make the trek is a new adventure and it is never the same." Jaymen smiled again before he walked away.

Roland felt he understood. Jaymen was an indigenous Peruvian and of Inca heritage. He, more than anyone, would feel the sense of the natural beauty of the land as well as the spirit of his Inca ancestors. Roland could only imagine the power of Jaymen's experiences every time he walked the trail. He grew an enormous respect for Jaymen and felt fortunate to be sharing the experience of the Inca trail with him.

The wakeup call was at 4.00 am. Theo, Paul, Fred and Roland were the first to start off with the early starters making it to the Sun Gate before sunrise at 6.15 am. The skies were clouded over and they waited there a while; however, it seemed that the sun would not be beaming through the Sun Gate that sunrise so they proceeded on to Machu Picchu.

The first to arrive at Machu Picchu got there just before 8.00 am. They were told by one of the guides that the picture postcard view of Huayna Picchu that towered above the ruins of Machu Picchu was just over the ridge. The tourists rushed to look, but the whole valley was clouded over.

The tourists expressed their disappointment, but the guide implored them to be patient. Some of the tourists refused to wait on the ridge and made their way down towards the ruins. Others persisted and remained affixed to the ridge with their eyes focused on the area where Machu Picchu was said to be. "The lost city of the Incas seems to be lost," Roland remarked.

The warmth of the sun started to take effect and one could commence to see a blurry vision appear. As the clouds dissipated and the vision became clearer, people's eyes grew larger. There were gasps, sighs and cries. "There it is; it's Machu Picchu!"

A scatter of photographic clicks went off from all directions. The view was changing as the clouds lifted and the majesty of Machu Picchu came into full view. Roland took numerous photos and then savoured the moment.

Roland then saw Jaymen. "Jaymen, hey Jaymen, I would really like to have a photo with you in front of Machu Picchu." Jaymen obliged and they both stood proudly in front of Machu Picchu where Malcolm took their photo.

Malcolm then suggested that there should be a group shot. They lined their cameras and the group had their Machu Picchu photos taken with Jaymen front and centre.

The group made its way down to the ruins and was introduced to another tour guide, Francisco. Francisco was extremely keen to provide just about every detail of the Incas and Machu Picchu. They were escorted through many attractions including the Tower of the Sun, the Temple of the Sun, the Sun Dial, the Sacred Rock and the Torture Chamber.

The porters prepared lunch and the group was later bussed down to the hot springs at Agua Calientes for their overnight stay.

The next morning, the group thanked and said goodbye to Jaymen, the other guides and the porters. They then caught their train down the Sacred Valley of the Incas, arriving back at the albergue in Cusco for dinner before heading to a bar in town for drinks.

Roland noticed an attractive lady enter the bar. She walked around as if she owned the place, seemingly looking for someone, and then exited in a huff and puff.

The group moved on to another bar and Roland noticed the same lady who was in the company of another young lady. The group headed back to the hotel, but Roland decided to stay. He noticed that the two ladies had parted company and the lady he was observing was now alone at the bar. He mustered enough courage to approach her.

Roland introduced himself and they engaged in some small talk. He learned that her name was Gina, she was from Lima and was on holidays in Cusco. Gina was reasonably friendly, although somewhat elusive. After more chatter and drinks, she said that she was leaving and invited him to go with her. He had some initial reservations, but accepted.

They went to Gina's hostel, which was of very basic, brick construction where she had a room with a single bed. They hit the sack and started making out. Gina was extremely intense and Roland tried to keep pace with her until she started with some freaky jolting and vibrating motions. He had little idea as to how to counter these actions so after a while he gave up. Gina seemed content to go to sleep.

Lying in bed, Roland tried to figure out why Gina approached sex in the most unusual way. *Maybe that's the way they sort of did it in this part of the world. Maybe the men from these countries were expected to be more forceful and domineering.* After exhausting himself of ideas, he fell asleep.

Roland awoke and began kissing Gina, but she shook him off. "Are you all right Gina?" he asked.

"Why do you ask me that?" she snapped back.

"I was going to leave and I wanted to know whether you were all right."

"I'm all right," she finally answered.

"Would you like to join me for dinner?" Roland asked.

"All right," Gina responded in a blasé fashion.

Roland said goodbye and struggled to give her a kiss on the forehead before he left.

Arriving back at the hotel, Roland had breakfast and set off to take advantage of his tourist ticket. He visited the Plaza de Armas, the cathedral, Museo Municipal de Arte Contemporaneo and the San Blas Church.

Needing to obtain some funds, Roland made his way to the market area. As he was walking down one of the busy streets, he felt a liquid, sticky substance hit him on the back of the neck. His reflexes caused him to slap and wipe the back of his neck with his left hand whilst grabbing his pocket containing his wallet with his right hand.

Roland looked up to where he thought the substance emanated and there were a number of balconies jutting over the street, but there was no sign of movement. At the same time, a man brushed past whilst Roland fixed his eyes on him and the man continued on.

Arriving at the bank, Roland spent almost two hours to get money. Once he was cashed up, he was on high alert all the way back to the hotel.

Roland showered to wash off the sticky substance and then met up with the group and other travellers. He told them of his experience and was surprised to learn that there had been other tourists who had been robbed using a similar process.

After a siesta, Roland spruced up for his date with Gina. He rushed to the Plaza de Armas, but still arrived ten minutes late. Gina was already there waiting. He apologized, but she didn't reply. She simply grabbed him by the hand and led him around the square.

Gina talked to many people and introduced Roland to a number of her friends. As they walked a little further, Roland bumped into his tour group and said hello. Gina said hello and quickly dragged him away.

Gina and Roland settled on a quaint pizzeria for dinner and took up window seats where they had a magnificent view out to the mountains and valleys. "It's raining," Roland commented.

"Why did you say that? Don't you think I can see that it's raining?" Gina curtly replied.

He started to laugh and she attempted to hide her smile.

The couple enjoyed a pleasant meal where Roland tried the cuy, being guinea pig, in a peanut sauce. He thought it was okay, even though the meal seemed to be mainly skin and bone.

They moved on to a nightspot where Gina knew many of the people and she went off to talk with them. Roland was chatting to some people and then excused himself to find Gina. "I'm feeling a little tired so I think I'll go back to my hotel," he advised. It was as if she hadn't heard him as she led him away and took him back to her place where they spent a wonderful night together.

Gina was heading home to Lima so Roland said goodbye, returned to his hotel and went to sleep. He got up around midday and went off for lunch. He then completed his sightseeing around Cusco, which included visits to Museo Arqueologico Qorikancha and Museo de Arte Religioso del Arzobispado.

In the early evening, the group went to an Indian restaurant for dinner. They then visited a number of the usual clubs, but Roland felt that they seemed to lack the usual spark and, after a couple drinks, he retired to his hotel room.

The group departed Cusco for Puno. It was a full day's journey by train on what was considered to be one of the most beautiful train trips. Roland slept most of the way; however, he still managed to get glimpses of the lovely scenery.

The train stopped at Juliaca where the group took a van to Puno. After checking into their hotel, they walked along the main drag of the town, grabbing a pizza and beer for dinner. Paul, Theo and Roland checked out a few nightspots, but they were all quiet so they returned to the hotel for a pisco sour nightcap before going to bed.

The group took a boat on Lake Titicaca and visited the floating reed islands of Uros where they were greeted by the locals. They were very unsteady on their feet as they walked around the miniature, reed islands.

They cruised on to Taquile Island where they climbed 500 steps to their night stay at Antonio's House. It was raining heavily, but Roland had a reasonable night's sleep in the mud-house accommodation.

The group enjoyed pancakes for breakfast and it was still raining when they walked to the village plaza. They spent the day exploring the small village and returned to Puno where they had time to rest before freshening up for dinner at a popular restaurant.

A local guide and his wife took them to a nightclub. It was their last night in Puno so they kicked up their heels and danced with the locals. Gema and Roland stayed drinking, talking and dancing, arriving back just before they had to get up.

The group had breakfast before being driven across the Peruvian/Bolivian border. They stopped at Copacabana for a quick set menu lunch and then changed buses with the new driver proving to be a dare devil over the mountain roads.

They had to catch a boat in order to cross Lake Titicaca and then boarded another bus to make their way to La Paz. This bus driver was more subdued as he manoeuvred his bus along the weaving mountain roads. The bus reached the top of the mountain range that led to La Paz, which translated to, "the peace." As they made their way around the mountain escarpment, the city came into view.

The group was amazed at the breathtaking vision of the city in its magnificent valley setting. The city sprawled over the whole valley floor of the mountain range. *If first impressions are anything to go by*, Roland thought, *I'm going to love this city.*

After checking into their hotel, members of the group went wandering the streets of the Spanish colonial city. It was a large city with a population of around one million people. It was like taking a step back in time with many of the people appearing to be indigenous Andeans who still wore traditional dress and made traditional handicrafts.

The group stopped at a restaurant for dinner. "You may wish to share a meal as the people in these parts are mountain people who eat a lot and the servings are very large," advised the waiter.

The meals were very cheap and the local people were generally small in stature so Roland figured that they couldn't possibly eat all that much. "I'll have the Llama Meat Casserole with rice all for myself," Roland replied.

It took a while for the dishes to be served, but when they emerged, they were indeed very large. "There you go, sir," the waiter said to Roland. "Is there anything else you wish?"

Roland felt diminutive as his giant casserole was placed before him. "No, I think this should do," he replied.

Roland got stuck into his meal and after more than an hour he had stuffed himself, although he hardly made an impression on his meal mountain.

The next day was the last day of the 14-day tour. The group had a continental breakfast before they visited the Tiwanaku Ruins and Moon Valley.

The group said their goodbyes and Roland proceeded with his sightseeing of La Paz. He visited Plaza Murillo, Palacio Legislativo, the cathedral and Iglesia San Francisco. He made it back to the hotel for a shower and finished his packing before he set off for his 20:15 Lloyd Aero Boliviano flight to Manaus, Brazil.

Chapter 33 – Last Stop Amazonas

The plane arrived in Manaus in the early hours of Monday morning, 16th March 1998.

After a good night's sleep, Roland took a bus to the city centre with his list of attractions. First up was the port area where there was a large wall upon which one could lean over for a view.

Vessels banked on the shore of red terrain, and large planks were laid down between the ships and the bank. They literally rolled out the barrels and hauled off the carts from the boats. All of the work was manual and the activity was frantic and continuous.

Roland found a vantage point to observe the other side of the Rio Negro and the contrast was amazing. Manaus was a metropolis of over a million people, situated on the one side of the river. On the other side of the river was the dense, enormous and natural Amazonian forest – *the lungs of the world.*

As Roland explored other parts of the grand city, it certainly lived up to its description as a city of contrasts. He read that the city of Manaus was built on the wealth of the rubber plantations, described as black gold, from the late 1800s to the early 1900s.

Reportedly, the British smuggled out rubber tree seeds, developed more resistant varieties and sent them to the colonies in Asia where they grew larger and more economical plantations. The Asian rubber, and the later development of synthetic rubber, resulted in the decline of Manuas, although symbols from its affluent past could still be evidenced.

Roland visited sites that manifested some of the rich trappings of Manaus's earlier history such as Palacio da Justica, Palacio Rio Negro, Praca da Matriz, the municipal market, the cathedral and the town clock. He particularly enjoyed a tour of Teatro Amazonas where he was the only person guided through the theatre by a delightful, young lady.

"Teatro Amazonas symbolizes the wealthy past of Manaus," the guide told Roland. "The opera house was built in 1896 and features crystal chandeliers, wrought iron banisters and Italian frescoes. Building materials were imported from various parts of the world, such as furniture from Paris, marble from Italy, steel from England and roofing tiles from Alsace. The external dome is covered with decorated ceramic tiles, which were painted in the colours of the Brazilian flag."

During the theatre tour, the guide also described a large curtain with the painting of the Meeting of the Waters. "What's that?" asked Roland.

The guide seemed surprised that he didn't know. "It is the confluence of the Negro River and the Solimões River, extending nine kilometres, being the final episode of the formation of the Amazon River."

Returning to his hotel, Roland freshened up and dined at the hotel restaurant. He then headed into the city centre and checked out a few bars, but he found them uninspiring so he made his way back towards his hotel. As he rounded a corner he came across a couple of strip clubs and he felt a sense of déjà vu as he entered one of them.

Roland ordered a beer, and like clockwork a lady sat beside him. Her name was Sylvia and she was slim, shapely and sexy. It took Sylvia little time to pop the question and it took Roland less time to accept.

The priority for Roland the next day was to book a cruise to witness the Meeting of the Waters. He rushed his breakfast and joined the other tourists in the foyer for the morning cruise. They hopped on a mini bus and were driven to the port where they boarded a medium sized boat.

Once they reached the Meeting of the Waters, the guide explained how the Negro, Solimoes and Amazon Rivers met at differing speeds and temperatures. What Roland found most astonishing was that one could visually evidence where the rivers flowed into each other.

The Negro River was true to its name as the black river; the Solimoes River, on the other hand, looked muddy and brown. Where the two rivers met, there was a distinctive demarcation; however, further on, the waters blended together.

The cruise continued to visit some of the riverbank inhabitants who lived in stilted houses and made many of the forest wildlife their pets.

One family had a variety of pets, including a sloth and a boa constrictor. The boa constrictor was enormous and the guide asked whether anyone wanted to hold the gigantic reptile. Roland stood back while a number of people lined up to hold the snake while they had their picture taken.

The standard routine wasn't enough for one lady tourist. She considered the snake to be a suitable dance partner and commenced to prance around with it. The swaying motions obviously didn't agree with the snake as it caused the beast to crap all over the place, with most of the green slime going all over the lady. She started shrieking, the onlookers didn't know what to do and Roland couldn't help but laugh. They had lunch before returning to the port to end their cruise.

Roland went into the city centre for dinner before a walk around town. It was raining and there didn't seem to be much happening around the city. Even though it was his last night in Manaus, he decided to retreat to his hotel.

The early morning wakeup call came in the form of a loud knock on the door. Roland had breakfast and set off for the airport for his flight to

Tabatinga, situated on the border of Brazil and Peru, which was where his Amazon River cruise was to commence.

On arrival at Tabatinga, Roland met Bernadette, a middle-aged lady from America, who was on the same cruise. They met their guides named Ricardo, Victor, and Daniel before they were introduced to some of the other passengers.

Ricardo was also the boat's cruise director and he gave a short briefing before allowing the passengers to board. He provided more detailed information about the cruise and delivered an extremely knowledgeable talk about life on the Amazon River where he had lived most of his life.

One of the passengers, Bruno, was an unusual character in a curious position. He described himself as a non-paying passenger who was an employee of the cruise company and, although he was not officially on duty, he was acting as an observer.

Passengers were grappling with the Bruno story when a young lady, Lisa, took over. She was a university student who was taking some time-out to travel. She was from Germany and lived with her mother; her father having left them when she was young.

The group made their way to the dinner tables where Roland was joined by Lisa, Sonya, Fred and Bruno. Sonya was an attractive, young lady from Argentina who was accompanying Fred, a middle-aged man from Scotland.

Most of the passengers retired after dinner, although Lisa, Bruno and Roland went on the top deck for a few more drinks. Lisa and Bruno had more in common as they were both German and often talked to each other in their native tongue. Before long, Bruno and Lisa retired to their cabins. Roland stayed on deck to finish his beer and take in the atmosphere of the Amazon jungle at night.

In the early morning, the group walked through the jungle, which was teeming with wildlife, including reptiles, birds and bullet ants. The advice to apply insect repellent and wear long sleeves and pants proved useful as the jungle was prime real estate for malaria carrying mosquitoes and disease spreading insects.

They returned to the boat for a rest, which was a relief given the hot and humid conditions. After lunch and another rest up, they visited a leper colony. Handicrafts were made at the colony, which were used by the inhabitants and to sell to the tourists.

The group proceeded on a cruise in a smaller motor boat to check out more wildlife before heading back for another rest. In the early evening, the passengers were offered a night cruise on the small motor boat up the Mayaruna River.

Ricardo explained much about the river, the jungle and the wildlife. The guides soon proved that they were attuned to all of them. Ricardo asked the passengers for silence and for all the torches to be switched off. He held on to Victor as Victor leaned over the side of the boat.

All of a sudden there was a violent jolt and the passengers' immediate thought was that Victor had fallen overboard or that something had captured him. The torches were switched back on to reveal that Victor had snatched a baby caiman from out of the water.

Ricardo again asked for silence and the torches were switched off again. The boat approached a tree on the bank, Ricardo leaned over the boat and there was another jolt. As the torches switched on, the lights shone on a night bird that Ricardo had plucked from the branches.

The group returned to the main vessel for dinner and drinks. After dinner, it was the usual top deck drinks attended by Lisa, Bruno and Roland. This time it was Roland who was the first to retire.

It was another morning small boat cruise where they ventured up the Ampiyacu River to visit the Bora people, being traditional Amazon tribal people who lived in huts. It was in a large hut where the Bora people entertained their visitors and encouraged them to join in the dancing.

Returning to the boat, children were selling souvenirs from their canoes. Roland was interested in purchasing a small blow gun, but he only had a five soles coin. "How much is a blow gun," he asked.

"Five soles," a boy replied and Roland bought one.

It wasn't long before the group was off on another cruise where they were treated to more fauna and flora, which featured various birdlife and giant water lilies.

After returning to the main vessel, they were invited to take a swim as there were pink dolphins in the area. Lisa and Roland were the only two who were keen to get wet. Lisa showed her usual elegance by striding down the steps, whilst Roland just jumped in, doing a water bomb.

Pink dolphins were gliding through the water very close to them and they attempted to swim towards the mammals, but in a flash the dolphins had vanished.

Making their way back on the boat, Lisa and Roland were advised that they could now fish for piranha. "How long will it take to travel to where the piranhas are?" Roland asked.

"The piranhas are swimming on the other side of the boat," Victor replied.

"What! We were swimming where piranhas are?" Lisa cried.

"It usually isn't a problem unless the fish sensed blood," Victor said with a smile.

Roland was sure Victor was having them on; however, his doubts were dismissed when he went to the other side of the boat where the passengers had caught eight piranhas that were piled in a bucket.

The group went for a final cruise and, when they returned, they spruced up for the last night of the tour where they were to celebrate with a special dinner and a party.

It was an enjoyable dinner with the first course being piranha soup.

The party started off slowly, but things picked up after a few more drinks. Latin music was playing and Lisa came into her own as she was an accomplished Latin dancer. Everyone got into the spirit of the evening and Roland danced with most of the ladies, although his favourite dance was the one he had with Lisa. During their dance, Lisa expressed her wish to share another dance with him later in the night.

When Roland finished dancing, Fred and Bruno started chatting with him. "So have you put the hard word on Lisa?" asked Bruno.

Roland was surprised by the question. "No, of course not."

"Young ladies on holidays usually like a bit of adventure," Fred stated. "You're a good looking guy and I'm sure she likes you."

Roland dismissed the suggestion, although it did start him thinking. He joined Lisa for their dance and he was brooding over whether he should pop the question.

"I've really enjoyed your company over the last few days," Roland said.

"I've enjoyed your company, too," Lisa told him.

"I got the feeling that maybe we could be good friends," Roland said with a smile.

Lisa returned his smile. "Yes, I also thought that we could be friends."

"I was also wondering whether you might like to spend the night together," Roland whispered.

"Oh, Roland, I like you, but I'm not interested in being anything more than friends," Lisa replied.

"That's fine; I'm happy being friends" Roland told her.

"Yes, I'm happy being very good friends," Lisa said.

The boat arrived in Iquitos early in the morning. Sonya, Lisa, Fred, Victor and Roland hung around together and they visited Quistococha zoo.

Lisa and Roland headed back to town together and she suggested that he could freshen up at her hotel. He showered and shaved, and as he exited the bathroom she started to make some suggestive comments and lay back on the bed. This made him question what this beautiful, young lady was playing at; however, Roland wasn't one to play games. "Come on, freshen up and I'll take you out to dinner," he said.

Lisa and Roland enjoyed a wonderful dinner together and he couldn't help letting her know how beautiful she looked. They returned to Lisa's hotel, exchanged addresses and said goodbye.

The Aeroperu flight arrived in Lima on time; however, Roland's connecting flight to Buenos Aires, which was scheduled to depart early afternoon, was now due to depart midday the following day. He was unimpressed, tired, and a little down in the dumps. He collected his baggage and proceeded to seek transport to a hotel in the suburb he was familiar with – Miraflores.

After a good night's sleep, Roland had breakfast before heading back to the airport where he caught his plane, and was soon checking into his Buenos Aires hotel.

Roland went for a walk around town and took note of many places that were familiar to him from his previous visit. After dinner, he was walking back to the hotel when a man from the other side of the street called out to him. Roland continued walking.

The man crossed the street and invited Roland to take a look inside his bar. "I'm not interested," Roland told him.

"Just take a look," the man said. "If you like the place you can stay for a drink, if you don't like it, you can leave; no obligation."

Roland didn't see the harm in just taking a look and the man escorted him into the bar. The place was very dark and it took his eyes a few moments to adjust. A couple of very unattractive ladies approached. "Would you like some company?" asked one of the ladies.

"I'm only here for a look," Roland informed them.

The ladies positioned themselves either side of him and tried to lead him to a small, round table. "Don't you want a drink or a lady?"

"I don't want anything," Roland stated.

During this time, a waiter came over holding a tray with a bottle of champagne and three glasses. "I don't want any of this," Roland pleaded as he tried to leave. One of the ladies moved back dramatically as if she was falling over.

"What's going on here?" yelled another waiter.

"He is trying to leave without paying!" shouted the first waiter. The barman then started yelling in Spanish. Pandemonium broke out and Roland started to sweat and feel light-headed. The barman continued yelling in Spanish, started rolling up his sleeves and charging from behind the bar.

"All right!" Roland shouted.

Roland pulled out his wallet and took out his money that amounted to $35US. "This is all the money I have," he revealed. The bill was $43US and the head waiter took $30US, leaving him $5US.

"You are invited to drink a beer at the bar," stated the first waiter.

"I just want to go," Roland replied.

Fuming about the extortion, Roland couldn't think of what he could possibly do so he returned to his hotel, went to bed and tried to forget about it.

Roland woke up feeling a little better. He had breakfast and set off for his last day of sightseeing. He passed by La Bombonera Stadium, home of Boca Juniors, and walked down Caminito Street in the suburb of La Boca. The street featured the multi-coloured houses for which La Boca was famous. He returned to the hotel to rest before going out for dinner and his last chance to enjoy an Argentine steak.

Returning to the hotel, Roland made sure everything was in order before he headed for the airport. He grabbed a cab and checked in with Aerolineas Argentinas for his 11:59 flight on 24 March 1998, relieved that he was going home.

Roland found his father well, although he noticed some deterioration in his mother's condition. He resumed his normal routine of working and regularly visiting his parents, but he soon became restless and his mind turned to travel and another trip.

Chapter 34 – European Reunions

Departure from Melbourne was at 19:00 on 5th July 1998. It was a 26½ hour flight with a one hour stopover in Singapore and a two hour stopover in Dubai before arrival in London. Roland took the train to Reading where he rang William, whom he had travelled with in Asia.

William picked Roland up from the train station and drove to his house. Roland was led into the living room where he backed up to manoeuvre his backpack through the doorway and as he turned around he was heartily greeted by Jane and Susan. "Surprise!"

They were excited to have the foursome back together and it was a joyous reunion. Susan had been living with William and Jane was invited to stay over to coincide with Roland's visit.

Roland shared the visitor's bedroom with Jane and after he settled in the foursome headed off to the pub for dinner where they spent the evening reminiscing.

Returning to the house, everyone soon retired to bed. Jane and Roland made some attempt to have sex; however, the outcome was feeble and they fell asleep.

The foursome spent the following few days going through numerous photographs and talking about their tour of China. Susan and William described how happy they were together and Roland could sense Jane staring at him, but he refrained from returning her gaze.

On the last night of Roland's stay the foursome spent the evening watching the World Cup final between France and Brazil. They witnessed history in the making as France won their first championship.

In the morning, Roland was off to London. He said goodbye and Jane promised to visit.

Roland spent his days in London roaming familiar areas. He attended a matinee session of *The Complete Works of Shakespeare* and then commuted to Waterloo Station to meet up with Jane. He took her out to dinner and they then enjoyed the *Blood Brothers* musical.

The following day, Jane and Roland went on an extensive walk to Buckingham Palace, the National Gallery and on to Covent Garden. They purchased some fresh rolls, cheese, ham and a bottle of Merlot and found a spot in St James's Park where they had a picnic. It turned out to be one of their most enjoyable times together.

After their last night together, Roland bid Jane farewell and departed for

Heathrow Airport to catch his KLM flight to Amsterdam.

Taking the train to Amsterdam Central Station, Roland checked into a hotel and took a long walk around the city. He rang Jorg, whom he travelled with on the US East Coast tour, and they arranged to meet in a couple of days.

Roland spruced up and had a few swigs from the bottle of scotch he'd purchased at the airport duty free. He hit the town and ended up on the main thoroughfare of Damrak. He grabbed a couple of falafels and downed them with a few beers. After further wandering, he found himself where all tourist roads lead in Amsterdam – the Red Light District. He walked up and down alleyways until he became sufficiently tired of the scene and headed back to his hotel.

Waking up mid-morning, Roland had brunch and then walked through Vogel Park and around the streets circuiting the Amstel River. He visited the Royal Palace and the National Monument before he returned to his hotel for an afternoon siesta. When he awoke, he freshened up, had a few more swigs of scotch and hit the town.

Roland returned to the only night attraction he knew – the Red Light District. He dined at a Chinese restaurant and then walked by the shop-front windows displaying the ladies of the night. He found the scene depressing so he thought he'd check out a different form of culture – a peep show.

Five guilders seemed to have been swallowed up in faster time than it took Roland to look at the stripper. Based on the rapid pace the machine consumed his money and the extraordinarily slow pace of the stripper, he figured it would take a mint of coins to witness a single strip.

Exiting the coin munching establishment, Roland returned to his hotel where he downed a couple of scotch nightcaps before enjoying a good night's sleep.

Roland caught a morning train to Sittard Station where Jorg picked him up and brought him home. Jorg introduced Roland to his wife Eva, his baby daughter Nora, and his two pet huskies.

Jorg arranged a meeting with the other three Dutch guys who travelled with them on the tour. They met up at Maastricht and the Dutchmen were overtly happy with the reunion as it re-ignited memories of their American adventures as well as giving them an excuse for a booze up.

Roland had a reasonable night's sleep and, after breakfast, joined Jorg to walk the dogs. It was back to Maastricht in the afternoon to explore the town by day. Returning to Jorg's house, it was another opportunity to walk the dogs.

In the evening, Jorg took Roland to Belgium to see the movie *Deep Rising*. "Why Belgium?" asked Roland.

"It's something different and the movies are cheaper there," Jorg replied.

After bidding Jorg and his family goodbye, Roland headed for Bonn to visit Lisa, whom he had travelled with on the Amazon River cruise. He arrived in Bonn and made his way to the main station, Bonn Hauptbahnof. He arranged accommodation at the station and walked ten minutes to arrive at the hotel.

Roland went for a stroll to a public telephone booth to call Lisa. He was surprised the phone card he purchased in Holland also worked in Germany. He rang the number and, to his delight, Lisa answered.

They arranged to meet at the Rathaus where Lisa picked Roland up and drove him around town. She pointed out the old and new government buildings before stopping off at a supermarket where they purchased some groceries and a bottle of wine. Lisa drove on and made another stop for firewood.

Roland was wondering about the firewood when Lisa revealed that she had a treat for him. She found a secluded place in a forest setting, got a fire going and barbequed some sausages. They ate the sausages with dips, crackers, sliced vegetables and bread. Not having any wine glasses, they took turns drinking from the wine bottle.

It was a light-hearted affair, which they both enjoyed immensely. When it became dark, Lisa drove up Petersburg Mountain for them to share the view of Bonn at night. She then drove them back to the city centre and Roland stole a kiss on her cheek before she dropped him off at his hotel.

They met at the Rathaus again the next morning and took the train to Cologne. The first attraction Lisa showed Roland was the Dome of Cologne – a large cathedral of gothic architecture said to have been the largest building in the world during the 19th century. The second attraction was the Eigelstaintor medieval gate. The third attraction seemed to be Lisa herself.

Lisa led Roland into a couple of trendy women's clothing stores and proceeded to try on a number of outfits and dresses. The gear was either tight fitting or free flowing garments that accentuated her slender and shapely body. Roland considered the fashion to be risqué, sexy and some even provocative.

Each time Lisa revealed herself from the change room, she would ask Roland his thoughts. He had to take a few moments to capture the view and civilize his words before he expressed his approval of what he beheld.

They proceeded to walk the streets of Cologne and dropped into a café for a spot of lunch. Returning to Bonn, they checked out the Munsterplatz, the Beethoven Monument and Beethoven Haus before heading to a Bavarian pub where they had dinner and indulged in wine and beer.

They strolled through the city centre and stopped off at a couple of bars for a few more drinks. Lisa suggested visiting her place and Roland politely declined. However, when she raised the suggestion a couple more times, his curiosity got the better of him and he finally agreed.

They caught the bus and went to her apartment. Lisa asked Roland what he would like to drink and he settled for red wine whilst she took some water with a vitamin pill. "Would you like to play a game?" she asked.

Roland sensed that they were already engaging in some sort of game and he agreed.

Lisa climbed on to her chair and reached to grab something from a shelf. The shelf came loose, it came down with a thud and she found herself sprawled on the floor with the shelf and various items on top of her.

"Are you all right?" Roland asked.

"I'm fine," Lisa replied, "but look at all this damage."

"It doesn't look bad, a couple of screws have come loose from the wall and they just need replacing," he reassured her. They cleared the mess before resuming with the game.

Lisa revealed a box of chess. "Would you like a game?" she asked.

Roland wasn't too keen; however, after all the trouble she had gone through, he agreed. They had a game, which he won. "Do you want to play again?" she asked, but this time he declined.

Lisa checked the bus timetable and the last bus was at 1.08 am. This gave them almost an hour and they spent the time to kick back, relax and have a pleasant chat.

"I'd better get a move on as we wouldn't want me to miss the bus; it may mean I'd have to sleep here with you," Roland joked.

"No, we wouldn't want that; my couch is too small for you to sleep on," Lisa replied and Roland thought, *touché*.

Lisa escorted Roland to the bus stop, they hugged and he stole a last kiss on her cheek before he caught the last bus back to the town centre.

On the Friday morning of 24th July 1998, Roland checked out of his hotel and took the train to Amsterdam. As he had five hours before his flight, he placed his backpack in a locker and walked around town. He rang Lisa to find out whether she and the shelf were all right, and they were. He then rang Jane to check on how she was faring, and she was all right too.

Roland then took a train to Amsterdam Schiphol Airport where he caught his 21:30 KLM flight to Casablanca.

Chapter 35 – A Moroccan Adventure

Arriving at Casablanca Airport just before midnight, Roland collected his backpack and went through the customs and immigration formalities. The airport appeared almost abandoned, with the taxi counters and other shops all closed.

There were a few suspect characters touting for business. Roland's information indicated that the going rate for a taxi fare from the airport to the city should be around 200 dirham. There were only a couple of guys offering transportation and they seemed to have settled between them who would take the job.

Roland's initial offer of 200 dirham was readily dismissed. From what he could determine, that rate was not valid this time of night where extortion reigned. There was much negotiation, but oddly the driver finally agreed on the original offer of 200 dirham.

They loaded Roland's gear in an old, beat up taxi and drove off. They'd been travelling for a while in silence, until the driver barked out. "400 dirham to hotel!"

Roland was taken aback. "What are you talking about? We've already agreed on 200 dirham."

"No, 400 dirham or I take you back to airport." It was at this point the driver abruptly stopped the taxi in the middle of nowhere and stared at Roland.

Roland looked at the driver, looked out at the dark wilderness outside and thought back to the almost abandoned airport. "Okay 400 dirham," he reluctantly agreed. The driver exhibited an amazing change in mood; he was obviously ecstatic now.

The next day, Roland attended the pre-departure tour meeting where they went through introductions and dealt with administrative matters. The group comprised the tour leader, named Brent, seven ladies and six guys. They were due to depart; however, two additional ladies who were scheduled to be on the tour had not shown up. By 11.00 am the two ladies still hadn't shown so the tour took off without them.

The group was driven to Rabat, on to Sale and then boarded a boat to the Medina. They viewed a crammed beach and wandered through the markets within the walls of the Medina. The markets supplied all sorts of exotic products, such as goats' heads and cats. Amy, a lady on the tour from Western Australia, and Roland got so immersed in the lively atmosphere of the markets that they were left behind. They managed to find their way back by circling the main Medina wall.

Arriving at their campsite, the group was instructed on how to organise their belongings. They were only permitted hand luggage containing items they required overnight with their larger luggage locked away in the truck. They had an enjoyable dinner and engaged in some banter before retiring to their tents. Having an odd number of men on the tour, Roland was delighted to have a two man tent all to himself.

The group arose and retrieved the belongings they needed for the day before having breakfast and setting off. They stopped at Tiflet to inspect the markets and then moved on to visit the fascinating Roman ruins situated in the flatlands at Volubilis.

Arriving in Fez, they settled into the campsite and sat around the pool with some of the locals. It was another easy-going night of dinner, drinks, chatter and bed.

After breakfast, the group was introduced to their guide, Ashid. They were guided through the Royal Palace, the Jewish Quarter and the Fez Medina. They were then taken to an elevated point for a panoramic view of Fez.

The group proceeded to visit a co-operative carpet factory where a number of the tour members were keen to purchase a traditional Moroccan carpet. They learned about the history of the craft and took photographs of the carpet factory, which had enormous dye vats outside. Back at camp, they freshened up and went out to dine at a restaurant.

On the fourth day of the tour, they left the camp and moved on to Azrou where they checked out the markets and completed the daily shopping. They proceeded to their campsite near the city of Midelt.

There was considerable discussion as to whether to set up their tents or whether they should risk the weather and sleep under the stars. Roland decided not to put up his tent, mainly due to laziness rather than any assessment of the odds for rain. They enjoyed a hearty meal and considerable volumes of wine, which primed them for bed.

It was in the early morning when the group had breakfast and headed towards the desert. They passed through the Legionnaires Tunnel, Berber villages, travelled along the winding roads of the Middle Atlas Mountains and stopped at the Aziz Gorge.

They continued on, passing through Er Rachidia, which was built as a French military outpost on the edge of the Sahara Desert. It was then on to the Meski Oasis where they had a refreshing dip in the cold water pools and relaxed amongst the lush ferns and palm trees.

Caitlin from London, Amy and Roland went for a walk around town. They enjoyed a café olé and checked out a few of the stores. Roland purchased a turban and Caitlan purchased a pouffe. "You're not interested in a pouffe?" enquired Caitlin.

"No," Roland responded. "I wouldn't feel comfortable on a pouffe."

Reaching the edge of the Sahara, the group picked up their guide, Hassan, and they camped in the area of the world famous sand dunes at Erg Chebbi.

The group went to the nearby bar for drinks after dinner where they enjoyed Moroccan music and joined in the dancing. It had taken a few days, but the passengers were now starting to feel more comfortable with each other.

They had an early morning wakeup call to witness the sunrise over the Sahara. The sunrise itself was not so impressive; however, this didn't detract from the spectacular views of the desert and the dunes as they became visible in the emerging light. They returned for breakfast and were then driven to Rissani.

Stopping at a Berber carpet place, they were offered mint tea and Moroccan pizza. Amy, Brent and Roland conducted the grocery shopping and, when they returned, the group headed for the Todra Gorge. They were pleased to be accommodated in dormitories, although they had to manage without electricity.

Gabbie and Beckie were the designated cooks for the evening and performed a miraculous feat. They cooked up pasta in a cream sauce on a makeshift wood fired cooker with candles providing the necessary lighting.

The group adjourned to a large tent, which comprised a bar and entertainment area. There was a band playing traditional Berber music and they participated in drinking, singing and smoking bongs.

Roland got bored with the scene and went for a walk along a stream. He dunked his head in the cold water before returning to the dorm and going to bed.

The next day, they set out for a trek up the Todra Gorge. They broke up into small groups with Roland joining Corina and Laura, two Swiss ladies travelling together on the tour, and George, a professor from London.

They trekked for a couple of hours and admired the stark scenery of the mountain gorge with its 300-metre-high walls and passages that narrowed to as little as a couple of metres wide. To their surprise, there was a hotel situated in the middle of the beautiful, natural wilderness.

Returning to their accommodation in the mid-afternoon, they had a siesta before freshening up. The group met up for dinner where they had chicken targine. It was then back to the tent bar for the usual drinking, singing and smoking bongs.

The group left the Todra Gorge after breakfast and headed for Zagora. It was the day of their desert adventure. They took the gear they needed for the overnight desert camp and were mounted on camels.

After settling into the desert camp, they were served mint tea. It was

11.00 pm by the time dinner arrived – a plentiful lamb and vegetable targine, which they ploughed through with their fingers. They were all chatting away, telling stories and cracking jokes. They then found positions with their sleeping bags on mattresses and amongst cushions.

Roland found himself lodged between Corina and George. It was a balmy night and they were lying outside, under the comfortable elements. Corina was whispering about the stunning, starry night. "Oh, did you see those shooting stars?" Corina asked.

Roland hadn't seen any shooting stars and he wondered whether she was having him on. He then spotted one, which made him relax and fall asleep.

The peaceful night's sleep was disturbed by the activity of the early morning rise. It was time to leave the desert haven and make their return camel ride. When they dismounted, the group took a dip in refreshing pool waters before conducting the grocery shopping and having lunch.

They took a group photo in front of a signboard with a picture of a camel train with a directional arrow with the words, *Tombouctou 52 Jours*, which was said to mean Timbuktu 52 days by camel. They were then driven to a rough campsite in the Middle Atlas Mountains.

It was Caitlan and Roland's turn to cook. "I really don't have a good reputation at cooking for groups," Roland forewarned her.

"Don't worry," Caitlin assured him. "I'm a great cook and I'm sure we'll cook up a storm."

Caitlan took charge as head chef and she decided to make up a vegetable casserole with her special sauce recipe. There was loads of fun had by all during the cooking process, which was aided by the copious consumption of beer.

Dinner was served and it gave off a wonderful aroma. As the group ate into the meal, it was obvious that something was amiss. After some analysis and discussion, it was concluded that the courgettes were off. They carefully separated the offending vegetable and, once the courgettes were avoided, the meal was found to be agreeable. However, by this time, Caitlin was distraught and Roland's bad cooking reputation remained intact.

The group left the rough campsite after breakfast and drove a few hours before stopping off at a restaurant for lunch. They then proceeded through the Draa Valley towards the High Atlas Mountains. Roland was having a pleasant snooze when he was woken by a loud thud and the truck came to a sudden stop.

They had allegedly hit a donkey, and the owner thoroughly examined the beast, insisting the donkey was injured. It was difficult to evidence any apparent injury to the donkey or whether, in fact, the donkey had been harmed at all. In the end, Brent and the donkey's owner reached a settlement of 300 dirham.

The group finally arrived at Mohammed's house – a mud brick house set in the mountain ranges. They had a tough day and even though the water at the house was cold they were eager to take a shower. They enjoyed a dinner of vegetables and lamb cous cous.

It was early morning when they went for a trek up the mountains. It was exceptionally hot and dry weather and it took almost five hours before all the group members reached the top. Some of the climbers were visibly distressed, but equally relieved upon reaching the summit. Their reward was magnificent views from Mount Toubkal, Morocco's highest mountain, down to the valleys and mountain ranges.

Back at Mohammed's house, they were served lunch before heading to Abdullah's house where they were given the opportunity to be treated to a massage at the Hammam and the women were to be first.

After over an hour, the women returned complaining about their torturous experience. The men trotted over to the Hammam for their turn, believing the women to be soft.

The guys were instructed to undress and were shown where to place their clothes. They were then allowed to use three separate rooms; hot, warm and cold. Buckets were available in each room that could be used to fill up with water as desired.

The staff provided general instructions of the ritual and the different stages. The impression they got was that there didn't seem to be any hard and fast rules, although in order to get acclimatised to the heat, it was recommended to go progressively from the cold to the hotter rooms.

Grabbing a bucket, Roland bypassed the cold room and went straight to the warm room. He filled his bucket with some water and doused the area he designated for him to lie down. He then splashed himself for a basic wash. After relaxing in the warm room, he was then off to the hot room, which was very hot.

Roland sat, relaxed and allowed his body to react to the hot, steamy conditions. With his pores opening up, his body started to perspire freely. He returned to the warm room and most of the others had or were in the process of enduring a scrub and a massage.

It seemed to be a fairly vigorous experience with the guys expressing a lot of verbal oohs, ahhs and ouches. Roland lined up and was soon summoned by a solid man with a large scrub glove who indicated that he should lay face down.

When the man started with an unexpected and decent slap square in the middle of Roland's back, he knew the man meant business. The man proceeded to scrub the living daylights out of him before indicating for Roland to turn over where he gave him a cracking slap in his midsection. On this occasion, Roland prepared himself and he took the pounding with a smile. By the end of the scrub, both of them were laughing, although

Roland felt that he had been stripped of a few layers of skin.

Roland didn't have too much of a break before he was led for a massage. He was seated on the floor and a man was kneeling. The man proceeded to interlock their bodies in all sorts of positions that provided the masseuse more leverage to stretch Roland's body.

As the man stretched and twisted various parts of Roland's torso and limbs, the masseuse would ask whether he was all right. Roland replied in the affirmative, although the experience was pushing his pain barrier. He then unintentionally reacted with a chuckle. The masseuse obviously didn't have the same sense of humour as the scrub man and masseuse pressed further.

Roland endured the massage, although he felt like he had been placed in a washing machine. He thanked the masseuse and made a sarcastic comment. "It was good, but it could have been a lot harder."

Bypassing the cold room again, Roland preferred to have his final wash with tepid water in the warm room. He then lay down on the stone slab to compose himself before getting dressed and limping out of the Hammam.

Leaving Abdullah's house, the group moved on to Marrakech. They travelled through a variety of landscapes, which dramatically changed from the deserts and dunes of the Kasbah region, to the oases with lush palms and ferns in the Atlas Mountain region. The scenery throughout Morocco was being more fully appreciated the more they travelled.

The group checked into their Marrakech hotel and had the day to themselves. Roland did some laundry and tended to some administrative matters before he met up with the others. They took the bus to the centre and were dropped off at the Djemaa el Fna, a large square adjacent to the Medina.

The square was lively and lined with eateries, orange juice stands, food stands, boys with chained monkeys, snake charmers, street entertainers and a mixture of many locals and tourists. The outside cooking filled the square with smoke and unique smells. It was a surreal experience of clashing noises and frenetic activity.

The group initially had some difficulty finding an outdoor eatery where they all could be seated. However, when the enterprising waiters noticed their plight, they took little time in clearing the tables and setting up benches to accommodate them all.

It was a production line of orders and serving. They enjoyed the novelty of the experience and thoroughly enjoyed their meals. They then meandered around the square to take in the atmosphere and activities. After they had satisfied their curiosity, they rounded each other up and headed off.

On the way back to the hotel, they grabbed a personal store of alcohol and ventured onto the rooftop for nightcaps. Amy was going on and on about how she hated the trip and some of the people on it. Roland put up with the whining by getting stuck into his bottle of whiskey. It was only him being sick on the balcony that put a stop to her complaining.

The next day was a visit to the Marrakech Medina. The group inspected the markets by weaving their way through the narrow streets of the old city. In the evening, they returned to the Djemaa el Fna for further adventures in the action packed town square.

Returning to the hotel rooftop for drinks, Roland took special care not to be cornered by Amy and was fortunate to enjoy the company of Corina, Laura and George.

The following day, the group left Marrakech and moved on to El Jadida. They stopped at a beach for lunch before making their way to their campsite near Casablanca, relieved it would be their last night in tents.

Roland woke early in the morning to find George already up. After their breakfast, they found a soccer ball and had a kick. When everyone was ready, they were driven to Casablanca and checked into their hotel.

After settling into their rooms, the group said goodbye to Brent and a few of the group members who were leaving the tour. Caitlan, Laura and Corina met up with Roland and they had lunch at a café near the hotel. Returning to the hotel, Roland had a siesta before joining the others for dinner at the hotel restaurant.

Amy, George and Roland were keen to kick on so they took a cab to La Corniche. They enjoyed walking along the boulevard and taking in the sea air. They stopped off at a bar for a couple of drinks before catching a cab back to the hotel.

Roland met up with Caitlan and Corina for breakfast. Amy and George joined them and rumours were spreading that the pair may have hit it off. When Gabbie and Beckie joined them, they made their way to the city centre where they checked out a number of shops and, notwithstanding Roland's protestations, went to McDonalds for lunch. It was then back to the hotel for a siesta.

In need of accommodation for his last night in Casablanca, Roland was fortunate to have Corina offer to share her room as Laura was going home a day early.

Corina had a siesta and Roland lay down for a rest on the other bed. The thought of crawling into bed with her crossed his mind, but he resisted. They slept until late afternoon before joining the others for dinner.

After dinner, it was time for the remaining tour members to say goodbye as they would be going their separate ways the following day. Roland's separation from Amy would be short-lived as they were on the same African tour starting in a few days.

Corina and Roland retired to their room, undressed and got into their respective beds. After a little time of tossing and turning, Roland considered how silly the situation was. "Would you like to join me in my bed?" he finally asked.

Corina was initially coy, but slowly made her way into his bed and they enjoyed the night together.

Receiving an early morning wake up call, Roland said goodbye to Corina and was soon on his 07:00 KLM flight to Amsterdam.

Roland had a night's stay in Amsterdam so he went to the tourist booth and booked a hotel room near the city centre. After checking in, he returned to the city and was again drawn to the Red Light District. He had a couple of beers at a pub he had frequented before and had a meal at the Chinese restaurant where he had eaten before. He then returned to his hotel.

Arriving at Amsterdam Airport, Roland heard an announcement over the loudspeaker about something to the effect that they were seeking volunteers. He had little idea what it was all about so he went over to the enquiries counter to find out.

Information advised that the flight was overbooked and they were looking for passengers to miss the flight and take a later one. In exchange, KLM would pay 625 guilders in cash as well as providing food vouchers for use in the airport. Roland didn't need much time to do the math before he accepted.

It would be a seven hours wait, which Roland expected would be a breeze. He paced himself and, before he knew it, heard the boarding call for his flight bound for Nairobi.

Chapter 36 – African Safaris

Roland arrived in Nairobi the following day and as he rode in the cab on the way to the hotel he was euphoric. Not only had he pocketed 625 Dutch guilders, he also saved on one night's accommodation in Nairobi.

After checking into his hotel, Roland tracked down Amy and they had lunch together. He thought it curious that Amy considered it appropriate to keep his change as well as the tip.

Setting off alone, Roland went sightseeing. As he walked through the streets of Nairobi, there were a number of people giving him serious looks, which made him feel insecure. He was also uncomfortable with the constant demands for money. He managed to visit Parliament House, the Town Hall, City Hall and the market before he retreated to the hotel.

Roland freshened up and went to the pre-departure meeting. Murray, the tour guide, and Matt, the driver, introduced themselves and then introduced the two helpers they referred to as couriers – Hayley and Rita. Roland counted 16 ladies, 10 men and four couples on the tour, which he considered to be a reasonable ratio of women to men.

The introductions seemed a little awkward as a number of the passengers already knew each other, having been travelling on the previous stage of the tour. The newcomers were made to feel like interlopers as they received a less than hospitable reception from the old guard.

The group sat down for dinner and drinks. Roland opted for the tilapia fish, which he thought was superb. However, he was not too impressed to hear the fish was introduced into Kenya to curb the mosquito malaria problems as the fish were omnivores and ate mosquito larvae.

On the first day of the tour, the passengers were off in all directions in an effort to purchase the required travel gear. Roland was in pursuit of a sleeping mat and he set off with Charlotte and Sue. They located the Nakumatt Supermarket and Roland readily found his sleeping mat. The ladies were also in need of mosquito nets and they had to seek out other stores to track them down.

When Roland returned to the hotel, he joined Hayley and Rita to prepare lunch. After lunch, the group left Nairobi for Tanzania, arriving at their camp in the Arusha National Park three hours late. After dinner and drinks, it was time for bed.

The group took off in the morning and after lunch they went to a Masai village. They had fun playing around with the tribal youngsters and experiencing the simple life of the village people.

The next stop was the central market in the town of MTO-WA-MBU, pronounced, "umtowambu", meaning mosquito creek. They had time to look around before moving on to their camp at Kudo.

Roland was relieved to have arrived at the camp until he learned that he and Carol were scheduled to clean the truck. He quickly put up his tent, cleaned the truck and was able to squeeze in a beer before Carol made an appearance just as dinner was being served. He saw little point staying up after dinner as the camp was in the middle of nowhere and the group appeared as lifeless as he felt.

The group woke early for their first safari in the Ngorongoro Crater. It was governed by the Ngorongoro Conservation Authority and was a UNESCO World Heritage Site, forming part of the Serengeti Ecosystem and reportedly the world's largest intact caldera.

The four-wheel drive vehicles turned up late, but the moment the vehicles arrived, they were off at high speed. The group witnessed an abundance of wildlife including zebras, wildebeests, white rhinocerosi, hippopotami, baboons, gazelles, jackals, elephants, buffalos, hartebeests and teems of birdlife.

The crater seemed to have entrapped the wildlife like an enormous natural zoo. Roland found the safari amazing, although the passengers sharing his vehicle may not have thought so, given he slept through parts of it. The group had dinner before they gingerly greeted their sleeping bags.

Arusha was the next destination, which was at the base of Mount Kilimanjaro. They stopped over at the Arusha Snake Farm for lunch and then at the markets of Arusha. Camp was near the little town of Moshi where they dined and downed a few beers before going to bed.

The days seemed to be following a pattern that involved early starts, driving, a stop for shopping, more driving, a stop for lunch and yet more driving to the next campsite. The tour members were rostered for chores, followed by dinner and washing up. The camps were usually in the middle of nowhere so after dinner their sleeping bags seemed to be the most attractive destination.

It was an arduous routine, which Roland was not overly happy about even though he appreciated that it was unavoidable given the long distances and the out-of-the-way places.

The next stop was Dar es Salaam, which was a relatively rich city of a couple of million people, set on a large natural harbour on the Indian Ocean.

It was Rita's birthday so the group hung around for a couple of drinks before most of them hit the sack. Rita, Hayley, Charlotte and Roland kicked on and they had quite a few drinks before Hayley came up with the idea of skinny dipping.

The ladies didn't lose any time getting their gear off and taking the plunge into the sea. Roland was left on the beach holding his beer. "Come on in Roland, you square," Rita called out.

"We won't look and it's very dark," Hayley said.

"It's not as if we'd be able to see anything anyway," Charlotte added.

Roland had never been skinny dipping, much less with three women. "Okay then," he said as he stripped. "I'm coming in!" As he got in, Hayley and Charlotte got out. "Take my clothes and you're dead," he shouted.

Rita and Roland fooled around in the water for a while before they also got out. It was 4.00 am when they retired to their tents, quite refreshed.

In the morning, the group rushed to catch their ferry to Zanzibar Island. Roland spent most the time on the top deck feeling very unwell. They went through customs, paid $20US for their Zanzibar visas and checked into an inn.

Amy, Sue, Charlotte and Roland went for a walk about Stone Town where they visited the city's old quarter and checked out the market. On the way back to the inn, they stopped off at the local takeaway for a bite. Roland sampled the meat and vegetable sambusas, which he elaborately described as, "nice."

The group visited Changuu Island where they inspected the prison ruins, admired the beautiful scenery and entertained themselves by observing the giant tortoises. They then went for a swim and sun-bathed before taking the boat back to the inn.

Dinner was at an Indian restaurant where changu fish, being Swahili for snapper, was the popular choice. The group walked around the market before heading back to the inn where they drank until one o'clock in the morning.

Roland woke early, as did his other roommates, Joanne, Blake and Matt. They headed off on the Spice Tour with their guide, Ali. The Spice Tour included a city tour where they got to see the Old Fort, the House of Wonder, the Slave Market, St. Monica's Cathedral, the CCM Revolutionary Ruling Party Building, Maruhubi Palace Ruins and the Persian Bath.

The main part of the Spice Tour was an educational experience where they sampled the exotic spices and fruits of the island – pineapple, liquorice, nutmeg, peppercorn, paw paw, custard fruit and jackfruit.

The group was driven to the North Beach where they were housed in bungalows. They had a siesta before being treated to dinner and stayed up drinking until 3.00 am.

Getting up early, Roland enjoyed breakfast and then went for a walk around the village of Nungwi. He stumbled upon Shelley, Joanne and Matt at the beach and they lay on the sand for some time waiting for the sun to come out. They persisted for some time and when the sun emerged they went for a swim. The water was cool and refreshing so they spent a few minutes splashing around before they headed back to their bungalows for a siesta.

The group went to a club for a few pre-dinner drinks and moved to a restaurant for dinner. It was then off to a bar for more drinks where they mingled with a number of other tourists before hitting the sack.

The next day, the group walked around Nungwi Village and along the beach before heading to Zanzibar Port where they caught a boat back to the port of Dar es Salaam.

Reaching the port, they were driven to the Ebony Market. Roland checked out the market and spent the rest of the time in a bar where he had chips and a couple of beers. When the others made it back to the truck, they proceeded to their next camp. Dinner was a filling three course meal, which was enough to satisfy the hungriest of travellers and it was midnight when they retired.

They had a full day's drive ahead of them with the monotony of the drive broken by the sight of elephants and giraffes. They had a roadside lunch stop and towards the end of the day they found a rough campsite.

The evening was very cold and Roland felt that he may have caught a chill. He was with a few of the passengers when he tried to speak, but he simply couldn't utter the words. He tried again, but still couldn't put together any coherent words. He was embarrassed, waved them goodbye and retired to his tent.

Roland experienced the shakes and a cold sweat with tingling and numbing sensations over his right hand. These sensations extended to his right arm, his tongue and the right side of his face. He stayed motionless for a few seconds, trying to comprehend what was happening to him. He then tried to rub some life into his numb body parts. He was experiencing a severe headache so he forced himself to seek out his paracetamol and managed to place two pills in his mouth. As he couldn't swallow, he sucked on them and eventually fell asleep.

After a very rough night, Roland got up, packed and joined the others for breakfast. As the group made no comment about his strange behaviour of the previous night, he made no mention of his experience.

The group took off for Malawi and endured another full day's drive. Passing over the border, they proceeded to Lake Malawi and on to a campsite near the small village of Chitimba.

The next day, they set off for a trek to Livingstonia, a small town named after David Livingstone, the Scottish pioneer, missionary, explorer and supposedly the first European to see Victoria Falls. It took four hours to trek up the Rift Valley escarpment where they checked out the Livingstonia National Monument Museum, the hospital and the Anglican Cathedral Church.

On the return leg of the trek, they viewed beautiful mountain scenery and the Manchewe Waterfall. It was a very tiring day and the trekkers took their time to enjoy their dinner before they moved on to the bar. There was a party atmosphere and the bar staff were providing an added service of a free haircut. The catch was that they only gave a number zero clippers cut.

Brent was game and, not to be outdone, Jim was also challenging to be the first. In order to service both customers, a second set of clippers was revealed. This led to other volunteers and before long all the guys had their heads shaved except for Hamish and Roland.

Hamish wasn't too concerned as he'd had his head shaved before; however, Erika, his fiancée, wasn't too keen for him to repeat the exercise and declined on his behalf. All attention then turned to Roland.

Roland spent a few minutes pondering the matter. *If one was ever going to get their head shaved, it would have to be on holidays in the middle of Africa.* "Okay, I'll do it," he declared. "But on one condition." Everyone's delight turned into anticipation. "On the condition that Hamish has it done as well." All eyes then turned back to Hamish.

Hamish meekly resisted as Erika gave him a staring down. He then decided that he couldn't be the only piker so he relented. He sat on one chair and Roland sat on the other. The cutting proceeded to the cheers and jeers of the crowd. As the night drew to a close, the ladies and the baldies went to bed.

It was an early morning start and after breakfast they attempted to clear away from the camp, but the truck got bogged. The group and hangers-on tried to push the truck out; however, the severe gradient of the track didn't allow enough purchase. This called for the grates to be pulled out from behind the truck and with an enormous collective effort they finally pulled, pushed and forced the truck free.

The group drove to Mazuzu where they took advantage of the money exchange. They then moved on to the market where they sought to purchase some gear for a fancy dress party. They moved onto Kande Beach where Roland undertook his now usual role of collecting the firewood and starting the camp fire.

Dinner comprised of more alcohol than food. Roland consumed numerous beers and half a bottle of scotch so he was well and truly sloshed as he followed the others to the bar. He was invited to take a seat on a large wooden swan and, not to be a party pooper, he assertively sat down.

The moment Roland's backside made contact with the big bird, there was uproar and a crowd appeared carrying a lifeguard and a yard glass filled with beer. He was fitted with the lifeguard and given his instructions to skull the beer.

Not feeling very well, Roland made an attempt to follow the orders to the chants of the revellers. He started tilting the glass and, after what seemed to be an eternity, the glass was empty. After he was released from his sanction, he managed to wobble to the bar where he soon fell asleep.

In the morning, it took Roland a while for him to come to his senses. He realised that he was nestled in his sleeping bag, which was scattered with the produce of his sickness. He struggled to clean up the mess before going for a long shower.

Roland had a light brunch, which consisted mainly of non-alcoholic liquids. He then went to the freshwater beach to fill the jerry cans whilst having a swim. He had a game of darts and chopped wood before he joined the others for dinner. He agreed to join the crew at the bar on the proviso that they kept him away from one thing – the dreaded swan.

The following day was a relaxing time where the group exploited all the activities on offer: darts, table tennis, swimming and sun-bathing. Roland chopped more wood before freshening up for dinner. The group went to the bar for a few drinks and then retired to bed. Given the now highly predictable routine of the stay at Kande Beach, Roland was glad that they would be moving on.

The group travelled to the town of Salima for a stopover and shopping. It was then on to their camp at Senga Bay. Roland had a drink with Joanne and Amy before helping out with dinner, which was another food-fest.

There was nothing to do at the rough campsites, which were usually some distance from civilisation so Roland got into the habit of stuffing his face. He was starting to put on weight and he didn't like it in the least. After dinner and a couple of drinks, he went for a walk along the beach by himself before returning to camp and going to bed.

The group left early in the morning for Lilongwe, the capital of Malawi. They stopped for a couple of hours to check out the city and spent their remaining Malawi currency on grog.

They proceeded over the Zambian border to their campsite near the small town of Chipata. A number of the group members were sick with various ailments so there was quietness about the camp. It was another filling dinner and the weary travellers had an early night.

The group made tracks and travelled to South Luangwa National Park, considered one of the greatest wildlife sanctuaries in the world. They went on a night drive that took five hours and were rewarded by witnessing zebras, warthogs, elephants, waterbucks and four lions that strode metres away from their four-wheel drive vehicle. Returning to camp, Hayley had prepared a scrumptious dinner, which was followed by a few drinks.

It was an especially early wakeup call for those that opted to go on the morning safari tour. They observed hippopotami, giraffes, warthogs, guinea fowls, crocodiles and egrets. When they returned from the tour they had brunch.

The group took off later in the morning and it was an extraordinarily long drive to the Zambian village of Sinda. They arrived in the early evening and, notwithstanding their tiredness, they put in a special effort to celebrate Amy's 19th birthday.

They set off on another long drive to the next campsite near the Zambia's capital city of Lusaka. Along the road, the tour truck passed another tour truck and they waved as Matt overtook them. Not to be outdone, the other truck overtook the tour truck with some of the passengers showing their panties or their bare buttocks. This was when the battle began.

The tour truck sped up and drove alongside the other truck, windows were opened and there was exchange fire of water bags and egg missiles. There was a short ceasefire when the other truck pulled back and, after enough time to reload, the other truck sped up alongside the tour truck and there was another exchange of water, flour and egg missiles. The other truck appeared to have mechanical problems as it slowed down and their tour truck pulled away.

The tour truck reached their camp where the group prepared and sat down to dinner. Later in the evening, they celebrated James's 33rd birthday with drinks and dancing.

It was another early morning get up and they set off straight after breakfast. The schedule was now religiously followed as the group appreciated the benefits of more time for stopovers and earlier arrival at the next camp.

Crossing the border from Zambia to Zimbabwe, the group took photos of the Kariba Dam from the Zimbabwean side. They stopped at the town of Kariba where they did their grocery shopping. When they arrived at camp, it was time to celebrate yet another birthday. This time it was Murray's 29th birthday where he led with the drinking, but lagged in going to bed.

Leaving camp the next day, the group dropped off their luggage and supplies at the houseboat launch area. They would be cruising on the houseboat on Lake Kariba, a manmade lake filled after the completion of the Kariba Dam.

Joanne, Katie, Blake and Roland were assigned the bar duties for the three day cruise. This involved a visit to the drinks company to buy the necessary beverages. The company allowed them to take as many bottles of beer and soft drinks they desired. They were required to pay the amount due and, when they returned the empty and full bottles, the company would provide a refund for the drinks not consumed.

Blake suggested they purchase the amount of alcohol he expected to consume and multiply it by the number of people. Roland agreed to his formula, but suggested they add another element to the calculation, which was to halve it. There was much negotiation before they settled on their liquid supplies. For the 24 people on the three day cruise, they loaded bottles comprising 500 beers, 100 diet cokes, 100 lemonades, 60 Fantas, 60 sodas and 60 tonics.

The group loaded the houseboat based on the order of highest priority. First was the alcohol, this was followed by the luggage, then the supplies and finally the food. They launched off, cracked open a drink and toasted each other as they waved goodbye to the people they were leaving behind.

They settled into life on the houseboat by making full use of the pool and spa. Roland was not a huge fan of life on a boat so he walked around a little before he read his book and had a nap. When he awoke, he freshened up and got into his costume for the fancy dress party. The passengers emerged from their cabins, dressed in their costumes, which prompted much discussion and laughter.

The costumes included pirates, sailors, mermaids, a maid who survived the Titanic, Huckleberry Finn, Ginger from Gilligan's Island, Popeye and Olive. There was even a catfish accompanied by seaweed. Roland chose a lifeguard outfit, although he soon ditched carrying around a real lifesaver and settled on carrying around a packet of Lifesavers candy instead.

There were pre-dinner drinks, dinner and after-dinner drinks. The music volume was increased and they commenced dancing and clowning around. It then developed into a wild party. Roland only lasted until midnight when he retired to his cabin. Others managed to turn the festivities into an all-nighter.

Roland woke to a continued banging in his head. He prepared himself a cup of hot chocolate and read more of his book. As the others dragged themselves out of bed, a few decided to jump off the side of the boat for a wake-up swim. Roland thought it was a good idea so he too took the plunge before joining the others for breakfast.

The group was taken for a boat ride where they spotted buffalos, hippopotami and elephants. They anchored for the evening and freshened up before dinner. The evening was a lot quieter from the one before, as they moved on to the top deck for a few quiet drinks before retiring to their bunks.

Roland was prepared for a pleasant night's sleep; however, he was awoken by the goings on of Jim, Blake, Joanne, Amy and Mindi. They were obviously drunk, except for Mindi who was a teetotaller. "I want to see willy, I want to see willy," the girls were shouting.

"Here's willy!" Jim yelled back and, going by the subsequent shrieks, Roland guessed that the girls most probably got their request.

Waking up early in the morning, Roland was in good spirits as it was the last day on the houseboat. He joined the bar people to pack the bottles in the drink crates. They had only drunk a little more than half of what they loaded, being a little more than a third of what Blake initially wanted to load. "I don't get it," Blake commented. "After all, I drank my quota."

The group had lunch before disembarking and dropping off the drink bottles. They stopped off for a short time in Kariba and then moved on to the Zimbabwean/Zambian border. It took a couple of hours to cross the border, followed by a very long drive to their next campsite. Dinner was whatever they could scrounge up and by the time they reached camp, put up their tents and crashed, it was 2.00 am.

They enjoyed an English breakfast and had enough time to go poolside to sun-bath and have a swim. There was an optional helicopter flight over Victoria Falls where they were blown away by the views of the falls, the canyon and the national park.

Returning to camp, the group visited a craft market and then moved on to a booze cruise on the Zambezi River. It was a civilised affair and the baldies sat in a row to have their picture taken at sunset. They returned to camp and continued drinking and dancing before going to bed.

Victoria Falls offered numerous water activities. Roland experienced the river boarding before lunch and then joined a few of the others to do the white water rafting. They were going very well until they got to Point 8 where the paddlers could choose the rapids they wished to tackle, which was based on the probability of flipping. It came down to a 40% chance of flipping, a 60% chance of flipping or, the rapids nicknamed Star Trek, which had a 95% chance of flipping.

Roland thought he would be adventurous and suggested the 60% chance; however, Paul had other ideas. "Why don't we do the 95%?" Paul yelled.

You don't have to be Einstein to know that 95% was not good odds, Roland thought and he queried the guide. "Just how dangerous is Star Trek?"

"It has taken at least one life," the guide advised.

With this reply, Roland was sure that the group would elect the 60% rapids, but Paul persisted. "So are we up to tackling the 95%?" Paul fervently asked.

The reply was equally fervent. "Yeah!"

Roland gave in to the proletariat and joined in with the cries. "Yeah, let's do it, yeah!"

The guide was screaming his instructions in an effort to hit the rapids at the correct angle and at the right speed. Jim and Roland were at the front. Amy and Charlotte were in the middle. Shelley, Paul and the guide were at the back.

The guide kept on stressing the importance of keeping up speed. Jim and Roland were doing a strong job in front, but the rest were either not strong enough or were just hanging on for dear life. In the end, the odds were proven right and their raft flipped.

The paddlers went in all directions and the guide took control, clasping the raft and barking instructions to his paddlers. They managed to bunch around one side of the raft and flip it the right way up. The guide, Jim, Paul and Roland helped each other on the raft and then used the ladies to practice their reverse buoyancy flip to bounce them back into the raft.

After their misadventure, they needed to make their way to the bank and carry their raft over some terrain. The rafters re-entered the river and continued along the various rapids. They seemed to have become a reasonable paddling unit by the time they arrived at Point 18.

They were trying to get their pace up to make the rapids, but they were all over the place and they were flipped by a huge wave. Roland was thrown clear of the raft and was submerged into a whirlpool. He tried to swim to the surface, but was being pulled under. He expected to surface at some stage, but he was being held down.

Starting to panic, Roland vigorously tried to swim to the surface. His head emerged from the water and he gave out a huge exhale before he sucked in as much air as he could. He caught a glimpse of Jim who was leaning over the side of the raft and Jim yelled Roland's name. Roland was panicked, but when he caught a glimpse of the gravely concerned looks on the faces of Jim and the guide, his panic escalated another notch. He was then dragged under water again.

Roland dug deep and drew as much energy as he could muster to swim to the surface. He eventually surfaced and fought his way towards the raft. The others had all been collected as a result of the Herculean efforts of the guide, ably assisted by Jim.

"Right Jim, do the reverse buoyancy and get Roland into the raft," commanded the guide.

"Okay Roland, you remember how we were instructed. One, two, three, dunk and pull," Jim ordered and Roland was flung back into the raft.

They continued tackling the few remaining rapids and, after they had arrived at the destination point on the bank, they relaxed thinking that their ordeal was over. However, to their exasperation they were advised that they still had a gruelling trek up a steep hill to complete their adventure.

The events of the day were excitedly discussed over a plentiful restaurant dinner where they got to sample local meats such as ostrich, impala and warthog.

Roland woke early and helped himself to breakfast. He then loitered around camp until the group departed to see the video of the previous day's rafting. To the paddlers' disappointment, the cameras didn't capture the more dramatic events so few sales were made that day.

Lunch was at a pizza restaurant and the group then ventured to a location in the wilderness between Zambia and Zimbabwe with Victoria Falls as the backdrop where there was the option for bungee jumping from the 111 metre bridge. They then returned to the township of Victoria Falls where they had dinner and drinks before going to bed.

Roland joined Joanne, Amy, Mindi and Jim for a hike around the Victoria Falls National Park. They took in a number of the attractions, including the David Livingstone Statue, the main falls and the part of the falls referred to as the Boiling Pot.

Back at camp, a few of the group headed off to the Victoria Falls Hotel. It was a stately hotel that exuded an old-world charm. They ordered the traditional high tea on the terrace, which had spectacular views of Victoria Falls Bridge set in the Batoka Gorge. They stuffed themselves before wobbling to the Explorers Bar for a few drinks.

The next day, Roland was getting bored just hanging around so he decided to go for a walk. He passed by the Victoria Falls Hotel to take in the lovely setting of the bridge and the Zambezi River. He then walked to the Zimbabwean/Zambian border, along Zambezi Drive and along the bank of the Zambezi River.

There was beautiful trail and river scenery with the devastation elephants caused easily evidenced by the broken branches, snapped trunks and uprooted trees. Roland took numerous photos, including one of an enormous 1,500-year-old Baobab tree.

Two of the ladies from the tour, Katie and Liz, invited Roland to join them for dinner at the Victoria Falls Safari Lodge. It was considered to be the best hotel in Zimbabwe with magnificent views, including the sunset view over the Zambezi National Game Park.

They walked onto the balcony where they could see a large expanse of desolate bush and a lake. The waterhole was under lights and it attracted elephants, buffalos, impalas and kudus. They had a drink on the balcony before they were led to their table and enjoyed a lovely meal. It was a pleasant walk back to camp, even though they were heading back to their primitive tent accommodation.

There were changes to the tour group with some leaving and others joining. The newly formed group departed for Botswana, crossed the border and eventually found a rough campsite on the edge of the Kalahari Desert. Annette and Roland had the added job of cleaning the truck, which they undertook before joining the others for dinner and huge portions of shepherd's pie.

The group moved on after breakfast and arrived at their next camp just after midday. Annette and Roland were required to fill the jerry cans, a new job assigned to the cleaners. After lunch, the group lazed around the pool and witnessed another overland truck pull in. Roland observed several lovely ladies descend the truck and thought, *that'd be right.*

Roland helped with the camp fire and grabbed a bottle of coke that he used to mix with his rum. The group had a stir-fry dinner and spent the evening at the bar.

The next day, the group headed for the Okovango Delta. They made their way to the airport and boarded a single-engine, six-seater plane. It was windy, which made the flight a little bumpy and it was a rough landing on the dirt runway.

The group was shown around the camp on Chief's Island before they had a drink at the bar and ate lunch. They set off in mokoros (dugout canoes), and passed a wide range of wildlife and birdlife. They found a rough camp, put up their tents and rested. They soon set off for a 2½ hour walk where they sighted impalas, zebras, elephants, wildebeests and hyenas.

Back at camp, a couple of passengers who elected not to do the walk had prepared dinner. After dinner, the guides told a few of the local stories before the group went to bed.

It was an early morning wakeup call and they had a cup of tea before setting off for their morning safari walk at 6.30 am. They left with two guides and walked for about three hours; however, they didn't observe anything more than they saw the previous day. The guides pointed out some animal droppings and explained from which animals they emanated. The guides also pointed out some lion and leopard footprints.

"So what are the chances of us seeing a lion?" Roland asked.

"It's possible," replied one of the guides.

"So what would you do if we came across a lion as you don't have a gun or any other defensive weapons?" Roland queried.

The guide looked at Roland before he replied. "You could run."

After breakfast, the group departed in the mokoros, arriving back at the main camp by midday. They went for a dip in the murky waters of the Delta and partook in a makeshift game of baseball. Late afternoon, they put up their tents, freshened up and had a few relaxing beers before they had dinner. It was then off to the bar for a few nightcaps and games of darts.

They left the camp for the runway where they took their uncomfortable, bumpy flights. When everyone completed their flights, they made their way to the town of Maun before travelling on to their rough camp stop in time to witness a lovely sunset over the Kalahari Desert.

Chapter 37 – Southern Africa

The group departed for their long drive to Windhoek, the capital of Namibia. Soon after crossing the border they stopped along the road for lunch. They reached the township of Gobabis, changed money and then moved on to Windhoek where they settled into their dormitory-style accommodation.

They went out for pizza and purchased enough for a small army, which they devoured at their hotel. They hung around the bar drinking beer and shooting pool. Roland retired and as he was lying in bed he over-heard Sue whispering happy birthday to Annette.

The travellers awoke amid discussions and accusations that thieves had ransacked a few of the tourist trucks. It appeared that the group's truck was untouched, but two other trucks had been broken into with numerous items taken.

The group had a full free day in Windhoek. Roland went for a walk and passed by the Government Building that housed the National Assembly and he took a photo. He also took photos of the German Lutheran Church and Independence Avenue with a statue of a springbok.

Roland proceeded to the markets in search of some wooden animal carvings. He was particularly interested in a giraffe, an elephant and a rhinoceros. It wasn't long before he came across exactly what he was after; three fine specimens and all located at the one stall.

Fairly confident of the going prices, Roland worked out a deal to secure the three carvings. "How much do you want?" Roland asked.

"I want $180 Namibian," replied the man.

"I'll make you a one, take it all leave it offer; I'll give you $100 Namibian for the three carvings," Roland confidently stated.

"No," the man immediately replied.

Roland was unprepared for the rapid rejection and stood there for a moment before he left empty handed.

Returning to the hotel, Roland learned they were moving to alternative accommodation due to the previous night's robbery. He quickly showered, packed and left with the tour truck. The group was split between two different backpacker establishments.

After settling into their new accommodation, they took taxi vans to a restaurant. Roland was keen to try the zebra rump steak, but they were all out so he went for the kudu loin in mushroom sauce instead. After dinner, they had a few drinks at a bar before moving on to a couple of nightspots.

Departing early the next day, Charlotte and Katie were in fine form after kicking on from the night before. They continued drinking in the truck, polishing off a bottle of vodka between them.

The group stopped off at a pie store near the Windhoek Royal Hotel for a bite to eat. They then moved on to their lunchtime stop by the side of the road. They continued on and observed giraffes, gemsboks, springboks and a dik-dik.

They reached their camp in Etosha, located on the edge of the Etosha Pan and set within an impressive, old German fort. The fort had a restaurant, a swimming pool and a waterhole where a giraffe and its baby were drinking under a spotlight.

After dinner, they returned to the waterhole where they observed several elephants drinking. The elephants eventually moved on and a tower of giraffe tentatively approached to drink from the waterhole. It was a civilised passing parade of different animals taking turns drinking from the waterhole. They also saw a jackal and heard a lion's roar echoing from a distance.

The fort was protected by high, electrical-wire fencing and armed guards. When the guards wandered off, it was a sure sign that further activity was unlikely to ensue so some of the crowd pulled away. Others stayed a little longer, taking in the quiet, eerie feeling of the jungle at night.

The group left camp for their morning driving safari. The safari took almost three hours and they saw giraffes, zebras, wildebeests, hartebeests, gemsboks, springboks and kudus. Upon witnessing the array of wildlife, there was much discussion as people started to get hooked onto their safari adventures.

Departing Namutoni mid-morning, the group stopped for lunch at Halali, a camp situated between the Namutoni Camp and the Okaukuejo Camp. Halali was said to be the German word signifying the bugle call made at the end of a hunt.

It was a very hot day and they relaxed around the pool, although Roland preferred to check out the Moringa Waterhole. He was the only person at the waterhole and there was no sign of animal life until a lonely springbok arrived. He stayed observing the creature for a few moments before he returned to camp.

The group was playing around by the pool when they saw Roland and waved him over. As he approached they asked why he wasn't going for a dip. "I don't feel like it," was his reply.

Eric, a burly man, got him in a bear hug. "I think you should go for a swim."

"Listen, I've got important items on my person and I really don't want them to get wet," Roland advised.

"So what are these important items?" Jim asked.

"There's my passport in my back pocket," Roland said.

Jim removed his passport.

"Okay, let's throw him in," Eric barked.

"Wait!" Roland snapped back. "I've got my wallet in my side pocket."

Jim removed his wallet and they were positioning themselves to throw him in.

"Wait!" Roland cried out. "I've got a gun in my other pocket and I'm not happy to see ya."

It was at this point that they threw him in the pool.

Roland's clothes were still drenched as the group boarded the truck to head for their night camp at Okaukuejo. Along the way, they saw the usual giraffes, springboks and zebras; however, there was more excitement when a lion and a cheetah were spotted.

They were happy with the sighting, even though the prized sighting of the rarest animal, being the black rhinoceros, had still eluded them. Sadly, the black rhino had been pushed to the brink of extinction due to the loss of habitat and illegal poaching.

Arriving at the camp at Okaukuejo, there was a bit of a scramble for tent space due to the presence of other tourist trucks. The group was commencing to put up their tents when they were told to hold off. Hayley entered negotiations with the other tour truck operators and the camp manager. The outcome was that another tent site had been arranged and they had to move.

After dinner, it was off to the waterhole for the wildlife procession at dusk. They saw giraffes, elephants and white rhinoceri. They then went to the bar for a few drinks before going to bed.

The group hurriedly prepared to be in time for their morning game drive. They drove around for over two hours sighting zebras, giraffes, honey badgers and squirrels.

Returning to camp, Roland learned that some of the tourists stayed up all night at the waterhole and apparently witnessed a lion and a cheetah darting through. He went to the waterhole later that morning and spent half an hour viewing the gemsboks, springboks and zebras. He then spent some time poolside, until it was time for the afternoon game drive.

A number of the tourists were tired of the drives and elected not to go. Those that did join the drive had low expectations so they grabbed a few beers to make the drive more enjoyable.

It took some time to get to the areas where the animals were more likely to roam. Roland had a beer and dozed off, but was awoken when the truck came to a sudden halt. There was a lioness on one end of a field and a white rhinoceros at the other end. They then visited a waterhole and saw two more lions. On the move again, they passed some dik-diks and came to a line of elephants crossing the road just ahead of them. Overall, it was their best game drive and they celebrated with beers all round.

Roland enjoyed dinner and then went to the waterhole for a little while. He was tired, but he didn't want to leave the waterhole in case he missed something, but ended up going to bed at around midnight without seeing much.

Waking up at various times during the night, Roland was too tired to go to the waterhole and sensed that this game watching was becoming an obsession. Even so, he got up and went to the waterhole at 5.00 am. He stayed there for an hour without evidencing any activity and walked back to camp where Annette was preparing breakfast.

Debbie ran to the camp. "There's a pride of lions at the waterhole," she declared. Annette cursed as she was on breakfast duty.

"You can go, as I've already seen heaps of lions," Roland stated. So Annette went off and Roland took over breakfast duty.

The group departed the Okaukuejo Camp for their long drive to the Namibian town of Outjo. They stopped for the shopping and then continued on to Twyfelfontein for lunch. They then inspected the animal rock engravings at one of Africa's finest rock art sites. They moved on, passing some elephants amongst a lovely remote setting before they arrived at their rough camp.

They got up to catch the sunrise with Matt making a cracking pace up the mountain. They made the top in time to see the sun come up and took a few photos of the Namib Desert and Brandberg Mountain. After breakfast, they packed up and took group photos with their truck in the background.

The group was on route to Swakopmund when they stopped to examine and take photos of the Welwitsches plant. It was a plant estimated at 1,000 years old that had its two leaves sprawling on the ground. Roland was fascinated by the plant and liked its local name that translated to, "two leaves never die."

As they approached the Skeleton Coast, they were warned that it would be somewhat cooler; however, they found the weather to be veritably cold. They stopped at Cape Cross Seal Colony and the passengers had to urge themselves to brave the elements in order to observe the sea lions.

Moving on, they stopped at Spitzkoppe Pub for a burger and a few games on the L and Y shaped pool tables. They were content to stay in the comfort of the pub; however, they were coaxed to continue. The journey was made slightly more agreeable by drinking beer and butternut schnapps.

When they arrived at the camp in Swakopmund, the passengers were allocated bunks in holiday bungalow chalets. After dinner, they marched to the pub for a few beers and shooters before retiring.

The following morning, the group was driven by combi vans to the sand dunes. They were given instructions and took turns to sand-board down the dunes. The 40 kilometres per hour run was found to be fairly tame and they were then given the option of a steeper run, which was estimated to be double the speed.

It was stressed how important it was to maintain a strong grip on the boards, particularly at the end, as the run finished up on a gravel surface. After the first few sand boarders came off, a couple of the others opted out. The next few that attempted the run survived intact. Roland made the run all right; however, he did find it hard to hold onto the board when he hit the gravel.

Burly Eric was the last to take off and he was doing it easy until he hit the gravel. The board stopped, but he continued, scraping himself along the ground for some distance. When he stood, his sleeves and pants were torn and his arms and legs were bloodied.

"You were supposed to hang on to the board," the onlookers reminded him.

The sand-boarders were treated to some bread rolls and beer before being driven back to the holiday bungalows. They then set off for a ride on quad bikes. They spent a bit of time at the office filling out the indemnity waivers and then set off for the sand dunes where they were distributed gloves, a helmet and a quad bike.

They dragged off on the quad bikes and the importance of following the guides and the correct lines was highlighted when they approached some gigantic dunes with steep falls. They had a welcome shower to wash off the sand from the day's activities.

After dinner, they kicked on at a nightclub where they partied until the early hours with a few travellers from another tour truck.

Roland woke up reasonably early, but couldn't make himself to get out of bed until almost midday. He had breakfast and did some laundry before hitting the town. He visited the Windhoek Bank in Swakopmund and changed his excess Namibian dollars for South African rand. He then went for a long walk around town and the nearby dunes to take a few photographs.

Returning to the municipal bungalows, the group gathered for dinner then set off to celebrate Nicky's birthday at the pub. They continued partying at a nightclub where Roland resisted the advances of lady, whom he found unattractive and her appearance did not seem to improve with extreme intoxication.

A few people were feeling hung-over as they left Swakopmund. They drove through the Namib Desert where the landscape featured craters, large sand dunes, baron plains, layered rocks and mountains. The vegetation and colours varied dramatically from baron land of grey, red and brown, to lush green vegetation. They were sights that captured their imaginations.

The group reached the camp at Sesriem where they had a drink before heading off to Sossusvlei in the Namib-Naukluft National Park. They were highly impressed by the sand dunes at Swakopmund and they found the dunes at Sossusvlei to be just as impressive. They moved on, heading for Aus and found a location about 50 kilometres from the town to set up a rough camp.

The group headed off in the morning in very cool climate. They arrived at the diamond mine ghost town of Kolmannskuppe and waited for the tour amongst cold winds and whirling sands. They visited a typical house, the casino with an entertainment hall and the old-style bowling alley where Charlotte got a strike and was awarded a certificate. They were allowed to explore more of the ghost town where they inspected the former doctor's house and the former mine manager's house.

They made sure everyone was present and accounted for before they left the ghost town and moved on to their lodge at the coastal port town of Luderitz. Roland took the spare time to go for a walk and visited the port, Shark Island, the town centre and the Lutheran Church situated high on a hill.

The group purchased booze from the bottle shop and had pre-dinner drinks. The evening activities were held at the lodge, which included games of cards, quoits, table tennis and more drinking.

They got up when it suited them and helped themselves to breakfast. They left Luderitz later than day, drove by Kolmannskuppe, through Aus and stopped for lunch. They then moved on to Fish River Canyon, the second largest canyon in the world.

They set off for a hike to the bottom of the canyon where they took in the views and had a dip in the river before heading back. They then drove to the main viewing point at Hell's Corner where they took in the view at sunset and stayed admiring the scenery until they were called for dinner.

The group was ready for their scheduled departure at six o'clock in the morning although the camp gates didn't open until 6.20 am. They drove for about three hours before having brunch on the side of the road. They continued until they hit the town of Springbok and stayed there for enough time to grab some lunch.

There was another stop at Gariep, with the bottle shop doing good business. They then travelled towards their camp at Citrusdale, drinking champagne along the way. After pitching their tents, they went for the ten minute hike up the track for the cold and hot pools. The hike to the toilet block took only five minutes.

After dinner, Roland took another five minute hike to the toilet before going to bed. It was very cold at night so he slept dressed in his track suit, buried in his sleeping bag. The cold caused him to have a much interrupted sleep and he got up a number of times for hikes to the toilet.

In the morning, the group went for a dip in the cold and hot pools before breakfast. Hayley handed out questionnaires for the trip, which Roland had some trouble filling out as he thought the 50 day camping safari felt more like work than a holiday.

The group headed off for Stellenbosch and freshened up before they went to a restaurant for dinner. They stayed on for a few shooters before they migrated to a pub with an open fire and enjoyed a few beers.

Roland woke to the sounds of Sue's voice. He went for a walk and took a photo of the Toy and Miniature Museum before he made his way back to his accommodation. The group headed off and visited two wineries before returning to Stellenbosch for lunch at a pub.

On the way to Cape Town, they stopped at the beach for an impressive view of the sunset over Table Mountain. As if they hadn't had enough to drink, they stopped off at yet another couple of pubs. The stops were appreciated as much for the use of the bathrooms as they were for more drinks.

The group made it to their lodge accommodation and took a while to settle in; however, everyone eventually found a home. A few of the group members had too much to drink and found their beds. The others went to a restaurant where Roland tried the Vetkoek pastry for starters and Springbok for mains. There was a band playing, which got the patrons dancing. They then embarked on a mini pub crawl on their way back to the lodge.

Roland was awoken by the noises made by the cleaner as well as visits from Hayley and Charlotte. He headed to the Cape Town city centre where he walked to Adelphi Shopping and the markets before visiting the Tourist Information to enquire about transport to Table Mountain.

Catching the Golden Arrow bus to Table Mountain, Roland took the cable car. He was enjoying the views of Cape Town and environs when he came across a lady from Sao Paulo. "Do you mind taking my photograph?" he asked and she happily obliged. "Would you like your picture taken?" he then asked and she was ecstatic with the return favour.

Returning to Cape Town, Roland visited the Botanical Gardens, the Houses of Parliament, St Georges Cathedral, Groote Kerk (Great Church), OK Bazaar, City Hall and Grand Parade.

On his way back to the lodge, Roland struck up a conversation with a man from Switzerland who was legally blind, on an invalid pension and travelling around Africa on his own. They walked together for a stretch and Roland found the talk inspirational.

After freshening up, Roland tried to contact a few of the tour members, but they weren't around so he set off alone. He walked to the waterfront where he checked out a few of the bars.

The Moulin Rouge was not quite like its Paris namesake, as it happened to be a strip joint. He paid the 30 rand entrance fee that included four beers with strippers performing a wrestling act. Roland didn't mind the performance; however, he was put off by a group of drunken louts who felt compelled to do their own, impromptu strip, which prompted him to leave.

The next day, the group set off on a peninsular tour. They visited Hout Bay where they took in views of the bay and the Twelve Apostles. They then moved on to Cape Point Nature Reserve. "The Cape Doctor is the wind that blows into Cape Town and is said to clear the city of pestilence and pollution," the tour guide explained.

They went to Cape Point where they enjoyed views from the lighthouse lookout. It was then off for a visit to the Cape of Good Hope where the signs *CAPE OF GOOD HOPE* and *KAAP DIE GOEIE HOOP* made a popular photo shoot backdrop.

The group moved on to see the penguins at Simon's Town and drove through Jamestown and Kalk (Chalk) Bay. They also made a stop to witness some of the 8,000 plus species of plants and the marvellous exhibits of Zimbabwean soap stone sculptures at Kirstenbosch. Returning to Cape Town, they spent a pleasant evening dining and drinking around the Cape Town waterfront.

In the morning, Roland had breakfast and said goodbye to Matt, Hayley and a few of the others. He made off to visit Green Point Stadium and Green Market Square. It was Sunday and the city was very quiet. Returning to the lodge along Martin Street, Roland came across a musical parade, which he thought may have been the Jewish celebration of the Feast of Tabernacles.

Continuing along Martin Street, Roland stopped off for a bite to eat. He then walked back to the lodge and waited for his shuttle to take him to the airport. He arrived at Cape Town International Airport for his flight from Cape Town to Johannesburg. As he was waiting in Johannesburg International Airport for his connecting flight, it dawned on him that he hadn't purchased any wooden carvings.

Scampering around, Roland located many carvings, but not the trio of animals of the size and detail he was seeking. Just as he was about to give up, he saw the common turned head giraffe, a lifelike elephant and a very unlifelike rhino. He made his purchase, which ironically cost him the exact amount that he offered the man at the market.

Heading for his flight, Roland could hear the sound of last call. It was an eight hour haul from Johannesburg to Perth and a further three hour flight to Melbourne.

Arriving home, Roland immediately set off to visit his dad. After a little while, he tentatively asked his dad, "How's Mum?"

"Your mother," his father replied, "oh she's all right."

On this reply, Roland hurried off to visit his mum.

Chapter 38 – The New Millennium

The moment Roland arrived at the nursing home, he was struck by the vision of his mother in her special chair – the one his father had bought for her. John saw Paola every day and changes in her were not that noticeable to him. However, it was obvious to Roland that his mother had become quite emaciated and her response was virtually negligible.

Roland assisted Paola on a small walk. Feeding was very difficult as his mother had problems chewing and swallowing her food. The carer suggested that gentle massaging of her throat may assist.

Roland cried all of the way home. He then paced his hallway trying to come to terms with the situation. The idea of ever travelling again was cast from his mind.

It was 3.00 am on Wednesday, 28th July 1999 when the phone rang, rousing Roland from sleep. He jumped from bed, rushed down the dark corridor and lifted the receiver. It was a lady from the nursing home. "Paola has passed away in her sleep," she said as kindly as she could.

"Has my father been advised?" Roland asked, holding himself together.

"No," she said. "We thought we would contact the son."

"That's okay, I'll let my father know. Thanks for the call."

The moment Roland replaced the receiver, he fell to his knees and broke down. He spent a few minutes on his knees crying before he realised he had to call his father.

Roland steeled himself for the dreadful moment, picked himself up and made the call. "Dad," he said, choking on the word. "The nursing home rang and advised that Mum has passed away."

"What do we need to do now?" John immediately asked.

"Sorry," Roland said; he'd not even considered that.

"Can we go and visit her now?" his father asked.

"I expect so, but I'm not sure."

"I will call the nursing home and find out," John said.

"I'm on my way; we can go together," Roland suggested.

"All right," his father replied.

Roland gathered some things then drove to his father's house.

John met him at the door. "We can go to the nursing home now and arrange the other things later," his father explained.

"Dad, I brought some of my things over to stay with you for a few days."

"That's good son, now let's go."

John's training and life experiences were such that he took control and was charged to do his duty. They visited the nursing home and saw both wife and mother seemingly at peace.

Roland stayed with his father for a couple of weeks before he returned to his own house. He gained tremendous support from his father and he liked to think that he gave his father some support too.

John was a tower of strength; however, the strain of taking care of his wife over so many years seemed to have taken its toll. He had a heart condition, which had been managed by medication, but he was often getting breathless and having increasing trouble managing his affairs.

The phone rang early one morning, and Roland had a premonition it would be his father so he rushed to the phone.

"I'm not feeling well," John said, short of breath.

"I'll be right over."

When Roland arrived, John was white, perspiring and shaking. Roland immediately called an ambulance. "I want to be seated on my chair," John stated. Roland helped his father to his favourite chair, placed a blanket on him and massaged his cold hands.

Roland noticed John's gaze seemed distant. "Dad…Dad…" but his father was quivering and unresponsive.

John eventually came to.

"Dad, why didn't you respond to me?" asked Roland.

"I don't know."

The ambulance arrived and the paramedics took over. "We'll have to take John to hospital as his heart is very weak."

When Roland arrived at the hospital, he was briefed by a cardiologist. "John's heart is functioning weakly and even if we are able to stabilise his condition we cannot guarantee his heart will be able to function normally," the doctor said gently. "I recommend a pacemaker be fitted. As his next of kin, do you approve this operation?"

Roland readily gave his approval.

Even though Roland's faith had left him, he prayed. "Lord, you've taken my mother, please don't take my father too, not now, I couldn't bear it."

The cardiologist emerged after a couple of hours. "The operation went well, and John is doing fine. Go home and try to get some sleep. You can visit your father later."

John recovered with the pacemaker giving him a new lease on life, and things returned to some form of normality. "Do you have any plans?" Roland's father asked him one day.

"No," Roland replied. "I don't have any plans."

Roland was still grieving his mother's death, and his father's heart episode had given him a further scare so he was content to spend time with his father. There may be a time when Roland would continue his travels, but now was not that time.

There was an enormous hullabaloo at New Year's Eve bringing in the year 2000. However, for John and Roland, it was a gathering at the family home of just the two of them.

The year 2000 was a quiet and reflective period where John and Roland spent much time together. In early 2001, Roland became restless and started thinking about travelling again.

Researching the Mesoamerican civilizations such as the Aztecs and Mayans, Roland was fascinated with the similarities between them and the ancient Egyptians. He was also interested in the history and circumstances surrounding Cuba. Since the fall of the Iron Curtain and the withdrawal of Russian support, Cuba appeared to be a country within a world of its own. He was also beguiled by the life and writings of Ernest Hemmingway, which were influenced by Cuba.

Given his interest in Cuba and its proximity to Central America, Roland began forming his travel ideas. He read various brochures and picked up on a tour referred to as The Lost World. This brought to mind Arthur Conan Doyle's fictional adventure of the expedition to a volcanic plateau above the Amazonian rainforest.

Venezuela featured the added attraction of Angel Falls. Roland had already visited Victoria Falls and Iguassu Falls – the largest and widest waterfalls in the world – he now had the chance to see the highest waterfalls in the world.

Roland made his plans then sat back to contemplate the prospect of embarking on his first trip in three years. It would be a journey that would take him to Cuba, Mexico, Central America and Venezuela.

The day before his scheduled departure, Roland visited his mother's grave then had dinner with his father before staying up all night performing his packing while he watched Wimbledon.

Chapter 39 – Cuba

It was early morning Wednesday, 4th July 2001, when Roland arrived at the airport for his 06:45 Qantas QF406 flight to Sydney and his connecting Japan Airlines JL772 flight to Tokyo. The free stopover in Narita gave him the opportunity to enjoy a good night's sleep, a wonderful buffet breakfast and a walk around the delightful township.

Roland checked out the Naritasan Shinshoji Temple, the Grand Pagoda and Naritasan Park, which had the largest gold fish he had ever seen. He took the shuttle back to Narita International Airport and caught his 17:45 Japan Airlines JL12 flight to Mexico City.

By the time Roland collected his luggage and went through the formalities at the Mexico City Airport, it was almost 9.00 pm. He had not booked accommodation and, as he had a very early morning flight the next day, he decided to spend the night in the airport. He placed his backpack in a locker and found a comfortable spot.

Roland had a sleepless night, doing quite a bit of walking around and spending long periods admiring the work of the cleaners as they undertook a masterly and meticulous job of buffing the floor tiles. He eventually caught his 07:55 Lacsa Airlines flight LR691 to San Jose, followed by his connecting 11:20 Lacsa flight LR622 to Havana.

Arriving in the early evening, Roland shared a cab with a couple of guys, apparently the done thing in Havana. He was dropped off a hundred metres or so from the entrance to his hotel so he lugged his baggage to the hotel reception. There were a few local kids playing in the street who were fascinated to observe the stranger struggling with his backpack.

The hotel was a delightful Spanish-style edifice with a lovely courtyard situated in the old part of Havana – Havana Vieja. The hotel was surrounded by some stunning, although rundown, Spanish colonial buildings.

Roland checked in, had a shower and headed off to experience the scene. It was a very warm and humid evening with intensity about the city. He made his way through some of the old, narrow streets, finding himself at the Malecon overlooking the old fort.

It was an impressive esplanade where waves from the Gulf of Mexico crashed against the rocky shore. Roland was soon being approached by a number of local opportunists, but managed to ward them off and returned to his hotel for a good night's sleep.

Roland embarked on a walking tour of Havana Vieja where he visited the Capitolio, Paseo de Marti, Museo de la Revolucion, Real Fabrica de Tobacos Partagas and Real Fabrica de Tobacos La Corona. He enjoyed his walk, although he was frustrated by the hustlers who tried to sell him an array of products, such as accommodation, rum, cigars and women.

Returning to the hotel for a rest, it was mid-evening when Roland freshened up and sought out a restaurant for dinner. He then went to a couple of bars before ending up at the National nightclub near the Capitolio where there was a floor show with a band playing salsa music.

Roland was seated at one end of a table and there were a few young ladies seated at the other end. He ordered a beer and was content to sit and watch the show. One of the ladies at his table approached him and asked whether he wanted to dance. He politely declined.

The lady started to play around and make a nuisance of herself. The other ladies thought it was all very amusing, but Roland was irritated by her and tried to ignore her antics.

"My name is Amelia. What's your name?" she asked in Spanish.

"Roland," he curtly replied.

Amelia proceeded to make herself comfortable next to Roland and helped herself to sips of his beer. He was less than impressed. "Could you leave me alone?" he asked.

"Why do you want to be alone? Don't you want to go with me?"

"I'm not interested," Roland responded.

Amelia obviously didn't put up with rejection, as she began to move to the music and made her way onto Roland's lap. It wasn't long after she buried her rump into select parts of his anatomy that he gave in. "That does it; vamos!" he declared.

"Can we go to your hotel?" asked Amelia.

"This is not possible," Roland stated, without actually knowing whether this was the case.

Amelia led him to a very old and rundown building where she stayed with a few of her girlfriends. It was a very basic and uncomfortable abode with no air-conditioning. He spent a couple of hours with her before he wandered back to the cool and comfort of his hotel room.

The next day, Roland set off on a very long walk to and around the Vedado area. He covered some of the newer suburbs of inner Havana and visited the Plaza de la Revolucion and the Necropolis Cristobal Colon, stated to be the second largest cemetery in the world.

Making his way back, Roland passed by the Hotel Nacional, which stood out on a cliff overlooking the Malecon. He then walked along the Malecon, taking in the sea wind from the Atlantic Ocean and the Straits of Florida. He was exhausted by the time he arrived back at his hotel so he thought he would rest up and ended up falling asleep, waking in the late evening.

It was Sunday night and Havana Vieja seemed quiet. Many of the establishments were closed, but Roland managed to find a restaurant that was still open and serving food. It was midnight when he ate his dinner, which he was enjoying until a small number of regular patrons partook in their group karaoke. The unpleasant sounds encouraged him to finish up his meal and leave for the peace of his hotel room.

Roland booked the hotel for only three nights, although he had details of a contact that ran a Casa Particular in Havana. A Casa Particular provided the opportunity to experience a stay with a Cuban family and gain an insight into the Cuban way of life.

Giving the contact a call, Roland was advised the owner was not available and to call back later. He went for a walk and found himself visiting the usual tourist spots of Havana Vieja. He came across Ernest Hemmingway's inscription. *My mojito in La Bodeguita My daiquiri in El Floridita.* This prompted him to follow the words by trying the two drinks at the designated bars.

Returning to the hotel, Roland booked a Vinales Tour then tried calling the guy from the Casa Particular and this time he was available. They agreed a price and he made his way to Vedado where he was met by Vera who lived in the apartment with her husband Gino. Gino was out, but was to return soon.

Roland was shown to his room and settled in. The apartment was in a high-rise, concrete building. It was very basic accommodation, but it was clean. The room had an air-conditioner, albeit Russian-built and sounding like a tractor.

Gino returned and took Roland to the local shops where they bought some groceries at Roland's expense before they returned to the apartment. "We are pleased to offer you an introductory dinner free of charge," Gino stated.

Roland got on very well with Gino and Vera. They told him quite a bit about life in Cuba and were happy to answer any of his questions. "I have no interest in politics," Gino advised. "I just try to make a reasonable living under whatever regime is in place."

After dinner, Roland went out to check out the nightlife in the Vedado precinct. He visited a couple of lively bars before trying a bar that Gino suggested. It was a strange bar with some performers seemingly just reciting Spanish words to music. He didn't find the place to his liking, thinking it all a bit too arty-farty.

There was a break in proceedings when a female compére asked where the various patrons were from. To Roland's surprise the people were largely tourists, with the young man next to him being from Ireland. "How did you ever end up in a hell hole like this?" Roland asked.

"I have no idea," replied the man.

"Well, I don't know about you, but I'm off to check out a nightclub that was recommended," Roland advised and the man was happy to tag along.

Kelvin was tall, fair haired and 20 years of age. He was studying in Cuba and spoke fluent Spanish. They shared a cab to the nightclub located close to the Plaza de la Revolucion. They entered the place and it was jumping. "Do you want a drink?" Roland asked Kelvin and beer was the predictable choice.

Whilst Roland was buying the beers, a few girls approached Kelvin. He was the stand-out tourist and the girls didn't waste much time pursuing their prey. Kelvin seemed a little uncomfortable with the attention so Roland handed him a beer and started chatting with him.

The guys were left alone for a little while before a few of the ladies led them onto the dance floor. It wasn't long before the infectious beat hit both of them and they were enjoying some basic Latin moves with their Cuban hosts. They danced for almost an hour when a show commenced and they took a seat.

Roland was chatting with one of the ladies he'd danced with, named Camila. She was a very slim, mature-aged, single mother. Kelvin was talking with an attractive, blonde lady who propositioned him. "I have a girlfriend back in Ireland and I'm not interested in any other women," Kelvin was quick to advise.

Once the lady learned Kelvin wasn't interested, she started on Roland. Speaking a little English, Camila translated on behalf of the blonde. "She wants to go with you Roland."

"I'm not interested in going with her," he responded.

"Why not? Don't you find her attractive?" Camila queried.

"Yes, I find her very attractive, but I like you."

Camila looked at Roland and was a little surprised as she assumed he would have preferred her much younger friend.

"Would you like to go with me?" Roland asked.

Camila looked at him again before she led him away. They took a cab to the Casa Particular and they went to bed. "What are you expecting?" Roland asked her.

"What do you mean?" Camila replied.

"I understand women in Cuba expect money to go with tourists," Roland explained.

"I know this is normally the case," Camila stated, "but I don't want to discuss money."

Feeling uncomfortable, Roland didn't know what to do or say. "It's okay," he eventually blurted out; however, Camila started foreplay. "It's not necessary," he stated.

"It's all right," Camila said, continuing the foreplay. "I want to."

Roland thought he had experienced some good sex in his time, but he had never experienced anything like what Camila lashed out. She was exceptionally gymnastic, flexible and obviously very sexually experienced. She engaged him in extensive foreplay and gave him pleasures that he couldn't have possibly imagined.

Camila departed in the early hours and left her contact details. Roland fell asleep and was fortunate to have Gino wake him in time for his tour to Vinales. He was still hung over from the previous night and felt like crap as the bus made its way through the picturesque countryside.

The tour visited a tobacco factory where Roland bought a cigar. They visited a rum factory where he was induced into tasting their renowned distilled produce. They then visited a liquor factory where he indulged in more of the local concoctions. Finally, it was off to the numerous caves with unusual rock paintings that abounded the areas of the Vinales and the Pinar del Rio.

Returning to the casa, Roland caught up with some overdue sleep. When he awoke, he rang Camila and invited her on an excursion for the following day. He was happy with his plans as he sat down to dinner with Vera and Gino.

After dinner, they watched the movie *Seven Years in Tibet* with Brad Pitt. Roland thought it both strange and ironic that he found himself in a Cuban Casa Particular, with strangers that felt like family, watching an American movie on cable television.

Gino borrowed a friend's beat up car for the day's excursion. Vera, Gino and Roland set off and Vera was dropped off at her work. Gino and Roland continued to Camila's address and tracked down her apartment block.

They made the long drive to Playa de Este and found a comfortable spot on the beach with a vendor who provided deck chairs, snacks and refreshments. Gino had a drink before he set off. "I've got a few errands to run," Gino stated. "I'll pick you up at around four."

"Would you like to go for a swim?" Roland asked Camila.

"I don't swim, and I'm not interested in going into the water," Camila advised. She seemed happy sun-bathing so Roland went for a swim.

Roland emerged from the ocean and they ordered pizza and sandwiches. After the food was served, Camila complained. "This pizza is not a pizza, it's rubbish."

"I think it is a pizza, but I must admit it is the first pizza I have ever made," the waiter confessed.

Roland tended to agree with both of them. "I think it is a pizza, but I also think it's rubbish."

Camila was not interested in eating the pizza and only nibbled on the sandwiches. "Would you like to order something else?" asked Roland.

"I wouldn't bother ordering anything else from this place." Camila replied.

"How about we go to the nearby hotel?" Roland suggested.

"You can go," Camila said, "but as I am Cuban, I won't be allowed in."

Roland thought this to be crazy. "Even if you're with me?"

"This makes no difference," Camila told him.

They went for a walk along the beach and when they returned they enjoyed ice cream.

Camila seemed to be in better spirits and finally agreed to join Roland for a dip in the sea. He drew her into the water at a depth where she was unsteady and sought his assistance. At this point of vulnerability, she seemed to let her guard down and started having some fun. A few of the waves rolled over her head and she grasped onto him. She broke out into a smile and then into laughter. It was the first time he'd seen her laugh.

They returned to their deck chairs, both invigorated by their refreshing bathe. "You seem to be having a good time," Gino commented as he returned and joined them for a drink.

Returning to the casa, Camila had a rest whilst dinner was being prepared. It was to be a special dinner that featured steak, a rarity in Cuba, which was enjoyed by all.

Camila and Roland went to the Capri Hotel to check out the show. In its halcyon days, the hotel was a Mecca for gambling, glamour and glitz; however, those days were long past. They checked out a few bars around the Vedado area before returning to the casa and spending the night together.

Camila and Roland arose at the same time, and he packed his belongings in preparation for his onward flight. After breakfast, Camila and Roland said goodbye to Vera and Gino, who saw them off. The taxi dropped Camila off at her apartment and Roland continued to the Havana Jose Marti International Airport.

After paying the taxi fare of $15US and the departure tax of $20US, Roland had $45US left. He checked out a few of the shops and came across a cigar shop. He saw a box of Romeo Y Julieta and enquired about the price. "The cost is $45US," the lady advised.

"Perfecto," Roland commented and he purchased them.

Chapter 40 – Central America

Roland arrived in San Jose and changed some money before catching a cab to his hotel. The cab driver took his own tip, returning only part of the change.

At reception the man behind the counter didn't seem too keen to provide any service. Seeing that Roland wasn't leaving, the man reluctantly attended to him and provided him with a room key.

Entering his room, Roland was not impressed with the standard of his accommodation. The television didn't work and the radio was ripped out of its cabinet. He left the dingy surroundings and went for a walk.

Roland checked out a few bars and restaurants where the people didn't seem to provide much service. He eventually found a diner where he managed to grab a couple of empanadas and a soda before retiring to his depressing hotel room.

The next day, Roland visited a bank, but service was scarce. He went to another bank, but it didn't open until 10.30 am. He walked around and came across a small shop with a shop owner who had a bit of animation about him so he ventured in and purchased two buns, a sweet bread and water. He sat on an outside bench and consumed his shopping items for breakfast.

Roland explored Parque Nacional before giving the banks another try. He was unsuccessful at the first bank, which couldn't provide currency exchange, but managed to obtain currency from the next bank.

Seeking out the attractions in San Jose, Roland visited the Parque Metropolitano La Sabana, Parque Morazan, Parque Francisco Morazan, Parque Central, Catedral Metropolitana and Teatro Nacional. He also visited a tourist agency where he booked a Costa Rica Highlights tour for the following day.

On his way back to the hotel, the heavens opened, drenching Roland. After he had a shower and spruced up he hit the town. He walked around for some time before he settled on a Chinese restaurant for dinner. There didn't seem to be much going on in the city and he didn't feel comfortable on the streets alone so he returned to his hotel.

Roland woke early for his day-tour and was picked up on time at 6.30 am. The tour bus collected others from various hotels before they stopped for breakfast.

The day-tour consisted of four separate attractions with the first being the Poas Volcano. They were perched at a barrier where the crater was located and would have been visible if it weren't for the heavy fog and low-level cloud. "Be patient as your patience will be rewarded," the guide promised.

They waited for some time before Roland piped up. "So how much patience is actually required?" he asked.

"Patience will be your reward," the guide curtly replied. However, the only reward the passengers received was their reprieve from waiting any longer when they left.

The group stopped at a tourist centre where they tried some of the famous Costa Rican coffee, which was stated to be the world's *fourth* best. They viewed the exhibits at the Hummingbird Gallery and also observed a roaming tarantula. They continued on before stopping for lunch at a mountain rainforest lodge.

The second attraction was a walk through the Cloud Forest and a view of La Paz Waterfalls. Roland thought this attraction was good, especially as it was one they could actually see.

The third attraction was a 1½ hour Sarapiqui Jungle River cruise. It was supposed to feature an array of wildlife such as monkeys, iguanas, crocodiles and birds; however, there was few wildlife to be seen. The passengers queried why the animals were not visible and the guide was conspicuous with his silence.

"The animals may have taken the day off," Roland quipped.

The guide was not amused.

The final attraction was a visit to Braulio Carrillo National Park. It was an impressive tropical rainforest rich with tropical plants, waterfalls and wildlife. Unfortunately, the tour bus could only park on the outskirts of the forest and the passengers were only allowed a short time to explore.

The tour took a total of twelve hours and Roland was exhausted upon his return. He had a rest before preparing himself for his last night in San Jose. He found a restaurant where he had a reasonable meal and then sought out some nightlife – a lifeless disco and a dingy bar. He found another bar where he sat down and ordered a beer.

It was a strange bar that showed porno on the television set. Roland struck up a conversation with a guy named Enrique from Mexico who was in San Jose on business. "I find this city a bit lifeless," Roland said.

"I tend to agree," said Enrique. "Although the hotel across the road is good. I was about to go there and you are welcome to join me."

Enrique and Roland strode into the hotel bar and it was teeming with people. Most of them were exquisitely dressed, attractive young ladies and it didn't take long before the two new entrants settled in. The place was abuzz and there was one main thing on the menu: the women.

"So what do you think?" Enrique asked Roland.

"This place is amazing!"

They were approached by an attractive Columbian lady who Enrique had once acquainted himself. "She's interested in going with you," Enrique advised. "The rate is $100US for an hour, room extra."

"Thanks for the offer," Roland responded, "but I think I'll give it a miss."

Once the women ascertained that Roland wasn't buying, they let him be. He felt he'd seen enough and decided to end proceedings. He thanked Enrique, said goodbye and returned to the snake pit of his hotel room.

Roland rose earlier than he needed for his flight to Panama in order to visit the National Museum. It was too early for the museum opening, but he waited until there was sufficient daylight to take a photo of the buildings. He returned to the hotel, grabbed his baggage and took a taxi to the airport.

Arriving in Panama City, Roland immediately looked around for a cambio. There was a team of poachers asking him whether he wanted a taxi, but he declined. One man pursued him. "What are you looking for, sir?" the man asked.

"I'm all right, thank you."

"You need taxi?" the man pestered.

"I'm all right," Roland replied.

Roland then noticed a sign indicating that the cambio was upstairs and he headed for it. Having obtained Panamanian balboa and US dollars, he now actually needed a taxi.

Roland returned into the fray and there was frenzy when he reappeared. A tall man noticed Roland had not yet been captured. "Are you travelling alone?" asked the man.

"I'm catching a cab," Roland said.

The man sensed his suspicion. "It's cheaper if you are willing to share a cab," the man explained.

"I'm willing to share," Roland replied.

The man haggled the price of the $25US single fare to a $15US fare to share. Roland hopped in the cab and gave the man a $1US tip.

The hotel was a little way out of the city centre and after checking in Roland trekked into town. He went through some ghetto-like suburbs, which made him feel a little uneasy. Along the way, he took photographs of San Felipe – Casco Viejo, Plaza de la Independencia, the cathedral and Avenida Central.

It took Roland an hour to get to the centre and he made his way to a lookout where he had fantastic views of the Panama City skyline and Bahia de Panama. He witnessed an amazing sight of a line of cargo ships proceeding to the Panama Canal and he took a photo. Walking around the street he was intrigued by the Diablo Rojo, or Red Devil. It was a bus that was customised and painted in bright colours, which prompted him to take more photos.

On the way back to the hotel, Roland took a different route in order to avoid the seedy areas. He dined at a restaurant near the hotel then stopped off at a supermarket where he stocked up on food for breakfast.

Roland slept in, then had breakfast in his room before sourcing a half-day tour to the Panama Canal for the following day.

Continuing to walk the Panama City streets Roland photographed festivities outside the Iglesia del Carmen then rested before going out for a bite to eat. After dinner, he walked into a bar for a drink and a floor show. It turned out to be a tasteless strip so he returned to his hotel.

In the morning, Roland was picked up for his tour to the Panama Canal in a comfortable air-conditioned van where he was the only passenger. He was taken to the Miraflores Locks and given time to inspect the visitors' centre.

The history of the canal dated back 400 years to King Carlos of Spain. The French attempted to build a canal in the late 1800s, but it wasn't until the early 1900s when the Americans overcame the malarial spreading mosquitoes before having the success of the canal's construction.

Roland saw the locks in action as a large container ship slowly made its way through the two chambers with literally inches to spare on either side.

As it was Roland's last night in Panama City, he planned for a night on the town. He dined at a local-cuisine restaurant and by the time he had finished eating it was approaching midnight. He had an early morning flight and didn't want to risk sleeping in so he decided to stay up all night. Since the only lively place was a strip joint, that's where he went.

The establishment cost $20US to enter, which also covered all the beer you could drink.

"Would you like some company sir?" asked a lady.

"No thanks," Roland replied. "I'll have a beer." He eventually got his beer and gave a $1US tip. The strip show was fairly ordinary, but he didn't mind as he was happy relaxing and drinking his beer.

A couple of ladies started chatting to Roland, but he didn't want to waste their time. "I'm not interested in any company," he revealed, "but I will have another beer." He consumed eight stubbies before he headed back to the hotel in time to catch his taxi.

Roland took the flight from Panama City to San Jose and then had to wait four hours for his connecting flight to Caracas. He relaxed, exhaustion overwhelmed him and he fell asleep. He was upset to have been woken up by the noises made by the unruly crowds until he realised that they actually did him a favour as his flight was boarding.

Arrival in Caracas was in the late afternoon. Roland caught a cab to his hotel and to his amazement neither the cabbie nor the busboy seemed interested in a tip. After checking into his hotel room he went for a walk.

The city was surrounded by mountains with barrios and squatter settlements scattered around. Roland tried an ATM, but it didn't work. As he didn't have enough money to buy dinner and was feeling exhausted he retired to bed.

Roland started the day with the hotel continental breakfast then managed to grab some Venezuelan bolivars from an ATM. He set off for a walk and visited Parque Los Caobas, Pateon Nacional, Plaza Bolivar and the Nuevo Circo Bullring. Having trouble with his bearings it took him a while to find his way to Boulevard Sabana Grande. When he finally arrived, he wrestled with the crowds for some time before he stopped for a bite to eat then headed back to his hotel.

After a rest and a shower, Roland set off to hit the town. "Most places will be closed and it may not be safe walking around on your own," the receptionist advised.

"Thanks for the advice," Roland replied as he walked out.

Roland found the city was very quiet. He stopped at a hotel bar where he had a couple of the local Polar beers. The waitresses were friendly, which was enough of an incentive for him to stay for dinner. He then tried to find some nightlife, but was unsuccessful so he returned to his hotel.

Waking up late, Roland went for a walk and stopped at a restaurant for breakfast. He moved on to the Jardin Botanico and found himself walking along a creek where he had to contend with a couple of local crackpots. The men turned out to be harmless and he was able to pass them by.

Palacio Miraflores caught Roland's eye as he walked to the Chacao area. On his way back to the hotel, he bought some fresh fruit for lunch.

Roland had a siesta before he headed out again. He stopped at a pizza joint for pizza and beer. He walked about town, but couldn't find anything worth investigating. He then stumbled upon a pub, but felt that it was too seedy so he returned to the hotel bar for a few drinks and then hit the sack.

The next day was the first day of The Lost World tour. Roland went in search of a bank to change some Venezuelan bolivars into US dollars, which he required for the tour. He found a cambio and, after eventually figuring out how the two-stage security doors worked and satisfying the guards that he was no threat, he changed his money.

The tour group meeting started off with brief introductions. Carlos, the tour guide, provided some general information before he led the group to a restaurant where they enjoyed a tapas dinner.

There was a total of 14 passengers made up of seven women and seven men. The group included an English family consisting of a professor, his wife, their teenage daughter and their younger teenage son. Of the passengers, 11 were English, there was one Scotsman and one Welshman. Roland was to share accommodation with the Welshman, named Gavin, a 22-year-old, happy-go-lucky guy.

After a restless sleep, Roland joined the group for breakfast. They were then off to explore the Avila National Park with its imposing mountain range that dominated the large city of Caracas.

It was a beautiful, sunny day and, being Sunday, the trail was packed with people. The tour group hiked up the Sabas Nieves route amongst many local hikers. Although it was mild when they set off, it was cool when they reached the top. They spent half an hour enjoying the magnificent views of Caracas before they strode down the mountain in a fraction of the time of their ascent and caught cabs back to the hotel.

Roland prepared his things for the upcoming trek then freshened up and joined the others at the hotel bar where they indulged in a light snack and a few drinks before having an early night.

The group caught their early morning flight from Caracas to Puerto Ordaz then took a bus where they passed through the area of El Dorado. Carlos provided a description of the penitentiary before he explained the fable.

"El Dorado, Spanish for the gilded one, developed into a story based partly on native mythology and partly on the tale of white explorers. The story was taken so seriously by a number of explorers from around the world that they tried in vain to find non-existent riches. For some of the explorers, the pursuit cost them their lives."

The group stopped for lunch near a bridge that was donated by the French Government and constructed by the company that made the Eiffel Tower. They then drove for eight hours and finally arrived at their camp at Kawe near Kaimouran. Mount Roraima, the destination of their trek, was now within their sights.

After breakfast, the group was driven by bus up to San Francisco de Yurani where they transferred onto four-wheel drive vehicles that took them to Peraitepui de Roraima. It was at this point where they would commence their six-day hike up the mountain.

Chapter 41 – The Lost World

Porters carried the food, tents and camping equipment, and each hiker could decide whether they would carry their own packs or have them carried by a porter. Roland was the odd one out and was without a porter. "If you want a porter to carry your pack, an extra porter could be called," Carlos advised.

Three of the younger male hikers had elected to carry their own packs and, rather than hold up the group to summon another porter, Roland decided to carry his pack as well.

The terrain was wet and the first half hour of the trek was steep and slippery. They hiked for about four hours and Roland found the going tough, but Carlos spurred him on with a few words of encouragement.

They came across a few hikers who were returning from their trek and they described their journey as torturous. The group dismissed the stories as high exaggeration. At the end of the first day of hiking, the group had a refreshing swim in a stream before dinner and resting their weary bones.

The second day was much easier and the hikers arrived at base camp to be greeted with bread and cold lemon tea. This was followed by tuna salad that included onions, an ingredient that was bound to repeat on Roland, and it did.

The group hung around base camp that afternoon with several other hikers. Dinner was a basic meal, although the group thoroughly enjoyed it as they quickly came to realise how good basic food could taste when one was really hungry.

On day three, Roland found the hike strenuous and was relieved to stop for lunch. They were soon encouraged to continue as they were approaching the hotel. They arrived at the top camp and it was revealed the so-called hotel was, in fact, a cave. Coffee, tea and bickies were served on their arrival and they were given a brief tour of the accommodation and surrounds.

Getting to the spot that was referred to as the toilet was precarious and required mountaineering skills. *If you think I'm going to go to all that trouble and risk my life for a crap, you are sadly mistaken,* Roland thought. *I'd rather crap my pants.*

The group surveyed the mountaintop and walked to the edge. "Take care," advised Colin, a mature-aged and experienced hiker. Before Roland had a chance to ask why, he looked down into a sheer drop of some 2,800 metres.

The views all around were spectacular, from the huge open areas of the Gran Sabana, to the plateau-shaped ranges of the tepuis with the clouds giving the scene a certain mystique. The views featured an abundance of unique plants and animal life within the Canaima National Park.

The group took turns in lying down to lean over the edge to take photos. The sheer-walled, flat-topped mountain of the tepui was a most eerie place. Its rock surface and unusual vegetation made them feel as though they were on the surface of another planet.

The group arose to a breakfast of porridge, coffee and tea. They then headed off for a morning hike to visit the other end of Mount Roraima. Along the way, Jim's boot fell apart and he was absolutely distraught. "How am I ever going to get down?" he cried.

Carlos lent Jim his Wellingtons. Carlos seemed comfortable walking around bare foot and he led the group back to the hotel with ease, arriving back in time for lunch.

Roland took an afternoon nap and was awoken by Theresa. "The clouds are breaking up and the sun is starting to shine through!" she advised excitedly.

The views were at their best and Roland rushed to get his camera to take another set of photos. After dinner, the group had an early night ahead of their return hike down the mountain the next day.

The group was preparing for the descent when nature called on Roland. He'd put it off for as long as he could, but he could wait no longer – he had to have a crap. He climbed the rock then made his way along the ledge to the crevice, which was the natural toilet. "Here goes," he muttered, "and let's hope I don't fall in." After quite a bit of trouble, he managed to exercise his bowels.

On his way back to the cave, Roland noticed Jim exercising his bowels, but not in the designated place. "Hey Jim, that's not the toilet," Roland pointed out.

"It is for me," answered Jim. "There's no way you'd get me climbing up to the toilet; I'd rather crap my pants."

Jim was ecstatic as Gavin gifted him a spare pair of boots that fit him perfectly. The group set off and Roland felt good, but still found the going tough. The river crossings were tricky as the currents had picked up, and it was rocky and slippery underfoot. Word had got around to take off their boots, walk in their socks and use a stick in each hand for support.

The final stages before base camp were very steep and slippery. They made it to base camp in three hours and had lunch before continuing on. The heavens then opened as they reached the final river crossing. Given the level of the water, Carlos decided that they shouldn't cross that day. They made camp to the delight of the exhausted travellers and had dinner encircled around a camp fire.

Roland's backpack was drenched. "You might want to try one of these plastic covers next time," Gavin suggested.

"Yeah right, thanks Gavin; like there's going to be a next time."

The group started off on the final day's hike. It was such a long and hard hike that a few of them, including Roland, really struggled. They finally reached the point named San Francisco and there were celebrations as Carlos handed the hikers a cold beer or cola.

There was a scale and a number of the hikers were weighing their packs. One of the guides, William, had a pack weighing over 30 kilograms. "Can I have my pack weighed?" Roland asked. "It was originally 18 kilograms, but with all the rain I reckon it'd be over 20 kilograms now."

"Not quite," the weigher declared. "It's 18 kilograms."

The group took the four-wheel drives to their lunch stop before they moved on to St. Helena where they checked into a hotel and it was a real hotel. They then went to indulge in an all-you-can-eat dinner.

Most of the group decided to retire so it was left to the younger lads and Roland to go off cruising with Carlos and William. They stopped off at a bar where they played pool and drank beer. Carlos then departed, which left William to take over and lead the group.

They stopped off at a discotheca, which was a sleazy strip joint where the younger lads were happy to be entertained by the ladies. A couple of the guys took out their cash to determine what their funds could afford. Roland wasn't interested in what was on offer and preferred to get stuck into the rum and coke. They returned to their accommodation with the younger lads eagerly discussing their experiences.

After breakfast, the group set off on a Cessna flight that allowed them to admire the expansive and spectacular views over the Grand Savanna. Roland found the experience rewarding, although also testing as he was well and truly hung over.

The group visited a waterfall featuring The Crack, which they reached by pulling themselves against the current along a rope suspended above the river. They relaxed for a couple of hours before being picked up in four-wheel drives and driven to a river bank.

They took motorized canoes to their overnight stay along the Carrao River where they were to sleep in hammocks. It was Roland's first time sleeping in a hammock and he was pleasantly surprised that he actually managed to get some good sleep.

The group continued on after breakfast in the motorized canoes up the Carrao River. They stopped to see a plane wreck and to examine a manioc plant, also referred to as a cassava plant, from which the locals made the alcoholic brew of chichi.

They walked through a souvenir precinct where there were local products, such as blow guns and necklaces. They arrived at camp and were treated to lunch before heading through the jungle for a swim. Back at camp, Roland watched a rain downpour from undercover before joining the others for dinner and going to bed soon after.

Roland had a restless night, partly due to the overnight storm. After breakfast, the group departed and arrived at their next camp at midday. They had lunch before setting off in motorized canoes towards Angel Falls.

They were in the canoes for only 15 minutes before they disembarked and hiked for a further 45 minutes. Angel Falls was in clear sight, a couple of hundred metres dead ahead. There wasn't much sound emanating from the waterfall and one had to focus to spot the water movement.

The waterfall started from its 975 metre high point with limited water coming over Auyan Tepui, also named Devil's Mountain. The water expanded and dissipated into a vaporized mist that seemed to hang like a cloud just above the lake. The group was initially disappointed with the lack of impact of the falls, but as they took in the subtle images and effects of the falls they became much more appreciative.

Canoes were positioned along the bank and they boarded in small groups. The canoes slowly floated towards the bottom of the falls where they could feel the spray that the mist gave off. They took a number of photos and after making it back to the bank they assembled for a group photo.

The group returned to camp and discussed their adventure over a cup of lime tea, coffee and bickies. It was a relaxing afternoon and they later sat down to dinner. A few of the travellers seemed to be drawn to view the falls by moonlight and, although the visuals of the falls seemed more illusionary than real, they could sense its presence.

Roland got up early in the morning after hearing the porters chatting away and he felt compelled to view the falls again. One of the porters, named Carluccio, noticed him wandering towards the falls. "I can show you a good view," Carluccio said.

The sun was rising and there was sunbeam that was filling the whole valley. Devil's Mountain was giving off a strong glow from the reflection of the sunbeam with Angel Falls featuring in the centre. Roland admired the glorious vision before he captured it in a photograph. Carluccio obligingly took a photograph of Roland with the good view in the background.

After breakfast, the group took the motorized canoes to visit the Sopa Waterfall. The travellers were able to go for an invigorating walk between the rock face and the falls with water crashing down into the lagoon right in front of them.

The group had lunch before they took the canoes to Canaima then walked to their hotel near the laguna. They visited the beach and went for a swim before they helped themselves to the mangos hanging off the trees that sprawled the area. They then freshened up and dressed for dinner at a restaurant where they stayed for a few after-dinner drinks and a dance before retiring.

It was the last full day of the tour and Roland sluggishly got up to have breakfast. He then joined Colin and Jim to check out the souvenir shop. He loitered around the snack bar and purchased some ginger bread and a cola to tide him over until lunchtime.

Leaving the hotel, the group was driven to Ciudad Bolivar Airport. On display was the 1930s vintage Flamingo monoplane, El Rio Caroni. It was the plane of the famous adventurer Jimmy Angel who first sighted Angel Falls in 1935. In 1937 Jimmy Angel rested his plane on the top of the falls where it remained for 33 years until it was airlifted out and placed on display.

The group took their flight from Canaima to Simon Bolivar Airport in Caracas and were transported to the beach resort town of Chichiriviche, situated on the Caribbean coast. It was a very long and tiring drive along a winding and undulating road. Parts of the road were unsealed and other parts were under reconstruction.

After their rough ride, they were relieved to check into their comfortable hotel rooms. They had dinner and then hit the town. There were limited options so they entered a quiet bar and were happy to have a few relaxing drinks before retiring to bed.

Rising when his alarm went off, Roland proceeded to the restaurant where a lady advised that breakfast was not served until 8.00 am. He returned to his room, picked up his camera and went for a stroll along the beach where he took a photo. He was eventually allowed into the restaurant and enjoyed the American breakfast.

Roland went to the pool area where he came across Carlos and enquired about his transfer back to Caracas. "I can arrange for a friend of mine to drive you, which will cost around 25,000 bolivars," Carlos said.

"The tour information states that the transfer to the airport is included," Roland advised.

"I don't know anything about this, and I don't have the money so you will have to pay," Carlos responded.

"I request that you contact the tour company to provide my transfer as stipulated in the tour dossier," Roland stated.

"I will see what I can do," Carlos replied.

Roland sun-bathed and had a swim at the hotel pool before he returned to his room to pack. He re-emerged to say goodbye to the group and then queried Carlos about the transfer arrangements.

"I couldn't find out anything," Carlos advised. "So you will have to pay for the transfer if you want to return to Caracas to make your flight."

"I thank you for the tour and I will pay for the transfer, but I will also be taking the matter up with your tour company," Roland said.

Roland took the ride to Caracas Airport in a very uncomfortable, rundown four-wheel drive vehicle. It was extremely hot and he was convinced that the heater was on so he checked with the driver. "I don't think so," the driver replied.

It was an enormous relief for Roland when they arrived at the airport, but he then had to contend with the usual harassment from the guys trying to carry his luggage. He fought his way through to reach the Grupo Taco check-in.

Roland had some spare bolivars so he took his place in the queue and, after having to put up with some fairly bad service, he purchased a can of cola for 950 bolivars. He then noticed a vending machine that had the same can of cola for 400 bolivars.

Taking a seat at a bar, Roland purchased a large coffee. He had to wait some time before boarding so he started reflecting on the tour and made the following entries in his diary.

The Lost World

14 made up of 11 English, 1 Welshman, 1 Scot and 1 me.

Gay, Amanda, Gary, Gavin and Colin were fun.

The professor, wife and kids were suitably know-it-alls.

Bill was incessantly trivial, but only rarely annoying.

Jim had a temper and was a gleeful receiver.

Chris and Lisa were pleasant honeymooners.

Caracas is a metropolis.

Outside of Caracas, Venezuela is a wilderness.

I survived the Mt Roraima hike, carrying my own pack.

Hey, I got to see Angel Falls. ✓

Chapter 42 – Mexico

It was early evening by the time Roland arrived in Cancun. The airport had a carefree feel about it until a security guard pulled him up. "I want to see your passport and I want to know where you have come from," was the demand.

Roland handed over his passport. "I've just flown in from San Jose," he replied.

"Are you telling me the truth?"

"Yes, I'm telling you the truth," Roland said. "I've travelled from Caracas via San Jose."

The security guard walked off with the passport and gestured for Roland to follow. The interrogation continued as he led Roland into a room. "Where do you come from? Do you speak Spanish? Have you been to Cuba?"

Roland tried to keep up with the questions. "I'm from Australia. I don't speak Spanish, and I've spent six days in Cuba."

The security guard checked with another man who went through Roland's documentation. The security guard continued with the questions. "What is your business in Mexico?"

"My business in Mexico is a holiday, which is part of a two months overseas holiday," Roland explained as he pointed out his tour itineraries for Venezuela and Mexico, as well as his return air ticket to Australia.

The men took a little time to digest the information and conferred with each other in Spanish before making their determination. "You may move on."

Roland proceeded through immigration and on to customs where he was told to push a button. He did so, and a green light blinked up: *PASEO*.

Roland purchased a ticket for a taxi, which he was required to share with a man from California, and a Latino couple. He checked into his hotel room where he met his tour roommate, Seppe, from the Netherlands.

"I'm going for a walk," Roland said. "Would you be interested in joining me?"

Seppe shook his head. "I'm tired, so I'll be going to bed early."

Needing to shake off his airport experience, Roland walked the streets of Cancun. Feeling a bit peckish, he stopped at a restaurant and ordered nachos with three sauces, grilled fish with melted cheese and cactus. He also took advantage of the two beers for the price of one offer.

After gorging himself, Roland moved on before stopping at a girlie bar for a drink. He continued on his way and came across a live jazz bar. He parked himself and had a couple of drinks before weariness got the better of him and he returned to his hotel.

The tour group assembled in the morning. There were six ladies, seven guys and the tour leader – Chrissie from Denmark.

Chrissie explained the tour details and recommended they leave Cancun for Isla Mujeres a day early. Roland was looking forward to the day in Cancun, as he liked the feel of the city. However, Chrissie was of the view that Cancun was just a tourist trap and an extra day on the Caribbean island was a better idea.

They took a ferry to the island and dropped off their luggage at their hotel. Whilst the rooms were being arranged, the group went to a nearby café and had licuados, a natural fruit blended with milk or water.

Returning to the hotel, they were allocated rooms and were soon off again, this time for a tacos lunch. After lunch, Seppe led Isabelle, Ingrid and Roland to the beach where they spent time relaxing.

The group reassembled for dinner. Roland was getting stuck into his chicken fajitas while Chrissie went over the tour itinerary. The group then moved on to a bar where they enjoyed a few cocktails before most of the group headed back to the hotel and Roland was left alone with Ingrid.

Ingrid and Roland had a few beers before going dancing at a nightclub. They then went for a stroll and came across a fair ground where they observed the activities. They continued their walk along the quiet, deserted beach promenade until she stopped to admire the moon and the stars.

Roland could feel Ingrid gazing at him, but he avoided her stare. He held out for some time, but he eventually returned her gaze. It was the obvious moment to lean towards and plant a kiss on her, but as much as he tried to warm to the idea, he simply couldn't make himself do it. "Oh well, we may as well go back to the hotel," he finally stated.

Ingrid remained for a moment before following him.

Setting off for a morning walk, Roland came across Hacienda Mundaca. There was no one at the admission booth so he ventured inside and saw a few animals, including spider monkeys.

As he was exiting, there was a lady at the booth. "There are animals to the left," she advised.

"I've already seen the animals, thank you. Is there any history to this place?"

"This was once a large hacienda, established in the early 1800s by a pirate, named Fermin Mundaca," the lady explained. "What are left of the estate are the gardens and the zoo. The pirate built the hacienda, including the stone archway with the inscription *El Paso de la Triguena*, for a young islander lady for whom he fell in love. The lady refused the pirate's advances and left him to live out his days in the hacienda alone."

Roland thanked the lady and took a photo of the front entrance of the hacienda featuring the stone archway. He proceeded to walk to the tip of the island where he came across the Mayan temple ruins and the lighthouse, which he inspected in dimming daylight and took photos.

Roland's new alarm, Seppe, woke him and they prepared for their departure. The group caught the ferry to Cancun and then stopped off at a supermarket where they purchased some Danish pastries and drinks for breakfast. They then proceeded to their campsite at Chichen Itza where they quickly made camp before heading for the archaeological site.

The former Mayan city still featured remarkable evidence of the lifestyle of the former civilization. There was the ball court, El Characol Observatory, the Temple of the Warriors and El Castillo, also known as the Pyramid of Kukulkan.

Roland was struck by the stark similarities between the Mayan and Egyptian civilizations and suspected that it was more than just a coincidence.

They had time to enjoy the pool at the camp and then freshened up for the sound and light show at Chichen Itza. The show was the main topic of conversation over dinner where quite a few drinks were consumed before they went to bed.

The group made their way to Valladolid, a small colonial town where they stopped off for lunch. They wandered the streets and observed a group of children looking cute in costumes and performing a traditional Spanish-style dance.

The next camp was at Tulum Beach where the group put up their tents before playing some volleyball and going for a swim. Tom and Uberta, two of the Germans on the tour, prepared dinner. They set up a taco production line, which proved to be loads of fun.

The group was scheduled to travel to Playa del Carmen later in the day, but as Roland was bored at the camp, he decided to hike there. Chrissie told him the distance from their camp to Playa del Carmen would be around 20 kilometres so he expected it would take him about three hours.

After two hours of solid walking, Roland came across a doctor from the United States who was on a cruise that docked around Puerto Aventuras. They walked together for a while before they parted ways.

It began to rain heavily and as there was no cover Roland got drenched. It took a total of 4½ hours before he reached Playa del Carmen. "I don't think it was 20 kilometres," he complained. "It was more like thirty."

Walking around the beach town, Roland's first priority was to somehow get dry. The weather was overcast and he found it unpleasant to be at the beach. He tried to find a location protected from the cool breeze and found a spot at a café where he grabbed a ham and cheese roll followed by a licuados of mango with milk.

Roland eventually bumped into the group in the early evening on the main drag of 5th Avenue and joined them for dinner. They spent some time at a bar where Roland drank a lime daiquiri, which he thought was the best thing he had done all day. They then made their way back to camp by van.

"I can't believe you walked all that way," Seppe said.

"I can believe it," Roland replied. "I can feel it."

The next day, the group visited Tulum where they explored the ruins and took photos of El Castillo with the beach backdrop. It was the first ancient buildings they had witnessed situated in an ocean setting and they enjoyed a swim and relaxing on the beach.

Papantla Flyers were performing their dedication to the sun god from the heights of a 90 foot pole. Dressed in native costume, the four flyers descended by revolving around the pole on ropes, making 13 revolutions. Four men making 13 revolutions totalled 52, which signified 52 years. In Aztec civilization, this marked the end of one life and the beginning of a new life. The four men represented earth, water, air and fire. The revolutions of the four elements also symbolised the creation of a new life.

The group continued on to the city of Chetumal where they had a chance to walk around and grab a bite to eat. They proceeded to Laguna where they offloaded their gear and had a swim before dinner and quite a few beers, which primed them for bed.

After breakfast, they packed up and headed for their jungle camp near Calakmul. Arriving at camp, they had lunch and proceeded to the ruins, spotting a wild turkey on the way. They spent 1½ hours exploring the ruins and then climbed the two largest pyramids. One pyramid was particularly steep, which made them descend on their haunches.

The jungle had overpowered the ancient buildings and, even with the recent clearing, it seemed a constant battle to keep the jungle from taking over. When they arrived back at camp they had a tent challenge with Seppe and Roland just losing out to Ingrid and Uberta.

It was the customary drinks after dinner before everyone went to bed. "There's not much nightlife on this tour," Ingrid said to Roland.

"I agree," Roland replied, "but it may be because it's more of a cultural tour."

Heading off the next morning, the group endured a five-hour drive to their campsite just outside the town of Palenque. They set up camp, had lunch and then set off for the Palenque ruins.

Roland entertained himself exploring the ancient Mayan city and took photos of the Temple of Inscriptions, the East Court Palace, the Temple of the Cross and the Temple of the Sun.

The group returned to camp and they had a swim in the pool before freshening up. Chrissie advised Seppe and Roland that they were going shopping.

"Why us?" asked Seppe.

"Because you guys are cooking tonight," Chrissie told them.

Roland didn't enjoy cooking for large numbers; large meaning greater than four people. Seppe; however, seemed to be even more useless. Roland decided on paella and sangria.

"Sangria? Why sangria?" Seppe asked.

"If we get the group drunk, they might not taste the food as much," Roland suggested.

Seppe had to have the ingredients explained to him a number of times. Roland then suggested that he would get the ingredients for the paella and Seppe could get the ingredients for the sangria. "So what do I need to get?" Seppe asked.

Roland's clarification was curt. "Me the vegetables and you the fruit!"

When they returned to camp, Roland was not impressed with the first thing he was asked: "When will dinner be served?"

Roland took a deep breath before he answered. "It might take a couple of hours; however, it would take less time if you could help."

Tom was keen to help and Roland suggested he make the sangria. "Sangria?" Tom asked. "What's in sangria?"

"It's a mixture of fruit and alcohol," Roland advised.

"Ya, sounds good," the tall German said with a smile.

Roland was required to do most of the cooking as Seppe provided little support. Fortunately, the English couple of Jane and Tim came to his aid.

Tom recruited the others and they entertained themselves making the sangria. Every stage in the process of concocting the drink was greeted with Tom making the standard comment. "This is going to be great!"

The paella was prepared in two pots, one for the vegetarians and one with meat. To finish off, Roland arranged for the left over chopped fruit from the sangria to be used with ice cream for dessert. Everyone complimented the meal and Roland was able to sit back while others cleaned up. He polished off his last cup of sangria before he hit the sack.

The following morning, the group packed up and headed for the city of Palenque. They walked around a little before going to the Misol-Ha Waterfall where they enjoyed a swim and a picnic lunch before they moved on to Osocingo.

"I'm going to have a milkshake as the milkshakes in Osocingo are particularly good," Chrissie advised. The group couldn't resist so they all followed her lead. They then broke up into smaller groups to walk around the town, although most of them ended up at the Indian market.

The group moved on to a ranch just outside of town where another tour had already settled in so they took up the remaining places. They enjoyed dinner, which they finished off with a cucaracha, consisting of tequila,

Kalhua and Cointreau.

"Do you want your cucaracha flamed?" Chrissie asked.

"It's sacrilege to burn alcohol," Roland replied, "and one definitely doesn't need a straw to down a shot."

It was a sedate evening where the group played backgammon and dominoes. Ingrid once again expressed her disappointment with the lack of nightlife before going to bed.

The following day, a number of the group opted to go horse riding across the country side of the Chiapas in the Ocosingo Valley. They rode for 1¼ hours to a farm where the riders were treated to lemonade, tortillas, black beans and chilli sauce. They admired the Tonino Mayan ruins on the ride back.

When the group returned, they ate lunch and had the afternoon to relax and play a few hands of Uno. It was a sedate evening and an early night.

The following day was spent at the local museum and then a visit to the ruins at Tonina. Returning to the ranch, they completed their packing, paid their bar bill and set off.

Arriving at the city of San Cristóbal de la Casas, they were taken to their accommodation in a Rancho that provided cabins. They had dinner at the Rancho with dessert consisting of marshmallows fired in the open fireplace.

After breakfast, the group departed to meet up with a local guide to visit the Indian communities of the area. They initially visited the Indian village at San Juan Chamula where they were taken to a typical house and had the chance to try the local home-brew. They then visited the local market, the plaza and the church.

Next on the agenda was the neighbouring Indian town of Zinacanton, or House of Bats. They visited one of the houses where they observed traditional weaving techniques and then checked out the local market.

Returning to San Cristóbal, the group stopped at a restaurant for lunch before Roland broke away to embark on one of his walks about town. After visiting the cathedral, he zigzagged along the path up the hill that led to the Santo Domingo Church. He later met up with the group for dinner and drinks in town.

The following day, the tour travelled to the city of Tuxtla Gutierrez. They took a speed boat ride through the Canon del Sumidero in the Sumidero National Park. It provided spectacular scenery of the canyon, the dam and waterfalls. They also got to see crocodiles, pelicans and vultures.

The group returned to San Cristóbal for lunch and some free time. They then headed to the Indian market to buy some souvenirs with Roland purchasing a couple of Aztec and Mayan calendars. They returned to their accommodation for an evening barbeque and an early night's sleep.

The next day, the group headed for the El Chiflon Waterfall and followed a trail to the spot that Chrissie referred to as the jacuzzi where they enjoyed playing around in the miniature rapids. They had lunch and returned to the city via an Indian village and were led to a house where women made pottery. They returned to camp for dinner and bed.

It was scheduled to be the longest driving day so the group rose early. Roland was sleeping intermittently in the van, but was constantly being disturbed by the antics of the Germans. The new love birds – Uberta and Tom – were seated in front of him and their romantic entanglements were quite loud. Ingrid was seated next to Roland and, with each amorous encounter between Uberta and Tom, Ingrid would peer longingly at him. He just played dead and the lunch stop provided a welcome break in proceedings.

The group continued on after lunch and arrived at their camp on the beach at Playa Zipolite where they had a refreshing swim in the surf. After dinner, Roland had a couple of beers and was then off to bed. "Why are you going to bed so early?" Ingrid asked.

"What else is there to do?" Roland replied.

After breakfast, Roland walked from Playa Zipolite to the small fishing port of Puerto Angel. He arrived back at Zipolite after a three hour hike and then went to the beach for a jog and a swim before lunch.

Having a siesta, Roland woke up to the banging noises of workmen. He was enjoying a beer after dinner when Ingrid asked him to go out. As he was out of excuses, he agreed to check out the disco bar. When they arrived, Ingrid couldn't believe to find the venue closed.

The following morning, Roland had a massive headache that paracetamol couldn't help and it persisted all day. The group stopped for a picnic lunch and inspected the ruins at Mont Albán, which was founded by the Zapotec and Mixtec civilizations.

They reached Oaxaca City and Roland went for a walk where he mailed some postcards and visited the Iglesia de Santo Domingo. The church looked fairly plain from the outside, although he was fascinated by the unique feature of the small cactus garden. He was pleasantly surprised with its interior, as it had exceptional and detailed artwork.

The group met at the zocalo – the town square – and headed for their campsite on the outskirts of Oaxaca. After setting up camp, Chrissie advised that it was Seppe and Roland's turn to cook. As Seppe was feeling unwell, Roland joined Chrissie to do the grocery shopping.

Roland prepared dinner with little help from Seppe as he was still claiming to be feeling unwell. Fortunately, Jane and Tim came to Roland's aid once again. To his relief, the group praised the meal and he was even more relieved with the fact that his cooking ordeals were over for the rest of the trip. He soon retired to bed with a splitting headache.

In the morning, the group visited the ruins at Mitla, another site founded by the Zapotec and Mixtec civilizations. A common practice of the

Spanish throughout the Americas was to demolish the heretic buildings of the old civilizations and impose their domineering Christian edifices to be constructed on top of them.

The cathedral in Mitla provided the starkest evidence of this practice as the foundations of the old civilization building were visible supporting the newer structure.

They moved on to the artisans in Mitla and then on to the city of Oaxaca. They stopped at the Mexcal factory, which produced an alcoholic beverage made from the agave cactus, similar to tequila that was made from the blue agave cactus. After sampling the produce and considering it to be drinkable, Roland purchased a bottle with a worm.

Visiting the town of Santa Maria del Tule, the group witnessed an enormous cypress, the national tree of Mexico, which was located adjacent to the church. They continued and then stopped off for lunch before making their way to the city of Oaxaca.

Roland visited the zocalo where a protest of sorts was taking place. He then visited the Basilica de la Soledad, the cathedral, the Juarez Market and the commercial market. He returned to the zocalo where he sat at a café, had a coffee and watched the activities around the town square.

During dinner, Roland got stuck into his bottle of Mexcal. As he drank from his bottle the worm swirled around at the bottom. He deliberated about what one was supposed to do with the worm before ultimately consuming the pickled creature.

The next day the group set off for the city of Puebla. They had lunch at a restaurant named VIPS where Roland tried the famous local mole poblano. He found the sauce, which had a mix of sweet, sour, rich and spicy flavours to be very unusual and concluded it must be an acquired taste.

Seppe and Roland went for a walk and visited La Victoria Market, the cathedral and the zocalo. They then went for a drink at a café before meeting the others to head for their trailer camp situated outside the city. They enjoyed their last camp cooked dinner with tequila and beer before going to bed.

It was off to Teotihuacan the following day and when they arrived at the ruins they were introduced to their guide – Gorilla. It wasn't too difficult to guess how the sizeable man acquired his nickname.

Gorilla took off with the ten people that opted for the Indian Adventure tour. They visited the platform symbolising the centre of the universe and viewed the pyramid that had been discovered beneath.

The Temple of Quetzalcoatl was next and they descended into the pyramid to partake in a fire ceremony. They were asked to imagine being a bird, like an eagle, flying over the pyramids and feeling the spirits. They then shared the fire around and were asked to say some words when the burner was passed to them.

Roland was the first and he was unprepared so he just stated what he felt. "I feel privileged to share in this ceremony and to learn of the Teotihuacan culture." As the words passed his lips he sensed that they sounded corny; however, he was heartened when a couple of the others echoed similar sentiments.

They continued on their tour, taking the fire with them and handing it to each other in turns. They visited the Avenue of the Dead, the Pyramid of the Feathered Serpent, the Pyramid of the Sun and the Pyramid of the Moon. Finally, they were taken to the Quetzalpapalotl Palace where the high priests once resided.

After the tour, Gorilla joined the group to view exhibits of obsidian stone sculptures. They also tried some pulque, a local beer-like brew made from the agave cactus with an alcohol content of around 5%. It was said to have been first brewed over 1,800 years ago and used by the Aztecs as a ritual and ceremonial drink.

Thanking Gorilla for the cultural adventure, the group departed for their campsite. They celebrated Paul's birthday with a piñata. He needed some directional support before he was able to break through the stuffed object and retrieve his presents.

The group went for dinner at a pizza restaurant where Roland had steak with cactus. They proceeded to a bar that had dance music playing and stayed there for a while. As the group was leaving, Ingrid grabbed hold of Roland and she seemed determined not to let him go. He expected she was about to make up for the lack of nightlife over the duration of the tour. They danced to everything that was played, from Pop to Hip Hop to Techno and left in the early hours of the morning.

Slow to rise the next morning, Roland was urged along by Seppe. Roland slowly rolled out of bed and undertook the tent clean-up. They had a group photo taken in front of the van before they moved on to visit the zocalo at Teotihuacan. It was then off for Mexico City, the largest populous city in the world.

Soon after they settled into their accommodation, the group set off for a city tour. They travelled part of the way by bus and then walked through the busy streets of the city centre. They ended up at the zocalo and it was here that Chrissie and Tom said their goodbyes and the group separation began.

Jane, Tim, Seppe and Roland decided to grab lunch and went to the Majestic Hotel where they were seated on a balcony overlooking the zocalo. It was midday, but this didn't stop Roland ordering the American buffet breakfast.

Seppe and Roland moved on to visit the Palacio Nacional and Catedral Metropolitana. They walked through the park Alameda Central and took photos of the monument of Juarez Hemiciclo, honouring the former President Benito Juarez. They then passed by the imposing monument of Cuauhtémoc, the last Aztec leader, and stood in admiration before taking a few photos.

Seppe and Roland parted ways with Roland moving on to the Plaza de la Republica where he took a photo of the Monumento a la Revolucion. He headed back to the hotel and said goodbye to Seppe who was leaving that evening.

Roland had a siesta and slept in, missing the rendezvous with the remaining group members. He freshened up and headed to the nightlife area of the Zona Rosa. He looked around before settling on a restaurant for dinner. Returning to the hotel, he bumped into Uberta and Ian who were leaving early the next day and they said goodbye.

The following morning, Jane and Tim said their goodbyes as they were making their way back to England. It was raining, but this didn't deter Roland from continuing to explore Mexico City. He went to the Museo Nacional de Anthropologia and took note of the time as he entered, which was 11.30 am. He examined his main attractions of the archaeological and anthropological artefacts of Mexico's pre-Columbian history and was content to exit the museum at 3.00 pm.

Roland visited the Museo de Arte Moderno and walked around the Bosque de Chapultepec, Mexico City's largest park. It was Sunday afternoon and the park was attended by many locals. He took photos of the forests and lakes, as well as the Monumento a los Ninos Heroes. The monument was dedicated to six young military cadets who died defending the Castle of Chapultepec from the American army that invaded Mexico in 1847.

The remaining group members met up and went to a Swiss/German restaurant for dinner. It was raining so they stayed at the restaurant for a couple of drinks before retiring to the hotel.

In the morning, Roland set off and checked out the artisan markets of Mercado Ciudadela and La Merced, one of the largest markets in the Americas. He then visited the Palacio Nacional and the Templo de Mayor where he spent some time examining the artefacts from the ruins of the temple.

Taking the elevator to the 42nd, 43rd and 44th floors of the Torre Latino Americana, Roland took photos of the Mexico City skyline. He also took a photo of the Palacio de Bellas Artes from the main thoroughfare of Avenida Juarez, amongst the motorized buzz of numerous green and white Volkswagen Beetle taxis. He returned to his hotel and freshened up for his last night in Mexico City and of his holidays.

Zona Rosa was Roland's destination for the evening and he checked out a couple of restaurants before taking the easy option of dining at VIPS. He wandered around after dinner, but he couldn't find much activity other than gentlemen's bars.

Roland ventured into one of the bars and ordered a beer. He declined the company of a couple of the ladies before he left and checked out another such bar. He had a couple more beers, declining all offers for a personal dance. When he'd had enough, he paid the bill with the waiter helping himself to the change.

Checking out of the hotel in the morning, Roland caught a cab where the driver seemed to be competing in a motorcar race, as he made the drive to the airport in half the usual time.

Roland had been on the prowl for Panama hats in Mexico, but he was unsuccessful and his attempts to find them at the airport were also futile. He then came across a cap with the words *Poco Loco* inscribed on it, which translated to, "little crazy." He thought his father may appreciate the humour so Roland purchased it for him.

Japan Airlines flight JL11 flew out of Mexico City to Vancouver. It was a half hour stopover before jetting off for Tokyo, which connected with his flight to Sydney. Roland walked around Sydney Airport and visited a duty free where he bought a bottle of gin for himself and an eau de toilette for his dad. It would be a break in tradition as John was a habitual Brut user.

Roland boarded Qantas flight QF421 to Melbourne. It was almost 11.00 am on Thursday, 30th August 2001 when the plane touched down at Melbourne International Airport. He couldn't wait to grab a taxi to drop off his luggage at his place before heading to the family home to see his dad.

Chapter 43 – Mexico Revisited

Roland was at pains to work out his next travel destinations with his priorities being Eastern Europe and Indo-China. He also desired to return to certain countries and catch up with family and friends overseas.

It was Tuesday, 25th June 2002 when Roland departed Melbourne on the 11:15 United Airlines flight UA862 to Sydney before transferring to a flight bound for Los Angeles. He listened to the audio of the air traffic control as they guided the plane into land with the co-ordinates, speed and altitude.

The twelve-hour flight experienced quite a bit of turbulence that Roland thought they really didn't need. The last message from the pilot was the World Cup soccer score: Germany 1, South Korea 0.

Anticipating high security at LA International Airport, Roland was surprised to experience a shambles. There was general confusion and he lost his way, finding himself outside at the front of the airport with cab drivers more than happy to take the alien wherever he wished to go. He cast his mind back to the impressive experiences he had at Disneyland and Universal Studios: *Americans, they can run theme parks, but can't run an airport.*

Mexican Airlines flight MX901 transported Roland to Mexico City. By the time he picked up his luggage and made his way through the red tape it was 8.00 pm. He enquired about a room at the airport hotel, but he thought the $175US per night to be a bit hefty so he settled on the $0US per night at the Mexico City Airport.

After a restless night, Roland woke at 6.00 am then carted his luggage to Wings Restaurant for breakfast as he watched the World Cup soccer match between Brazil and Turkey, which Brazil won one to nil.

Roland caught his flight to Acapulco where he took a Collectivo taxi ride that cost $35US, which he thought was a little expensivo for a Collectivo. The taxi driver was giving him his hard luck life story and indicated an expectation for a good tip. The 30 pesos tip the driver was given didn't seem to impress.

It was around midday when Roland arrived at the hotel. He was rather disgusted with the standard of the accommodation, which prompted him to go for a long walk in the heat and humidity.

Roland ended up at La Perla Restaurant in El Mirador Hotel and took advantage of the two drinks and show for 150 pesos. He was the only person seated on the balcony and he ordered a Pina Colada as he waited patiently for the famous La Quebrada cliff divers.

The divers soon emerged as Roland ordered his second Pina Colada. The divers went through a form of ceremonial procession and then steadied themselves on the diving platforms.

The divers seemed to take an eternity before committing themselves, which was little wonder as La Quebrada had jagged and perilous cliffs jutting out over the waters that camouflaged a rocky bottom. The timing of their jump needed to coincide with the incoming waves in order to cushion the impact and protect them from landing in the shallows of the rocks. One by one the men hurled themselves into the narrow inlet.

The show concluded and Roland remained sucking at the remains of his Pina Colada, making a slurping sound with the straw. With the show and his Pina Colada now finished, he returned to his hotel room where he performed his own dive onto his bed.

Roland awoke after a hell of a night's sleep. He rose, went for a walk and stopped off for a buffet breakfast. He then set off and visited old Acapulco, the zocalo, Nuestra Señora de la Soledad Cathedral, Museo Historico de Acapulco - Fuerte de San Diego and La Costera Malecon Acapulco.

After a rest at his hotel, Roland booked a Taxco day tour at a local travel agent.

On his way back to the hotel, Roland was consistently hassled by men wanting to sell tickets for cabarets. The tickets supposedly offered 80 pesos worth of value for 50 pesos. He resisted all offers, but so impressed was he with the last salesman's performance, he ended up purchasing a ticket.

Roland had a couple of hours sleep before he set off for the nightlife. He had dinner and then thought he'd make use of his cabaret ticket. He caught a cab to one of the clubs, but it was closed. He then tried another club, but he thought it was rubbish so he retired to his hotel room.

After receiving his wakeup call, Roland was just coming around when he received a second wakeup call. The second call confirmed he needed to get up and not fall back to sleep. He prepared himself and was in the lobby by the tour pickup time of 6.30 am.

The driver rolled up in a Dodge Stratus and Roland was driven a short distance to another hotel where they picked up a couple and their young son before setting off for their day tour to Taxco.

The driver stopped off for breakfast then continued to a photo stop at the Papagayo River before arriving at Taxco around midday. They visited a silver factory where they were treated to a complimentary drink.

Taxco was famous for its silver, but Roland learned that Taxco was also famous for its local cocktail, named Bertha. Dona Bertha, who owned a cantina in Taxco, came up with her tequila cocktail in the 1940s and its popularity had grown ever since. Roland was not a fan of tequila, but found mixing it with lime juice, syrup and soda water made it a most refreshing beverage.

The group had a delightful lunch at the Hotel De La Borda, which was situated on a hill and provided wonderful views of the picturesque town. They continued on their tour of the charming, colonial town with cobbled stoned streets and buildings that featured tiled rooves. They visited the zocalo and the impressive Santa Prisca Cathedral before returning to Acapulco.

Roland freshened up before having dinner and setting off for the tabares. He thought they were clubs; however, the strict translation was strip clubs. He sought out a couple of them, stayed for a beer at each and then retired to bed.

On the cab ride to the airport it dawned on Roland that he neglected to take a dip in Acapulco Bay. He was a little depressed when he arrived at the airport and he had a five hour wait until his flight.

Roaming the airport, Roland noticed the soccer match between Turkey and South Korea showing on the television in a café. He found a seat and watched the game whilst munching on a ham and cheese baguette. Turkey won 3 goals to 2 and the entertaining game placed him in better spirits.

Roland caught his flight for Mexico City, which connected with his flight to Merida. It was a smooth flight where he slept most of the way, although he cursed the fact that he had missed out on his airplane food.

Roland was pleasantly surprised that his hotel was located right on the zocalo. It was around midnight when he freshened up and went for a walk around the block. There was quite a bit of activity with a band playing Latin music, which got the locals as well as the tourists dancing. He had a beer and took in the scene before returning to his hotel.

The front door was locked so Roland had to knock in order to be allowed entry. He got to his room, settled into bed and turned on the television where the World Cup final between Brazil and Germany was showing. He started watching the game when he began to perspire profusely and felt very ill.

Roland stayed in bed for a while and then had to use the bathroom. He had the problem of which end of his anatomy to place over the toilet bowl first as there was activity at both ends. He spent quite some time in the lavatory and was somewhat grateful that the television was partially visible from the toilet seat. He shed quite a bit of fluid, and when he felt he had stabilised he returned to bed.

Ronaldo slotted in a goal for Brazil in the 67th minute, which Roland celebrated by drinking electrolytes, glucose and loads of water. Ronaldo scored his second goal in the 79th minute, which completed the 2 to nil score line and awarded Brazil its fifth championship.

Roland stayed in bed until he recovered and went for a walk around town. It was mid-afternoon and the zocalo was very active with dancing, singing and stall owners selling food and souvenirs. After a bite to eat, he passed by an internet café, but he couldn't send any emails so he moved on to visit the cathedral and the Parque Santa Luccia.

The following morning, Roland took a seat at the outside café. He had to ward off some menacing mosquitoes that disturbed an otherwise delightful breakfast. He then walked around the zocalo and the artesian market where he came across a small shop selling hats, including his much sought-after Panama hats. He purchased two: one for his dad and one for himself.

Roland packed his Panama hats in the manner he was instructed, being assured that they would not lose their shape. He took a cab to the airport and, two hours later, caught his flight to Mexico City.

Mexico City Airport was a hive of activity. Roland roamed around a while before considering which of the three airport restaurants he would eat at, being Wings, Wings or Wings.

Deciding on his preferred Wings, Roland ordered a Mixteca Platter and coca. The spicy steak and chorizo sausages were repeating on him and he expected it was going to be a long night at his customary accommodation at the Mexico City Airport.

Roland was fixated on the cleaners who operated like a small, blue army. He was in awe of the floor cleaners who systematically and meticulously polished and buffed the tiled floors.

In the early hours of the morning, as Roland lay asleep on a bench seat, he was nudged awake by a security guard and ordered to get up. He checked in his luggage and did some window shopping before he caught his flight to Havana.

Chapter 44 – Circuiting Cuba

Roland agreed to the $15US fare with the taxi driver, and after arriving at the hotel, he handed over $20US. The driver took the money with a smile and drove off, withholding his own tip.

Proceeding to the hotel check-in, Roland presented his hotel voucher. "Your name does not appear on our system," the receptionist advised. "This indicates that the hotel accommodation has not been paid by the tourist agency. As our lines are down, we cannot get a telephone line to the tour agency to investigate so you will have to pay the accommodation to get a room."

Roland wasn't happy having to pay for his accommodation a second time, but he paid the $35US for one night's accommodation.

It was a very modest standard of accommodation, although it had a great view of the Malecon. Roland slept for a few hours then set off to explore the city. Even though he had been to Havana before, he was being frustrated by the incessant hassling by the locals on the streets. After dinner, he walked about town, amongst more hassling and it wasn't long before he had enough and returned to his hotel.

Waking the next morning, Roland was totally pissed off with the world. He had breakfast, which he thought was crap, and set off for some sightseeing. On the way out of the hotel, he checked with reception as to the status of his accommodation and they advised the problem had not been fixed.

Roland went to Hotel New York where he looked for the bus stop for the ciclobus. It was the bus that accommodated bicycles and travelled through the Havana Bay Tunnel. He eventually found the bus stop and, as he didn't know the cost of the fare, he handed the teller a $1US note. The lady took the money and provided a ticket without change. He thus assumed that the fare must have been precisely $1US.

The bus arrived and Roland boarded. Emerging from the tunnel, the bus made the next stop and he jumped off. He then walked to the Castillo de los tres reyes del Morro.

Roland explored the fortress, which also housed a lighthouse. He then made his way to the suburb of Casablanca, which he got to by going through vegetation and openings in fences. He came to a monument of Christ, took a photo and found it a peaceful spot for a rest. He continued and found the port for the ferry back to Havana Vieja.

Again not knowing the fare, Roland found 35 centavos in his pocket and handed it over. The man gave him a ticket with no sign of change. He thus assumed that the fare was precisely 35 centavos. He then checked the ticket and it appeared to have *10 centavos* printed on it. He concluded that whatever amount was provided at or above the going rate was graciously accepted.

Arriving back in Havana Vieja, Roland ignored all approaches by the hustlers. He returned to his hotel and the receptionist waved him over. He suspected she was after another $35US.

"Hello sir," the receptionist stated. "The tourist agency has confirmed your payment, the problem has been fixed and here is your $35 refund." He was pleasantly surprised, thanked them and returned to his room sporting half a smile.

After resting for a few hours, Roland had dinner and then tried out a few of the more popular tourist bars. They were all quiet until he came across La Casa de la Musica. He paid the $5US entrance fee and ordered a $2.50US beer. He enjoyed the big sound of the Latin band and observed the patrons who took to the dance floor.

Roland thought the salsa steps the dancers were performing were fairly basic; however, when the tempo of the music increased, the dancers picked up their act. It was apparent that the warm up was over and it was now down to business. The dancers performed impressive spins, turns, neck drops and other salsa drops. He was amazed by the performances and as the activities slowed, he finished his beer and returned to his hotel.

Forcing down an unpalatable breakfast, Roland was off to buy some edible supplies for his train trip to Santiago de Cuba.

Arriving at Central Station, Roland learned that the Especiale train to Santiago de Cuba was not running that day, although a train that went through San Luis, situated 20 kilometres from Santiago to Cuba, was running. He paid the $29US for a ticket and joined the crowd.

There was general uncertainty as to when the train was expected and from which platform it would depart. After a few false alarms, the passengers were called for the train to San Luis.

Finding his window seat, Roland was soon joined by an elderly lady. She nestled herself in amongst her numerous bags, trapping him into his seat. It was a position he was corralled in for the entire journey.

Roland purchased some fried chicken on board that, together with his coffee cakes and water, satisfied his hunger. He gained little sleep and experienced a journey that ranged from uncomfortable to agonising. He was hugely relieved when the conductress advised San Luis was nigh. His relief turned into ecstasy when he excused himself to the lady and extricated himself from his train incarceration.

The San Luis Station was in the middle of nowhere. There was a number of beat up yank tanks parked outside the station that were used as makeshift taxis and the drivers were scurrying around for business.

Roland rejected initial offers of $20US. He sat down to observe the frenzied activity and ate his last coffee cake. It became apparent that as soon as the taxis were full, or beyond full, they would drag off and the number of automobiles was dwindling before his eyes.

A man approached Roland, seemingly surprised he was not pursuing a ride. The man appeared to indicate that he should grab a ride while he could. "I can give you a ride for $10US," the man offered. Roland countered with $5US, which was readily accepted.

Roland got the distinct impression that he still paid over the odds as the family he shared the Buick with handed over a dollar per person. The driver, mum and dad rode in the front with three kids seated in the back with Roland. He was also called upon to hold onto one of the family's bags.

It was a short ride to the Santiago de Cuba Station where Roland was dropped off. He organised himself and went in search of accommodation. He walked through the town centre with his backpack on his back and his list of Casa Particulars in his hand. He was receiving a number of odd stares from the locals and was also being hassled by a number of people who offered him transport, accommodation, rum and cigars.

At the first casa, Roland was met by a guy he assumed was gay, given his effeminate disposition. Roland introduced himself and, in response to the guy's question, he advised that he was from Australia. The guy introduced himself as Amadeo and told him to wait a minute before he summoned him with a musical, "AUSTRALIAAAA!"

Roland followed Amadeo down a narrow passage, through a kitchen where a lady sat quietly, and into a room. He noticed the room had rising damp and found it very small and uncomfortable. "This is the first place I have seen so I would like to inspect other places before making a decision," Roland explained.

Amadeo examined Roland for a moment. "There is another casa that is more central, costs the same rate and is highly recommended," Amadeo suggested. Even though the casa did not feature on Roland's list, he agreed to check it out.

Soon after Amadeo made a telephone call, a young lady greeted them. She introduced herself as Lucrecia and asked Roland to follow her. Lucrecia brought him to the other casa and introduced him to the owner, named Maribel. Maribel confirmed the prices of $15US for the room, $2US for breakfast and $7US for dinner. After short deliberation, he accepted.

Roland settled into his room and then set off for some sightseeing. He came across an El Rapido takeaway and tried to purchase two bocadillos and a drink, but was upset when the vendor didn't accept his money. He then realised he was trying to hand over Mexican pesos. The vendor graciously accepted his US dollars.

Continuing on his walk, Roland arrived at Parque Ferriero where he bought a litre of water and guzzled it as he was dehydrated. He took a couple of photos of Parque Ferriero and Plaza de Marte, being the former location for firing squads. He returned to the casa where he chatted to Lucrecia for some time before having a siesta.

Maribel had dinner prepared at the time of Roland's awakening. After dinner, he headed into town to check out the Festival del Caribe (the Caribbean Festival), and Fiesta del Fuego (the Festival of Fire). The centre was packed with people and traffic as well as being filled with music and general commotion. He found a club and had a drink before seeking out other places. He visited Hotel Las Americas where a young lady asked whether she could enter with him as ladies were not allowed to enter alone.

Sonja introduced Roland to a few of her friends. "Would you like to dance?" she asked.

"No thanks, I'm not a great Latin dancer," Roland replied. He observed her friends grinding away on the dance floor and he thought, *get a room*.

Roland bought a drink for Sonja and one for himself. "Why don't you dance?" she asked again. "I can show you how."

Roland accepted and she showed him a few basic steps. They danced for a little while, until he tired of the scene. He thanked her for the dance and said goodbye. He walked back to the casa, observing the festivities along the way.

The next day, Roland was about to head off for some sightseeing, but procrastinated around the casa to chat with Lucrecia. He would have liked to have talked with her more freely, but Maribel's young son stifled his designs by persisting to hang around like a little chaperon.

Eventually setting off, Roland visited Parque Alameda and continued walking along Paseo de Marti and Felix Pena until he arrived at Parque Cespedes where he took a photo of the park and the cathedral.

Roland walked to Plaza de Marte and Parque Historico Abel Santamaria and reflected on the site where Abel Santamaria and Fidel Castro led revolutionaries during the attack on the adjacent Moncada Barracks and the site where Castro made his famous, *History Will Absolve Me*, defence speech.

Walking along Avenida de los Liberadores, Roland made it to the bus station where he purchased his ticket to Trinidad for the following evening.

Roland spruced up for his last night in Santiago de Cuba. He walked around town and it was the usual commotion, traffic and smog of the Festival del Caribe and Fiesta del Fuego. He didn't find the atmosphere comfortable, but was willing to put up with it in order to enjoy the live bands playing a combination of African, Reggae and Latin music.

Visiting the usual clubs and bars, Roland had a beer at each stop. He took in more of the festivities and music from a rooftop bar then tried a nightclub that appeared to be a family affair, including children and babies in nappies. At this point he considered that it may be an appropriate time to retire.

After a restless night, Roland got up convinced he'd been bitten by bugs or mosquitoes; however, the morning light revealed no visible signs of any bites at all. He had breakfast and then aimlessly walked about town until he got fed up with being hassled and returned to his room. He took the time to write postcards to his dad and friends.

Mirabel and Lucrecia were not around at the time Roland was set to leave with Mirabel entrusting her son to see him off. Roland left disappointed he could not farewell Lucrecia.

Roland trekked to the bus station where he watched television. One television set was showing the World's Strongest Man and the other television set was showing a speech by Fidel Castro.

The bus arrived and Roland assembled in the line to board. The driver loaded his bag and seemed to insist on a tip. Roland grudgingly handed over $1US, boarded and found his seat on the air-conditioned Viazul coach. He felt unwell and tried to settle in, but found the air-conditioning very cold. He wrapped himself in his top and eventually fell asleep.

After an interrupted and restless night, Roland arrived in Trinidad. He went to collect his backpack from the cargo hold and a man took it upon himself to retrieve the bags and was expecting a tip. Roland pulled out the coins he had in his pocket and, as he took his backpack, he handed over the coins. The man hardly had time to establish the value of the coins before Roland was off. He wasn't sure how much he handed over, but he was sure that the man would not have been impressed with some measly centavos.

Finding a bench near the bus station, Roland pulled out his remaining food comprising sweet bread and water, which he consumed for breakfast. He contemplated whether he should stay in Trinidad for the night or move on to Cienfuegos that day.

Trinidad was a UNESCO world heritage site that featured prominently on Roland's map of Cuba. He estimated that the attractions wouldn't take much more than three hours to see. He checked the bus timetable and noted that there was a bus to Cienfuegos at 3.00 pm. He was quick to reserve a seat and then made enquiries as to where he could store his backpack.

Roland was directed to a man that could mind his bag and, low and behold, it was the same man that he gave the loose centavos. He considered carrying his pack around, but this was not a practical option as it was an extremely hot and humid day. He then approached the man and communicated his requirements.

The man routinely revealed his bare hand, which opened up like flower blooming. Roland reached in his pocket, pulled out a $1US note and handed it over. The man pocketed the dollar and then re-opened his hand. Roland proceeded to pull out another $1US note and it also found its place in the man's palm. The man then took custody of the backpack.

Roland visited the Plaza Mayor before he checked out the church on the hill and was saddened by the extent to which the building was dilapidated. He purchased water and drank a large quantity as he was very dehydrated. He checked the time and noted that it was only 9.30 am.

It was a Monday morning and the town centre was almost deserted until a small wedding party rolled up. The first automobile was a convertible yank tank with the bride and the groom riding in the back. It was the most impressive activity in town, which prompted Roland to take a photo.

Continuing on his walk, Roland stopped off at a café where he bought a hamburger, an orange juice and a bottle of water. He returned to the town square, found a cool spot under the shade of a tree and spent the remainder of his time in Trinidad watching the peaceful world go by.

Roland returned to the bus station and obtained his ticket. He then noticed the bag man who seemed to be guarding his backpack with the utmost priority. He approached to collect his backpack and the man assisted him to load it on the bus. Another man welcomed Roland on board. "Havana?" asked the man.

"Cienfuegos," Roland countered and the man nodded.

Arriving in Cienfuegos, Roland didn't know what to expect as it was another UNESCO's world heritage site that also featured prominently on his map of Cuba. The bus was greeted by a hoard of local entrepreneurs. "Sir, try my casa. Sir, come see my casa."

Roland declined all offers and proceeded on his way when a smiling man approached him. "You may come to visit my casa. It is close, clean and cheap. If you don't like it, it's no problem."

"I have a list of casas, but I am willing to inspect your casa first," Roland replied.

The man's name was Manuel and he led Roland to the casa that wasn't far from the bus station. It cost $10US for the room, $2.50US for breakfast and $5US for dinner. Roland glanced around the house before he accepted.

Roland shaved and showered before he emerged from his room and joined Manuel and his brother Chico in the backyard where he was handed a beer. He was chatting with Manuel and Chico when food started to be paraded out of the kitchen. "This is our mother, Margarita," advised Manuel. Margarita smiled at the sound of her name.

The procession culminated in items consisting of a jug of mango juice, a plate of black beans and rice, a plate of string beans, a plate of sliced cucumbers and tomatoes, a plate of fried chicken, a plate of French fries and a plate of oranges and mangos. Roland thought it was quite a bit of food for the four of them.

Manuel led Roland to a seat at the table situated in the middle of the courtyard while Margarita brought out a single plate of soup for entrée. "Aren't you having any soup?" Roland asked.

"We have already eaten," Manuel replied. "This is all for you."

Roland finished the soup then tried a bit of everything. There was still a load of food on the table when he indicated that he had enough. He was then presented with a percolator full of coffee.

After dinner, Roland went for a walk along Paseo del Prado, Calle 37 and Marti Avenida 48. He proceeded to Punta Gorda before he made his way back. There was a bit of outdoor activity along the Paseo de Prado, but he passed it by.

Roland entered the Benny More café that had a $3US cover charge and $1US beers. He ordered a beer, found a table and settled into a chair. He observed the ladies who were dancing to the sounds of a Latin band. He had another couple of beers before heading off.

As Manuel and Chico lived with their respective families, Margarita lived in the casa alone. Roland was advised that the front door lock was broken so he had to ring the bell to be allowed entry. It was around midnight when he returned to the casa and he felt guilty Margarita was required to get out of bed to let him in.

Breakfast was perfectly timed for when Roland arose in the morning and it was another feast.

Setting off, Roland walked in a northerly direction up Paseo del Prado. On the return, he cut into Avenida 58 and checked out the Mercado. He then moved on to Parque de Jose Marti, which featured a statue of Jose Marti and a statue of the Madonna.

Roland referred to his guidebook and it noted there was a view from Casa de la Cultura Benjamin Duarte. He went there and was greeted by a lady. "May I enter?" he asked.

"You may climb the tower and give a donation," she advised. He gave $1US and made his way up the circular metal staircase to the Mirador. He admired the view and took a few photos of the panorama of Cienfuegos.

Returning to Parque de Marti, Roland found a seat and was approached by an old man who proceeded to talk in English about his life. He found the man to be well spoken and very interesting. The man then started to ramble on and complain that he needed US dollars to buy a special soap for his wife.

Interrupting the monologue, Roland excused himself and made his way around the park and into the Catedral de la Purisma Conception. The man momentarily stayed on the bench before moving on.

Roland inspected the cathedral and noticed a donation box. He searched through his pockets and found a few coins, which he deposited in the box before exiting the cathedral. He was walking away from the Parque de Marti when the same man that spoke to him moments earlier approached him again.

The man introduced himself as if they had never met and commenced reciting the exact same monologue he delivered before. It was as if the man was making the speech for the first time. When the man reached the point where he complained that he needed US dollars to buy the special soap for his wife, Roland felt a surge of sorrow come over him and excused himself once more.

Roland was upset by the experience and continued walking for a while until he found himself at the bus station where he checked the cost and departure times for buses to Varadero.

On the way back to the casa it started pouring rain and Roland got drenched. He walked at an even pace, not particularly bothered by the sudden downpour. Arriving back at the casa, he dried off and rested before freshening up for the usual dinner extravaganza. He then set out for the nightlife.

After a drink at the Fernandina Bar, Roland checked out Disco La Carabena where he ordered a beer. He was soon approached by a tall, thin lady and her shorter friend. The tall lady spoke English. "Do you want to dance?" she asked.

"No, thank you," Roland replied.

The two ladies departed, soon to return. "Do you want fuckie fuckie?" asked the shorter lady.

Roland was at a loss as to how to respond, but his mind turned to ringing the bell at the casa and mamma Margarita answering the door. His mind then turned to the man in Parque de Marti. He looked at the ladies, gave them a smile and shook his head.

Roland returned to the casa and rang the bell. Margarita answered the door and they greeted each other by exchanging smiles.

Waking up with a sore throat, Roland had a shower and prepared his belongings for departure. He had another feast for breakfast and settled his account, which came to $35US. He handed them $40US and thanked them.

"One moment, I will go and get your change," Manuel said.

"It's not necessary," Roland stated. "The money is all for you."

"Thank you," Manuel humbly said and Margarita gave Roland a big hug.

Roland was appreciative of their hospitality and felt that Margarita treated him like family. He gathered his things, said his goodbyes and headed for the bus station.

Roland had a couple of hours before the scheduled departure so he walked into a panaderia and purchased water and a loaf of, who knew how old, bread. The bus finally pulled up, which was a non air-conditioned, rundown, local Astro bus and he knew he'd be doing it tough.

The Astro bus took off on time transporting a large number of passengers and stopped numerous times to pick up even more passengers. It was half past five in the afternoon, the time scheduled to arrive at Varadero, when the bus came to a halt. Roland enquired and confirmed that it was, in fact, Varadero. He looked around the deserted area, sat down on his pack and started munching on his bread rock.

After washing his dry loaf down with water, Roland consulted his map and checked the address of a recommended hotel. He made his way towards the direction that he guessed would take him to the main road, Avenida 1ra. Once he found the main drag, it was a further hike to the hotel.

The hotel deal was $55US all inclusive, meals and drinks. Roland paid for one night's accommodation and a man tried to grab his bag in a rough manner. "It's okay, I can carry my bag," Roland said. The man snatched the bag and, without uttering a word, led him to the room.

The man allowed Roland to open the door before he barged in, dropped the bag on the floor and placed his hand out for a tip. Roland searched through his pockets and found a half US dollar coin and handed it to him.

"No, one US dollar for me," stated the man.

Roland pulled out his wallet and exchanged the half US dollar coin for a $1US note. The man exited the room with a grunt.

Roland went to dinner and was greeted by an elegantly-dressed, beautiful lady attendant. He smiled as she waved him through, motioning for him to take a seat. He surveyed the area, but couldn't find a spot where he felt comfortable. The lady noticed his indecision and escorted him to a candle-lit table for two in an inconspicuous position and not far from the buffet.

After a filling meal, Roland left the dining room and smiled, evoked by the lady attendant. He walked to the poolside bar where most of the guests were seated for the evening show. He noted that the bar was open till 11 pm so he took advantage of the included drinks, sampling the range of cocktails listed on the board.

There was a modest show with dancing, singing and music. There were a number of animal acts that included a horse, a collie, a poodle, a snake and a small crocodile. As the show finished and the bar was about to close, Roland made his last cocktail orders.

The crowd started to disperse and a young guy who worked at the hotel noticed Roland. "A number of us are heading out for a nightclub," the guy said. "You are welcome to join us."

Several people assembled at the front of the hotel where the staff arranged taxis, placing a couple of tourists and a couple of hotel staff in each cab. Roland found himself in a cab with two staff members and a 20-year-old guy named Marco. Marco was travelling alone; bankrolled by his rich parents.

Arriving at their destination, a staff member told Marco to pay the taxi fare and escorted Marco and Roland to the entrance of a club, which had a $10US entrance fee. "You can go in," encouraged the staff member.

"Would you like a drink?" Roland asked Marco as they entered the club.

"No, that's all right," Marco replied. "I find it easier to get my own drinks when it's an open bar."

"Open bar?" Roland queried.

"Yes," Marco confirmed. "The nightclub's entrance fee includes all-you-can-drink."

Roland felt ridiculous as he reflected back to how he scoffed down as many cocktails as he could before the hotel bar closed.

Roland chatted with Marco and a Belgian lady before going for a wander. He began talking to a Brazilian lady and they had a few dances before she said she needed to go to the Ladies. Roland also went to the bathroom and, when he returned, he noticed that the Brazilian lady was conversing with another guy.

The bar crowd was made up of mainly tourists with the hotel staff failing to make an appearance. Roland tried to find Marco, but Marco was nowhere to be found so he returned to the hotel.

After breakfast, Roland explored the hotel resort and decided to return to Havana later that day. He booked a seat on the bus to Havana departing 4.00 pm and returned to the hotel where he enjoyed a swim at the beach, a swim in the pool and had a quick shower.

Roland was told he could take advantage of lunch so he did. He then checked out of the hotel, left his backpack in storage and departed for some sightseeing.

Roland purchased some water and headed down Avenida 1ra, passing Parque Central. He visited Parque Jasone where he slowly wandered through the well maintained and manicured park, which he found very peaceful.

The Dupont Mansion and Mirador didn't appear to have any tours so Roland took a photo from the outside. He noted that he had been walking for an hour, which meant he only had half an hour left so he hurriedly made his way back to the hotel.

"May I have my bag please?" Roland asked.

"You'll have to wait," the receptionist replied.

After five minutes, he again requested his bag, although the lady seemed more interested in her social chit-chat. "It should be here soon," the lady said.

"I have a bus to catch," Roland pleaded, but the lady was unmoved.

After another five minutes a man appeared with Roland's bag. Roland thanked the man, gave him a tip and darted off. It was 3.45 pm and he had to struggle to make it to the bus station. He noticed a bus at a platform with the motor running. He checked his watch as it ticked over to 4.00 pm and the bus took off.

Startled, Roland enquired whether the bus was the 4.00 pm bus to Havana. The teller was unsure and suggested that he check the platforms at the back of the station. He went to the back of the station and there was another bus. "Is this the 4.00 pm bus to Havana?" he asked and, to his great relief, it was.

The bus arrived at the Havana Bus Station situated in the suburb of Vedado at 6.45 pm. Roland made his way to Gino and Vera's Casa Particular, purchasing a bottle of whisky for Gino and cola for Vera on the way. He settled into his room before freshening up and joining them for dinner.

Roland chatted to his hosts for a while before going out for a walk about town. He ventured down the main thoroughfare of La Rampa and noticed a club. He descended the stairs into a small bar, which was packed with local patrons with a live band playing Latin music.

Settling in with a few beers, Roland was approached by a young, attractive lady. They struck up a conversation, although communication was strained due to the language barrier. The scene commenced to wind down when another lady approached him. Her name was Isleta and she suggested a nightcap at another bar on La Rampa.

Isleta and Roland headed off and sat down at an outdoor café. They ordered drinks and a friend of Isleta, named Jesus, joined them. Jesus facilitated an active conversation and suggested Roland take Isleta back to the casa. Roland declined and soon departed.

Roland was making his way back to the casa when he somehow bumped into Isleta. He was sure that she hadn't followed him, she was alone and appeared depressed. Isleta stopped and looked at him; he gave her a smile and continued on. He walked a few steps past her then looked around. Isleta was staring at him.

"Would you like to come to my casa?" Roland impulsively asked.

Isleta beamed a large smile and ran to him.

They spent the night together, although Roland found the experience unpleasant. He was even less impressed when she started nagging and suggesting plans for the next couple of days.

"I'm sorry, but I'm busy for the next few days," Roland advised.

"I'd better leave," Isleta eventually stated and he escorted her to the door.

Now free to get himself organised, Roland visited the Hotel Habana Libre where he confirmed his flights and changed travellers' cheques. After stashing his cash, he embarked on a long walk to Marina Hemingway.

It was a hot and humid day with a strong breeze circling the marina, which was very quiet and devoid of people. Roland roamed around for a while before entering a restaurant where he indulged in seafood paella and a couple of beers. He took a picture of the marina before departing.

Crossing a bridge over Rio Jaimanitas, Roland stopped for the view and took a photograph of the stilted houses perched along the river bank. It looked like a shanty town, which was in stark contrast to the affluent surroundings of the adjacent suburb of Marina Hemingway. He continued and a taxi stopped along the road. Negotiations ensued on the fare to Vedado and they settled on $5US.

Roland ended up sleeping in, but as soon as he woke, he set off for the Macumba Club. In his search for a taxi, he was side-tracked by a lady who was keen to chat and he found himself in a bar having a drink with her. He initially found Mirela interesting; however, she soon became a drag. She insisted that he escort her to a club, but he told her that he had a headache, which wasn't entirely untrue.

Leaving Mirela, Roland caught a cab to the Macumba Club. As he got out of the cab, he stumbled on a young lady. "Could you be my partner so that I can enter the club?" asked the lady. She presented him with the $15 US entrance fee and he obliged. Once inside, the lady hung around so he asked her if she would like a drink.

"We could share a beer," she suggested reluctantly.

He thought it was a most unusual suggestion until he noted the exorbitant prices on drinks list.

Roland purchased two beers and handed the lady one. There was a fashion show followed by a salsa band, which triggered some crowd activity and they had a couple of dances.

Roland thought the lady was pretty, but for some reason he wasn't attracted to her. He soon tired of the scene and decided to return to the casa. He said goodbye to the lady and left. As he was leaving, he was disappointed that he hadn't even thought to have the courtesy to ask the lady her name.

Waking up the next day, Roland contemplated what to do. He was determined to see the show at the Tropicana Club in the evening, but he didn't know what to do that day. Gino mentioned that some of the hotels had deals whereby one paid a fixed amount for lunch and the use of the pool. He checked out the pools at the Hotel Habana Libre and the Hotel Nacional, but they were both quiet. He then made his way to the Hotel Copacabana.

The Copacabana had a deal of lunch and use of the pool for $8US. The pool area was jam-packed with people taking up all the available deck chairs and most of the paved areas. Already wearing his bathers, Roland stripped off his top and sought out some spare space in a prominent position where he piled his belongings. He went for a swim, which he found most refreshing on that typical hot and humid day.

After drying himself and getting dressed, Roland was off to take advantage of the included meal. He checked out a couple of the outdoor restaurants, but there was too much confusion and disorganisation for his liking so he opted for the quieter indoor restaurant.

Arriving back at the casa, Roland was introduced to a breathtakingly beautiful, young lady, named Katy. They struggled through a conversation and arranged to go to the Tropicana Club that evening for the dinner and show.

After a siesta, Roland rose with a spring in his step. He spruced up and took a taxi to Katy's house where he was introduced to her mother. Katy and Roland proceeded to the club where he purchased two tickets and they were escorted to prominent seats near the stage.

The show started while they were sipping their cocktails. They were then provided with some snacks, champagne, rum and coke. "I've rehearsed at the Tropicana Club, but I have never performed in any of the shows," Katy advised in Spanish. "In fact, I've never even seen the show so I'm very excited to have this opportunity."

Katy continued to point out a number of details about the performers and the show, which made Roland think. *Well that's all very interesting, but let's not overdo the exaggeration concerning your involvement with the club.*

The show proceeded and Roland marvelled at the music, dancing and acrobatics. The show developed into a big dance production and a number of the dancers spilled off the stage and moved around the tables.

"Oh, I recognise that man," Katy mentioned excitedly. The male dancer spotted her, conga danced his way over to her and opened up his hand. The moment Katy received the open hand invitation, she catapulted herself off her chair and joined her male partner in an energetic performance that was worthy of the show.

The spotlights made their way to Roland's table and as Katy completed her routine her male dancer gave her a peck on the cheek. She resumed her seat, the male dancer started applauding her and the audience joined in with rapturous applause. Roland also applauded, although the dazzling spotlights gave him the urge to crawl under the table.

The spotlights were eventually turned away and Roland congratulated Katy on her dancing. She was ecstatic and thanked him over and over for taking her.

After the show, they headed for the adjacent nightclub. There was a long line and they amazingly bumped into the lady that Roland escorted into the Macumba Club the previous evening. He said hello and felt a little odd waiting in line with the lady and Katy eyeing each other.

Katy was tired of waiting in line. "We could go to another club," she suggested.

"Which other club?" Roland queried.

Katy took him by the hand and led him to the taxi rank. "Mi casa," she said.

They arrived back at Katy's house at around midnight, and to Roland's surprise, they were greeted by her mother. Katy led Roland into the living room where she put on some contemporary American music. Her mother plonked herself in the armchair, was smiling excessively and watched with anticipation.

Katy and Roland started dancing. Katy and her mother were making intermittent sounds of approval, suggesting how impressed they were with his moves. Katy then changed the music to salsa and led him with some salsa moves. Again, Katy and her mother wowed with approval. Katy soon turned off the music. "Should we call you a taxi?" she asked.

Roland looked at her and then at her smiling mother. "Yes," he responded. "I think that's probably a good idea."

Vera was cleaning the walls when Roland got up the next morning. "Buenos dias," he said and she offered him mango juice and coffee. "I've arranged to pick up Katy today," he informed. Vera rang Katy's house and confirmed the arrangement.

Making his way to Katy's apartment, Roland was introduced to her aunty, cousin and brother. Katy and Roland then set off for Havana Vieja where they visited the cathedral and a few shops. As they wandered through the streets, Roland noticed how many men's eyes were following Katy's progress.

Roland suggested a stop for lunch and Katy selected the Oro Bar, which had live music. After lunch, Katy advised that she had a family commitment and asked him to take her home. "I'd like to take you to a cool jazz club this evening," Katy stated. "I'll be at your casa at 9.00 pm."

After a siesta, Roland went out for a bite to eat. On the way back, he stopped off at the nearby El Rapido and purchased some smokes and beer for Gino. He returned to the casa just before 9.00 pm and waited until 11.00 pm before he resigned to the fact that Katy wasn't going to show.

Roland headed off to the nightclub where he met Camila the previous year. The place was different and the ladies were very aggressive and affronting. A lady approached Roland and lost no time in vigorously propositioning him. "You me fuckie fuckie?" the lady offered.

Roland was astonished how much the lady resembled Natalie Imbruglia and he was even more astonished when the words, "No gracias," passed his lips.

Looking around, Roland didn't like what he saw. It was his last night in Havana and he pondered on what to do as the time ticked over to 2.00 am. It then came to him. *Why don't I try the nightclub at the Tropicana Club?*

Roland rushed off, but couldn't find a cab so he started towards the Tropicana Club on foot. It was very warm and he started perspiring. A taxi driver was passing and beeped his horn. The driver offered to take him to the club for $3US and he readily accepted.

"It's very dangerous to be walking around on your own," the driver advised.

"I didn't know that," Roland admitted.

Arriving at the Arc Crystal Disco, Roland gave the taxi driver $5US, went to the disco entrance and paid his $5US entrance fee. "Vine rapido," the teller commented. Roland had indeed rushed there and he quickly entered the club, but he was immediately disheartened with what confronted him. The club was very quiet with very few patrons. He ordered a beer and sat on a stool at the bar.

Having given up all hope of a big last night in Havana, Roland gazed at the coloured lights that reflected off the dance floor. His eyes then caught a small light that was glimmering intermittently and noticed that it was caused by the provocative movements of a young lady on the dance floor.

Roland couldn't take his eyes off her as she danced in the most sensual way. She was swivelling down with her legs apart to the point where her groin almost met the floor. She suddenly stopped dancing, swept off the dance floor and exited the club.

As Roland was about to depart, the lady made a re-appearance. She was passing him by when he tried to introduce himself and she grabbed him by the arm. "Wait a minute," she said in Spanish.

She then walked off and spoke to a guy who started towards him. "What do you want?" the guy asked.

"I just saw the lady and I tried to talk to her," Roland replied.

The guy looked him over. "She's a friend of mine. Do you like her?"

"Yes I do," Roland responded.

The guy went off and returned with the lady. "Would you like to join me for a dance?" she asked. Roland hardly had a chance to respond when she led him onto the dance floor. The lady weaved herself around him and he did his best not to hinder her suave moves. After a while, she led him back to the guy.

"She's interested in going with you; how much are you prepared to pay for her?" asked the guy.

"I would have thought $50US was reasonable," Roland responded.

"She'll go with you for $50US, but only if you give me $10US," the guy proposed.

With hardly any time to think, Roland readily accepted.

The lady's name was Jaimica and she strangely reminded Roland of Kylie Minogue. He then thought it curious that he knocked back a lady that resembled Natalie Imbruglia to end up with a lady that reminded him of Kylie Minogue.

Jaimica led Roland to a fast food place where she got him to purchase some fried chicken, chips and beer. She then grabbed hold of him and took him to a taxi, asking the driver if it was all right if they feasted in his cab. He was fine with it.

On the way to Roland's casa, Jaimica scoffed down her chicken and chips, offering some to him. He declined, but she wasn't interested in his reply. She continued to tear the chicken meat from the bone with her teeth, sensually place her mouth over his mouth and he obligingly accepted it.

Arriving at the casa, Roland paid the driver and gave him a tip. Jaimica seemed to respect the fact that he gave a tip and she rewarded him with a passionate kiss. She then left a couple of beers in the cab, indicating that they were for the driver and he returned an appreciative smile.

Roland placed his index finger on his lips, indicating to keep the noise down and Jaimica automatically obeyed. They tiptoed to his room and indulged in aggressive and passionate sex. They slept the rest of the night and when he woke he was aroused. As if she anticipated it, she automatically responded and they had sex once more.

Jaimica and Roland seemed to hit it off pretty well and she was keen to meet up with him again. They exchanged details and she was off. He failed to tell her that he was leaving Cuba that day.

Gino advised that a man would be passing by to drop off some cigars and he wanted to give a box to his Australian friend who recommended Gino's casa to Roland. Roland indicated that he'd also be interested in buying a box.

The cigar man arrived and dropped off two boxes. Gino claimed that each box retailed for $175US, but he would sell a box to Roland for $30US.

Roland packed, said goodbye to Vera and Gino and headed off to the airport. He had plenty of time before his flight to Mexico City so he did some window shopping. He happened to notice a box of cigars identical to those he purchased from Gino and the retail price was indeed $175US.

The Mexican Airlines flight arrived in Mexico City on schedule; however, Roland was confused that his connecting flight was to depart in a very short time. He rushed to collect his bag from the baggage claim, but had trouble locating the carousel. He eventually found his baggage, but then had to contend with security, immigration and customs.

Roland felt like throwing his arms in the air and giving up when he looked at the clock. He compared the time on the clock to his watch and realized that he had failed to adjust his watch for the time difference between Havana and Mexico City. In actual fact, he had plenty of time before his Lufthansa flight to Frankfurt so he could relax.

Chapter 45 – Europeans Friends

Roland arrived in Frankfurt after a sleepless flight where he was continuously disturbed by a rowdy group. He was pleased with the orderly procedures at the Frankfurt Airport and took the train to Frankfurt Hauptbahnhof. He inspected a couple of hotels near the main train station and settled on a room with a television, its own bathroom, and breakfast for 40 euros.

Taking off for a walk around town, Roland visited the Dom Church and the Romerberg Platz that housed the city hall. He continued to explore further areas of Frankfurt and took pictures of the city from the Altebrucke and the Untermainbrucke bridges.

After freshening up, Roland headed out for a bite to eat. He walked around the immediate area of Bahnhofsviertel, wandered down Munchenerstrasse and ended up at the railway station where he purchased a bratwurst, a pizza and a beer.

It was almost midnight and it started to drizzle. Roland walked around the seedy areas near the station and was appalled by the degenerate rows of sleazy adult video shops, brothels and peep shows. He walked by drunken men along the streets and saw homeless people settling on a little piece of real estate to sleep the night. He was disgusted by the sight of drug addicts, some of whom were shooting up on the footpath. Feeling very uneasy, he returned to his hotel.

After a sound sleep, Roland enjoyed the buffet breakfast before heading to the station where he rang Lisa and her mother answered. "Lisa is not home; she is studying at University in Cologne; however, since you are in town you are welcome to visit me."

Roland took a moment to absorb the news and reflected on the unexpected invitation. "I'd love to visit you," he eventually replied.

Roland returned to the hotel to collect some items and then caught the train to Bad Nauheim. Lisa's mother, Helga, met him at the train station and he could immediately see the resemblance between mother and daughter. It was raining and Helga came prepared with umbrellas.

Helga drove Roland to her house where he handed over an Australian Aboriginal souvenir painting he had brought for Lisa. Helga expressed her gratitude on Lisa's behalf and then showed him around the house where there were many photographs that featured Lisa growing up.

Helga served lunch before she drove Roland to the town centre where they walked around. She then drove them to the elevated point of Johannisberg, which provided views over the town and environs with its lush green, rolling hills.

"You must come back to my place for dinner," Helga offered.

"I'd love to," Roland responded. "However, I really should be returning to Frankfurt." Helga drove Roland to the station and he thanked her for being the perfect host. They kissed on both cheeks, said goodbye and he was off to catch his train back to Frankfurt.

Roland washed up and went back to Frankfurt Hauptbahnhof to call his dad. He was in good spirits after his enjoyable day and this seemed to place his father in good spirits as well.

Looking around the depressing railway station, Roland ordered an apple strudel and hot chocolate, which he consumed at the station before returning to his hotel.

The following morning, Roland over-indulged at the buffet breakfast before he set off sightseeing on his last full day in Frankfurt. He passed by the opera house and visited the Goethe-Haus Museum. He then visited the Romerberg where he sat down to drink a half litre of apfelwien and watch the world go by.

Roland walked through the area he dubbed 'Drugland' and took a photo of Kaiserstrasse featuring the Hauptbahnhof in the background and stalls where the locals were indulging in beer and their staple snack of sausages and bread rolls.

Roland enjoyed his buffet breakfast again, then checked out of the hotel and travelled to the airport. He had time to browse the duty free stores where he bought a bottle of herb liqueur before boarding his Lufthansa flight to Zurich.

Making it to the Zurich Hauptbahnhof by mid-afternoon, Roland went in search of accommodation. He used his list of accommodation and inspected them one by one before he settled on a modest hotel for 60 Swiss francs. He went for a stroll and took a few photos of the Hauptbahnhof, Limmat-Quai Street and the Limmat River. He then walked around the old Zurich area and stopped off at a restaurant.

Keen to try the famous Swiss cheese fondue, Roland examined the menu closely, but couldn't spot it. "We do not offer fondue in the summer months; however, I can recommend Raclette, which is an alternative cheese dish that is also a Swiss tradition," the waiter told him.

Roland had his heart set on cheese fondue, but settled for the alternative. He was served a plate with round pieces of cheese, accompanied by potatoes, gherkins, sliced peppers, tomato, onions, mushrooms and dried meats. By the time he finished his meal and went for a short walk it was approaching midnight so he decided to retire.

After breakfast, Roland rang Corina, whom he travelled with in

Morocco and she gave him instructions for Schwanden. He checked out of the hotel and went to the station where he purchased a ticket for the next train.

Corina was waiting at the station and they gave each other the traditional three Swiss kisses on alternate cheeks. She drove to a house that she shared with Matt, Chris and Vivienne. After the introductions, Corina was keen to show Roland around the township so he dropped off his belongings and they headed out.

Corina drove to a café that had a pleasant courtyard overlooking some beautiful mountain scenery where she bought iced chocolate drinks and chocolates. They sat down and playfully consumed them.

Corina then drove to Lake Klontal and they sun-bathed near the bank before she invited Roland to go for a swim. "It's only 20 degrees and the water will be too cold," he complained.

"The climate is warm and the water temperature is 18 degrees," Corina advised as she undressed and proceeded into the lake.

"But I don't have any bathers!" Roland yelled.

"So?" she replied.

Corina was playing around in the water and again called on Roland to join her. He eventually relented, slowly stripped down to his underpants and proceeded to the water's edge. He placed a toe into the water and yelped. "This water isn't 18 degrees, it's more like eight degrees!"

Corina called out. "You're a baby!"

Roland slowly made his way into the lake and submerged his body, inch by inch. When he reached Corina, she splashed him and he reacted by dunking her. They played around for a little while before he gave up. "Sorry, this water is too cold for me; I'm starting to get a headache; I'm getting out."

Dragging himself out of the water, Roland was shivering and he quickly dried himself with a blanket. Corina followed him and tried to grab the blanket from him.

"What's your problem Corina? You're not cold are you?" Roland asked.

Corina laughed, flicked him with her top and the chase was on.

After the frivolities, they returned to the house, stopping off at a supermarket where Roland bought some beers. There was a large group of Corina's friends at the house who were cooking up a barbeque dinner. Corina had a shower and joined the group. Roland then had a shower and, when he re-emerged, Corina smiled and Matt handed him a beer. "I could get used to this Swiss hospitality," Roland commented.

Corina's friends were curious to know about Australia and about Roland. He was happy to talk about Australia, but was uncomfortable talking about himself. He was conscious that the group was quite a bit younger. He was over forty, Corina was thirty, but the others were in their twenties.

"I'm going to bed now so I'll show you where you can sleep," Corina said.

Roland followed Corina to a guestroom and she then showed him her room. "This is where I sleep in case you need anything."

Roland gave her a quizzical look. "Why can't we just sleep together?" he promptly asked.

"No reason," she said with a smile. "We can sleep together."

Corina opened the blinds and the window before getting into bed.

"Why did you do that?" Roland asked.

"I like to feel the sun and to see the scenery when I wake up in the morning. It helps me start the day with a smile."

"That makes sense, but you've also opened the window."

"It's healthier to have fresh air."

"It may be healthier, but it's also colder."

Corina laughed and they settled on leaving the window half open. They cuddled up in bed and fell asleep.

Roland heard the church bells chiming in the morning. It was Sunday and he didn't get out of bed until one o'clock in the afternoon. He presented Corina with a gift of an Australian Aboriginal painting.

Corina drove to Restaurant Bergli situated high on a hill, which had some magnificent mountain views. Roland took a couple of photos of Corina and of the views before they sat down to eat a wonderful meal.

They returned to the house and Corina said she needed to step out to make final arrangements for a short holiday she was embarking on the following day with her girlfriend. Being left in the house alone, Roland fell asleep.

When Roland woke, he showered and was dressing when Corina returned. They had a light snack and nestled on the couch for a while before they went to bed.

Roland woke to the sound of cows mooing and got out of bed to admire the view of the small town settled in the mountain range. Corina joined him and after a short, pensive period she suggested that they'd better get going.

Corina's friends, Kaja and Chris, arrived and they all left together. Chris drove them to the Zurich Fluhafen Airport. Roland checked in for his flight as Corina and Kaja checked in for their holiday flight. They reunited for a short time to say goodbye.

Roland caught his Lufthansa flight from Zurich to Munich that connected with his flight to Milan. He took the Malpensa Airport shuttle bus to the Milan Central Station, arriving mid-afternoon. He purchased a phone card and rang an old friend of his father's.

Gavino had a loud and lively voice, typical of John's home town. "I'm glad to hear from you; I was awaiting your call. Wait at the front of the station and I'll pick you up," Gavino said in Italian.

Appearing out of nowhere, Gavino introduced himself. "Good day, I'm Gavino; I immediately recognized you as John's son," Gavino stated before Roland had time to enquire how he knew it was him.

Gavino drove Roland to his house and introduced his wife, Esta. She served iced peach tea while they got acquainted. Gavino's daughter, Mia, arrived home and was introduced to Roland. Mia was an extremely shy and timid creature.

"My house is too small to accommodate you, but I can drive you back to central Milan to find some accommodation," Gavino explained.

"That's fine," Roland said. "I have a list of hotels situated near Milan Central Station."

The first hotel on the list offered basic accommodation with a communal bath. "At 40 euros, it's very reasonable for central Milan," Gavino suggested and this was enough for Roland to take the room. He dropped off his baggage and Gavino drove him back to the house for dinner.

After their feast, Roland gifted them souvenirs of an Australian Aboriginal painting and a boomerang. Gavino escorted him back to central Milan and onto a train via the Metropolitana. On the way back to the hotel, Gavino showed him the sights of the Duomo, the Galleria and La Scala opera house. He then led Roland all the way to the hotel reception where he bid him goodnight.

The next day, Roland took the Metropolitana train to visit Gavino. He stopped off at a supermarket where it took him a little time to figure out that the two prices shown for the products were for euros and Italian lire. He purchased a pineapple juice and drank it as he made his way to Gavino's place.

After lunch, Gavino rang John and then let Roland speak to his dad. They were lively conversations that left the three of them in good spirits.

Gavino insisted on taking Roland to the shopping complex, a place where Gavino spent many hours of his retirement. He introduced Roland to many of his acquaintances where he led lively discussions, mainly monopolised by his lotto strategy to win himself a fortune. It was a strategy that had been in place for some years, but had not yet produced the desired result.

They returned to the house and Roland re-acquainted himself with Esta and Mia as well as being introduced to Gavino's other daughter, Traviata. Unlike Mia, Traviata was extroverted and outgoing. They all sat down to a hearty dinner and Traviata arranged to meet up with Roland the next day.

Gavino drove Roland along the river where there were many people patronising the cafés, restaurants, bars, bookshops and art shops. They stopped for a drink and observed the nightlife. Gavino was intent on conversing with a number of strangers and proudly pointed out that he was with a friend from Australia.

They drove to the railway station and even though Roland assured Gavino that he could make his own way to the hotel, Gavino insisted on taking the train with him and escorting him all the way to the hotel reception. By this time it was 11.30 pm and Gavino had to rush to the station to catch the train back to his house.

Roland went walking in the morning and visited Giardini Publici, Castello Sforzesco and Stazione Cordona. He considered stopping for something to eat, but continued to Chiesa Santa Maria Della Grazia. He noted that the church was closed until 3.00 pm and proceeded to enter the cashier's office for the gallery, being the location of Da Vinci's painting of *The Last Supper.*

The cashiers were ignoring Roland, which upset him and he left. He returned to Cordona Station where he purchased a focaccia and a multi-vitamin drink. He felt a little better and returned to the Chiesa Santa Maria Della Grazia.

Entering the cashier's office, Roland firmly declared that he wished to purchase a ticket. The cashiers seemed to respect this assertive request and they enthusiastically sold him a ticket and stated that he could join the next tour.

It was a short wait before Roland was led to the gallery where he viewed Da Vinci's painting of *The Last Supper.* He considered it to be impressive; however, he also marvelled at the painting by Giovanni Donato Montorfano of *The Crucifixion,* which was hanging opposite.

Roland was in fine spirits as he continued on to visit Piazza La Scala, Piazza Del Duomo, Galleria Emmanuelle II and the Duomo. He returned to his hotel where he had a quick shower and a shave then rushed off to Castello Sforzesco where he had arranged to meet with Traviata at 4.30 pm. He didn't arrive at the meeting place until 5.00 pm and he apologised profusely.

"Don't worry," Traviata told him. "I was also late."

They went to a nearby bar for a drink before she took him to inspect the Roman columns of San Lorenzo. She then escorted him back to her parent's house.

As they entered the house, Gavino was intently checking his lotto numbers, but he was not to be a rich man that day. They sat down to dinner and engaged in continuous conversation. Time passed by very quickly and it soon came around for Roland's departure.

It was Roland's last night in Milan so he said goodbye. "I'll escort you back to your hotel," Gavino said.

"That's not necessary," Roland assured him, but Gavino insisted that he at least walk him to the station where they wished each other farewell.

Roland checked out of the hotel the next morning, made his way to the Milan Central Station and purchased a ticket to Genoa. After some difficulty, he managed to locate the train and arrived at Genoa in just over an hour.

Stopping at the telephone booths at the front of the station, Roland rang his relatives whom he met 14 years earlier and let them know of his arrival. He then made his way to their apartment on the same bus and trekked up the same hill as he had done all those years before.

Roland was greeted by Alba, Nina, Filomena and Chiara. He presented the family with a few Australian souvenirs of Aboriginal paintings and boomerangs. He then joined the family for dinner. It was like a homecoming for him as he recalled his happy visit years earlier and he was comforted that things didn't seem to have changed.

Nina woke Roland up and served him breakfast. "Ricardo is going into town and you are invited to go with him," she said.

Ricardo and Roland caught the bus to the city centre where Ricardo showed Roland around the various markets. Ricardo purchased some seafood before having to leave for his volunteer work at the hospital. Roland stayed to further explore the city.

It was a warm and sunny day, and there were many people and much activity. Roland was happy to roam the busy streets, taking photos along the way. He walked by Stazione Bignale, around the quaint shops near the station, along Via San Vicenza, through the little market area of Mercato Orientale and down Via XX Settembre to Piazza Ferrari.

Roland proceeded down to the port and took a photo of the ship, named *Neptune*. He then went to Ponte Spinola and to the Acquario di Genova, the largest aquarium in Europe and the second largest in the world.

Roland passed by San Lorenzo and Stazione Principe, then walked along Via Garibaldi. He sighted Palazzo Bianco, Palazzo Rosso and Palazzo Doria Tursi before stumbling upon Panificio Mario. The bakehouse sold Focaccia Genovese, a renowned traditional food of Genoa, which he simply had to try before heading back.

During dinner, Roland was asked about the passing of his mother. It was a topic he had great difficulty broaching; however, he explained with pride how his father dedicatedly cared for her. They then changed the subject to some lighter topics. It was fairly late by the time the discussion wound down and everyone went to bed.

Roland woke to Nina's delicate wakeup call and she served him breakfast. She mentioned that it was forecast to be a hot day and, as it was Saturday, Angelo was thinking about going to the beach. Roland hadn't been to a beach on the Italian Riviera so he was quick to express his interest.

Angelo drove through the southern Genoa suburb of Nervi and on to the beach at Bogliasco, which had the added attraction of being a free beach. They descended the stairs, climbed down the rocks and went in for a dip.

Roland had tremendous problems dealing with the slippery rocks, but finally got clear and was able to enjoy the warm waters of the Ligurian Sea. He had to contend with the rocks again on his way out and managed to cut a toe on his left foot and the heel of his right foot. He tended to his cuts with his first aid kit.

They returned to the apartment where lunch was awaiting them. After lunch, Roland freshened up and set off with the men for a trip into the city centre.

Angelo took the driver's seat of his 1990 Alfa Romeo 33, Ricardo jumped into the front passenger seat with Pino and Roland squeezing in the back. They parked the car and walked to the port area where they relaxed on a bench and admired the views of Porto Vecchio. They continued to the church of San Pietro in Bianchi, also named San Maria Immacolata in gratitude to the Madonna for ending a plague.

They returned to the apartment where they found that the women had already eaten, but they had dinner ready for the men. It was Roland's last night with his relatives and they presented him with a T-shirt of Genoa.

Nina gave Roland an early wakeup call, which was fortuitous as he had failed to hear his alarm. He gathered his things, thanked Nina for all her help and departed.

As there were no buses in sight, Roland trekked to Stazione Brignole where he was to catch the No.100 Velobus to the airport. He offered to pay the driver, but the driver did not take the fare. He expected that the passengers were to pay later. Another passenger boarded, enquired about payment and ascertained that all the passengers were travelling gratis.

Roland caught his flight to Munich on an Air Dolomiti plane, an airline based in Verona and part of the Lufthansa group. He touched down in Munich and transited to his flight to Frankfurt and then to his last connecting flight to Prague.

Chapter 46 – Eastern Europe

After orientating himself in Prague airport, Roland withdrew Czech koruna from an ATM. He needed coins for a bus ticket to the city centre so he used the converter machine to change $5US. The converter machine indicated that he should receive 145 koruna; however, this did not include 50 koruna commission. Roland was not impressed.

Roland took the bus to the Dejvicka Metro Station and studied his Prague city map. The city centre appeared a long distance from the station, but this did not deter him from loading up his backpack and making his way there.

It took Roland a long time to arrive at the Vltava River and the views of the city from high on a hill in the parklands of Letenske Sady were spectacular. He continued towards the city centre and ended up in the Lesser Town Square.

Roland used his list of accommodation, but couldn't find anything suitable. It was a warm, sunny day and he took a rest in the parklands at Kampa overlooking the river and Charles Bridge. He then set off to try and find accommodation in the old town.

The next place on his list was the Pension Unitas. The pension used to serve as interrogation cells for the Communist secret police, and was also a former convent before being run as a hostel by the Christian charity of Unitas. Vaclav Havel, the president of the Czech Republic, was reported to have been a guest there.

If it was good enough for the president of the Czech Republic then it's good enough for me, Roland thought and he accepted a room. His room was in the basement and had steel doors, bunks and truly resembled a prison.

Roland freshened up before walking around the old town. He sat down and ate at a restaurant with Czech cuisine. After an exceptionally filling dinner, he went for a walk and stopped off at a bar where he had a beer before returning to his cell and fell asleep.

After breakfast, Roland felt compelled to take a couple of photos of the art prison hostel before taking a walk up Wenceslas Square to visit the National Museum. The museum had a large range of exhibits, including rocks, fossils, taxidermy, tools, utensils and art from the Middle Ages. There were also many items and memorabilia from political prisoners under the Iron Curtain.

Roland took a photo down Wenceslas Square from the National

Museum before moving on to Hlavni Nadrazi Station where he checked out train journeys to Budapest. He drank a lemon flavoured mineral water whilst lazing on the lawn in front of the station. There were many amazingly attractive women, and he concluded that it must be fashion week in Prague.

Continuing on his walking tour, Roland passed by the Municipal House and visited the Old Town Square with its astrological clock. He scoffed down a stracciatella and tiramisu ice cream waffle before returning to his prison cell.

After a short rest, Roland had a shower at the pension communal facility. He had a quiet meal in town and a few beers at a couple of uneventful nightclubs before he retired to bed.

Roland had breakfast then headed out to continue his walking tour. He followed his map over Charles Bridge and on to visit Prague Castle and St. Vitus Cathedral. He then walked to the Singing Fountain in the Royal Gardens.

It was a fine, warm day and Roland found a bench under the shade of a tree and took his time with lunch while enjoying the views of the beautiful gardens and the Singing Fountain.

A few people approached the fountain and attempted to hear the singing. It appeared that some people were successful, while others weren't. Roland finished his food and went to check it out. He placed his ear at various places on the metal base and at certain points he could distinctly hear musical chimes.

Roland walked through the Royal Gardens before going on to see the Changing of the Guard. He saw the ceremony, but failed to get a photograph. As the Changing of the Guard occurred every hour, he decided to hang around. It was bang on 2.00 pm when the ceremony came around again and this time he was at the ready to take some photographs.

Continuing to walk through the gardens, Roland arrived at the Metronome overlooking the Vltava River and the city of Prague. He crossed Manes Bridge and visited the Wallenstein Palace, being the seat of the Senate of the Czech Republic. He then made his way along Kampa to the funicular railway.

Roland purchased an ice cream, which provided him with the change he required to purchase a ticket from the machine for the funicular. He enjoyed the views of the city before he took the return ride. He walked to the Dancing Building and tried to take a photo, but his camera malfunctioned.

Returning to his prison hotel, Roland had a rest before he washed up and went to a traditional Czech restaurant on Wenceslas Square where he had an enjoyable feast of substantial proportions.

Next was a visit to a nightclub. It was quiet, but he had a couple of beers before making his way back to his hotel. Along the way, he passed a few women of the night before reaching the safety of his prison cell.

During breakfast, Roland struck up conversations with some tourists, including a lovely, young lady from America. It was almost midday by the time he checked out and he placed his backpack in storage. As he was leaving the hotel, the American lady gave him a big smile. *That'd be right*, he thought. *I'm leaving today.*

Heading off to the station, Roland purchased a ticket for Budapest and then went shopping for a new camera with quick success. He continued to roam the city centre and admired the large number of stunning women walking the streets. He then reconsidered his previous conclusion that it must be fashion week in Prague and entertained the possibility that it just might be that Prague contained the most beautiful women in the world.

Roland returned to the Unitas Pension, picked up his backpack and trekked to the railway station. It was at the railway station that he realized that he hadn't taken a photograph of the Dancing Building. *Oh well.*

After boarding the train, Roland squeezed his backpack into the storage area of the carriage then found the cabin that contained his seat: number 65. The cabin door was closed and the light was on so he knocked. Eventually, the door opened and there were two men who reluctantly made way to allow him entry. He found his seat and settled in.

The train started off and soon after the cabin door was opening. A backpacker entered and found a seat. Sometime after there was another knock on the door. This time it was the conductor to inspect the tickets.

The two men produced their tickets and they got the nod. Roland produced his ticket and all was in order. The conductor then turned to the backpacker who reluctantly produced his ticket. "Why have you not filled in your departure?" the conductor asked in a firm voice.

"It's not a problem," the backpacker responded, "I can do it now."

"You are required to do it before you travel. Now is too late. Now you are required to pay the fare," the conductor stated, again in a firm voice.

"I shouldn't have to pay," the backpacker shouted back. "I can just fill in the ticket now."

"The requirements are clear," the conductor said. "You are required to fill in the ticket beforehand and it is now too late. If you do not pay you will be put off the train at the next station." This instigated a shouting match with both castigators holding firm. There was an impasse.

The conductor stormed off and repeated his decree. "If you don't pay, I will order you off the train at the next station!" The backpacker continued asserting his case. The two other men and Roland looked at one another and shrugged their shoulders.

Before long the train was stopping. The backpacker collected his belongings and left the cabin. Moments later the conductor entered the cabin and enquired about the whereabouts of the backpacker. The two men and Roland looked at one another and shrugged their shoulders.

The conductor shot off while the two men and Roland started quizzing each other as to what may have happened. They got up and stood guard at the cabin door to see if there were any developments. The train eventually took off and the three men started laughing and hypothesizing as to what may have happened. The backpacker was not to be seen again.

Arriving in Budapest, Roland visited the Information counter where they provided him with a map and some guidance about the city's orientation. He settled on a bench outside the station and ate the last of his stale bread and drank it down with water.

Roland walked long distances in search of accommodation and managed to find an economic single room. He had a couple of hours rest before he set off again.

Passing the Parliament Building, Roland visited Margaret Island. He enjoyed walking on the island and viewing the lovely gardens, sporting venues and parks. The island contained the ruins of the Dominican Convent and Church, which was where Saint Margaret of Hungary once lived.

Venturing up to the Citadella on Gellert Hill, Roland took a number of panoramic photographs of Budapest. He then made his way back to the hotel, passing the Independence Monument where he came across two young women involved in a vicious fight. They were pulling each other's hair, punching and kicking. He felt no compulsion to intervene as there were a number of spectators who seemed to find the incident most amusing.

For dinner, Roland settled on a local restaurant. He then checked out a nightclub where there were only a few people. Nevertheless, he stayed for a couple of warm Heineken beers before returning to his hotel.

Roland had a restless night, he was dehydrated and woke up with a slight hangover. He had a shower and struggled through his breakfast before heading off for his day of sightseeing. He walked by the State Opera House and St Stephen's Basilica. The basilica was externally covered with scaffolding, but he was impressed with the highly decorative interior.

Climbing up the steps to the right of the funicular Siklo tram, Roland strolled around the old town of Buda, taking photos of Fisherman's Bastion and the Holy Trinity Statue. He then visited the Budapest History Museum and the Royal Palace, also named Buda Castle.

Roland made his way down the steps on the other side of the Siklo tram, meandered his way to the National Museum and admired the exhibits. He stopped at the Keleti Station where he purchased a pizza and a multi-vitamin drink. He then made his way to Varosliget City Park and found a quiet spot to eat.

Wandering around the lovely park, Roland eventually located Vajdaunyad Castle. He visited Heroes Square where he took a photo of the monument that featured statues of the fourteen leaders of the seven tribes that founded Hungary.

The city was exceptionally quiet until a fireworks display started to go off in the city. It was Friday 2nd August 2002 and Roland had no idea why there were fireworks, but he enjoyed the display nonetheless. He popped into a club for a few drinks before he returned to his hotel.

After breakfast, Roland checked out of the hotel and headed for the Kelenti Station. On the way, he witnessed a minor crash between two motor vehicles. He was bemused by the fact that neither of the drivers considered it necessary to stop.

Roland enquired about tickets to Zagreb and was recommended to take a return ticket as for some reason a return ticket was cheaper than a one way ticket. Purchasing a return ticket, he boarded the train and entered his cabin. He was joined by a family of four made up of mum, dad, daughter and son.

After some initial concerns, Roland found the family to be very pleasant. The family left after a few stops and was replaced by a bunch of reasonably well behaved school kids who also stayed for only a few stops.

As the school kids departed, a team of customs and immigration officers entered ahead of the Bulgarian/Croatian border. All was in order and the train continued into Croatia where Roland had the whole cabin to himself.

Chapter 47 – The Balkans

Arriving in Zagreb, Roland searched for a hotel and finally settled on one in the city centre. He soon set off, armed with his walking tour map and camera. He trekked to Lotrscak Tower and took a few panoramic photographs of the city. On the way back to the hotel, he took a photograph of the Croatian National Theatre.

Hungry by the time he returned to his hotel room, Roland spruced up and was off in search of a place to eat. The places on his list located nearby were either closed or did not appeal to him so he continued walking until he came across Restaurant Vinodol.

After outdoing himself at dinner, Roland walked around town. It was fairly quiet, which he considered surprising for a Saturday night. He stopped off for a couple of drinks at a bar where he learned that Monday was a public holiday and most people had gone away for the weekend. He returned to his hotel and watched television before going to sleep.

Roland had breakfast, checked out of the hotel and left his backpack in storage. He was wandering the streets when he stepped into a pile of dog turd. He was particularly upset as he tried to come to terms with the quandary of how he managed to land himself in the pile of crap in such a clean city.

It was an overcast day with intermittent showers. Roland walked through puddles in an effort to remove the stinking problem; however, the crap was very much embedded into his treaded boots. He reached the Dolac Market and the first thing he noted were the public toilets. He rummaged for two krona and gained entry.

"There is a God!" Roland exclaimed at the sight of a toilet brush in the cubicle and he quickly got to work. It was quite a struggle, but he managed to free himself of the unwanted debris. He thought it was the best two krona he had spent in Zagreb.

Roland inspected the Dolac Market where the enormity and freshness of the fruit blew him away. He then went to the Historical Museum of Croatia, walking through puddles for no particular reason. The museum was closed so he took a photo of the baroque style mansion and moved on.

Passing the Tolkien House, Roland decided to indulge in the tourist experience of drinking a hot chocolate at the Tolkien themed café. He then walked to the Lotrscak Tower. It was approaching midday, which was when the canon was due to fire. The daily event was supposed to assist the locals to set their time. He waited as the second hand of his watch past midday, but there was no canon fire. He waited for a few more moments and the canon went off with smoke emerging from the tower. *Am I early? Or, the canon late?*

Finding a seat in the park at Tomislav Square, Roland stopped for a rest. Minutes later, a man in his mid-60s sat on the other end of the bench. "Where are you from?" queried the man.

"I'm from Australia," Roland replied.

"Would you like to join me for a drive to my small town?" the man asked.

"No thanks," Roland responded.

The man departed and left Roland wondering. *What in the hell was that all about?*

Roland continued his sightseeing and took a couple of photos of Tomislav Square and the Exhibition Pavillion before visiting the Botanical Gardens. He veered around the streets taking photographs of Jurisiceva Street, St Mark's Church and Tomiceva Funicular Railway. He stopped for a pizza before returning to the hotel where he collected his backpack and walked to the station.

Purchasing a return ticket for Split, Roland managed to locate his carriage with the help of a few fellow travellers. He was sharing the cabin with an elderly couple, a young couple and another man. He slept for most of the journey and woke as the train arrived in Split at 6.30 am. He made his way to a bench seat at the front of the station where he ate a salami roll and took in some water. He then loaded his backpack and trekked to a hotel.

"We're full, but I can recommend private accommodation," the receptionist advised.

"Okay," Roland replied and the receptionist made a call.

A lady soon arrived, introduced herself as Rose and led Roland to the accommodation. It was a four-storey apartment block where he was shown a cramped room with a small window, a television and a communal bath. He thought it was acceptable so he took it.

After settling in, Roland thought about heading out; however, he dozed off. When he woke, Rose offered him Turkish coffee. They sat down to enjoy coffee and wafer chocolate biscuits as they had a chat.

Roland set off and strolled around the old city. He visited Narodni Trg Praca – the people's square – and the location of the once occupied Palace of Diocletian. He checked out the Croatian National Theatre before heading to the palace's Golden Gate. It was here that he laid eyes on the imposing sculpture of Gregorius of Nin. He couldn't resist rubbing the big toe of the sculpture, which was supposed to bring luck.

Proceeding to inspect inside the old city, Roland saw the Peristyle, the Temple of Jupiter, the cathedral and the three entry gates. He continued to walk around Sustipan and the harbour before returning to the hotel for a snooze.

Waking up late in the evening, Roland quickly shaved and showered before he headed out. To his amazement, the restaurants seemed to be closing up. He approached a gentleman standing outside a shop. "Do you know a place to eat?" he asked.

"There should be a place a little further up the road," the man suggested.

Not being able to locate any restaurants that were open, Roland found a couple of takeaways near the station where he settled for a hamburger and a beer before returning to his hotel room.

Roland woke after a restless night and washed up. Rose offered orange juice and coffee, but he declined as he had decided to depart Split that morning. "Could you tie the house keys onto a string after you have locked the front doors?" Rose asked as he was leaving.

After making his way down the stairs and onto the street, Roland locked the front doors and tied the keys to the string that Rose had lowered. He waved to her and she hauled the keys up then waved to him. He waved once more before he headed off and, as he made his way to the station, he wondered how many times the keys had been pulled up that way.

Roland purchased a ticket for the next bus to Dubrovnik before heading to the supermarket for food and drink. When he returned to the bus platform, the No.001 bus was not there and the departure time had come and gone.

Another bus to Dubrovnik finally arrived and there was a rush to get on board whilst the arriving passengers on the bus were attempting to get off. Roland stood back to observe the mayhem. He then casually submitted his backpack for loading and got on the bus. All the seats were taken and there were people standing. He now appreciated why there was such a mad rush to get on board.

Roland had to stand for four hours before a seat was made available and he sat down for the remaining 1½ hours of the trip. He had a splitting headache as the bus arrived at Dubrovnik and he made his way to a hotel, but it was full. The receptionist suggested private accommodation, Roland agreed and the receptionist made the call.

A man by the name of Antonio arrived and drove Roland to a house in close proximity to the city centre. He settled into his room, took two paracetamol tablets and went to sleep.

Roland's headache had abated when he woke, so he spruced up and headed out. He found his way to the walled old town, entered the side gate and located a place for dinner.

Roland couldn't find any nightlife with the main pastime seeming to be groups of people sitting around drinking and chatting. After a little more wandering around, it was after midnight so he decided to return to his accommodation.

After lapses in and out of sleep, Roland got up, showered and set off for the old town. He then took a ferry to Lokrum Island where he visited the old monastery, the old fort, the pine forest, the Botanic Gardens and Charlotte's Well. He trekked a little way to take a picture of the stunning view back to Dubrovnik before he caught the return ferry.

Roland walked to the Lazareti Art & Craft Market, which was quiet, and then returned to the old town. He visited St. Blaise's Church, the Praca that featured a clock tower, and the Pile Gate with the statue of St. Blaise, the city's patron saint.

Finding an ATM, Roland withdrew 500 krona, hoping that it would be enough for the rest of his stay in Croatia. He then headed back to his accommodation for a siesta.

Roland hit the town for a final attempt to find some nightlife. He passed by the Express Restaurant and noted the all-you-can-fit-on-a-plate offer for 25 krona, which he felt he couldn't pass up.

On a full stomach, Roland went to an internet café; however, it was full. He then went to the Nautilus nightclub, which had a number of guys, but no girls. "The nightlife seems pretty quiet," he commented to the barman.

"Things don't really get started until around one in the morning," the barman advised.

After having a few beers it was 1.30 am. Roland went for a walk and found the same scene as the previous night with groups of people sitting around drinking and chatting. At this point, he thought it was time to retreat to his room.

The next morning, Roland paid Antonio and said goodbye. He went to the bus station and bought a ticket returning to Split. The bus arrived and there were only a few people so there was no mad rush to get on and he had a seat.

Arriving in Split, Roland had enough time to get some food and visit an internet café before catching his train to Zagreb. Roland shared a cabin with a young man, Suresh, from Sydney. They shared their respective experiences of Eastern Europe and their stories had striking similarities.

Roland arrived in Zagreb roughly on time and he immediately checked the times for trains to Budapest. The ticket office wasn't open and he was uncertain as to what to do so he just hung around the station along with several other lost souls.

A train named Venezia Express rolled up, but it appeared to be heading for Belgrade. Another train appeared out of nowhere and the people boarded. The passengers didn't appear to be too concerned about confirming its destination; they seemed more intent on getting out of the cool, morning air.

Roland shared a cabin with an English couple and a Croatian chap. They all seemed content to keep to themselves and it was a fairly relaxed journey until the train stopped suddenly. This caused an empty glass bottle that was stowed in the overhead rack to fall on the lady's head. Her husband spent the remainder of the journey consoling her.

The train arrived in Budapest and Roland enquired about train tickets to Bucharest. The cost was 15,400 forints, but he only had 15,200 forints. He exchanged his remaining kronas, which provided him with the currency for a ticket and an extra 4,200 forints. He spent the additional money on goulash and a half litre bottle of Kaiser beer from the station restaurant as well as the 30 forints required to use the public facilities.

Roland shared a cabin with a couple from Spain and two guys from Denmark. He was tired, but couldn't sleep. He went for a wander and noticed that there was an empty cabin so he made himself comfortable and managed to doze off. He came to as the train pulled into Bucharest Nordi at which time he was recharged and ready to go.

Setting off to find accommodation, Roland dodged the advances from the awaiting crowd of entrepreneurs. He tried unsuccessfully to locate the first couple of hotels on his list, and the next couple of hotels quoted double the price he expected. He wasn't feeling too hopeful, but he forged on. The next hotel was the Hotel Carpati where they quoted $16US for a room with a TV and a shared bathroom, which he gladly accepted.

Heading off, Roland visited Piata Revolutiei, being the Revolution Square, which featured the former Royal Palace that housed the National Art Museum. He then viewed the Romanian Athenaeum and the Cretulescu Church where he was doing spins taking photographs of the impressive buildings.

Roland went to a foreign exchange where he consolidated a variety of currency notes into Romanian lei. He also checked out a few travel agencies with the idea of doing a Dracula tour around the city of Brasov. It was Saturday and most of the agencies were closed or the tours were full so he aborted the idea.

Stumbling upon the Dracula Club, Roland found the place to be dead, which he thought was appropriate. He then strolled along the two main thoroughfares of Calea Victoriei and Bulevardul Nicolas Balescu, ending up at Piata Uniril.

Looking down Bulevardul Uniril, Roland gained his first sight of the Palace of Parliament. The building must have been a few kilometres down the boulevard with fountains lining the street that led to the enormous edifice. It was indeed a most imposing building, being the second largest administrative building in the world behind the Pentagon.

Drawn towards the Parliament building, Roland strolled along the Dimbovita River. He walked around the Parliament building and proceeded towards the Botanic Gardens, Cotroceni Palace and Cotroceni Museum.

Roland proceeded in the direction he believed would lead towards his hotel via the Gara de Nord train station. He followed the perimeter of the gardens and reached a river. He recalled that a river flowed near the Gara Basarab train station and from there he hoped to find Gara de Nord.

Continuing on, Roland came across two middle-aged men involved in an altercation, which seemed to provide a group of onlookers with entertainment. He moved on and, just as he was convinced he was lost, he reached Gara de Nord.

Roland tried to enter the station; however, an old lady positioned at the entrance gave out a yelp, stopped him in his tracks and was holding out for money. He was unaware why he was being asked for money as he simply wished to enquire about trains to Sofia. He knew there was another entrance on the side of the station and he made his way there.

Again there was a lady at the entrance. This lady was young, attractive and spoke English. "You have to pay 4,000 lei to enter unless you have a ticket," explained the lady. Roland was gazing at the lady's lovely face when he remembered that he had a return ticket to Budapest and this was sufficient to gain him entry.

After obtaining the train information, Roland's stomach reminded him he hadn't eaten anything since his schnitzel roll at 6.00 am. He bought a sandwich and a gogosi sugar coated pastry, which he ate before heading back to his hotel.

Roland was exhausted and it was starting to get dark. He had trouble finding his hotel and ended up in Parcui Cismigui Park where a flock of screeching birds greeted his arrival. He knew that the park was located near the hotel, but he simply couldn't find the right street. He was going in circles when he was approached by a man.

"Do you want a woman?" asked the man.

"No thanks!" Roland barked back in frustration.

Roland moved on and ended up at the park for the second time. The birds had ceased screeching so he decided to take a rest and admire the scenery. The park was pretty and was popular with the locals. He regained his composure and continued to make another assault on his hotel. Like magic, his quaint, nondescript hotel appeared in front of him.

After a short period watching television and relaxing, Roland got caught up in the movie *As Good as it Gets* with Helen Hunt and Jack Nicholson. It was fairly late when the movie finished, but it was a Saturday night and he was determined to check out the nightlife.

In search of a restaurant with local cuisine, Roland settled on a place named Boema. After some initial language difficulty, he managed to communicate his order of soup, a pork dish and a bottle of Vampire Cabernet Sauvignon. He was full and happily drunk as he took off to roam the streets.

Roland found himself outside a nightclub where a guy greeted him with a smile. He walked inside, looked to one side and then the other, but noticed few patrons. He thought the place had good music and a reasonable feel, but he decided to move on.

Reaching Piata Victoriei, Roland went in search of the Sydney Bar & Grill. The square was quiet and he couldn't locate the club. He then tried to locate the Swing House, but he couldn't find that either.

Roland stumbled across a bar named Backstage. "So what's the score?" he asked the doorman.

"It's 500,000 lei entry and there are quite a few people inside," the doorman replied.

Roland looked at the doorman and thought about the prospect of going inside. He sensed that he was sobering up and started to feel flat so he decided to return to his hotel.

Roland didn't have much luck locating places that night and he wasn't confident of finding his hotel either. He located the Cretulescu Church and knew that the hotel was somewhere behind it. He walked behind the church, through a high rise office building and found his beloved hotel.

Taking his time to get up the next morning, Roland slowly prepared himself and switched on the television. The time featured on the television was 10.00 am. He looked at his watch and it was showing 9.00 am.

Roland then cast his mind back to a discussion he had with the Danish guys on the train when they asked what he was doing. He replied that he was changing his watch by one hour as there was a one hour time difference between Budapest and Bucharest. He thought he had changed his watch, but he didn't – he'd been operating one hour behind for the last two days.

What disappointed Roland even more was the realization that he had missed out on breakfast. He was moping around his room when he came across a piece of paper that had information about the hotel, including the breakfast times from 7.00 am to 10.30 am. "I've got twenty minutes to have breakfast" he stated with glee. "You beauty!"

Stuffing himself at breakfast, Roland returned to his room to recover. He took his time over the next couple of hours packing and putting his things in order. He checked out and loaded up his backpack for the trek to Gara de Nord.

Roland had an eight-hour wait and he considered what to do. He checked his backpack into storage for 50,000 lei and walked around the nearby streets. He was bored so he took a couple of photographs of the station. He then came across a sex shop and thought about venturing inside to kill some time; however, he decided against it and returned to the station.

After great deliberation over the eating options, Roland purchased a half litre of Timisoreana beer and a slice of Panipan pizza. It was now 6.00 pm and he thought he'd venture over to purchase his ticket. The lady at the counter stated that he would need to return at 7.00 pm.

Roland wandered outside the station and found a seat. He was happy watching the locals, some sitting, some talking and others walking their dogs. He then returned to the station to purchase his ticket and used his remaining Romanian currency to buy some food for the train journey and a bottle of Dracula Paprika Palinca.

Palinca was double distilled plum concentrated at 50% alcohol. Roland had heard the plum, brandy-like beverage was a traditional drink, mainly produced in Transylvania and reputedly good for one's digestion.

With the train due to leave in ten minutes, Roland rushed to collect his backpack. There was a group of four young ladies who were taking their sweet time collecting their bags and chatting to the storage man, who seemed to be relishing the attention.

Roland eventually collected his bag and rushed to the train. He again came across the four ladies as they were catching the same train. They entered a cabin alongside his, which he shared with a Korean, a Japanese, two Austrians and a Pole.

After finding a place for his bags, Roland went into the corridor to stretch his legs and to take in the view from the other side of the train. A couple of the four ladies also spilled into the corridor and they started chatting. The ladies were from Finland and were travelling together on holidays. They talked for almost an hour before they retired to their respective cabins to get some sleep.

The train arrived at Sofia and Roland did his usual thing of finding an out-of-the-way place to sit and avoid the mayhem. He consumed the remainder of his food and water before he slowly loaded his backpack and set off to look for accommodation.

The first few hotels Roland inspected were expensive or full. He then came across Hotel Enny and accepted a room with a shower and television for $20US per night.

It was raining a little when Roland left the hotel and the clouds looked ominous. He walked towards the city centre and his sightseeing was being greatly interrupted by the rain, which at times was torrential. He was soaked by the time he made it to Tsar Boris Park when the rain subsided and where he discovered the Soviet Army Monument.

The monument was set on a 34-metre pillar depicting a Soviet army soldier leading a Bulgarian couple to the land of Communism. Roland took a photo of the monument, which also captured the small skateboard park that had been set up in the foreground.

Roland visited the Aleksander Nevski Cathedral and walked to the former Communist Party Building. He couldn't resist taking a photo of the edifice as he found it ironic that the stark, grey building, typical of former Eastern Bloc, featured a large colourful billboard of a provocative, young lady advertising a cocktail.

It began to pour again and Roland took refuge in an underground shopping area around the Sveta Petka Samardjiska Church. When the rain ceased, he surfaced from the underground and continued his walking tour. It was peak hour and Roland took a photo down Maria Louiza Boulevard with the Banya Bashi Mosque in the background.

Returning to the hotel, Roland had a rest before he set out again. He followed his habit of walking around until he found a restaurant serving traditional, local cuisine. He was his usual tipsy self as he exited the restaurant and set off for some nightlife.

Roland stumbled upon a small club with a good vibe where he stayed for a few drinks with the locals before returning to the hotel.

After a restless night, with the television left on and having intermittent battles with Kamikaze mosquitoes, Roland got up, washed and ate his remaining food. He checked out of the hotel and headed for the railway station under glorious sunshine.

Roland purchased a ticket to Athens, stored his backpack and inspected the shops around the station. It was midday and he sat down at the station café for a bite to eat and an espresso. The coffee was awful, but it did the job of keeping him awake.

Roland purchased two rolls and sweet bread for his train journey, and as he headed for the station, a man approached. "Would you like to sit down for a coffee?" the man asked.

"No thanks," Roland replied and made his way to the platform.

As Roland arrived on the platform, the man reappeared and tried to carry his pack. He pulled his pack away from the man's reach. "No thanks," he stated again and continued along the platform.

Roland stopped alongside two young Irish ladies and was relieved to strike up a conversation with them until his train arrived.

Chapter 48 – Greek Islands

Passengers were walking from one end of the platform to the other in an effort to find their carriage. In the end, passengers hopped on wherever they could and tried to find a place in one of the cabins. Roland shared a cabin with an Italian lady, an Israeli guy and a Swiss guy.

They arrived in Thessaloniki three hours late and Roland booked a seat for his connecting train to Athens where he shared a cabin with three Greek men and an American lady who was in Bulgaria on a two-year stint with the Peace Corp. The Greek guys protected the remaining seat from any potential interloper.

They arrived at Larissa Station in Athens in the early evening. Roland took the Metro train to the port at Piraeus and had dinner at a nearby hamburger joint.

Roland boarded the Blue Star Ferry destined for Rhodes and as he didn't have a cabin he roamed the decks to find a place to stow his pack. Without success, he enquired at reception who advised that he could place his bag in the Pullman. He had no idea where the Pullman was so he found a small corner and dropped his bag amongst a number of other bags.

Unable to sleep, Roland got the idea of getting stuck into his Dracula Paprika Palinca. He purchased a coke, found a spot to sit and took a swig of the palinca neat. He considered it to be ghastly stuff, but he was determined to get plastered. He took a few more swigs, but rather than tasting more palatable, it only got worse.

Roland then tried the palinca with a little coke, but it didn't seem to aid the taste. In fact, the plum brandy and coke seemed to take on a uniquely awful taste. "How bad can this stuff get?" he grumbled. He got the point where he'd drunk most of the bottle, but couldn't stomach any more. *How can this drink possibly be good for one's digestion? Maybe it's an acquired taste and needs to be taken in moderation.*

Spending the rest of the night toing and froing, Roland was delighted when the ferry neared the port. He looked at a navigational screen, which showed that the island was not Rhodes, but the island of Kos. The consensus was that they still had three hours before they would get to Rhodes.

The ferry eventually arrived at Rhodes and Roland tried to find the Municipal Information, but he was unsuccessful. He came across Hellas Aegean Information, but contrary to the listed timetable it was closed. He then set off to find accommodation.

The going rate for a hotel room appeared to be around 50 euros until he came across the Amphitryon Hotel, which offered a single room with a bathroom, breakfast and swimming pool for 30 euros. He was tired of looking and the nice lady at reception assured him that he would not find anything better so he took it.

Roland immediately set off with his first priority to head for the harbour where he attempted to visualise the possible location of the Colossus of Rhodes. Accounts varied, but the more popular account placed the statue near the entrance of Mandraki Harbour. He could imagine how a monstrous statue of the Greek god Helios could have towered at the entrance of the Rhodes Harbour around 280 BC, prior to the earthquake that supposedly caused its destruction in 226 BC.

Heading to the old town, Roland walked through the Eleftheria (Liberty) Gate then visited the Palace of the Grand Master of the Knights of Rhodes. He was impressed with the imposing walled, old town and the palace. He took a number of photographs, including the gate, the main courtyard in the palace and Ippoton – the Avenue of the Knights.

Roland visited the Byzantine Clock Tower and as he climbed the tower he bumped into a pleasant couple from Italy. He heard the sound of a young boy who emerged from behind his mother and took Roland by the hand.

The boy enthusiastically led Roland away to show him that he had discovered a bell and wished to share the discovery with him. The boy seemed to have a developmental difficulty and Roland's Italian language was limited, but even so they were able to communicate.

Roland led the boy back to his parents and when he said goodbye the boy gave him a big hug. Roland was touched. "This boy is really special," Roland remarked in Italian.

"Yes, he is special," the mother replied and both parents smiled.

Returning to his hotel, Roland had a swim in the pool before taking a siesta, which turned into a deep sleep and didn't wake up until 10.30 pm. He headed out and settled on the first restaurant he came across for dinner. He then walked to the old town in search of some nightlife.

Roland visited the Blue Lagoon where there were several groups of tourists. He stopped for a drink before moving on. He then came across a hub of nightlife activity in Orfanidoy Street, which was lined with pubs and clubs. He encountered hordes of very young European tourists who had obviously drunk more than they could responsibly handle. He checked out a couple of the clubs and had a beer at each before returning to his hotel.

After taking advantage of the buffet breakfast, Roland caught the bus to the town of Lindos. He inspected the site of the ruins and was impressed with spectacular views of the Acropolis and the surrounding seas. He then went to the beach where he spent an hour of swimming, sun-bathing and admiring the scenery.

Returning to Rhodes Town, Roland was curious about the Acropolis of Rhodes and was determined to visit the site. Notwithstanding the restoration work that had spanned many years, the ruins were only a fragment of the original buildings due to weathering and the bombings during World War II. Nevertheless, he still found the site and the remaining columns inspiring.

Roland sat on a wall to drink some water and further admire the ruins when two young guys approached on their hired motorised scooters and they fooled around on the dirt track. "Do you mind taking my photo with the Acropolis in the background?" Roland asked and one of the guys obliged.

The guy then asked if Roland could take his photo on the scooter. Roland was happy to reciprocate and was handed the guy's camera. The guy was riding along and Roland clicked a photo at the moment the guy found a soft bit of dirt and came off. The guy brushed himself off while the other guy was in hysterics.

The other guy then asked if Roland could take his photo. Again, Roland was happy to oblige. The other guy revved his machine rather aggressively and started riding. Roland clicked a photo the moment the other guy lost control of his scooter and ploughed straight into a small tree. Roland had to contain himself from breaking out into laughter.

The two guys spent a few moments to check on each other to ensure that they were both all right and they limped back to their scooters.

"Do you want any more photos?" Roland asked.

"No, thank you," they replied. "We've had enough."

Returning to his hotel, Roland freshened up and was off for the evening. He settled on an eatery that was advertised as *The Best of the Best*. He then proceeded to the Blue Lagoon, which was surprisingly quiet so he went to Orfanidoy Street. It too was quiet, but he stayed for a drink at Bad Boys Club. After a while, he asked a lady to dance and she responded by puffing up her cheeks like a blow fish and moved on. He found the lady's reaction comical.

Moving on to the Ozzie Pub, Roland struck up a conversation with a lady and she introduced him to a number of her friends. They were about to head to a club and invited him to tag along. He followed the crowd and was about to pay the eight euros entrance fee when one of the group stopped him. "You don't need to pay if you're with us," the guy stated.

The place was a jungle with wall to wall partying people. It was near impossible to move, much less get a drink, although many of the crowd already seemed to be smashed or stoned.

Roland soon lost touch with his new-found friends and struggled around for a short time before he decided to leave. He witnessed a number of sickly people lining the gutters with one young lady having to be taken away in an ambulance.

Waking up well and truly hung over, Roland went down for a liquid breakfast. He returned to his room for further rest and was being regularly disturbed by the cleaning lady.

Checking out of the hotel, Roland visited a travel agent where he purchased a ferry ticket bound for Piraeus for a connecting ferry to Santorini. He then settled on a bench seat under the shade of a tree and sipped on water as he waited for the ferry.

Roland hung around the port area and when he saw no sign of the ferry he enquired at GA Ferries. The teller advised the ferry was running late and should arrive soon. The Marina ferry reached the port and it was pandemonium as the arriving passengers disembarked while the departing passengers rushed to get on board.

The ferry departed an hour late at 7.30 pm. Roland found the Pullman area where he was able to shove his backpack in a rack. He then visited the cafeteria and had a bite to eat before wandering into the first-class area. A cheery staff member advised that he could take a seat, although he was not permitted to sleep there. He took a seat and rested for a while.

The ferry stopped at an island and it was raided by an additional batch of passengers. The reasonably comfortable ferry had now turned into a crowded tub. Roland tried to find a spot to get some sleep, but the options were limited.

Roland finally found an available spot on the upper deck, but it was cramped and exposed to the wind. There were a couple of other available empty spaces; however, they were in the way of passing passengers. In the end, he found a spot near the cafeteria where he managed to get a few hours of intermittent sleep.

No longer able to bear the uncomfortable position, Roland went for another walk. It was during this time there was another island stop and a new group of raiders boarded the ferry. The ferry was more cramped and the passengers became more feral.

The crowds sought out every available spot, with some of the passengers placing their belongings all over the benches and seats in order to secure as much space as they could. Roland was in dire need of sleep so he returned to the cramped and windy upper deck.

Tossing and turning most of the night and early morning, Roland went to the cafeteria where he was resigned to sit out the remainder of the journey. The estimated time of arrival at Piraeus was around midday, but then came the public announcement that the ferry was not likely to arrive at Piraeus until 4.00 pm.

Roland had been depressed before, but now he was positively

demoralised. He thought he would go to the outer deck to absorb the afternoon sun and see in the entry to the port of Piraeus. Approaching the estimated time of arrival, Roland spotted land and was relieved the epic journey would soon be over. However, as they neared land, it became apparent the land was not Piraeus, and the ferry cruised on.

The ferry arrived at Piraeus 6½ hours late at 5.00 pm. Roland disembarked and passed a number of irate people yelling and complaining. He went to the office and purchased a ticket to Santorini, which was scheduled to depart at 10.00 pm.

The ferry departed roughly on time and Roland put into action his developed ferry routine. He commenced by finding the Pullman area where he shoved his backpack in a rack. He then found a bench seat in a protected area outside that he assessed to be acceptable for his tenancy.

Spending the night on the outside bench, Roland enjoyed moments of good sleep, although he had to put up with sporadic singing by groups of passengers. At first he found the singing interesting, but after a while it just pissed him off.

By morning, Roland had migrated to one of his favourite haunts on the ferry – the cafeteria – where he spent the rest of the cruise sitting on a plastic chair.

As Santorini came into view, Roland was intrigued by the island's formation. Layered rocks formed the base of the surrounding hills with the township perched on the hilltop. The ferry docked at the port of Athinias and he followed the crowd to catch the bus to the township of Thira.

Once in town, Roland went hunting for accommodation. He wasn't having much luck when, out of the blue, a lady noticed him walking around with his backpack. "Are you looking for a room?" the lady asked. "I can show you one."

Roland inspected the accommodation, a single room with its own bath for 30 euros, and he readily accepted it.

Visiting a travel agency, Roland enquired what cruises were available and he opted for the popular full day cruise that was departing soon.

The tour commenced with a visit to the volcano at Nea Kameni Island with its unusual island formations. They then visited the hot springs at Palea Kameni Island where Roland had a swim. The next stop was at Thirasia Island, also known as little Santorini, at the port of Korfos where he had another swim. The tour visited Oia Village before returning to Thira.

After climbing the steps of Marinatou, Roland strolled around town and checked out a number of the shops and restaurants. He returned to his room for a rest before seeking out the nightlife. He had dinner at one of the restaurants he noted earlier that day. He then went for a walk off the beaten track that provided beautiful night views of the township.

It took Roland some time to find his way back and he stopped off at a bar that had two cocktails for the price of one. There were a number of young, attractive ladies; however, they only showed interest in the DJ.

Roland moved on to the Tropical Club, paying four euros to enter. He ordered a beer and enjoyed the music. He chatted to a lady from Athens and then two ladies from Madrid. After the Spanish ladies moved on he decided to retire.

Waking up after a rather ordinary night, Roland took his time to get ready until he realised that he had to rush to make the early ferry. He quickly packed and sped off to catch the bus for the port at Athinios. He then embarked on the ferry headed for the island of Ios.

Failing to make any preparations for Ios, Roland had no idea where to go. He saw a group of people apparently making accommodation arrangements so he joined in. The man offering accommodation had no available single rooms left; however, a lady overheard Roland's requirements. "I can offer you a single room for 20 euros," the lady stated.

Roland was asked to board a small van with an Australian lady and two French ladies. The Australian lady was the first to be dropped off then the two French ladies. Naturally, Roland was last and was directed to a house… or rather, a concrete block.

Roland was shown a room with three beds and he gave the lady an odd look. "The room accommodates three, but it's just for you and you'll only be charged the single room rate," she reassured him.

After settling into his room, Roland set off for a walk. He purchased a ferry ticket from Ios to Piraeus for the following day. He returned to his accommodation and was greeted by a young lady who was staying at the same house. Her name was Claire, she was from Scotland and was travelling with three friends.

Heading off again, Roland made his way to the port and went to the port beach. It was reported to be the worst beach on the island, but this didn't deter him from having a swim. It was late afternoon when he returned to his room, stopping off at the supermarket to buy a few beers.

Arriving back at the house, Roland met a young Irish guy, Kieran, and they engaged in conversation. "I'm 19 years old," Kieran told him. "So how old are you?"

As most of the tourists on the island appeared to be students at around twenty years of age, Roland said he was 35 rather than his true age of 41. However, the response didn't alter Kieran's reaction as he still referred to Roland as, "the old man." At this point, Roland excused himself. "I think I might go for a nap."

Roland awoke, washed up and was heading off for some dinner when Claire saw him. "It may be a little early to head off for the nightlife," she said.

Kieran then made an appearance. "She's right, you know. I'll be going out with some of my friends at around midnight and you're welcome to join us."

"I'm going for a bite now, but I might meet up with you later," Roland said.

There really was no nightlife at that time, so Roland grabbed a souvlaki and a beer before heading back to the house, buying a slab of beer from the supermarket on the way.

Roland was drinking a beer on his private balcony that provided a good view of the village when Kieran and a couple of his mates arrived armed with bottles of local wine. "We'll be heading off to a number of the nightclubs after we're smashed on this local plonk," Kieran advised. "This local wine is crap, but it's a dirt cheap way of getting drunk before going clubbing."

Kieran gave Roland a taste of the local wine and he was able to confirm that it was crap.

Roland, Kieran and his friends went on a club crawl. Roland was tipsy; however, the boys were well and truly plastered. "There are hefty entrance fees to the clubs," Kieran explained, "but as I work at one of them and know quite a few of the staff, I should be able to get us in for free."

They started at the Dubliner and then moved on to the Fun Bar, having a few cocktails on the house at both. They then moved on to the Q Club and Kieran was starting to act aggressively. He was helping himself to other guys' beers and when they queried what he was doing, he abruptly told them where to go. Ladies were not spared his abuse as he swiftly told them to suck him off. It was at this time that Roland decided to part company.

A young lady approached Roland and it wasn't long before they were kissing. She was then being called over by some people. "I'm going to talk to my friends and I'll be back in a couple of minutes," the lady stated.

"Okay, I'll time you," Roland said. After several minutes, it was no surprise that the lady hadn't returned.

Roland started talking to a couple of young ladies, but they seemed uninterested. He then came across a pretty lady and started talking with her. She was on holidays from Athens and she agreed to a dance. Things seemed to be going fine until he attempted to kiss her, at which time, she abruptly thanked him for the dance and stormed off.

The club was closing and Roland moved outside. There were a number of people assembled and he struck up a conversation with an Irish lady. "My friends and I are going to the only place likely to be open called La Cuva," she advised.

"I could do with a beer so I may head over there too," Roland said.

Roland had a couple of beers at La Cuva and struck up a conversation with a young lady from England. They talked for a while before he had enough. He finished his beer and called it quits.

With hardly any sleep, Roland forced himself to get up and have a shower. There was one thing that he wanted to do before leaving Ios, which was to track down Homer's Tomb. He was unsure about his chances of success, as no one he asked could tell him exactly where it was.

Determined to at least make an attempt, Roland hired a moped and followed the direction of a sign that pointed to Homer's Tomb. He rode endlessly to locate it, but saw no further signs so he gave up.

It was midday when Roland checked out. Kieran was nowhere to be seen, but he was able to say farewell to Claire. He went to the bus station taking a couple of photos of Chora Village before arriving at the port. He found a shaded spot under a statue of an anchor where he spent some time sipping on water.

Roland visited an internet café and sent off some postcards. He walked around and took some photos, including one of Homer's statue. He then enjoyed a meal of stuffed vine leaves, stuffed tomatoes, stuffed peppers and an iced coffee frappé.

Boarding the ferry, Roland discovered that the set up was different to the other ferries he had encountered. He could only avail himself to three levels of outside decking and there were no chairs or benches available.

Roland settled in a small corner on the top deck where he used a beach towel as an under blanket and placed his backpack as a pillow and wind break. As the ferry took off, there was a gale blowing and the majority of the people retreated to less exposed areas; however, Roland stuck it out, withstanding the windy onslaught.

The ferry arrived on schedule, docking at Piraeus at 7.00 am. Roland took a couple of photos of the port before catching the train to Larissa Station in Athens where he sought information about train travel to Istanbul. He discovered he had to travel via Thessaloniki and his best chance to make it in time was by bus.

Roland trekked over the bridge to the nearby bus station where he bought a 67.50 euros ticket for the bus to Istanbul departing 7.00 pm. He then stored his backpack and set off to make the most of his eleven hours in Athens.

Arriving at the Parliament Building, Roland noted people heading toward the Tomb of the Unknown Soldier. He observed the Changing of the Guard ceremony, which he found most unusual, particularly the uniforms with the frilly skirts and the slipper-like shoes with pom poms.

Roland walked around the Temple of Zeus, the Acropolis and Ancient Agora. He then visited Athens Cathedral and the Tower of the Winds. He passed by the City of Athens Museum, but for reasons unbeknownst to him it didn't open on Thursdays until 6.00 pm.

Returning to Larissa Station, Roland stocked up on some food and drink. He then went to the nearby square where he sat down on a bench until it was time to catch the bus for Istanbul.

Roland got quite a bit of sleep during the course of the journey with the bus stopping every two to three hours. Before he knew it, it was early morning and they were making another stop to pick up more passengers, at which time, he ate his remaining food and water.

The next stop was just ahead of the border where passengers disembarked and there was a brisk trade. Roland thought he might as well use up his remaining few euros on food and a large bottle of water. He had 20 eurocents remaining, which was the precise fee for a visit to the toilet.

They got back on the bus and drove to the Greek/Turkish border where there were long lines of traffic going both ways. Roland needed to purchase a visa, which cost him $20US. The customs and immigration formalities took two hours and this was even though the police gave their bus priority passage.

The bus continued on, again stopping every two to three hours. Roland ate his food supplies and managed to sleep until eventually arriving in Istanbul 1½ hours late at 4.30 pm.

Chapter 49 – A Flying Carpet Tour

Roland was armed with his central Istanbul map, and thought he had an idea of the way to the city centre so he started walking. However, he soon realised the roads didn't align with his map and he felt daunted by the complex road system and the busy traffic.

Returning to the bus station, Roland came across a man and enquired about the way to Sultanahmet. "Sultanahmet is a long way away; you will need to take the Metro," the man explained.

Roland spotted an ATM at the Metro station and withdrew some local currency then noticed a map of greater Istanbul and discovered he was miles away from the centre, which was totally off his central Istanbul map.

Roland caught the Metro from Otogar Station to Aksaray Station. Another man guided him to the tramway at Yusufpasn Station. After catching the tram and receiving more assistance, he disembarked in the area of the Sultanahmet.

Without details of where his tour commenced, Roland managed to locate the travel agency for the tour, arriving just minutes before their closing time. They advised him of the hotel from where the tour commenced and were able to book him that night's accommodation at the hotel.

Roland had a brief rest in his room before heading out for the evening. He settled on a restaurant near the Blue Mosque where they had live Turkish music and an unusual, colourful fountain. He had a special kebab and, as alcohol was not permitted in close proximity to the mosque, he had a coke.

After dinner was the time to check out the nightlife. Roland crossed the tram tracks and found a few restaurants and bars where he stopped for a large beer. The beer cost the equivalent of $6AUS, which he considered to be relatively expensive. *Since alcohol is against their religion, why not let the infidels pay?* He took his time to drink his beer before he returned to his hotel.

Roland spent the night tossing and turning before he eventually rose. He had a quick shower and went downstairs for a hearty breakfast. He confirmed his room for another night before he set off for a walk.

Arriving at the Yenikapi Port, Roland inspected the fish markets then moved on to the large Kapali Carsi Market, also referred to as the Grand Bazaar. He inspected a few of the leather jackets and notwithstanding the pressure from the vendors, he resisted purchasing anything for one reason or another. He found the purchase of a takul kebab and a fresh orange juice much easier to negotiate.

Roland took a few photos around the bazaar before walking to the Golden Horn and crossing the Galata Bridge. He stopped to admire the spectacular views looking back to the Eminonu area with its numerous mosques and other famous landmarks.

Visiting the Galata Tower, Roland was able to enjoy the panoramic views it offered. He then visited Suleymanije Camii, Aya Sofya, Sultan Ahmet Camii and Topkapi Palace. He found the views from every quarter stunning. He was highly impressed with the bustling, ancient city and was amazed how the chaotic metropolis could function in such a well-orchestrated way.

On his way back to the hotel, Roland stopped at a mini mart to purchase a bottle of water and a few beers. He was pleasantly surprised that a half-litre bottle of beer only cost the equivalent of $1AUS.

Roland turned on the television whilst he prepared for the tour group meeting. An episode of Seinfeld was showing so he relaxed to watch whilst having a beer. He then made his way to the rooftop bar where he joined the rest of the tour group.

The tour leader, Ayhan, provided information including some cultural observances and security matters. The group then went to the Doy Doy Restaurant where they enjoyed dinner in a lovely rooftop setting with magnificent views.

They went downstairs to the bar for complementary apple tea and the group members got to know each other a little better. There were twenty-five travellers with four couples, fourteen single ladies and only three single guys. Roland suspected that this may be a problem.

After breakfast, the group headed off on a city tour. They visited the Hippodrome where they saw the Egyptian Obelisk and the Serpentine Column. They then visited the Blue Mosque followed by Saint Sofia and the Basilica Cistern, the largest cistern that lay beneath the city of Istanbul. They stopped for lunch with some of the group opting for the Pudding Shop. Roland preferred to buy a kebab, which he ate under a shaded spot in a public square.

The group reassembled and proceeded to the Topkapi Palace. They had the choice of visiting the Museum, the Treasury or both. Roland opted to visit the Museum and took his time to explore the various courts and exhibitions. The highlight was the sacred safekeeping rooms that stored the holy (prophet) relics.

They made their way back to the hotel where the travellers split up and went their separate ways. Roland stepped out for a light dinner and then stopped off at an internet café. He popped into the mini mart to replenish his beer stocks before he returned to his room for some TV, beer and bed.

The group departed and had a few stops spaced a few hours apart before lunch. They then headed for Gallipoli where they commenced with a visit to the Anzac Museum. Certain members of the group were noticeably moved, which was understandable as they had close family connections. The next stop was Anzac Cove and there was a sombre mood as they approached the beach.

They peered over the hilltop and were dumbfounded by what they beheld. The vantage point on top of the hill provided a clear view of the open seas and the hill was a virtual drop. They stood and stared in silence as they attempted to comprehend the landing and reflected in awe of the diggers.

The group slowly made their way to visit the Ari Burni Cemetery and Lone Pine. They didn't speak very much, seemingly compelled to quietly pay their respects.

They proceeded to a ferry, which was running an hour late so some of the the group indulged in ice cream while others had a beer.

They got back on the bus, which was driven onto the ferry. A number of passengers disembarked, but Roland preferred to stay on the bus and enjoyed conversations with Kelly and Phillip.

On arrival at the Canakkale Port, it was a short drive to their hotel where they were allocated room keys and given 45 minutes to freshen up before they met up again.

They took a short walk around the block to a restaurant for dinner. They then went looking for some nightlife and stumbled upon a bar where they enjoyed drinks, light-hearted conversation and games of backgammon before they eventually wobbled back to their hotel.

The group headed south along the Aegean Coast to the ancient city of Troy. Roland was surprised to learn that there were in fact several cities built one on top of the other. Troy I dated from the third millennium BC and Troy IX dated back to the first century BC. Homeric Troy was considered to be Troy VIIa, dating around 1300 BC to 1190 BC. They toured the ruins and took numerous photographs including the Bouleuterion, being the former Parliament building.

They had a buffet style lunch in the city of Bergama and then visited the ruins of Pergamon. The ruins boasted the steepest amphitheatre in the world and there was also a large statue of a Roman soldier that was missing its head. "Do you mind taking a photo of the statue with me standing behind," Roland asked Cameron.

Kate was in the shot and she proceeded to get out of the way.

"Don't go, Kate," Roland insisted. "I'd prefer it if you were in the foreground of my photo."

Cameron was about to take the photo when Roland looked down at Kate. "Hey Kate, looking down at you at my feet like that, you know what?" Roland asked.

"What?" Kate replied.

"I could really go for you!"

The overnight stay was at the Barbados Hotel in Kusadasi and soon after they arrived, dinner was served. Roland returned to his room to unpack and noticed that some of his clothes were wet, which made him reflect on the merits of plastic linings. He hung up his wet clothes, put on his bathers and joined the group at the pool.

Most of the group was drinking poolside and Roland joined Trisha in the pool where they played around with an inflatable ball.

Trisha was a very attractive, elegant lady with a beautiful body. Going by her confident manner, Roland expected she knew she was attractive. He also expected she knew that he knew that she knew she was attractive. Further, he suspected that she was teasing him. He also suspected that she knew that he knew that she was teasing him.

"I really enjoyed the swim and I'm now going to bed," Trisha announced. As she emerged from the water she had a glint in her eye. Roland really would have liked to have joined her in bed and he suspected that she knew this.

Receiving an early morning wakeup call, the group had breakfast and headed off. They passed by an ATM where they pulled out some necessary funds, part of which was required to pay for the upcoming gullet cruise.

The group visited Ephesus and Roland was overwhelmed by the impressive ruins. He took photos of the statue of Nike, the Goddess of Victory, the partially restored Roman Celsus Library and the Grand Theatre.

The group was off to visit the house of the Virgin Mary. Roland wasn't feeling well and when Kate, Trisha and a few of the others opted not to visit the house, he also decided to remain behind.

After lunch, they had one of the obligatory stops at a carpet place before visiting the Cave of the Seven Sleepers.

The Seven Sleepers referred to a legend of seven young Christian men who fell asleep in the cave and woke up after a couple of hundred years. When the men died, they were buried in the cave and over the years, a number of people who wished to be buried close to the Seven Sleepers were also buried there.

The group then visited the Temple of Artemis, one of the seven wonders of the ancient world. It was once the greatest Greek temple ever built, but now lay in fragmented ruins .

The last stop for the day was a mandatory stop at a leather factory. Roland was still on the hunt for a leather jacket; however, he couldn't find anything to his liking and considered the prices to be high so he passed up all offers.

They enjoyed a buffet style dinner then went to the popular location by the pool. Trisha was taking a swim and when she emerged from the water she advised that she would be leaving the tour the next day and bid them goodnight.

It was an early morning wakeup call and the group set off at 7.00 am. They had a long drive to their first stop – the ruins at Hieropolos. This was followed by the amazing calcium white terraces at Pamukkale, which meant cotton castle in Turkish. The white layers of travertine and limestone had a cascading effect resembling a frozen waterfall. It was an unusual natural phenomenon of white cliffs, hot springs and pools.

They had a buffet lunch and Roland had the pleasure of sitting next to Trisha. "I'd really like to hear from you about the rest of the tour," she said. They exchanged contact details and after lunch the bus drove to the railway station where she was dropped off.

The group continued on to Marmaris and its lovely, colourful port. They went to a supermarket where they picked up some supplies for their three day gullet cruise.

They were taken back to the port where they were broken up into smaller groups, placed onto boats and transported to the gullet. Roland settled into his cabin, which he had to share with Judith and Clair. The two ladies shared a double bed while he took the single.

The group enjoyed drinks whilst the gullet was anchored in the harbour; the port city of Marmaris in view. Roland peered over and listened to the festivities taking place in town and wondered why they had to be stuck on the yacht. Once he finished his beer he went to bed.

Roland tossed and turned most of the night and gladly welcomed the morning. The yacht headed off after breakfast to commence their cruise around the Mediterranean; however, Roland noticed that the boat wasn't rigged for sailing. "Where are the sails?" he asked the captain.

"It's a sailing ship, but we'll be using the motors," the captain advised.

"The promotional material clearly indicated that we would be sailing in a gullet, but we're not actually sailing the Med, we'll be motorising the Med," Roland said disappointingly.

The captain didn't say a word and Roland left him to the wheel.

The group spent the day sun-bathing, swimming and drinking. The only interruption was the buffet lunch and the only excitement was when Clair was stung by a bee. Roland had a siesta and didn't wake until he was disturbed by the ladies sharing his bunk. They were dolling themselves up in preparation for dinner.

Arriving late for dinner, Roland was disappointed to hear that he'd missed out on the serving of the chicken and vegetable shish kebab so he settled for the salad, vegetables and rice. He was settling down to eat his meal when Kate handed over some of the chicken shish kebab she'd put aside for him.

Roland thought Kate was a genuinely lovely person; however, other ladies on the tour were less kind. They suggested that Kate wasn't genuine at all because, as an airline hostess, she was just putting on an act.

That evening, the group danced a little and drank a lot. It was early in the morning when they finally hit the sack.

Having very little sleep, Roland stayed in bed tossing and turning until 8.30 am. He rose, said good morning to Clair and was greeted with silence. Judith came out of the shower and gave him a similar reception. Roland was at a loss to understand why the ladies acted like bitches towards him and it gave him an added incentive to look forward to the end of the cruise.

The yacht anchored in a cove while the group had breakfast. They then boarded a small boat that took them to the beach where they climbed a few hills to view some ruins. Some considered the ruins to be a waste of time, but Roland found them interesting.

Returning to the yacht, the group had some time for a swim before lunch. They were given the option of parasailing, although Roland preferred to take a rest on the top-deck lounges. They were then given the option of riding a banana boat; however, Roland thought it looked too tame. They were later offered cakes with tea and coffee, which was an option Roland was happy to accept.

In the late afternoon, Roland went for a swim. The crew soon called him in as they were about to dump some waste and he didn't have to be told a second time. He freshened up and joined the others for pre-dinner drinks.

The group enjoyed dinner and after-dinner drinks where Roland chatted with Kate and Sofia until the ladies retired. He stayed on deck and fell asleep until he was woken by droplets of rain when he retired to his cabin.

Opening his eyes in the morning, Roland noticed that Clair was still in bed. This meant the noise coming from the bathroom was Judith having her shower. He was happy to stay in bed until the two ladies had done their thing and vacated the cabin before he rose.

Roland was comforted in the knowledge that he had endured the last night of the cruise and having to be cooped up in the cabin with the two ladies. He joined the group for breakfast and then couldn't be bothered doing anything else other than loaf about until lunch.

After lunch, Roland did some more loafing about, then went to the lounge area on the top deck where he noticed that Ann was unwell. "Is there anything I can do?" he asked.

"I'm fine," Ann stated, but Roland wasn't convinced. He called on Mia and Pam, two nurses travelling on the tour.

"She's probably dehydrated," the nurses diagnosed.

On this advice, Roland fetched a bottle of water for Ann and a beer for himself.

The group arrived at the port of Fethiye and was driven to their hotel. Roland dropped off his things and walked into town with Sofia and Kate. The ladies were in search of a travel agent and he was after an internet café.

It was Sunday 1ˢᵗ September 2002 – Father's Day. Roland had 62 email messages to attend to, but sent a happy Father's Day message first. He returned to the hotel, freshened up and joined the others for dinner. It was a special occasion – Kate's birthday.

Roland woke after a deep sleep, thankful that he was off the gullet. A few members of the group were leaving the tour, Kate being one of them. They exchanged contact details and said goodbye.

The remainder of the group headed for Saklikent Gorge, which Roland walked through with Kerrie and Cameron. They took a few photos of the gorge with its smooth rock formations and returned in time for lunch.

The group proceeded to their next hotel stop in the city of Antalya. After they settled in, they took the tour bus to a restaurant for dinner. It was early in the evening when they arrived back at the hotel, which was located in a quiet area. Antalya was renowned for its nightlife so Phillip and Roland decided catch a cab to the city centre.

They checked one of the biggest nightspots – Club Ally, which had a large outdoor disco with fancy lighting and a huge screen. It was quiet with a few seemingly well-to-do young people. After a beer, they left and walked around town trying to seek out other clubs.

They were approached by a middle-aged Englishman who struck up a conversation with them and who then took the liberty of joining them in their pursuit of nightlife. Roland attempted to shake off the Englishman, but the man persisted.

They got to Club 29 where Phillip and Roland were refused entry on the basis that they did not permit singles. "You could have said that you two were a couple," the Englishman suggested. This was enough for Roland who stormed off and Phillip quickly followed.

The group had breakfast and set off soon after. With the departure of Trisha and more recently Kate, Roland lacked motivation. He sat alone on the bus and was in a pensive state all day. The lunch stop was at the city of Konya, the religious capital of Turkey.

Roland ordered one of the traditional Konya dishes of Itsarits, which was described as a bed of chopped lamb and bread pieces topped with peppers and yogurt. He was then asked what drink he would like. "I'd like a beer," he stated without thinking. He looked around the room and noticed that all eyes were upon him.

It then dawned on Roland that they were in the religious capital of Turkey. It was one of the world's oldest settlements in the midst of numerous revered mosques and the home of Meylana Celaleddin Rumi,

Konya's Islamic hero and founder of the Sufi Order, the Whirling Dervishes. Roland placed his head in his hands. "I am very sorry, excuse me," he pleaded. "I'll have a coke please." The waiter smiled, noted down the order and went off.

The group proceeded for a couple of hours along the Anatolian Plain and stopped off at Sultanhani where they visited the Caravansary, the English term for Caravanerai. A simple translation would be a hotel; however, it had a greater historical significance. The venue and buildings, including lodgings and stables, had once served merchants travelling along the Silk Road. The complex was like a mini fortress with high external walls that once provided protection against thieves and the elements.

The group was driven to their hotel at Cappadocia where they were greeted with a small cup of red wine. They were handed their room keys and had a couple of hours to settle in and prepare for dinner. They feasted on a buffet and then hung around the hotel where they drank, chatted and played backgammon and darts. Most of the group retired, but Roland was keen to kick on and Phillip jumped at the opportunity to join him.

They wandered around the area surrounding the hotel and went into the small town centre of Ortahisar. The town was dominated by the imposing castle set on an 86-metre-high cave. It was a pleasant scene; however, there was no visible nightlife so they slowly made their way back to their hotel.

The next morning, Roland lay in bed until he could muster the motivation to have a shower and go down to breakfast. He took his time through breakfast, picking at his food before joining the group ahead of their departure.

The group visited the Open Air Museum, being the most popular tourist site in Cappadocia. It comprised churches, chapels, monasteries and other buildings carved out of the soft rock formed from the eruptions of Mount Erciyes. Roland inspected a number of the buildings and was impressed by the superb religious frescoes.

They headed off to a restaurant for lunch where they were greeted with a complimentary glass of wine then visited underground caves that housed a number of dwellings that formed the previous underground cities. The caves contained everything one would expect to find in a city, including schoolrooms and kitchens.

There was another obligatory stop, this time to visit a pottery factory. After being shown a demonstration, the group was allowed to view the exhibits and purchase items for sale. There were numerous pottery pieces, many that depicted sexual positions from which they gained much amusement.

The group visited the rock formations in the area known as the fairy chimneys including Clinton Valley. Roland asked why it was named Clinton Valley and it was suggested he wait and see. On viewing the valley, Roland took a photo and queried. "Why didn't they just refer to it as Phallic Valley and be done with it?"

Returning to the hotel, the group prepared for a traditional Turkish-folklore evening. It was a large food fair with various plates laid out on tables. They were asked not to take photographs during the performance by the Whirling Dervishes. When the mesmerizing performance concluded, they were advised that photos could now be taken and alcohol was served.

The group was entertained by folk dancers followed by a belly dancer. The finale was a form of conga dance. Roland had declined all invitations to join the dancing; he preferred to get stuck into the vodka, beer, red wine, white wine and the Turkish aperitif of Raki. He was eventually dragged onto the dance floor at the point when he was sufficiently tanked. They then headed for a disco where they continued to party until the early hours.

Roland woke, but stayed in bed due to his hangover. He went down to breakfast where he joined a few of the tour members and caught up with the gossip. He then prepared himself for a walk to the township of Goreme six kilometres away.

Arriving at the town, Roland visited the internet café for a couple of hours. He then went to a restaurant for lunch and visited a mini mart where he bought a large bottle of water. He made his way back to the hotel, taking a few photos of the landscape along the way.

On his way back, Roland was approached by an old man with a donkey. The man insisted that he take a bunch of grapes. The grapes didn't look very nice and he declined, but the old man shoved them into his hand. Roland walked on, carrying the grapes for a distance before dumping them on the side of the road.

Roland joined the group at the pool where he had a refreshing swim and relaxed sun-bathing. Arrangements were made to visit the Turkish bathhouse and the males made their way there.

The men took off their footwear and put on a pair of plastic slippers then went through to the change rooms and got into their bathers. They piled into the sauna to sweat it out for a while. They splashed themselves with cold water and it was back into the sauna to sweat it out again.

They lay on a large marble slab and were selected in turn to have a scrub and by the sound of it, some hard slaps. At this moment, Roland cast his mind back to the torturous massage he'd had years ago in Morocco and prepared himself for the worst.

The scrub was bearable and Roland tensed up at the sign of any slap. The massage was firm and invigorating, which made him feel good. After everyone had completed their massage, they rejoined the group for dinner and an early night.

It was a five hour drive to Ankara with a couple of stops along the way. They visited the Ataturk Museum with Ataturk's symbolic monument sarcophagus. The museum included various paintings and items that belonged to Ataturk. They viewed the mausoleum and also witnessed the Changing of the Guard.

The group was taken to a shopping complex in Ankara where they had lunch in the food court. Roland then strolled around the complex and noted how modern the establishment was and how fashionable the people were dressed. It was a stark contrast to the more traditional cities they had visited in Turkey. They purchased some snacks and drinks for the long haul to Istanbul.

Arriving at the Grand Yavuz Hotel, it was the juncture where Ayhan was to leave the tour. Cameron made a thank you speech on behalf of the group and handed Ayhan a present and an envelope containing a tip. Ayhan seemed genuinely appreciative and thanked everyone before departing.

As soon as Ayhan left, the group seemed lost. They finally arranged to go to the same place they patronised on the first evening of the tour – the rooftop of the Doy Doy Restaurant.

After dinner, as most of them were heading off in the morning, they returned to their hotel. Unsurprisingly, Phillip and Roland decided to experience the nightlife and headed off to Taksim Square.

They roamed around trying to find a place to have a drink, before finally finding a bar and ordering beers. They struck up a conversation with a man who recommended a disco, named Laila. Phillip and Roland caught a taxi there, but they were told that it was closed. They strolled to another bar and were told that they could not enter as it was a private function. They then went to a place named The Mix and were allowed entry.

They tried to order two beers and the waiter advised that it was an open bar for a fixed price of 25 million Turkish lira. Their eyes lit up and they eagerly accepted. Turkish music was playing, and whereas other nightspots were mainly frequented by men, to their surprise there was an even mix of men and women. "Makes sense, given the name of the joint," Roland quipped.

Phillip drew Roland's attention to the front table where a bride and groom were seated. "That'd be right," Roland commented. "We couldn't get into the standard clubs, but we're allowed at a wedding reception." It was early morning when they were asked to leave, and they were the last to leave.

Roland dragged himself out of bed to see off several members of the group. He then joined the remaining group members for breakfast. He still had six days in Istanbul and as the Grand Yavuz was booked out he needed to find alternative accommodation. A couple of the group members had switched to the Tayhan Hotel so he migrated there as well.

Walking along the thoroughfare of Ordu Cadessi, Roland inspected a few leather places, but he couldn't quite find a jacket he wanted so he moved on.

The Grand Bazaar was Roland's next destination where he purchased pistachio gelati. He contemplated making another attack on more leather places; however, it was getting late so he returned to his hotel room. He dozed off and woke up in time to meet up with Kelly and Shirley for dinner at the Sultanahmet Chicken Restaurant.

Roland found the dinner enjoyable and the company pleasant; however, he was depressed about the dwindling group numbers and the fact that he had lost his only drinking partner in Phillip. After dinner, he watched some television in his hotel room before going to sleep.

The next morning, Roland found a message from Kelly advising that she was planning to go for a cruise up the Bosphorus and she'd be at breakfast at 9.00 am. He joined her for breakfast before they set off along Ordu Cadessi and followed the tramline to the ferry port.

They had heard that one could purchase a return ticket for a Bosphorus cruise including a small snack for a meagre five million Turkish lira. They were hassled by numerous men to purchase tickets; however, the prices quoted seemed exorbitant. After some enquiries, they managed to find return tickets for Rumeli Kavagia for five million Turkish lira.

Kelly and Roland boarded the midday ferry and were greeted with a toasted cheese sandwich and an orange juice. Roland graciously accepted the offer as did Kelly. The waiter continued with the offerings to others and then reappeared soon after as Roland was licking his chops. The waiter then demanded eight million Turkish lira for the snack.

"I thought the snack was included in the price of the ticket?" Kelly queried.

"That's what I thought," Roland said, "but don't worry, the snack is on me."

Kelly and Roland found a comfortable spot inside the cabin, venturing out to take photographs of the Rumeli Fortress. They reached their destination at Rumeli where they walked around for a while. They stopped for a bite to eat and the competition between the food vendors was fierce.

Roland wasn't very hungry and settled for an Ayran yogurt drink. Kelly was able to negotiate a cheap meal of calamari and mixed salad. Roland was impressed with her negotiating skills until he evidenced the food that was presented to her. She managed to obtain a 20% discount, but they appeared to have halved the serving.

They returned to the ferry and arrived back at the hotel. "I'll be stepping out to dinner around seven in the evening," Roland told her.

"You can knock on my door," Kelly said with a smile.

Kelly wished to dine somewhere close so they ambled towards the sea of Mamara and came across a couple of seafood restaurants where she chose the one where she felt more comfortable. They had a fascinating chat, with Kelly opening up about some of her personal experiences during her time in Turkey.

Kelly was an attractive, middle-aged English lady with blonde hair and blue eyes. "Men had made a number of what I felt were improper advances towards me," she divulged. "I really appreciate you being with me because, had I been on my own, I expect I wouldn't be going out at all."

"It's my pleasure, and I also appreciate you being here as I've enjoyed your company," Roland said. They exchanged smiles and toasted each other.

Roland joined Kelly for breakfast and they discussed their options for the day. They decided to go shopping at the Grand Bazaar where Kelly purchased a baby's T-shirt for her niece and 30 bookmarks for her school students. Roland still hadn't purchased anything and was resigned to the prospect that he may not be purchasing any souvenirs in Istanbul.

Roland knocked on Kelly's door at the pre-arranged time for dinner. They walked around the nearby streets and decided to eat at the Divan Pizza Restaurant.

Making their way back to the hotel, they witnessed a load of people around a police van. There were a couple of police cars with policemen scattered around wielding guns. They avoided the scene, not even curious to know what was happening and returned to the relative safety of their hotel.

Kelly was heading off the following morning and she met up with Roland for breakfast before they said goodbye. Roland couldn't secure his room for his final two days but managed to find alternative accommodation at the Park Hotel.

Walking to the Grand Bazaar, Roland inspected more leather places and finally found a jacket he thought looked good. "I will offer the jacket to you for the special price of 385 million Turkish lira," stated the salesman.

Roland interpreted the term special price to be a high price. "I've seen a similar jacket for only $85US," Roland claimed.

"I'll match it," the salesman immediately replied.

Roland looked at the jacket again. "I'll take another look around, but I may come back later."

Roland walked around the shops in the area of the Suleymaniye Mosque before crossing the Galata Bridge and moving on to Galata Tower. He took the lift to the panoramic level and snapped a few photos of the city. He then travelled to Taksim Square and took a photo of the Republic Monument. The thoroughfare of Istiklal Caddesi in the suburb of Galatasaray was lively and he took a photograph of the scene with one of the characteristic trams.

Crossing the Galata Bridge, Roland came across the many vendors on boats along the bank. Amongst the products on sale were grilled and fried fish fillets in a roll. He purchased one, which the vendor included tomatoes and added some lemon sauce. He crunched through the small fish bones and considered it to be a reasonable snack for around $1.50AUS.

Roland went through the Egyptian Bazaar, also known as the Spice Market. He sampled the pistachio flavoured Turkish delight, which he liked, but didn't buy. He then returned once more to the Grand Bazaar determined to buy the leather jacket he'd seen earlier that day.

The salesman immediately recognised him and before Roland could utter a word the salesman questioned him. "Why didn't you buy the other jacket?"

Roland was unprepared for the question and didn't know what to say so he blurted out the first thing that popped into his head. "They didn't take credit card."

The salesman seemed unimpressed with the reply. "That's a pity as my jacket is more expensive."

Roland was puzzled by the statement. "I thought you were willing to accept $85US?"

"No the price is $185US," the salesman asserted.

"Forget it!" Roland stated and stormed off.

Walking by the shop where Kelly purchased her bookmarks, Roland considered they would make good token souvenirs so he purchased a bunch. He went back to the hotel and later stepped out briefly for dinner before going to bed.

In the morning, Roland made his way to the rooftop terrace where he had magnificent views of the Blue Mosque, Saint Sofia and the Bosphorus. Classical music was playing and he enjoyed a relaxing breakfast in the warmth of a clear morning.

Having dropped off his laundry, Roland headed for the port where he took the ferry to Buyukada. It was the largest of nine islands that made up the Princes Islands in the Sea of Marmara.

The beaches near the port appeared dirty, which discouraged Roland from going for a swim. Motorised vehicles were forbidden on the island so he went for a hike. He walked for about an hour before he decided to head back to the town. He admired the quaint suburban areas containing tree-lined streets that featured lovely weatherboard houses, horse drawn carriages and fruit shops displaying fresh produce of enormous size.

Taking the ferry back to Istanbul, Roland took a photograph of the Buyukada Port as they cruised off. He was uncertain of the ferry route so he disembarked at Kabatas about four kilometres from his hotel in Eminonu. He commenced walking and saw the ferry turn and go directly to the Eminonu Port.

Roland picked up his laundry and returned to the hotel. He had a snooze before he set off and found a restaurant that took credit card and served alcohol. After dinner, he went to the Taksim area and looked around for a club or a bar. He ended up in the Regina Club that had a Crazy Horse Show. He entered at midnight and had a couple of drinks before he left.

Roland then dropped into a club on the bank of the Golden Horn, which drew in patrons with a large beam of light and thumping, loud music. The patrons were made up of mainly men so he finished his drink and headed back to his hotel.

Managing to get a couple of hours sleep, Roland went to breakfast where he enjoyed the lovely views from the rooftop terrace for the last time. He checked out, had his backpack stored at the hotel and strolled to an internet café. He spent three hours dealing with his messages and then went for a walk. He continued walking to the point where he could capture a view of the Bozdogan Aqueduct.

Roland moved to the seating area near the Blue Mosque for a rest. He then returned to the hotel, collected his bag and caught the airport shuttle. The driver went like a bat out of hell, which was hardly necessary as Roland had a thirteen hour wait before his flight.

Placing his luggage in storage, Roland wandered around the airport to figure out how he could spend his remaining Turkish lira. He bought some sandwiches and Turkish delight as well as a drink from the vending machine where the prices were almost half the price of those in the shops.

Roland rested on a bench where he dozed off. When he awoke he wondered what he could do next. He pulled out one of his sandwiches and ate it. He then shuffled around, laid out on the bench and went to sleep again. When he awoke, he pulled out his remaining sandwich and ate that one too. He then opened his box of Turkish delight and before long he had eaten the lot.

Noticing that the Lufthansa check-in counter was open, Roland collected his backpack, joined the queue and caught his Lufthansa flight LH3399 to Frankfurt. He went to the transit service counter and was directed to the boarding gate where the passengers were progressively allowed to board Thai Airlines TG921 flight to Bangkok.

Chapter 50 – Indo-China

After picking up his bag, Roland withdrew 10,000 baht from the ATM and went to the train station. The ticket salesman couldn't give change for a 1,000 baht note so Roland went to the nearby 711 store and purchased a bottle of water that provided the change he required.

Roland took the train to the Hua Lampong Station in Bangkok, loaded his backpack and was quickly on his way. He had to deviate around a number of people who were offering their services and products, but eventually made it to the street. He scurried along; however, it didn't take long before he felt that he was lost so he returned to the station.

Picking up on Roland's uncertainty, the locals were even more persistent in their offerings. He reluctantly replied to some of their questions. "Yes I have a hotel... it's in Chinatown... the Grand China Princess Hotel." Once he cooperated with the locals, he actually found that they were extremely helpful.

Arriving at the hotel, Roland freshened up and considered his options for a walk about the city. He headed down Rama I Road, Ratchadamri Road and Patpong Road. The streets were quiet as the markets and bars were closed; however, this didn't stop him being hassled.

Making it back to Chinatown, Roland looked around for a bite to eat. The restaurants seemed pricey so he checked out the street vendors, most of whom didn't speak English, but his hunger got the better of him and he took a seat. He pointed to a bowl showing through a glass cabinet and the vendor stated something. He had no idea what the vendor said, but he nodded and was soon presented with dumplings soup.

Roland returned to his hotel and commenced taking his malaria pills. After a snooze, he headed out for the evening. He checked out a number of restaurants and finally selected the Tip Top Restaurant. It was a strange choice of restaurant as it was where he fell ill the previous time he ate at Patpong. He was reasonably satisfied with his meal and took off to see if he could find some nightlife.

Roaming around the Patpong streets, Roland couldn't locate anything that appealed so he headed back to the hotel. As he was walking off, he came across a person with the looks of a woman, but the voice of a man. "Can I do anything for you?" the person asked.

"No thanks," Roland replied as he rushed away.

Waking up in the early morning, Roland made his way to the buffet breakfast, which often proved a problem as he tended to overeat. He made his way to reception and checked on the room situation as he was due to commence his Indo-China tour that day. "You will need to check out of your room and check into a twin share room where you will be sharing with Miss Crimmins."

Roland was sure they meant Mr Crimmins; however, they confirmed that it was in fact Miss Crimmins. He went off, packed and returned to reception. During that time, Miss Crimmins had apparently changed to Mr Crimmins, and Mr Crimmins was currently in the room. Roland proceeded to the room to meet Mr Crimmins.

Damian Crimmins was an amateur rugby player from Brisbane. After they became acquainted, they went in search of an internet café. They went to the train station and were directed to an internet place costing one baht per minute. They spent a couple of hours at the internet café before they returned to the hotel and had a workout at the gym then visited an establishment that advertised traditional Thai massages.

Damian was called up first by a young, attractive lady who led him away. Another lady entered the room and she was a middle-aged lady with severe body odour. Roland was looking into space and hoped that she didn't call him, but she did.

Roland was led into a small room and was asked to undress. He was given a reasonable massage and the lady then pointed to his testicles. "Would you like your eggs massaged?" she asked.

"Is this part of the massage?" he naively queried.

"Yes, it is," she replied, "and the locals love it."

Roland gave the go ahead and the lady massaged his eggs.

"Would you like…?" the lady asked as she gestured a hand job.

"Is this part of the massage?" he again naively queried.

"No, it isn't; this will cost you extra," she replied.

Roland declined and the lady then advised that the massage was over.

Returning to the room, Roland found Damian lying on his bed with a big smile. "What extra services did your lady provide in order to give you that smile?" Roland pried.

"She gave me a head job," Damian responded.

"You're a lucky bastard to get the good looking, young lady. Was it part of the standard massage or did you have to pay extra?" Roland asked.

"I had to pay extra," Damian advised, still sporting a broad smile.

Damian and Roland freshened up and went to the tour meeting in the lobby. The group took care of some paperwork and received a rundown of the itinerary before they went out for dinner at a Chinese restaurant.

After dinner, the group headed off to Kao San Road and found a bar where they got stuck into the local Chang and Leo beers. As they got inebriated, they also sampled the delicacies of silk worms and scorpion.

Damian and Roland inspected one of the nightclubs and reported back. The report was good enough to attract most of the group and it was in the early hours of the morning before they headed back to their hotel by tuk tuk.

Damian and Roland received an unexpected wakeup call. Roland was hung over and struggled to get up a couple of times before he managed to sit up in bed. He had a quick shower and headed down to breakfast where he managed to consume fluids.

The group met up and was introduced to their guide, Susan. Susan escorted them for a tour of Wat Phra Kaoe and the Grand Palace. She provided a detailed explanation of various buildings and highlighted the Emerald Buddha. They then visited Wat Pho, the largest wat in Bangkok and the location of the famous Reclining Buddha. Although Roland had visited these attractions before, this visit with the added explanations made him even more appreciative.

They were given the option of returning to the hotel or hitting Kao San Road. They opted for Kao San Road and jumped on a boat that cruised along the Chao Phray River. Arriving at their destination, Susan provided some information and they were allowed to do as they pleased; however, they tended to stay together and went to a restaurant.

After lunch, Damian and Roland walked back to the hotel via the Democracy Monument. When they arrived at the hotel they hit the pool and had a short rest prior to meeting up with the group again. They took taxis to the Patpong area where they had dinner then Susan said they could spend the evening doing their own thing.

Damian and Roland chose to go off to check out the Patpong bars. They went upstairs to watch a girlie show, which was promoted as 100 baht per beer with no cover charge. They ordered a beer and were soon approached by some ladies who tried to pressure them to pay 300 baht for the show.

"We agreed to enter the bar on the basis that there was no cover charge," Damian explained; however, the ladies insisted.

"If you persist in asking us for money, I will leave as soon as I finish my beer!" Roland stated. The ladies seemed to have accepted his assertion as they moved on to harass other tourists.

Damian and Roland sat back with their beers and over the duration of a couple of hours they saw some amazing acts. Roland was most impressed with the vaginal dart shooting of balloons at 10 metres where the stripper achieved a perfect score. When they noticed that the acts were starting to repeat, they considered it to be an appropriate time to leave.

They were heading back to the hotel when a couple of bar girls bailed them up. They stayed for a beer and a traditional game of Connect Four. Of course the girls won and they were soon propositioning the men for other pursuits.

Roland was highly attracted to his lady friend, although Damian was understandably not keen on his. It was no surprise when Roland went off with his lady and Damian returned to the hotel. Roland's lady friend was particularly playful and they spent half the night together before he returned to the hotel.

The group was scheduled to depart early in the morning; however, they were delayed twenty minutes due to Mira being late. Mira didn't see how the group having to wait for her was a problem.

They visited the Floating Markets where there was a hive of activity. Canoes floated around containing various foods with all sorts of dishes being cooked up on boats along the banks and they were offered various produce to sample.

The group then visited a wood carving place before they had lunch and moved on to the JEATH War Museum. JEATH was the acronym for the six countries involved, being Japan, England, America, Australia, Thailand and Holland. The war museum was housed in bamboo huts like those the prisoners were kept in on the banks of the Mae Klong River.

The museum was a memorial to the construction of the Thai-Burma Railway, also known as the Death Railway. The group learned quite a bit about the atrocities perpetrated against the prisoner of war labourers and the historic events of the area during World War II.

They were driven a short distance to the bridge over the River Kwai and they pensively walked across. Roland took a photo of the bridge and then had one taken with Damian. The group travelled by long tail boat to their overnight stay at a hotel along the River Kwai.

Roland and Damian went for breakfast and had their fill by the time the others joined them. The group took a hike where they admired the scenery of the Kanchanaburi area on their way to the Lave Cave.

It was very hot and humid so they were relieved to have reached the coolness of the cave. The lighting in the cave was on the blink and no one had a torch so they only ventured in a short distance before they returned. When they arrived back at the hotel, they gained some respite from the hot and humid weather by hitting the pool.

The group had lunch and at the time when the group was due to leave in the early afternoon it started pouring rain. They were given umbrellas and scampered to their rooms to pack. They continued their travel by long tail boat and then by vans to Bangkok.

Reaching Hua Lampong Station, the group piled their bags in the food court. A few members of the group took turns standing guard of the bags, whilst the others ventured around the station to get a bite to eat and stock up on supplies before their overnight train journey to Chiang Mai.

Chapter 51 – The Hill Tribe

The group boarded the train and found their seats. Damian and Roland lost no time to settle in and popped open a couple of beers. Roland soon got restless so he went for a wander down the corridors and peered into each carriage as he passed. He spent some time in the restaurant carriage before returning to his seat.

The train staff systematically made up the beds and when Roland's bed was done it was a position he cramped into for the duration of the 14-hour trip.

The train arrived in Chiang Mai over 1½ hours late. The group boarded a van and was driven to their accommodation at the Suan Doi House where they settled into their rooms and were given a couple of hours of free time.

Damian and Roland checked out some of the shops before finding a restaurant where they enjoyed a meal with complimentary Chinese tea. They dropped into an internet café before making their way back to the hotel. It started to rain and returning to the hotel, they quickly towelled down, changed into dry clothes and met up with the others.

The group was driven by bus up the mountains to the Doi Sudthep Temple and climbed the 309 steps to the top where they took photos of the temple and the panoramic views of the sprawling city of Chiang Mai.

They made their way to a jade factory where they were provided with complimentary jasmine tea, shown a video and given a demonstration of jade outlining and polishing. They were then provided with complimentary rice crackers and more tea before being given time to examine the products and make purchases.

The group was given a couple of hours to freshen up before they took a songthaew to the Night Bazaar. They were shown the food court where they could purchase vouchers, which were traded for food and drink. There was live entertainment in the form of Thai dancers on one stage and Thai boxing on another stage. They explored the night market before joining up again for the ride back to the hotel.

The next day, they were driven in songthaews to an elephant pickup point. Each elephant had a rider and places for two passengers. Damian and Roland shared an elephant and they rode for about an hour before they were dropped off.

The group trekked a short distance where they were provided with a lunch box. They proceeded on their trek along the trail, which was fairly steep in parts, so they set a leisurely pace with regular stops. They were joined for the last part of the trek by a guide named Dell.

It had begun to rain before the group arrived at the hill tribe huts in the Lahu Village. They were shown their huts with two people being accommodated in each one. They joined the locals who had started a fire for their wet visitors and were offered drinks of sprite, coke and beer.

The group sat around the fire and waited for their turn to have a shower. During their wait they tried some food that had a distinct peanut taste. It was later revealed that the food was fried larvae worms.

Roland thought it was close to his turn to have a wash when they were told that the water had run out. Damian didn't seem too fussed about not being able to shower; however, Roland was seated, gazing into the fire, feeling wet, dirty and miserable.

The group was served dinner and entertainment was provided by way of music and singing with children dressed in traditional costumes. The guests didn't need much encouragement to participate in well-known Western songs.

The food and entertainment had taken Roland's mind away from his sad state and he was further uplifted when Dell said he could take them to the adjoining village for a wash.

Damian and Roland hiked to the adjoining village where they were handed buckets filled with water and then shown to a veranda with small torches hanging overhead. They were stumbling around trying to shine the torches in a direction that assisted them while trying to juggle their buckets and soap.

Damian finished his wash whilst Roland had just managed to get steadied and organised. Damian headed off and Roland continued on, stopping momentarily to admire the magical view of the cloudy, moonlit sky when he realised he was standing in the open air, nude.

Finally completing his wash to the point where he felt reasonably clean, Roland dried off, dressed and slowly made his way back towards the hill tribe huts. It was dark, and he had trouble finding the trail. The track was muddy, and in his flip flops, very slippery. By the time he managed to find his way back, he felt almost as dirty as before his wash.

Roland rejoined the others around the fire where they listened to stories about the hill tribe people who originally came from Burma and China. Some of them did not really know the country in which they were born or the country in which they lived. They just considered themselves to be people from the mountains and the hills.

It was a long night of unfamiliar jungle and animal noises, and as the group emerged from their slumber they were greeted with breakfast. Most of the group opted for an elephant ride whilst Mira, Adrian, Damian and Roland opted for a hike to the Huay Sadan Waterfall with Dell as their guide.

The pace was comfortable with the initial part of the hike being reasonably flat, although there were some steeper parts as they continued. On their arrival at the waterfall, the hikers jumped in the waters for a ceremonial dip.

They returned after 2½ hours of hiking and they met up with the others at the Mae Tang Elephant Camp where they finished their adventure with a group photo. Lunch was served and the group had time to digest their meal before they embarked on a white water rafting adventure.

Roland was a bit apprehensive as he recalled the drama of his white water rafting at Victoria Falls years before. However, the rapids on this occasion were only rated grade three and found to be very tame. The only way they managed to get wet was by tossing each other into the water.

The group visited the Akha Village whose people originated from China. The Akha people had a witch doctor to deal with the swamp spirits. The group visited a hut house and was provided with green tea and bananas before taking songthaews to another camp.

The group picked up mountain bikes and rode to their next overnight stop at Lisu Lodge where they had an opportunity for a warm shower before drinks and dinner.

Roland tossed and turned all night, going to the toilet several times and being irritated by the animal and jungle noises. He had a sore throat and chest congestion and suspected that staying wet for such a long time after the hill tribe trek had resulted in him catching a cold.

After managing only a couple of hours sleep, Roland decided to get up. He had a shower, packed his things and walked out on the veranda where he sat for some time, gazing out at the lovely mountain scenery until breakfast was served.

The group visited the Lisu Village and was invited into a hut house where Dell delivered a wealth of information about the Lisu people. They then visited a Spirit House followed by a Sharman's House where Dell provided more intriguing information.

They returned to their lodge and later that morning went for an ox-cart ride through the farmlands. They visited the village of Baan Pang Mai Daeng before returning by songthaew to Lisu Lodge for lunch.

They returned to Chiang Mai, packed their main luggage and loaded them into the van. They then headed towards the Thai/Laos border, stopping every hour or so. Their overnight stop was at a guest house in Chiang Khong where they dined before preparing their belongings for their two-day boat ride in Laos.

Chapter 52 – Laos

In the morning, the group settled their accounts at the guesthouse and took some time to admire the lovely views of the surrounding area set along the banks of the Mekong River before being driven to the town of Huay Xai.

They proceeded to the Thai border where they took a long tail boat to the Laos side of the river. After a quick stop to convert their Thai baht into Laos kip, it was off on another long tail boat to their cruise boat, the *Pak Ou*.

Roland sat on one of the comfortable chairs on the side deck where he could feel the cool breeze and a touch of river spray. He took a photo of the Mekong River taking in the lovely scenery of both banks on the Thai and Laos sides before he was interrupted by the call for lunch.

The group stopped at Yao Village and was shown around by a local guide. The town was quaint and quiet, other than a group of carefree children playing. They boarded their cruise boat and travelled until they reached their overnight stay at the guesthouse Villa Salika in Pak Beng, Northern Laos.

The accommodation was set on the Mekong with magnificent views. Roland had a snooze and when he woke, no one from the group was around and the boat was no longer where it had berthed. He decided to go for a walk before it got dark. Leaving the room key at reception, he strolled up the main street where he came across the group sitting at a café and he joined them for a lemon iced tea.

The group returned to their accommodation where they had dinner and tasted rice spirit before moving to the balcony to continue drinking and socialising. Roland had an early night in an effort to get over his cold.

The next morning, the group was escorted to the market but the merchandise was already sold out. They then moved for a visit to a Buddhist temple before returning to the guesthouse.

They boarded the *Pak Ou* and set off for their second day of cruising. At midday, the sound of a spoon chiming against a glass was the call for lunch.

The group stopped at the Pak Ou Caves, also referred to as the Caves of a Thousand Buddhas. They explored both the upper and lower caves where they could view the various Buddha images.

Resuming their cruise, they stopped off at a village where they tasted various types of flavoured rice wine. They continued on until they arrived at

Luang Prabang and were driven to the Sene Souk Guesthouse in the middle of town where they were allowed 30 minutes to settle in before reassembling for a briefing.

It was a short briefing and they were then given 2½ hours of free time. When they reunited, they headed off to the Café D'Arte for dinner. They walked off their dinner by passing some shops and moving on to the night market before they returned to the guesthouse.

After breakfast, the group visited the Royal Palace Museum where they admired exhibits from several centuries of the Lao past. They soon set off again and were taken to Kuang Si Waterfall where they took a short hike up a cliff to enjoy the scenery. On their way back to the guesthouse, they had a glancing view of an Indochinese Corbett's tiger.

It was a short rest before they were taken to Mount Phousi to climb the steps and enjoy the panoramic views over Luang Prabang at sunset.

Waking up a number of times throughout the night, Roland finally rose early and kept a lookout to see if the Buddhist monks were out to collect their food donated by the town folk. He saw no sign of them and joined Damian for breakfast.

The group left the town of Luang Pabang and moved along with relief stops every couple of hours. It had developed into a very hot and humid day so when they stopped for lunch the travellers stripped down to their underwear. They continued on and encountered a very windy and bumpy road. Roland felt the full impact of every bump as he was stranded down the back of the van.

They arrived at the town of Vang Vieng and were handed their room keys. Roland rested on his bed and felt miserable. When the time came to visit some caves, he declined, preferring to rest. He admired the lovely views of the Nam Song River, the forest and the misty mountains.

The group set off after breakfast for the capital of Laos, Vientiane. Without stopping, they managed to arrive by midday where they were distributed their room keys and given some free time.

Damian and Roland went for a walk down one of the main drags, named Setthaithirath, and along the Mekong Promenade. They walked by the Presidential Cabinet and the Presidential Palace then visited Talat Sao, which was called the Morning Market even though it was open all day.

The market was the centre of life in Vientiane with a wide variety of fruits, vegetables, meats and handicrafts. Surrounding the market were banks, government buildings, the tourist office and the bus station.

Damian and Roland passed by That Dam (the Black Stupor) before stopping off at the Kua Loa Restaurant for lunch. They made it back to the hotel in time for the group gathering.

The group visited Wat Si Saket and Haw Pha Kaew – once a royal temple but now a museum with excellent Buddhist sculptures. They moved on to view Pha That Luang and the Golden Stupa, being the national symbol of Laos, with the statue of King Luang in the foreground.

They visited the Patuxai Victory Arch Monument, which was stated to resemble the Arc de Triomphe in Paris. It was ironic that a structure, said to resemble the Parisian arc, was built as a memorial to the victory of independence from France.

The group was driven to the Morning Market where they were allowed a short visit before returning to the hotel for dinner. They walked to the Wildside Restaurant where Roland and Susan shared a Laos Discovery meal.

After dinner, Damian and Roland broke away to check out the nightlife. They tried the Broadway Club at the Plaza Hotel that seemed like a karaoke with a few people on the dance floor doing a form of dancing with unusual finger movements. They stayed for a beer before they moved on.

Their next stop was the Anou Hotel Cabaret. The establishment seemed to offer a similar deal and the guys had their customary beer. They tried one more bar and had one more beer before they returned to their hotel.

The group set off for the airport and had to wait to check in and pay the airport tax. They used the time to change their remaining kip and Mirella allowed Roland to lump his small sum of kip together with her kip to minimize the fee. She also loaned him $10US for the airport tax.

It was yet another wait until they were allowed to board their two engine propeller plane to Hanoi.

Chapter 53 – Vietnam

Damian and Roland settled into their room. Damian switched on the television and the 2002 AFL Grand Final was showing. They sat and watched the remainder of the game and witnessed Brisbane beat Collingwood by nine points.

The group went to the Kangaroo Café for lunch and then followed Roland on his walking tour. They headed for the Old Quarter where the setting and the character of the area captured their imagination.

The streets were tree-lined and packed with small motorcycles and foot traffic. There were a number of local people going about their business transporting their produce in large carry baskets. Roland took a photo of Cua O Quan Chuong – the Old East Gate of Hanoi – before they slowly made their way back to the hotel.

The guide for the next day gave a briefing before the group returned to the Old Quarter for dinner. They enjoyed a set menu and lots of beer. It was then off to another bar for more beer. They kicked on at the New Century Disco where the tourists proved popular with the locals and they danced until the early hours.

The group visited the Ho Chi Minh Mausoleum and viewed Uncle Ho's body before they moved on to the Presidential Palace. Uncle Ho did not live in the palace, preferring to live in a modest, small stilt house beside a lake.

They visited Uncle Ho's House before heading to the One Pillar Pagoda and the Temple of Literature. Their last visit was to the Army Museum where they spent some time viewing the many exhibits depicting the Vietnamese wars. They were driven back to the hotel at midday and had the afternoon to themselves.

Damian and Roland continued on Roland's walking tour around the Old Quarter where each street had its own theme. There was a street with leather shops, another street with tin products, another street of fruit shops and so it went on. Passing St Joseph Cathedral, they noticed a unisex hairdresser and Damian decided to have a haircut. He was being attended to by one hairdresser and Roland struck up a conversation with the other hairdresser.

Roland agreed that Damian's haircut looked good. "You have hair cut?" the other hairdresser asked Roland. They confirmed the price of 30,000 dong and Roland gave him the go ahead. The hairdresser kicked a local guy off the seat, welcomed Roland onto the seat and gave him a masterly haircut.

The guys returned to the hotel and got ready to meet up with the group. They were booked for a showing of the Water Puppets and were handed their tickets and a cassette recording of the show's music. They had dinner before they attended the Thang Long Water Puppet Theatre.

Roland spent some time trying to figure out how they managed to work the puppets on the water stage. He eventually gave up trying to figure it out and just sat back to enjoy the show.

The group stopped off for some bia hoi where the vendors quickly gathered additional plastic stools to accommodate them. They had quite a few glasses of the local brew before they returned to their hotel.

The next morning, Roland awoke ahead of Damian. "Do you want to go to Lake Hoan Kiem?" Roland asked. The attraction was to witness the locals going about the early morning regular exercise routines, including tai chi and badminton.

"No, not really; why, do you?" Damian responded.

Roland thought about it and was comfortable in bed. "No, not really."

Damian and Roland headed off after breakfast to complete Roland's walking tour. They went to Lake Hoan Kiem — lake of the restored sword and home to freshwater tortoises — to view the Tortoise Tower in the centre of the lake. The tower was dedicated to the legend of the tortoise who gave the King a magic sword to defeat invaders.

They then visited the Jade Mountain Temple and the Huc Bridge. The Huc Bridge, or the Bridge of the Rising Sun, was the pathway to reach the Ngoc Son Pagoda.

It was a hot and humid day, so they were happy to spend some time relaxing around the beautiful lake. They exchanged some pleasantries with the locals and purchased doughnuts and custard sweet bread from a street vendor. They returned to the hotel, packed and joined the others to set off on the four hour drive to Halong Bay.

They first stopped off at a craft factory where they saw potters at work and shopped for handicrafts.

Arriving at Halong Bay, the group was greeted with sweetened orange juice. They checked into their rooms and hung around until they headed off to a restaurant.

After dinner, they went to an establishment that offered bia hoi. They consumed a few glasses before they shifted to a karaoke bar where Karen and Damian performed a duet. They reunited in Anne and Archie's room to consume more beer while they watched MTV and a replay of the AFL Grand Final.

The group left for the port at Halong Bay where they boarded their private boat and set off for their five-hour cruise to enjoy the views of the spectacular scenery of islands and limestone outcrops for which Halong Bay was renowned.

They stopped off to view a grotto and a cave before cruising on to a spot where they dived off the boat, had a swim and sun-bathed. The tranquil environment was temporarily interrupted by the call for lunch. They made it back to the port around three o'clock in the afternoon and returned to Hanoi before their overnight train trip to Hue.

The group gathered their bags and was ready ahead of the departure time, although one of the passengers, named Ben, was unseen. They waited for almost half an hour. "We have no option but to leave without him," Susan stated.

They were heading down one of the main streets of the town when Ben was spotted at a fast food place about to order some food. They called out to attract his attention, and he boarded the bus, totally bemused. "I lost track of time."

The bus returned to the hotel for Ben to collect his belongings before proceeding to the train station. Roland shared a cabin with Anne, Archie and Damian where they enjoyed some lotus flavoured Vietnamese tea before bed.

They arrived in Hue, considered to be the cultural capital of Vietnam, and were driven to their accommodation at Hotel Morin. The group was then taken to the Citadel where they were given a guided tour of the Main Ceremonial Hall, the King's Library and the Worship Building of the 13 Kings.

Later that afternoon, they were taken to the Bang Do Market. Roland came across a bottle of local rice wine brew, Minh Mang Thang, which was for medicinal purposes and a reputed aphrodisiac. Roland decided to buy a bottle. "If it was good enough for Emperor Minh Mang, then it's good enough for me," he declared.

Only about half of the group showed up to meet for dinner. They dined at the Mandarin Café before migrating to the DMZ Bar. The bar was fairly quiet, but they stayed for a few beers before returning to the hotel.

After breakfast, the group walked to the river port where they took a tourist boat along the Huong River, which translated to the Perfume River. They visited the Thien Mu Pagoda, also known as the Pagoda of the Heavenly Lady. They took a bus to visit the mausoleums of two kings from the Nguyen Dynasty, being the Khai Dinh Mausoleum and the Tu Duc Mausoleum. They then stopped off at a village that made incense sticks before they returned to the hotel.

Damian and Roland walked to a small restaurant for lunch and then returned to the hotel for a siesta. When they awoke, they decided to miss the group dinner in order to check out the nightlife.

They stopped for a bite to eat and then found a bia hoi place.

Communication was difficult so they took a cyclo ride to another bar where they struck up a conversation with an attractive, local lady. "I am going to the DMZ Bar with my friends tonight," the lady stated. "You can join us if you like."

The guys joined the ladies at the DMZ Bar and, although they found that it had the same atmosphere as their previous visit, the company of the lady and her friends made it a much more enjoyable experience. They were having a great time until they heard their names being called out. It was Mirella and Karen, who had arrived and soon muscled in.

Mirella and Karen were all over Roland and Damian and the local ladies soon left. The guys were fuming, but they had to hand it to the girls for getting one up on them. They stayed drinking at the bar, with Mirella and Karen sticking to the guys like glue for the rest of the night.

The group left Hue the next day and drove along the scenic mountain roads of the Hai Van Pass, also referred to as the Pass of the Ocean Clouds. Roland therefore considered it appropriate that it was overcast.

They were driven through the Marble Mountains and stopped off at the fishing village of Lang Co where there was a flotilla of traditional boats anchored in the harbour.

The group stopped to explore the caves. It was raining and they were unprepared; however, as they descended the bus an enthusiastic vendor appeared out of nowhere selling plastic ponchos.

It was around midday when the group proceeded to climb the steps and observe the caves that were adorned with Buddha statues.

After a couple of hours, they'd had enough. They were struggling with their plastic ponchos, they were hot, wet and had mosquito bites. They hung around until the bus arrived when they dumped their ponchos and jumped on board.

The group continued on and reached Hoi An in the late afternoon. They checked in at the Vinh Hung 2 Hotel and settled into their rooms before attending a tour briefing. The rest of the afternoon was given over as free time.

Damian and Roland walked along the bank of the Thu Bon River and stopped at a restaurant for lunch. Hoi An had a good reputation for tailor-made suits so they went to check out a couple of clothing stores at the market, but failed to make a purchase and returned to the hotel for a short rest.

Mirella, Mira, Anne, Archie, Damian and Roland went for dinner aboard a floating restaurant and selected the seafood steamboat. They were presented with a large pot that was still on the boil with coals continuing to burn and keeping the meal hot. The meal was thoroughly enjoyed by all, even though they were being interrupted by young children trying to sell their wares.

The group set off the next day and was driven for an hour before they walked a stretch and then travelled on jeeps to the Cham religious ruins of My Son. After inspecting the ruins of the abandoned Hindu temples they returned to their hotel.

Damian and Roland visited the Japanese Covered Bridge and walked along the river bank where they dropped into a restaurant for lunch and enjoyed a meal on the balcony.

After lunch, they walked about the quaint town with its traditional, well preserved buildings and old-style charm. Roland took photos of life along the Thu Bon River and Nguyen Thai Hoc Street before they returned to the hotel for a siesta.

The group had to wait for Mira who had gone to pick up her tailor-made clothes and have them posted home. When she turned up, they departed for dinner, which was another enjoyable meal on a floating restaurant.

The next morning, they drove for a few hours with a couple of stops until they came to Son My, also known as My Lai.

Roland was still half asleep as the group was taken to where the village once existed. He had heard about the incident; however, he had not appreciated the extent of the atrocities or the circumstances of the events. It was a very moving and humbling experience where the group saw graves and monuments to the villagers where generations of families had been wiped out – from small babies to the elderly.

Many of the village people were slaughtered, exact numbers were uncertain. Justification for the incident was based on the order by the Americans to attack combatants and Viet Cong suspects. Roland shook his head as he tried to come to terms with how the elderly, children, babies and animals could have possibly been considered combatants or suspects.

The group continued their drive before they stopped for lunch. Roland and a few of the group members walked over to a small, wooden bridge and sat down. It was a hot and humid day with a cool sea breeze. They stared out over the beach and the waters of the South China Sea, pondering the events of the day.

The group continued on their drive and reached their overnight stay at the Seagull Hotel just outside the township of Qui Nhon. They freshened up and reunited for the hotel dinner.

After dinner, Mirella and Roland went for a walk along the beach. Roland got on well with Mirella and considered her a good friend. They hardly spoke while they were on the beach and they both instinctively walked back to their hotel, wishing each other goodnight.

The group headed off early in the morning for their next destination, the city of Nha Trang. They had a few stops along the way, including a stop at a fishing town. Roland was constantly drawn by the great views of mountain scenery, rice paddies, sailing boats and stunning beaches. They arrived at Nha Trang around midday and were welcomed at the Vien Dong Hotel with a drink of coconut juice.

They settled into their rooms and it wasn't long before Damian and Roland were off for a walk. They strolled along the beach and found the Dam Market where they settled in a café and had lunch. On the way back to the hotel, they stopped at a shop and purchased a large bottle of cola and a bottle of Vietnamese whisky.

The guys freshened up and were joined in their hotel room by Mirella, Karen and Mira to indulge in whisky and cola. After polishing off their drinks, they met up with the group and went to the Red Star Restaurant. On the way, Damian saw some paintings and felt compelled to buy two of them.

Ordering the barbequed squid, Roland was presented with steamed rice, sauces and fresh squid. "I thought the squid was supposed to be barbequed?" he queried. A barbeque was then promptly placed on the table.

Roland scrunched up his face at the realisation that he was expected to cook his own meal. His dejection turned to glee when Susan, who had ordered the same dish, was happy to do the honours of cooking for both of them.

After dinner, they went to Crazy Kim's Bar. Damian and Adrian had drunk quite a bit and ordered some cocktails, which were huge. Damian downed a couple of the cocktails and was exhibiting some uncharacteristic, obnoxious behaviour. He was performing all sorts of improper gestures, which included pouring the remainder of Ben's beer all over him.

Roland could see the situation getting out of hand so he convinced Damian that they should leave. Roland took hold of the paintings Damian had purchased and commenced to escort him out, only to witness Cindy and Mira haul him back in. Roland was left standing outside holding the paintings so he decided to return to the hotel.

It was midnight when Roland heard a knock on the door. It was Mirella and she was being pushed into his room by Mira. "Damian is sleeping with Karen in my room so can I sleep in your room?" Mirella asked.

"That's fine, you can sleep in Damian's bed," Roland replied.

"You're strange, Roland. The other ladies on the tour are sure that you're keen on me," Mirella said.

"I like you, but just as friends," Roland explained.

Mirella was disappointed with his response, but accepted the news and after some lighter discussion they went to sleep.

In the morning, the group set off for Mama Linh's Boat Trip. The cruise kicked off with a visit to Mun Island where they did some snorkelling and observed exotic fish and colourful coral.

Mot Island was the next stop where they were treated to a plentiful buffet with a wide variety of dishes. As the passengers ate their meal, the crew formed a small band and provided some fun entertainment.

The next activity was the local version of a floating bar. It involved the passengers floating about the waters on lifesavers as they waited for the barman to float around to serve them a special concoction of wine with pineapple.

The group proceeded to Tam Island where they could disembark and spend some time on the beach. They went for a stroll and then sat on deck chairs. The cool sea breeze caressed their faces as they admired the ocean views. Re-boarding the boat, the passengers were provided with fresh fruits.

They cruised near Mieu Island where some of the passengers tried floating around in bamboo baskets. They had great difficulty navigating the baskets whilst a couple of the local kids made it look easy. The boat returned to the harbour, which ended the full day cruise.

The group went to an Italian restaurant for dinner and then proceeded to the Coconut Cave followed by the Log Bar where they had beers and played pool. Karen and Damian went off for a walk whilst Mirella and Mira decided to return to the hotel. Left alone, Roland decided to try the Lodge Hotel Disco. The music was loud and thumping with the patrons being mostly young locals. He felt out of place and decided to try Crazy Kim's Bar.

Roland ordered a UFO cocktail, settled onto one of the bar stools and noticed a very slim, attractive barmaid. He was happy sipping on his cocktail and admiring her. He finished his UFO cocktail and then tried a Jungle Juice cocktail. The cocktails were enormous and they really packed a punch.

The barmaid noticed Roland staring at her, and introduced herself as Mai. "I put on the French music to discourage customers from hanging around," she said.

Roland had no idea how to take the comment, but was happy to continue sipping on his cocktail and admire her.

"The bar is closing," Mai told him.

Roland excused himself to go to the bathroom and when he returned Mai invited him to join her group for drinks. Roland had no desire for any more drinks, but he did want to go with Mai so he accepted.

They joined locals sitting on plastic chairs in front of the bar. The moment Roland's backside settled into his chair, he started dozing off. The party was to move on to another place. "Would you like to join us for a bite to eat?" Mai asked.

Roland had no desire for food, but he did want to go with Mai so he accepted.

Mai and Roland walked to the other place hand in hand. It was drizzling and he was slightly sobering up. He felt strange as he walked down the street, hand in hand with a stranger who had invited him for food and drinks. He sensed that Mai was a genuinely lovely person and felt fortunate to be walking with her.

They arrived at an outside area by the road where there was a group of people eating and drinking. Roland sat beside Mai, accepted some tea and felt comfortable observing the social gathering. "I'm heading off now," Mai eventually stated. "You should take a cyclo back to your hotel."

Just the thought of riding on a cyclo made Roland's head spin. "It's okay," he responded. "I prefer to walk and I'd like to thank you very much for your generosity."

Roland awoke and saw Mirella in Damian's bed. *Damian must have spent the night with Karen again.* He had a shower and Damian made an appearance shortly after. Mirella returned to her room and the guys went down to the buffet breakfast.

Going for a stroll on his own, Roland arrived at the beach and gazed out to the sea where the waves were pounding against the shore. He reflected on the events of the last few days as he walked along the beach and then returned to the hotel.

The group departed Nha Trang and arrived at the airport where they boarded their Vietnam Airlines flight for Ho Chi Minh City (HCMC).

Damian and Roland relaxed a while before going for a walk to the Ben Thanh Market. They found a seat at some food stalls next to some lovely, young ladies. The ladies seemed to find the visitors' speak very humorous.

Damian and Roland had a serve of seafood noodles soup where they added some green herbs. They then checked out some of the shops at the market and along the streets before returning to their hotel room.

The group had dinner at the Lemon Grass Restaurant and then unanimously agreed to go for bia hoi. On the way, a boy carrying a number of small toys and gum approached Mirella. "You buy something from me," the boy stated.

"I don't want to buy anything," Mirella replied.

The boy insisted, but Mirella again declined. The boy then hit her and ran away.

The group sat down at a bia hoi establishment and had a few beers. They then went to the Blue Gecko Bar where there were a few young waitresses serving mainly middle-aged tourists and businessmen. They settled in and the bartender gave them a complimentary chocolate vodka. They drank quite a few beers before they returned to their hotel.

Damian repeated his habit of sleeping with Karen in her room and Mirella slept in Damian's bed in Roland's room.

In the morning, the group drove for over an hour to reach the Chu Chi Tunnels. Local guides provided fascinating information about the tunnels, describing various guerrilla warfare tactics and providing examples of booby traps.

The group was then given the option of firing a selection of firearms. Roland shared a set of bullets with Mirella, Mira and Adrian. Roland had very little knowledge of firearms so he just followed instructions. He was handed an AK47 by a staff member and was shown how to set up and fire. He shot the AK47 a few times where he felt a slight kickback. He had no idea where the bullets ended up and handed the rifle back to the staff member who looked bewildered.

The group returned to HCMC and was allowed an hour of free time for lunch. Damian chose to hang around the hotel whilst Roland went for lunch at the BBQ Restaurant. He ordered frogs' legs and had a bit of a wait before frogs' legs were placed on the table with some greens, rice and a sauce.

Roland inspected the frogs' legs and they were raw. A small BBQ was placed on the table and this time there was no Susan to cook his meal for him. He was fortunate to have the waiter assist him cook before he scoffed the meal down and rushed back to the hotel for the city tour.

The group visited the Presidential Palace, renamed the Reunification Palace, where they spent some time inspecting the various exhibitions. They then drove on and parked near the American Embassy. They visited a department store, the Notre Dame Cathedral, the Post Office and the War Remnants Museum. The museum presented a graphically gruesome video of an account of the Vietnam War and they viewed equally gruesome photographs and other displays.

Roland was appalled by the exhibits and considered the previous name of the venue, being the Exhibition House of American War Crimes, to be a more apt description. He found the outdoor exhibits of planes and tanks much less confronting. The group was taken to a lacquer factory before returning to their hotel.

Damian and Roland went for a short walk and came across the City Hall, named the People Committee Hall. Roland liked the cream and red brick, French colonial building so he took a photo. It was getting dark and the traffic quickly grew to an army of motorbikes, cars and trucks. They walked back to their hotel along the bustling streets as the vehicles progressively switched on their headlights.

Damian decided to have dinner with Karen and a few of the other ladies. Roland decided to do his own thing, but agreed to meet up with Damian later at the bar named Apocalypse Now.

Walking down Da Lo Le Loi Street, Roland stopped at a street side food stall for some dinner. Moving on, he came across an establishment with bia hoi and sat down for a couple of beers before he went to Apocalypse Now.

Roland walked around the bar looking for Damian, but he couldn't find him. He walked around again, but still couldn't find him. He suspected that

Damian must have come and gone. It was pretty dark and dingy in the bar and he felt uncomfortable being on his own so he left.

Roland walked onto the street and a motorbike rider approached him. "I can take you to a good bar," the motorbike rider offered, but Roland declined. The motorbike rider persisted. "Sir, these tourist bars no good; I take you to good local bar." Roland still refused.

The motorbike rider made more attempts to lure his potential customer. Roland then considered that it was still early and he didn't know where else to go. Negotiations ensued and they agreed on a price.

Roland hopped on the motorbike and the rider scooted through the busy traffic. The local people on motorbikes were riding up and making enquiries about the tourist passenger. Roland got a buzz out of the ride and enjoyed the attention of the passers-by.

The motorbike rider stopped at a bar that had little clientele and a couple of ladies. Roland was led upstairs where a lady invited him to stay and play a game of pool. He thanked her for the offer, but declined.

The motorbike rider took Roland away and it was another round of zipping through traffic and being approached by other motorbike riders. Amongst them were young ladies offering their services.

"You want a girl?" asked the motorbike rider.

"No, I don't want a girl," Roland responded.

"It would only cost $20US for a girl."

"I don't have $20US for a girl."

"How much you have?"

Roland was uncomfortable with the question and didn't know how to respond so he just said the first thing that popped into his head. "I don't know, maybe around $10US."

Another motorbike rider who was hovering around rode up to Roland's motorbike rider and they engaged in a short conversation before the other motorbike rider rode off.

The motorbike rider then went to another place. As Roland dismounted, the only establishment he saw was a restaurant. "This isn't a bar," he stated.

"It's the same," the motorbike rider said. "You go upstairs to look."

Roland was escorted upstairs to an empty room with a long table and was seated at the far end. Shortly after, a Mama-san entered and offered him drinks while a line of young ladies entered. "No, I don't want any of this," he cried.

As Roland was communicating his disapproval, he was being offered ladies while drinks were being poured. He continued in vain to decline all offers and the motorbike rider, who was in the room earlier, had disappeared.

"I wish to leave," Roland pleaded.

"You can leave after you pay your bill," Mama-san advised.

A bill appeared with the total of 100,000 dong, being around $10US.

Roland thought he had 50,000 dong and some US dollars in the open compartment of his wallet and another 50,000 dong and more US dollars in the zipped up compartment of his wallet. *If I was stripped of all my money, I'd be stranded in the middle of nowhere, penniless.* He then thought that if he could get some privacy he could take out the required money. "May I use the toilet?" Roland asked

Mama-san's response was stern and immediate. "No!"

Roland then blew his top and demanded to see his motorbike rider. He charged down the stairs and onto the street in search of the motorbike rider and located him.

"If you can lend me 50,000 dong, I will repay you as well as pay your 20,000 dong fare after you drop me off at the hotel," Roland suggested.

The motorbike rider looked extremely worried. "I don't have the money," he claimed.

By this time, a large group had milled around with people hurling abuse at Roland and others spitting towards him. Another motorbike rider then approached. "I can loan the money and take you to your hotel."

Roland recognised him as the rider that had previously rode up when they were on the road. He had an uneasy feel about the man, but saw no other way out. He paid over the 50,000 dong and the rider paid the other 50,000 dong. They then set off amongst further abuse and spitting.

The rider rode around for quite some time. Roland had no idea where they were and found the surroundings strange. "Do you know where the hotel is?" he queried, but the rider ignored him. The rider then stopped abruptly in the middle of a quiet road and hailed down a taxi.

Roland thought the rider was going to ask for directions when he ordered Roland off the bike. The rider approached the taxi. "Get in!" he shouted.

"I thought you were going to take me to the hotel?" Roland questioned.

The rider was silent and had the taxi door opened for him to get in. Roland looked around the deserted streets and saw no other viable option.

As Roland sat in the front seat of the taxi, the rider wound down the window, closed the door, struck him and demanded money. Roland was stunned as was the taxi driver. Roland took out his wallet and the rider snatched it, opened all compartments and took all the money. There was a total amount of around $25US. The rider handed the taxi driver $5US, threw Roland his emptied wallet and rode off.

The taxi driver started driving. "The rider said you drank beer and did not want to pay; what happened?"

Roland told him what happened.

"Motorbike rider no good," commented the taxi driver.

Roland was awake when Damian got up. "So what did you get up to last night?" Damian asked.

"I was briefly at Apocalypse Now, but I didn't see you there," Roland advised.

"I actually didn't get there until very late," Damian said.

"That's great," Roland remarked. "If only I had hung around a while, everything would have been fine."

"What do you mean?"

Roland then briefed Damian about the evening events.

The group headed off for the Mekong Delta. After a short drive on the bus, they boarded a boat and cruised along the river. They stopped at a place where they were shown how popping rice was made and were given samples of popping rice, peanuts, ginger and other savouries to try with green tea.

They proceeded to another stop where they were shown how coconut candy was made and were provided with samples of various candies to try with tea.

They set off cruising again with the next stop featuring a python with the opportunity to hold the reptile. They were then provided with tea as well as some rice wine and snake wine to taste.

They returned to the boat for the last part of the cruise where they admired the river scenery and the small villages along the bank.

Returning to the hotel after dinner, Mirella and Karen joined Damian and Roland in their room for a few nightcaps of local whisky and cola. Their discussion reflected on the trip, particularly as Karen was about to leave the tour the next day.

The group met up in the morning and said goodbye to the passengers who were leaving the tour. Those that were to continue were driven to the Vietnamese/Cambodian border.

They changed their Vietnamese dong for Cambodian riel before taking off on another vehicle and stopping in a small, dusty settlement in Cambodia. Roland couldn't ascertain the name of the town, but he was so fascinated by the place that he started taking photos.

The group was wandering around the settlement when they noticed their van being driven on a boat and there were loud calls to get on board. They scampered onto the boat with Susan counting the numbers as they boarded. She was relieved when the last of the group made it on board, which just happened to be Roland after he took his last photo.

Chapter 54 – Cambodia

After the river crossing, the group crammed into a van and was driven to Phnom Penh. As they travelled through the city, the dramatic variation from grandiose buildings and new estates to poor areas and shanty towns was striking.

The group arrived at their hotel and was given two hours of free time before they met up for dinner at a restaurant by the Tonle Sap River followed by drinks at the Riverside Bar.

After breakfast, the group walked across the road to visit the Royal Palace. They inspected various buildings in the large complex, including the Throne Hall and Silver Pagoda. They were taken to Psar Tuol Tom Pong (Russian market), which stocked craft items and artefacts. They then visited the National Museum where they were guided through the exhibits of Cambodian history from the Pre-Angkor, Angkor and Post-Angkor periods.

The group had lunch at the Boddhi Tree Guesthouse and then walked to Tuol Sleng Genocide Museum. The museum was a former school that was turned into a prison. It was Security Prison 21 (SP21) during Pol Pot's, Khmer Rouge regime of the 1970s and 1980s.

The tour guide was a middle-aged lady who delivered the information with utmost deliberation and intent. Roland was impressed with the guide, particularly as he expected that she had recounted the same story many times over.

The group was shown through the various classrooms that had been converted into small cells and torture chambers. They were also shown graphic photographs of the many prisoners and the atrocities perpetrated against them. It was some of the most gruesome forms of torture imaginable.

They were taken by bus to Choeung Ek, the Killing Fields, and told about the thousands of Cambodians that were slain and buried in mass graves. They were shown the Memorial Stupa, which was filled with thousands of human skulls that had been dug up from the graves. They were then allowed to walk around where they could witness human bones and pieces of clothing scattered around.

Again the tour guide was very passionate about her description. "There were few families that remained untouched by the atrocities," she explained.

"Did you know of anyone who was affected?" asked a tourist.

"I lost half of my family to the regime," the tour guide stated unflinchingly.

All were shocked to hear how she was so dramatically and personally impacted. They were humbled and greatly respected the courage she displayed.

The group returned to the hotel and had time to have a rest and freshen up before they went out for dinner.

Mira's dinner had not arrived after a lengthy period and the others offered her portions of their meal. After some enquiry and another lengthy period her meal finally arrived. She ate a bit of her meal, but when she noticed a long hair she pushed her plate away.

"Is there anything wrong?" asked the waiter. When he heard about the series of events and as she was not interested in ordering anything else the waiter did not charge her.

They took cyclos back to the hotel and Roland shared a cyclo with Mira who sat partly on the seat and partly on his lap. Noticing Mira having fun and being carefree was very much out of character for her, and it made him wonder about her true nature.

The group headed off after breakfast and driven to the harbour for their journey to Siam Reap. They boarded a speed boat that looked more like a space capsule. They dumped their packs at the back of the vessel and found some seats in the hull. There was so little room to move that they felt like they were in straitjackets.

The boat set off and sped along the mighty waterways of the Mekong Delta. For the 5½ hour journey, they had to endure hard bumps and solid thumps. Damian and Roland hardly moved a muscle and gave each other a glance and a smile the moment they hit a proper wave. They edged out of their seats as they neared the pier and took a few photos of the floating houses along the Tonle Sap Lake.

Arriving at Siam Reap there were chaotic scenes as passengers tried to collect their luggage and disembark. There were also hordes of locals trying to sell accommodation and transportation. The group located their designated bus, squeezed on board and was driven to their hotel.

It didn't take long before Damian and Roland headed off for a walk. They stopped off at a café on Pokambor Street along the Siam Reap River for a bite to eat then visited the Old Market where they purchased tablecloths, shirts and placemats. The purchases were influenced more so by the beautiful nature of the lady vendors rather than their desire to buy the products.

Returning to the hotel, the guys joined the group to head for Angkor Wat. Cindy, Mandy, Damian and Roland didn't bring passport photos with them, which were required for the three day pass into the Angkor Archaeological Park so they went to the office to have them taken.

A jovial man in a uniform greeted them at the door and welcomed them to enter. "Who wants to have their photo taken first?" asked the man.

"The girls can go first," Roland said.

"I ask you again, who wants to go first?" the man asked with a smile and this started some chuckling.

"Yeah, Roland," Damian said. "Why don't you go first, you're a big girl."

"Well, at least I'm not a big c…," Roland started to say then trailed off.

Mandy sat first and the man placed his hat on her head. "How does that look?" asked the man and the others were wowing.

"I really like women in uniform," Damian stated.

Mandy gave a broad smile and the man took the photo.

Cindy was up next and she was giggling. "Don't I get to try on the hat?" she queried.

"Maybe this hat too small for you," the man responded.

"Or just maybe her head is too big," Damian suggested.

Cindy gave a beaming smile and the man took the photo.

Roland sat down next. "Where am I supposed to look?" Roland asked.

"You look at the little birdie," the man instructed.

"Little birdie?" Roland queried. "I ask you again, where am I supposed to look?"

Everyone was cracking up and the man took the photo.

By the time Damian got on the seat, everyone was in hysterics. Mandy hurled the hat. "Talking about big heads, yours will need a wide angled lens," Cindy joked.

"Don't forget to look at the little birdie," Roland reminded Damian.

Damian was in stitches and the man took the photo.

"It shouldn't take too long," the man advised.

"That's okay as the ladies are used to that," Roland commented.

The photographs were made up into their passes and revealed to them one by one, which started a new batch of hysterics.

The man escorted them out of the office, along the path and onto the bus. "Why did it take so long and what's so funny?" Mirella asked. The passes were handed around and this got all the passengers laughing.

The group drove towards Angkor Wat and had a photo stop with a view of the towers reflecting off a pond. Entering from the Western Gateway, it was their first full view of the majestic temples that housed the ruins of classical Khmer architecture with its Hindu and Buddhist influences.

The temple was built in the early 12th century for the Khmer King Suryavarman II. After a quick tour, which did little more than whet their appetites, they left, but they were assured that they would return the next day for more extensive exploration.

Angkor Thom was their next destination. Roland took photos of the

Bayon main temple, the South Entrance and the Demon side statues of the walkway entrance of the South Gate. They were taken to climb the Temple of Phnom Bakeng where they enjoyed the sunset.

After dinner, Damian and Roland told the group they were going to check out a few bars and the others decided to tag along. They passed by the Angkor What, but it was full so they settled into the place next door, named Le Tigre e Papier where they had some beers and chatted away with the courteous barmaids.

After breakfast, the group headed off for a return visit to Angkor Wat. On the way, Roland took a photo of families collecting wood and reeds from a pond where even the children were pitching in.

The group was shown the various temples and bas-reliefs, which included the longest running bas-relief in the world, depicting Hindu religious epics.

They admired the five towers of the mythical mountain upon which Angkor Wat was situated. From the front end view only three towers were visible. These represented the three Gods of Vishnu, Brahma and Shiva. Roland took a photo of a bas-relief of Apsaras Dancers inside the West Wall Gate and the Vishnu God at the South Tower.

They walked to Angkor Wat's main temple and were shown the three distinct levels of the temple and the various walls. Roland was particularly impressed by the bas-relief depicting Heaven, Earth and Hell with the Demons being the dominant theme.

They moved to the east side of Angkor Wat and proceeded to climb the 70-degree steps that took in the views from the top, which highlighted the majesty of the temple complex – the largest religious monument in the world.

They descended from the south side, which also had 70-degree steps, although the descent was assisted by a hand rail. They headed back to the hotel at midday and were given a couple of hours of free time.

Damian and Roland returned to the Old Market where they purchased whisky, cola, Angkor beer, Bayon beer and Black Panther stout. They dropped off their booze at the hotel and had lunch. They then walked to the Grand Hotel D'Angkor and around the Royal Gardens before returning to their hotel to meet up with the others.

The group headed off for Angkor Thom where Roland took photos of the Bayon reflecting off a pond, the Bayon from the south entrance and the three towers featuring face statues. One of the faces was identified as the Khmer Buddhist King Jayavarman VII in whose time, during the late 12th and early 13th centuries, the State Temple was built. They then visited Phimeanakas and the Terrace of the Elephants before returning to the hotel.

Roland shaved, showered and turned on the television. To his surprise, the program *Aerobics Oz Style* was showing. There was a knock on the door and it was Mira. "Were you and Damian interested in joining us for dinner?" she asked.

Roland checked with Damian who preferred they do their own thing. This suited Roland and he let her know.

Damian and Roland headed off and found themselves at the Martini Club. They made themselves comfortable in the beer garden and they both ordered fried noodles with chicken and large bottles of Angkor beer. They were intrigued with the bar girls who were wearing different uniforms that promoted different beers.

"Do you want another Angkor beer?" Roland asked.

"I don't know, I think I might fancy the Bayon beer this time," Damian replied. After their small talk and beers, they entered the disco.

The disco was patronised by loads of local guys, a few tourists and a couple of middle-aged men accompanied by young ladies. They moved on to Zanzibar where there were local ladies who appeared happy with their own company. They then moved on to check out the Bakheng Nightclub where they struck up a conversation with a man who recommended another bar.

They managed to find the other bar and were guided onto two stools. The moment they sat down there was an immediate encroachment by a number of ladies. They ordered beers and were approached by more ladies.

One of the ladies started a conversation with Roland. "Would you like a massage?" she asked.

"No thanks," Roland replied.

Damian was involved in repartee with a couple of the ladies when Roland noticed a petite, attractive lady walking by and she immediately started talking to him.

"Would you like a drink?" Roland asked.

"No," she responded.

Looking around, Roland noticed the pool table. "Do you play?" he asked.

"Yes I play," the lady replied and she led him away.

Roland noticed Damian looking on. "Can my friend play too?" he asked.

"I can arrange my friend to join us to play doubles," the lady suggested and the moment Damian saw her lovely friend, he jumped from his stool and was chalking up.

Kiri and Roland introduced themselves as they paired up. They started playing and were continually exchanging glances. Then all hell broke loose. It was a police raid and people were scattering all over the place.

Women situated in the front part of the bar were taken into custody. The women at the rear of the bar, including Kiri, got away through the back door. Before they knew it, both Damian and Roland were left alone holding their cues. They looked at each other and continued playing.

After they finished the game and their beers, they returned to their hotel thinking about what could have been. They banged on Mira and Mirella's hotel room door before they rushed off to bed.

The group made another assault on the Angkor temples where they travelled the big circuit, which involved visiting the Preah Khan, Northern Baray (Snake Temple), Eastern Baray, Pre Rup and Ta Prohm. Ta Prohm, also known as the Jungle Temple, was said to be a location for the filming of the movie *Tomb Raider*.

Roland separated from the group after lunch and went to the internet café before heading to the Old Market. He thought about purchasing a traditional local print of Angkor Wat, but after much deliberation he failed to make a purchase and returned to the hotel.

The group went to the Forest Hut Restaurant for dinner followed by a karaoke place where they had a couple of beers. Damian and Cindy performed a duet before the group ventured off to the Martini Club. They had a couple of beers served by the Angkor beer waitress and then staggered to the disco to dance the night away.

Cindy knocked on Roland's door the next morning to say goodbye, and they made tentative plans to meet up in Bangkok in a few days. Roland stayed in bed until he eventually got up and went down to breakfast with Damian.

Damian and the other remaining members of the tour were departing and they amassed outside for their transport to the airport. Roland said his goodbyes and as they were leaving they waved him farewell. He stayed seated in the hotel garden until he felt uncomfortable in the heat and humidity, at which time, he retreated to the comfort of his air-conditioned room.

At midday, Roland decided to go for a walk. He went to the Old Market and then on to the Central Market. After strolling up and down the aisles, he ventured into one of the shops and purchased a couple of prints of Angkor Wat.

Roland dropped off his purchases at the hotel, had lunch and then walked to the internet café where he spent a couple of hours dealing with his messages. He considered having a massage, but decided against it and ended up back at the hotel.

After a while, Roland again thought about having a massage and made the effort to go to a massage place. They didn't take credit card so he headed back to the hotel.

Roland went to the Forest Hut Restaurant for dinner and ordered the Cambodian Amok. He also took advantage of happy hour by ordering the Angkor draft beers with a two for the price of one offer. He thoroughly enjoyed his meal, considering it to be the best he'd had.

Walking about town, Roland ended up outside Le Tigre e Papier and the Angkor What bars, but they were both quiet. He continued on to the bar that was raided a couple of nights before. The moment he set foot into the bar he received immediate attention by the ladies. They flocked all around him and, as he was slightly overwhelmed, he didn't break stride and walked straight through to the toilet.

When Roland emerged, he approached the bar and a young lady pulled up a stool next to him. Her name was Cam, she was from Vietnam and it didn't take her long before she was offering him her services.

"I will spend the night with you for $20US," Cam offered.

"I don't think I have that much to spare," Roland advised.

"Okay, you give me $5US and I give you a good, one hour massage."

Roland was after a massage all day so the moment Cam made the offer, he automatically accepted.

They strolled the short distance to the hotel and Cam quickly stripped him down and then she stripped off. Cam proceeded to give Roland a very thorough and strong massage. He was pleased with his massage and estimated that it lasted precisely one hour.

"Okay, I sleep here," Cam blurted out.

"That's fine by me," Roland was quick to confirm.

There was an early morning wakeup call with a knock on the door. "I should go," Cam stated. Roland rustled up whatever money he could spare, which amounted to $10US and his remaining Cambodian riel. Cam thanked him, said goodbye and was off.

Roland stayed in bed contemplating things for a while before he placed his belongings in order and went down to breakfast. He headed to the airport and after paying his departure tax he found some loose change, which he deposited in the Red Cross box.

Chapter 55 – A Bangkok Stopover

Roland caught his 07:20 Siam Reap Airways flight, which arrived in Phnom Penh in less than an hour. He collected his bags and walked from the domestic terminal to the international terminal where he caught his connecting Thai Airlines flight to Bangkok.

A man greeted Roland and provided the transfer to the hotel. Roland had arranged to rendezvous with a few of the group members from his Indo-China tour at Kao San Road and he immediately set off. He walked to the Laksi Station, caught the train to Samsen Station and walked the rest of the way to Gulliver's.

Roland ordered a drink and it wasn't too long before Cindy arrived, then Mirella and finally Mira. They chatted for some time before going for a bite to eat and a walk through the markets. They then went to another bar for a couple more drinks. As it was getting late, Roland said goodbye and headed off.

With only 200 baht left, Roland thought he had just enough for a cab back to his hotel.

"How much to my hotel?" Roland asked a group of cab drivers.

"500 baht," one cab driver said.

"100 baht," Roland countered.

"300 baht," the driver fired back.

Roland was now confident that he would clinch the deal. "Okay, 200 baht."

The cab driver thought about it for a moment. "No, 300 baht," the cab driver repeated.

"Come on, 200 baht is a fair price," Roland pleaded.

"Not at this time and not where you want to go," the cab driver told him.

Not prepared for rejection, Roland walked to the train station but the trains were not running that late. He then set upon walking all the way to his hotel – a distance of about 10 kilometres, which he expected would take him one hour and forty minutes.

Roland figured that the hotel should be easy to locate as it was situated near the railway line so all he had to do was walk alongside the tracks. He encountered a narrowing of the road that departed from the train track, then found himself walking along a narrow, wooden path with small, old wooden houses either side. A number of dogs started growling and barking, which started off the whole dog community.

Reaching a dead end, Roland couldn't figure out where in the hell he was. The surroundings were completely alien so he decided to backtrack to the railway line where he began walking on the actual railway track. The dogs from the nearby houses were now going berserk. The occurrence of someone walking on the track at that time of night was obviously unique.

Roland had been walking for ages when he finally got to a main road. He decided to get off the railway track to try to orientate himself, but there were no apparent signs so he just started walking in one direction along the main road. There wasn't a lot of traffic nor was there much activity.

Headlights approached from down the road, and Roland stood transfixed as the vehicle stopped before him. "Do you need a taxi?" asked the driver.

"Yes," Roland replied.

The driver indicated that he knew Roland's hotel. "How much will it cost?" Roland asked.

"150 baht," the driver quoted.

"Eureka!" Roland exclaimed as he jumped in the taxi.

The taxi driver drove for about twenty minutes in all sorts of directions before arriving at a road that was familiar to Roland – the road that led to the Don Muan Airport. The taxi driver revealed that there was a point along the railway line where it split; one track veered left and this was the track Roland was following; it was the wrong track.

The driver had to go up and down the main road a few times before he managed to locate the correct turn off, eventually finding the hotel. "Is this the right hotel?" asked the driver.

"Yes it is," Roland advised as he clapped his hands.

Roland gave the driver the agreed fare of 150 baht plus a 50 baht tip.

"Thank you," the driver said and joined in the celebratory applause.

Roland made it to his room and collapsed on the bed before dragging himself up for a shower. He then found his breakfast voucher and went down for the buffet breakfast.

Returning to his room, Roland packed and was downstairs for his transfer to the airport. He checked in his backpack and did some window shopping before boarding his 08:10 Thai Airlines flight. He slept most of the way with the plane finally touching down in Sydney where he soon boarded his flight bound for Melbourne.

Completing his last-chance duty free shopping, Roland continued through immigration and customs. They inspected the items he declared and he was allowed to go through. He then rushed and caught a cab to his house.

Even though it was almost midnight on Saturday, 19th October 2002 when Roland arrived home, he rang John. "Hello, Dad, I hope I didn't wake you?”

"No son, you didn’t wake me. I was expecting your call.”

Chapter 56 – Where to Last?

Roland settled back into his routine existence, content in some ways and disillusioned in other ways. Now in his mid-forties, he sensed that he needed to get over his obsession with overseas travel and concentrate on a more stable life in Australia. At the same time, he was determined to do one last overseas trip.

There were two particular destinations Roland had yet to experience, but considered to be most intriguing: the Galapagos Islands and Patagonia.

Researching the Galapagos Islands, Roland was shocked to discover that it was one of the few places on earth that did not have an indigenous population – those that now lived there having largely emigrated from Ecuador over the last fifty years.

The Galapagos was a unique group of islands that contained one of the most unadulterated examples of ecosystems in the world, and provided the scene for Charles Darwin's formulation of the theory of evolution by natural selection.

What disturbed Roland was that the rapidly growing human population was destroying the natural habitat. Faced with this fact, he crossed the Galapagos off his list and he was left with a list of one.

Patagonia incorporated Tierra del Fuego, or Land of Fire, which was also known as The End of the World. The scenery was described as some of the most beautiful and spectacular on earth, comprising deep turquoise lakes, towering mountain peaks and a large variety of wildlife.

If these weren't enough reasons to visit the exotic area, what increased Roland's enthusiasm was the story concerning the writer, Bruce Chatwin. Bruce worked for The Sunday Times when he interviewed the architect and furniture designer Eileen Gray in her Paris salon. As the story goes, he noticed a map of Patagonia and commented that he always wanted to go there. Eileen stated that she did too and that he should go there for her and so he did.

The trip inspired Bruce Chatwin's first book entitled *In Patagonia* published in 1977. The story behind the book captured Roland's imagination in a similar way that Arthur Conan Doyle's 1912 novel *The Lost World* captured his imagination of Venezuela and Ernest Hemmingway's life story and 1952 novel *The Old Man and the Sea* captured his imagination of Cuba.

Roland considered it appropriate, if not his destiny, that his last overseas trip would be to The End of the World. It sparked an enthusiasm like that of his younger days. He had eight months to wait and he was very much looking forward to the trip, although the wait was proving to be a testing time.

Catching up with an old workmate, named Peter, Roland briefed him of his trip. Peter examined the travel plans and noted the tour dates. "These dates roughly coincide with when a couple of my friends and I are going to be in Brazil so we could meet up."

Roland thought this a great idea and examined Peter's itinerary. He noted the cities in Brazil that Peter was visiting and worked out the dates when they could meet up prior to the commencement of his Patagonia tour. He incorporated visits to Fortaleza, Natal, Recife, Salvadore and Rio de Janeiro where he would meet up with Peter and his friends in Recife and Rio. Having finalised his travel plans, the countdown had begun.

Chapter 57 – First Stop Fortaleza

On Thursday morning of 9th October 2003, Roland stayed up watching television and packed ahead of his departure. He had a light breakfast, made final preparations and waited for the taxi.

Arriving at the airport, Roland went directly to the Qantas check-in. The lady was exceptionally friendly, particularly when she heard that he was going to Brazil. "I've been to Brazil during the Carnivale," she stated and the excitement was evident in her voice. "I wish I was going with you," she said as he moved on.

Roland checked out a couple of shops and duty free stores. He then waited until the final call before he purposefully made his way to the gate and boarded his Qantas flight QF01.

The plane arrived in Sydney and he rushed to the international transfer desk where they took their sweet time. "We need to telex for your suitcase," they stated. The boarding card had a boarding time of 08:35 and it was 09:00.

Roland rushed to the gate where there was an attractive, Latino lady attendant. "Is this Aerolineas Argentinas flight AR1183?" he asked. The lady confirmed that it was and, as people were lined up, he took the opportunity to pay the toilet a visit before boarding.

The pilot predicted that it should be a smooth flight to Auckland; however, this did not take into account the buffeting Roland received from an out of control family. He was relieved to have arrived in Auckland where they had an hour stopover before re-boarding for Buenos Aires. He was hoping the family wasn't seated next to him all the way to South America.

Being one of the last passengers to re-board, Roland looked intently to see where the family was seated. They took up different seats a few rows in front of him and he thought things wouldn't be as bad.

Roland settled into his seat and all of a sudden he felt as if he was being ejected. An old man got up, but could not manage it under his own steam so he raised himself by holding on to the top of Roland's headrest and hurling himself up.

The old man was travelling with his wife and they were being escorted by their middle-aged daughter. They were all seated in the row just behind Roland. The flight steward instructed the old man to be seated and Roland took off again.

The aircraft took off and Roland thought he would have some respite.

"

However, the family who had taken seats a few rows in front of him started off with a ruckus. It seemed to reach a crescendo; however, the crescendo never seemed to progress to a denouement, much less an end.

As the family continued their noisy antics, the seat belt sign went off and the daughter immediately asked the old man if he could let her up. Roland was prepared for the next take off and leaned forward as the old man rose; however, he was totally unprepared for the take off created by the daughter as she leveraged herself through.

The daughter followed this with a backhander to the top of Roland's head and finally gave him an elbow on the side of his head for good measure.

For most of the trip, Roland had to put up with the chaos of the family seated in front of him. He also had to deal with those behind as he had to dodge, weave and manoeuvre around the incessant movements of the old man and the daughter. The old woman wasn't totally left out as she made her regular sojourns. What helped Roland endure the ordeal were the cognac, Tia Maria and wine from the Argentine Mendoza region.

As the plane arrived in Buenos Aires, Roland couldn't get off the plane quick enough. He rushed to catch his connecting Aerolineas Argentinas flight AR1256 to Rio de Janeiro. The plane was due to take off at 13:55, which gave him 25 minutes and he got there with time to spare.

The flight to Rio was a little bumpy, but Roland thought it was heaven compared to the family and company. He collected his luggage and was about to enquire at Information about his connecting flight to Fortaleza when a man approached him.

The man was wearing a uniform with some wings pinned to his jacket. "What do you need?" asked the man.

"I don't really need anything," Roland replied.

The man proceeded to ask a series of questions, although Roland couldn't make much sense of them. "I'm simply catching a connecting flight to Fortaleza," Roland advised.

"You'll need to catch a cab to the other terminal and pay a departure tax," the man instructed.

"I don't have any Brazilian currency; in any case, all airport taxes were to be included and I'm unaware of any domestic departure taxes," Roland said.

The man didn't make any further comment and walked off. Roland continued on his way to Information where the staff advised that Varig Airlines was at Terminal 2. It was only a short walk and Roland checked into his Varig flight RG2376. There were no departure taxes payable.

It was a basic meal on the flight to Fortaleza, but Roland found it adequate for the journey. The flight was stopping at Sao Paulo, which didn't mean much until it dawned on him they should be served another meal. Touch down at Fortaleza was at 1.00 am and as it was so early he hung around the airport.

Roland caught a community taxi to Peter's recommended Olympo Praia Hotel, which was across the road from Praia de Meireles. Reception couldn't secure a room for him, but suggested that he return in the afternoon.

Dropping off his suitcase, Roland went for a casual walk in 30-degrees-centigrade heat and high humidity. It was little wonder a few of the locals pulled him up to query his sanity in wearing slacks and a long sleeve shirt.

Roland walked along the beach and through some shanty town suburbs where he arrived at the Fortaleza Museum, which was formerly a lighthouse. It was a rundown tower with a few photographs of Fortaleza inside. He climbed the stairs to look out at the views.

As Roland exited, a man showed him the sardines he had caught. "Do you wish to buy some?" asked the man.

"No thanks," Roland replied.

"Do you need a tour guide, a woman or a taxi?" the man queried. "It's very dangerous walking around this area so you should take a taxi."

It was at this time Roland realised that he had his wallet and his daypack that contained all his prized possessions. "I'll be fine," he stated as he headed back towards the hotel. He got to the shanty town areas that appeared a little dodgy and he hurried along.

Making it safely back to more civilised surroundings, Roland was very hot and bothered so he stopped off at La Florentina Restaurant for lunch.

Roland returned to the hotel and scored accommodation for three nights. He settled into his room and slept for the rest of the day. When he awoke, he freshened up and headed off in search of some nightlife. As he had a big lunch, he didn't bother with dinner and walked to Praia de Iracema.

Stumbling on a series of bars and clubs, Roland dropped into the Desiguays bar. It was quiet, dark and dingy, but he stayed for a beer. He then passed by the Café del Mar where they wanted six reais to enter. As it didn't look too active inside, he decided to move on.

Roland came across the Zip Bar where he pulled up a stool. He had a couple of beers and enjoyed chatting to the friendly barmaid. There were a couple of tourists having a good time with a few of the local women and he observed the goings on for a while before he returned to his hotel.

In the morning, Roland went to the nearby supermarket where he bought some fruit juice, bananas, grapes, oranges, yoghurt drinks and water, which he took back to his hotel room for breakfast.

Roland headed for the city centre where he visited the Centro de Turismo. He was directed to catch the No.14 bus, which got him to the main bus terminal where he purchased an overnight bus ticket to Natal for Tuesday, 14th October 2003 – in three days time.

Returning to the city centre, Roland continued with his sightseeing. A guy approached him and asked a number of questions. Roland's travel experiences taught him that if you wanted to shake off an undesirable, you didn't stop, you just keep on walking. However, his theory didn't seem to be working on this occasion.

The guy continued to follow Roland. "Do you want me to show you around?" asked the guy.

"No thanks, I prefer to walk alone," Roland responded.

The man was about to ask another question when he ploughed head-on into a steel, street post. The collision gave off a loud, bell sound. "Are you all right?" Roland asked.

"I'm fine," the man replied, although he was noticeably shaken up.

Roland walked on, but this time the guy did not follow.

Roland inspected the cathedral and then explored the central market. It was a colossal building that housed various items of food, artefacts and a craft market.

Completing his walking tour around the city centre, Roland returned to his hotel. He rested and when he awoke he was recharged to attack the nightlife. He returned to La Florentina Restaurant for dinner and after a filling meal he wobbled towards the clubs.

Roland's first stop was Africas, which was quiet. He moved on to Desiguays, which was packed and he stayed for a couple of beers. He tried to chat with a few ladies, but they showed little interest. He then moved on to the Bikini Club for a beer and finally the Café del Mar for another beer. By this time he felt sufficiently dejected that he returned to his hotel.

After enjoying his own breakfast in his room, Roland visited an internet café. On his way back to the hotel, he stopped off at the supermarket to replenish his stores.

Roland caught the bus to Praia do Futuro, which passed through some of the poorer suburbs before arriving at the beach. On one side of the road were miles of pristine beaches with thatched umbrellas and tourist facilities housed under hut shelters. The other side of the road was fairly deserted with low class housing and the odd high-rise, unit complex.

Roland had a ceremonial dip in the sea and then went in search of a place to sit. There were loads of people, but once the waiters noticed his plight they escorted him to a plastic chair in an ideal location – a shaded spot where he could relax and take in the views.

Inspecting a menu, Roland thought he might as well live it up and ordered lagosta and a cerveja grande. He was served a monstrous plate of lobster, vegetables and salad. He indulged himself so much that he almost felt guilty...almost.

Roland went for a short stroll along the beach before he caught the bus back to the hotel where he had a swim in the pool followed by a siesta.

Considering his options for dinner, Roland returned to La Florentina Restaurant yet again. He then went to check out the nightlife. He passed by the Zip Bar and Africas before he moved on to Desiguays. He thought about stopping for a drink; however, the waitresses gave him little attention so he moved on.

Roland walked into the nightclub named Don Angelos, which was an establishment with two levels. The ground level had a live band. The top level had an area with pool tables, a bar and a door that led to a thumping disco. He bought a beer and alternated between the three areas.

There were a few ladies in the disco and Roland attempted to speak to one of them; however, she quickly shied away, giving him a peck on the cheek as she moved on.

Roland was admiring a couple of ladies and although they were initially on their own, they were soon approached by a group of men. He tried to talk to a couple of other ladies, but they were dismissive of his response. "Nao falo Portugues." The fact that he did not speak Portuguese seemed to be a distinct handicap. He finished off his second beer and called it quits.

Waking up early the next morning, Roland had breakfast in his room before he set off. Passing the dining room, it crossed his mind whether breakfast was included in his accommodation. He left the hotel and went to the internet café with this question playing on his mind.

Roland received a couple of email messages from home and one from his friend Peter. He dealt with his emails before returning to the hotel. Passing a receptionist, he felt compelled to ask whether breakfast was included. "Of course, sir, breakfast *is* included," the receptionist confirmed.

Of course you idiot, Roland thought. *Breakfast is obviously included!*

Roland went for a walk to the nearby beach and watched the fishermen pulling in their nets with their labour producing only a small catch. There were few people on the beach and a number of vendors who tried to sell him various items such as sunglasses, sun cream, lobsters, prawns and ice cream.

Returning to the hotel, Roland noticed three lovely, young ladies at the pool. He considered going for a swim; however, he needed to use the shower to get the sand off his feet. The ladies were hovering around the shower and it all seemed too complicated so he returned to his room.

Roland had a shower and finished off his remaining fruit, as breakfast was included. He then had a siesta until the early evening when he got up and prepared for his last night in Fortaleza. It promised to be a party atmosphere as it was Monday night, which was Pirata Night.

Praia Iracema was abuzz and Roland walked around trying to find a good place to eat. He ended up being seated on a terrace overlooking one of the main drags. He enjoyed his meal and was entertained by the activities all around him. The place had a carnival and circus atmosphere with street performers, bands and loads of beautiful, fun-loving people.

Moving on, Roland ended up at a small bar with outside seating where he enjoyed a large beer and watched the world go by. An old man produced a small, plastic cup, which Roland obligingly filled with beer. The old man toasted, drank up and sauntered away.

A young, slim, attractive lady with a pony tail then caught Roland's eye. She spoke Italian and introduced herself as Julieta. "I'll be going to Don Angelo's disco; you may want to catch up with me there," she stated, giving him a peck on the cheek before she walked off.

Being in good spirits, Roland felt it was time to hit Pirata. Pirata was a bar on Praia de Iracema that featured live lambada and traditional forró music. He paid the 20 reais entrance fee, walked in, went straight to the bar and purchased a can of beer.

Roland's first impressions were not good as the same band played the same music over and over and over. If this wasn't bad enough, the band featured his least preferred musical instrument, being the ear splitting noises of the piano accordion. He thought the only saving grace of the establishment was the cheap beer so he made the most of it. He endured a little over an hour of the music and the family-type crowd before he decided to leave.

Africas was quiet so Roland moved on to Desiguays where he bumped into Julieta. "I'll be back in a minute," she said; however, she failed to reappear. He then chatted with another lady. "Would you like to dance?" he asked.

The lady started walking away as she responded. "Maybe later."

Interpreting this to mean *definitely never*, Roland decided to hit Don Angelo's.

Roland asked a couple of ladies to dance, but they politely declined, giving him a peck on his cheek as they departed. He was just about to write the night off when he saw a trendy lady dressed in a tight, black dress and fitted with a silver studded, black leather cap and matching belt. "Would you like to dance?" he routinely asked her. She promptly took him by the hand and led him onto the dance floor.

There were only a few people on the dance floor, which was being hit with all sorts of modern lighting effects and foam sprinkling down from the ceiling. *This is really cool*, Roland thought, *and at least a fun way to leave Fortaleza.*

Roland was feeling tired and decided to go. "Larisa, I'm leaving now, but I'd like to buy you a drink before I go."

"I don't want a drink," Larisa replied. "I will go with you."

Roland saw no point in questioning her statement and he led her away to catch a cab back to his hotel room.

The moment the door closed, Larisa wasted no time; she was all over him. The activities went on for most the night and it was due to sheer exhaustion that they eventually managed to get some sleep.

Roland woke and Larisa was still sleeping. He made some advances, but she brushed him off. He had a shower and as he returned to the bedroom she was awake and sporting a wide smile. She went for a shower whilst Roland prepared his belongings.

Larisa emerged from the bathroom with a towel around her head to harness her wet hair and otherwise nude. They starting chatting and she seemed a little coy talking about herself.

Initially stating that she worked in a hairdressing salon, Larisa then indicated that she did other stuff. It finally emerged that she in fact worked in a massage parlour. She further advised that most of the women in the Don Angelo's club were working girls.

Roland didn't immediately realise the significance of the statement, but then it struck him. *I was rejected by prostitutes?*

Roland checked out at midday and they took a cab to the bus terminus. He placed his suitcase in storage and they then took a cab to Larisa's apartment. It consisted of a bathroom, a balcony and a main room, which accommodated three single beds and a lot of junk.

"Hello Jessica," Larisa called out as she walked into the bathroom. Roland could hear the two ladies chatting for a short time before Larisa emerged and a lingerie-clad, young lady with a stunning body followed.

Larisa introduced her to Roland and Jessica started dressing whilst sitting next to him on one of the beds. Before he could come to his senses, Larisa started taking off her clothes in order to change into something more casual.

After the ladies finished dressing, Roland pulled himself together and the three of them went for a walk along the street, which was lined with cafés and restaurants. They sat in a street-side bar, had drinks and a light lunch. The ladies were often talking amongst themselves, glancing at Roland and giggling.

Larisa went to the toilet and Jessica started playing footsies with Roland. This triggered him to fantasise about a threesome and he couldn't get the idea out of his head. Larisa returned to the table and Jessica continued with the footsies.

Larisa mentioned something about how expensive their apartment was and Jessica said something about wanting to go shopping. Roland wasn't at all happy with the direction of the conversation and wasn't keen on the idea of shopping. "I think I'll be returning to the bus terminus," he stated.

They jumped into a cab and the ladies directed the driver to the market. The ladies hopped out of the taxi and made one last attempt to get Roland to go shopping with them, but he declined. Larisa gave him a kiss and he continued on to the bus terminus.

Chapter 58 – One Long Day in Natal

Arriving at the terminus, Roland had six hours to kill prior to departure. He spent some time at an internet café and then went to a restaurant for a meal. He spent the last couple of hours waiting outside, fighting off a couple of mosquitoes and warding off a drunken salesman.

Spending an extra night in Fortaleza than Roland had initially planned meant he only had one night in Natal before his flight to Recife. The bus journey from Fortaleza to Natal took eight hours and he slept most of the way, arriving just after 7.00 am.

Whilst waiting for the crowds to diminish, Roland consumed the food and water that he had stowed in his daypack. He then took a taxi to the beach suburb of Ponta Negra.

On Peter's recommendation, Roland sought accommodation at the Hotel Pousada Sol where the receptionist led him to a room. "I can offer this room for 60 reais," the receptionist stated. He confirmed that breakfast was included before he took it.

The room had to be made up, so Roland left his suitcase at the hotel and went for a walk up the esplanade. He travelled some distance when it dawned on him that he was carrying his daypack with all of his prized possessions. *You idiot, you'll never learn.*

Roland returned to the hotel and his room was ready. He settled in, had a shower and headed off for central Natal. The No.56 bus took over an hour to get there and he was fortunate there were a few guys on the bus who told him where to get off, in a nice way.

Totally losing his bearings, Roland had to do a few circuits before finding his way. He walked around the Centro area and viewed the city attractions before he made his way towards the main attraction: Forte dos Reis Magos (the fort).

Roland couldn't ascertain how far the fort was going by his map, but he started walking. After a while, he came to a road that overlooked the beach area and the fort was in sight. He took a photograph of the beach view before he made his way down the steep road that led to the entertainment precinct at Praia dos Artistas. He strolled through the precinct before proceeding toward the fort.

It was a hot day, although there was a cooling breeze. After an hour of walking, Roland got to the end of the main road, which narrowed into a dirt path. He was disheartened when he saw there was another road leading to the fort, which jutted from the other end and it looked a long way away.

Roland surrendered the idea of walking to the fort. He adjusted his camera to full zoom, pointed it towards the fort and took a photograph. He then returned the way he came, cooling himself down by walking through several sprinklers.

Coming across a self-service restaurant, Roland considered stopping to eat, but then wondered how long the food had been sitting there and walked on. He came across a bar and was befriended by a man. "I don't work here, but I can vow that they serve good food," the man advised.

Sitting down at an outside table, Roland ordered a large beer and the recommended fish. He enjoyed his meal, which he finished off with a coffee. He bade farewell to the man, thanked the waiter and left a tip. The waiter seemed as much surprised as he was grateful for the tip.

Roland tried to catch the No.56 bus from where he'd disembarked, but the driver was thumbing backwards. It wasn't until an onlooker advised that he needed to catch the bus from the side street that he got the message.

Being peak hour, the No.56 bus was full. As the bus chugged along, it started to get dark. They travelled for what seemed to be an eternity and Roland was starting to worry as he couldn't locate where to get off. To his relief, the bright lights of Ponta Negra emerged.

Returning to the pousada, Roland had a rest before he spruced up and headed out for dinner. He had a roadside seat at the Blue Bayou Restaurant, which was across from the beach and he watched the passing foot traffic.

Roland enquired about the Bife a Cavalo, which he thought may have been horse meat, but the waiter assured him that it was beef. He enjoyed his feast as did the cat that parked itself under his table and took advantage of the discarded leftovers.

Setting off to seek out the nightlife, Roland stopped at the Rio Dance Bar. The barmaid was very friendly and he ordered a beer. "The nightlife changes between the clubs and tonight the Baraonda Nightclub is the place to go," she advised.

Walking in the direction the barmaid pointed, Roland came across a large number of plastic tables and chairs where numerous people were seated. "Would you like to sit and drink cerveja?" asked a waiter.

Roland took a seat and ordered a beer. He was on his second beer when he was approached by a lady whom he found unattractive and she started propositioning him. In his desperation, he looked around and caught the eye of a young lady who was sitting down with a friend.

Contrary to his character, Roland propelled himself out of his chair and joined the two women. Before he knew it, the two ladies were offering their company to him for 100 reais each. Stunned by the unexpected offer, he was unsure how to respond.

In Fortaleza, Roland was fantasising about a threesome and now had an actual opportunity. However, he felt uneasy about these women and got cold feet. "I might go for a walk, but might catch up with you later," he eventually replied.

Roland climbed a hill, walked by a strip joint and reached a couple of bars where there were a few people drinking and chatting. He found the environment too laid-back for his liking and decided to go back to the club.

The crowds had left the seating area so Roland entered the disco. He found it dark and uninspiring, but he grabbed a beer. As usual, another lady whom he found unattractive approached him.

Again, Roland looked every which way and caught the eye of one of the two ladies that he spoke to earlier and she approached him. "My friend Tristina has found an amigo and I'm looking for an amigo too," she advised.

The lady's name was Carina and she appeared desperate, which made Roland feel uneasy. "Go with me," she begged.

"I'm just checking out the disco and I'll be leaving soon," Roland replied.

Roland returned to the bars at the other end of the beach and started putting away the beers. He chatted to a few people and it wasn't long before the bar was closing and the sun was rising.

Walking along the esplanade on his way back to the hotel, Roland realised that he hadn't been for a swim at the beach. He returned to the hotel and quickly changed. He went for a run along the sand, had a swim and sat on the beach to take in the sea breeze. By the time he returned to the hotel and had a shower, it was time for breakfast.

After breakfast, Roland returned to his room, packed his bags and rested until midday when he checked out of the hotel and took a walk along the esplanade. He stopped at a takeaway and purchased three pastels. They were like pies filled with chicken, beef and lobster. He also purchased a coconut, which was punctured and ready to drink. He found a shaded area where he drank his coconut milk and ate his pastels.

Roland returned to the hotel and ordered a cab to the airport. It wasn't long before he caught his 17:20 Varig flight RG2343 to Recife, very much looking forward to meeting up with his friend Peter.

Chapter 59 – Meeting the Gang

Arriving in Recife, Roland was exiting the airport when Peter appeared sporting a large grin. They jumped into a cab and it was a very short drive to their hotel at the Praia de Boa Viagem.

Roland settled into his room and then met the rest of the gang. Henry was a former veterinarian who'd opted for semi-retirement. Saverio, or Sav, was a former teacher who gave up teaching to pursue day trading on the share market.

They went to a buffet-style, por quilo restaurant where the food was paid for by the weight. They over-indulged in food and drinks, finishing off with liqueurs and coffee before retiring to their rooms for a spell to meet up again later in the evening.

They walked a couple of blocks to a bar where they sat around a table in the outdoor seating area and ordered beers. They engaged in conversation on a broad range of topics and the topic of performance enhancing drugs of the sexual kind came up.

"Have you ever tried the pill?" Sav asked Roland.

"No, I've never even considered it," Roland admitted.

"My whole life has changed since I've been on the pill," Sav divulged and he handed Roland one. "You've gotta at least try it."

After a couple of beers, Henry and Sav headed back to the hotel. Peter and Roland checked out the downstairs disco and two attractive, young ladies started dancing around them. It wasn't long before the ladies selected their man and commenced dancing with them. They started kissing and there wasn't much discussion before they all headed back to the hotel.

"Have you made any arrangements with the girls?" Roland asked Peter.

"No I haven't," Peter replied.

"Wouldn't it be a good idea to arrive at an understanding with them?" Roland said.

"Don't worry about it," Peter stated reassuringly.

It turned out that the two ladies were sisters. Roland's lady was named Regina and was the younger of the two sisters at twenty years of age. She was a real live wire so Roland thought he would try out the pill. Regina was all over him at the bar and she didn't let up when they got into the sack. He thought the sex was good, although he didn't feel the pill made any difference.

In the morning, Regina commenced discussion about being paid.

Roland expected that the issue of money might come up and, based on what Peter had previously indicated, he expected the going rate to be 100 reais; however, Regina had other ideas.

Seeking clarification, Roland phoned Peter. "Hey Peter, I'm having a discussion with Regina about how much I should give her. Is it correct that the standard rate is 100 reais?"

"Yeah, that's right; that's all I'm giving my bird," Peter confirmed.

"I've checked with Peter and he's paying Nadia 100 reais so you should also be happy with 100 reais," Roland said.

"This is rubbish! You should pay 200 reais," Regina stated.

There was a knock on the door and it was Nadia. "You should pay Regina 200 reais as this is the amount that Peter paid me," Nadia advised.

Roland was on the phone again to Peter. "Peter, exactly how much did you pay Nadia?"

Peter procrastinated a little. "Yeah well, I did sort of pay her 200 reais," he eventually admitted.

Roland handed over 200 reais and as the ladies were about to walk out the door Nadia stopped and turned around. "Peter also paid me twenty reais for a taxi," she stated.

"Since you are sisters and live together won't you be sharing the cab?" Roland asked.

Nadia rolled her eyes and the sisters walked out.

Going down to breakfast, Roland sampled most of the offerings at the buffet. After he returned to his room, he received a call from Peter. "I'm going to the bank and, as it's overcast with the forecast of rain, Sav and I thought it might be a good day to go to the shopping complex."

It was early in the afternoon when Sav, Peter and Roland grabbed a taxi for the shopping centre. They walked around the various levels and admired a number of lovely ladies. "Gee, there are a lot of pretty lady shop assistants," Roland commented.

"I think they specifically hire them to attract customers," Peter said.

"I guess this explains why you're such an avid shopper," Roland said with a smile.

"I'm going to purchase some more pills," Sav advised.

"Don't you require a prescription?" Roland asked.

"No, you can buy the pills over the counter in Brazil," Sav said.

As Roland owed Sav a pill, he thought he'd also buy a packet.

The guys met up for dinner and selected another of their regular places: Ponteio Grill. It was an establishment that had a rodizio – all-you-can-eat. They would naturally overindulge and again finished off the feast by alternating their sips of Argentine wine with liqueurs and coffee. They retired to their rooms for a while and met up again to head off for the bars. Roland sensed that there was a strict routine going on here.

They grabbed a cab to a nightclub, which happened to be a strip joint. They took up seats on the lounges and ordered drinks. Sav noticed three familiar ladies and invited the ladies to join them.

"Are these ladies working girls?" Roland asked.

"Of course they are," said Peter.

Sav, Peter and Henry took one each of the ladies for a dance. It was dark in the club and as Roland was walking around the dance floor someone grabbed him and started dancing cheek to cheek. He had no idea who it was, but they were soon all over him. They were dirty dancing, groping him and kissing him passionately. He had to come up for air and tried to get a look at the person.

Catching a glimpse, Roland considered it to be a lady and not totally unattractive so he reciprocated a little. He then managed to pull himself free. "I have to go to the banos," he stated.

"Are you coming back?" asked the lady.

"I don't know, as I might go to talk with my friends," Roland replied.

Exiting the toilet, Roland was going to talk with the guys when another lady touched him on the hand. He looked around and it was a lady that he hadn't seen before. They started chatting and he found her to be delightful. "Would you like to go to the lounge area to sit down and talk?" he asked her and she nodded.

As Roland was passing the guys, the first lady positioned herself next to them and grabbed him by the arm. "What are you doing?" she questioned.

"I'm going to sit down with my lady friend to talk," Roland explained.

The first lady grabbed Sav's drink out of his hand and poured it over Roland's head. The bouncers took no time dragging her away.

"That lady poured out my drink and it's all your fault," Sav complained.

"You didn't have to hand over your drink, so it's actually all your fault and now I've got vodka and orange all over me," Roland countered.

"It wasn't vodka and orange, it was a double vodka and orange," Sav corrected.

Roland was glad to see that his new lady friend had hung around. "Do you still want to sit with me?" he asked her and she nodded.

Roland chatted with Tatiana for ages and, although she didn't speak English, the communication was fluid and enjoyable. "Would you like to go back my hotel?" he asked her and again she nodded.

Recalling the disagreement of the previous night, Roland didn't want a repeat performance so he asked how much she wanted. Tatiana quoted 150 reais and he couldn't get out of the place fast enough.

They took a cab back to Roland's hotel room and he thought he might as well make use of a pill. They engaged in foreplay for a lengthy period and he noticed things were developing in a most dramatic way. He got one of the hardest erections he had ever experienced. They had sex in numerous positions and it was almost an hour before he could orgasm.

Early in the morning, Roland woke with an erection so hard that it felt uncomfortable. He struggled with the situation for a short time until he considered there was only one way of gaining relief. He started foreplay and Tatiana freely reciprocated. Intercourse endured for a prolonged period; however, he failed to climax.

They had a break for a while, but Roland's erection returned as hard and as uncomfortable as before. It took almost another hour of intercourse before he managed to come. He was so exhausted, excited, and out of breath that he fell back on the bed, gasping for air.

Tatiana and Roland stayed in bed until midday. He then escorted her to her modest accommodation in central Recife. She took him on a tour of the city where they visited Catedral de Sao Pedro Dos Clerigos and the Mercado De Sao Jose. He was snapping away with his camera, taking as many photos of Tatiana as he was of the sites.

Tatiana was returning home to her folks that day so they grabbed a cab and headed off to the bus station, called TIP, an acronym for Terminal Integrado de Passageiros. They exchanged details, said goodbye and Tatiana was gone.

Roland arrived back at his hotel and Peter advised they were meeting up for dinner. It was a return visit to Ponteio Grill where they had the standard feast. They returned to their hotel and freshened up before going to a bar.

Peter came across another one of his acquaintances and Roland was introduced to her friend, Cassia. Roland tried to talk to Cassia and, although he found her to be very attractive, he sensed that there wasn't much chemistry. They were seated in the outdoor seating area when it commenced to drizzle and they retreated to the disco.

Roland bought beers for the lads and stood next to Sav at the edge of the dance floor. He noticed Cassia dancing and she caught a glimpse of him watching her. She slowly danced her way in front of him and continued to edge closer.

It didn't take long before Cassia was in Roland's arms and they were moving to the music. They started kissing and he eventually popped the question. "Would like to go back to my hotel?" She accepted and as if she could read his mind she immediately quoted the price of 100 reais.

They went back to Roland's hotel room and were engaging in foreplay when, out of the blue, Cassia confessed that she had featured in three porno movies and that she loved anal sex. He had never indulged in anal sex, nor did he particularly have any urge or curiosity to do so. To his relief, they engaged in conventional sex.

Cassia and Roland arranged to meet up later that day at her favourite bar. Cassia departed and Roland went down for breakfast where he saw Peter who quizzed him about his experience.

Roland set off to join the guys at the beach with a skip in his step. He walked up and down the beach in search of the guys whilst various vendors made numerous offers for him to take a seat. He gained a glimpse of a familiar figure out of the corner of his eye.

Taking a closer look, Roland could identify the statuesque figure of Henry as he surfaced from the sea, brushed back his silver hair and caressed his rotund tummy. Roland waved, Henry waved back and pointed to the location where Sav and Peter were settled.

There wasn't enough space for all of them, but the staff was quick to rearrange the patrons to ensure everyone was happily accommodated.

Roland had heard a lot from the guys about the Brazilian beach culture; however, this was the first time he had the opportunity to fully experience it.

It was a Sunday afternoon and there was a large crowd. It was a festive atmosphere and Roland was immediately impressed with the organised chaos. There were baraccas that hired out beach umbrellas, plastic tables and deck chairs as well as selling food and drink. It was instantaneous service with a smile. There was also a continuous stream of freelance salespeople who roamed up and down the beach selling their wares.

Roland's toughest decision was what to do first. Order a beverage, order some food, take a swim, go for a jog, sun-bathe, read his book, or just relax under the shade of a beach umbrella and watch the world go by.

The time advanced and when the tide came in the guys migrated to the café across the road for afternoon drinks.

After a while, Roland headed off to freshen up before he went to Cassia's favourite bar. He arrived on time, but the bar was closed. He was waiting outside when a man arrived and allowed him to enter. He had a couple of drinks whilst chatting to the barmaid.

Cassia arrived and they talked for a little while before heading off to dinner at the Ponteio Grill. It was the third night in a row that Roland dined at that restaurant. They enjoyed the meal and Cassia came up with the idea of going to Recife Antiga.

They caught a taxi to the old town; however, most of the establishments were closed. It was a warm night and they strolled through the old streets admiring the colonial-styled buildings. They came across a small bar and stopped for a beer. It was midnight and Roland was feeling a little tired. "Do you want to go to my hotel?" he asked and Cassia agreed.

"I've got a surprise for you," Cassia revealed as they entered Roland's hotel room. She went into the bathroom with her bag. He had no idea what the surprise might be, but he decided to take a pill.

Roland was lying on the bed when the bathroom door burst open. Cassia was in a schoolgirl's uniform and started doing a provocative strip to the sound of recorded music from her ghetto blaster. *Terrific*, he thought.

Cassia enthusiastically performed her routine using Roland as a prop and plaything. He was pretty impressed with the act and was ready for sex; however, she wasn't done. "Nao," she said.

Going back into the bathroom, Cassia closed the door. It was about 10 minutes when the bathroom door burst open again. This time she was in a nurse's uniform. *What else?*

Roland was now busting for sex, but Cassia still wasn't done. "Nao," she said again. This time it was because she wanted a shower. He was exasperated until she clarified that she wanted to have a shower together.

They washed each other and started foreplay, which made him even more aroused. Cassia exited the bathroom first and Roland followed; however, she was nowhere to be seen and he couldn't figure out where she had gone.

Checking under the bed and behind the couch, Roland found no trace of Cassia. He then looked around and saw the cupboard. He swung open the cupboard door and there she was, playing with herself. Taking her by the arm, he threw her on the bed and they engaged in foreplay and then intense sex. She was highly excited when she cried out. "Screw me up the arse!"

Roland wasn't keen, but didn't want to disappoint her so he agreed. Cassia scrambled for the lubricant and jumped on top of him. She was moaning. "Do you like it?" she asked.

Roland wasn't certain whether he was inside her and he wasn't sure what she meant. "What do you mean?" he asked.

Cassia reacted by immediately getting off him, ripped off the condom, placed another condom on him and screwed him in the conventional manner. *She's cracked the shits,* Roland thought as they fell asleep in each other's arms.

Early the next morning, Cassia left and Roland struggled to breakfast. He found Peter and they updated each other with the latest gossip. It was a Monday and they arranged to go to the shopping centre.

Most of the shops were closed, although the banks were open so they took the opportunity to cash up. They returned to the hotel, stashed their money and met up with Sav and Henry at the beach.

There was a ball game going on with the locals showing off their soccer prowess on a beach volleyball court. Roland took a couple of photos and it was no accident that many of them featured ladies in their G-string bikinis.

Sav and Peter struck up a conversation with a threesome of young ladies. "Are these ladies more working girls?" Roland asked.

"Of course they are," Peter advised.

Roland wondered whether there were any normal ladies in this town.

It had reached the time when the crowd migrated to the café across the road for afternoon drinks. Whilst the guys socialised with the ladies, Roland returned to the hotel.

Roland was asleep when he heard the telephone ring. It was Peter who invited him to go out with the guys and the ladies. "I'll have to pass up the offer as I'm meeting up with Cassia," Roland advised.

There was another ring and this time it was Cassia at the door. She led Roland outside and hailed down a cab. He had no idea where they were going as she directed the cab along the beach. They stopped at a seafood restaurant where Cassia ordered for both of them.

The waiter poured glasses of white wine and served an entrée of savouries stuffed with prawns. The main course was a platter of barbequed lobster, grilled fish and prawns, which they shared.

Cassia was very playful during the meal and she had her own version of footsies, which involved taking off her shoes and playing with parts of Roland's anatomy that didn't exactly concentrate on his feet.

After dinner, Cassia grabbed a cab and stopped off at her favourite bar where she started getting intimate. Roland wasn't comfortable as she was kissing him passionately. *Okay this completes the repertoire*, he thought. *She's a porno star, a prostitute, a stripper and also an exhibitionist.* They retired to his hotel room where they spent a wonderful night together.

Roland was to depart Recife that day so he bid Cassia farewell. The guys had left Recife earlier in the day and he went for a walk along the beach on his own. The beach was very quiet and he stopped off at a café for lunch.

Grabbing his suitcase, Roland caught a cab to the TIP. He fell asleep in the cab and woke up as the driver parked at the bus terminus. He purchased a couple of pastels, a beer and a bottle of water to go.

Roland caught the bus for Salvadore and sat next to a pretty lady. He helped her with her bag and she started to converse with him in Portuguese. As the level of the Portuguese was well beyond his grasp he had to revert to his standard response. "Desculpa, nao falo Portugues." The statement that he didn't speak Portuguese effectively killed the conversation.

Chapter 60 – Salvadore

The bus arrived in Salvadore and Roland walked around to find a secluded spot to eat the snacks he was provided on the bus. He then set off to check out the accommodation on his list for Pelourinho. The city's name of Pelourinho meant whipping post.

Roland went to the Hotel Pelourinho, which he considered to be an impressive building, although he decided to inspect other places before he made a decision. He had to climb a steep hill to get to the next accommodation on his list.

The pousada provided basic rooms, but it was cheap so Roland took it. He paid for two night's accommodation and settled into his room. He had planned to go on his walking tour, but he made the mistake of lying on the double bed and fell asleep.

It was midday when Roland was awoken by the sound of music and singing. He washed up and started on his walking tour. He walked down the street and into the Largo do Pelourinho, which was a former slave auction site. The square was not where he had expected to end up. As usual he had trouble with his bearings. He took a couple of pictures of the square before he moved on.

It was a hot, sunny day and Roland purchased a bottle of water from a pleasant lady. He continued on his walking tour, but was still having trouble with his bearings. This time he ended up at the square named Terreiro de Jesus. He took a couple of photos before he moved on.

Arriving at Praca da Sé, Roland was approached by a friendly lady. "I'd like to give you a present," she said.

"Thank you, but I cannot accept it," Roland replied.

"It's a tradition and a gift at no charge," she insisted.

Roland wasn't comfortable accepting the gift, but he didn't want to offend the lady and he certainly didn't want to break with tradition so he allowed her to tie two ribbons around his wrist.

Thanking the lady, Roland tried to walk off, but she stopped him. "You now have to buy something from me," she demanded.

Roland wasn't impressed with her nor was he impressed with himself for falling for the stunt. "I'm not buying anything from you," he stated as he tried to walk away.

The lady became hostile and took a hold of him. He extricated himself from her grasp, managed to break away and ripped off the ribbons.

Roland walked to the Praca Tome de Souza, which had a viewing area on a balcony overlooking the Mercado Modelo and the Baia de Todos os Santos. He admired the views and took a couple of photographs.

A couple of guys with piles of ribbons in their hands were approaching Roland and he dashed away. He ended up at Praca de Sousa where he took a photograph of the Palacio Rio Blanco before entering the ornate building. He walked onto the balcony and took a photograph of the harbour.

There was an elevator, named Elevador Lacerda, which took people between the upper and lower cities. As there was a queue, Roland decided to walk down the steep road to the lower city. He continued to the Mercado Modelo and a lady approached him to ascertain whether he was interested in some comida. Feeling hungry, he took a seat.

Roland completed his meal and had a quick look around the market before he headed off. He took the Elevador Lacerda up to the upper city and returned to Terreiro de Jesus. He took a photograph of one of the local ladies of Salvadore Bahia, named Bahianas, in her traditional dress.

The African influence was noticeable in many aspects of Bahian life due to the strong African roots and the slave history of the area. Roland continued on his walking tour and arrived at Largo do Carmo. He reached the lower station of the funicular railway and caught the funicular back up.

Roland made his way back to his accommodation where he cooled down by washing his face and drinking water. He dozed off and was woken up by the sound of drums. It was as if they were beckoning him.

After a shave and shower, Roland was off for the evening activities. He stopped at the Dona Chika Ka Restaurant and had the specialty of the house, Bobo de Camarao, which was a hot pot of prawns in a cream sauce served with rice. He found the meal to be enjoyable and with two large beers and a coffee, very filling.

Venturing off to find some nightlife, Roland went to Pelourinho Dia e Noite, but it was quiet. He moved on and located an outdoor bar with music. He bought a beer and hung back to enjoy the live band. The venue was popular with young people and he stayed for a few beers before he tired of the scene and headed back to his pousada.

Roland had a disrupted night's sleep, mainly due to dodging mosquitoes most the night and being on the lookout for the odd giant ant. However, his efforts were not entirely successful as he still woke up with a series of bites.

After breakfast, the lady from the pousada arranged a car to take Roland to the airport. The lady and her male partner loaded his suitcase in the boot of a car and guided him into the back seat. They placed a young boy in the back seat to sit next to him and the couple assumed the front seats.

There were no seat belts and as they sped along Roland had to steady the boy to stop him from falling about. Arriving at the airport, he paid them the 40 reais fare and said goodbye.

Roland checked the departure screens and noted that his flight was due to take off in 40 minutes. He rushed through check-in and made it to the gate with minutes to spare.

Boarding his Varig flight RG2315, Roland found his seat where he was sandwiched in between two big, burly men with noticeably unpleasant body odour. It was a really bumpy flight and he felt like a kangaroo trying to paw at his airline food. He was most relieved when the flight touched down safely in Rio at 2.20 pm.

Chapter 61 – Rio de Janeiro

Roland grabbed his suitcase, headed for the exit and stopped at the taxi counter. "Do you have a hotel reservation?" the lady asked.

"No I don't," Roland admitted and she directed him to the Tourist Information.

"There's a convention in town and most of the hotels are booked out," informed an assistant. "But I will make some calls for you."

The hotel where Peter was staying was booked out as were a couple more that the assistant contacted. Roland eventually managed to score a room at a hotel only a block away from where Peter was staying. He returned to the lady at the taxi counter and booked a ride to the South American Copacabana Hotel.

After settling into the hotel room, Roland went to the hotel where Peter was situated, but he wasn't in. He found an internet café and dealt with a couple of messages. He considered what to do next and it was one of those rare occasions where he was at a loss for ideas.

It was cool and overcast when Roland went for a walk along Copacabana Beach and stopped at a Sindicato do Chopp for dinner then made his way to a club Peter had mentioned.

There was a long line at the entrance and when Roland turned around he spotted Peter wearing a bright orange top and sporting a big grin. Roland returned his grin. "What a surprise to bump into you here."

"Where else would I go?" Peter replied.

Sav then made an appearance. "Henry returned to his room; he's got an upset stomach." It seemed to be a regular after-dinner ailment for Henry.

"I'm tired so I'll be heading back to my room, too" Peter said.

Roland then looked to Sav. "I'm keen to kick on at the club," Sav said and Roland was happy to join him.

It was a Thursday night and even though there was a sizeable crowd outside the club there were few people inside. Sav got into the swing of things and soon had a mixed drink in one hand, a smoke in the other, and was chatting to an attractive, blonde lady.

It took a while before Roland felt at all comfortable, which was assisted by the consumption of alcohol. He started off with a caipirinha, then a couple of beers and then a Cuba libre. He was able to relax a little and found himself talking to a few ladies.

An attractive lady with blue eyes and bleached-blonde hair led him onto the dance floor and they had a few dances. "Can I have a Red Bull?" she asked. *You would have to choose one of the most expensive drinks on the board*, Roland thought. She took her drink and led him to the upstairs seating area.

The lady started negotiating and it then hit Roland that the establishment was one of those working girl places. He declined the offer and she was soon on her way.

Returning downstairs, Roland saw Sav still talking to the same blonde who appeared to be giving him some grief. Roland went to let Sav know he was ready to leave. "Wait for me as I'm about to leave as well," Sav said and had some further exchanges with the lady before following Roland.

Roland walked onto the street and turned around, but Sav was nowhere to be seen. He looked up and down the street and waited a few minutes before concluding that Sav must have had a change of heart so he made his way back to his hotel on his own.

The next morning, Roland lay in bed a while before finally getting up to take advantage of the buffet breakfast.

It was a fine, warm day and Roland went to the guy's hotel. Peter and Sav were on their way to Rio Sul Shopping and Roland tagged along. They bumped into Henry who was bound for the hotel pool and told him that they'd catch up with him later.

It was a short cab ride to Rio Sul and they walked around the shopping centre where they admired an abundance of beautiful women. After a coffee and further window shopping, they returned to Peter's hotel.

The conference in Rio was causing havoc with the accommodation, and Sav couldn't secure a room for all the days he was to be in Rio so he moved to the nearby Copa Sul Hotel for five nights. As Roland had only one more night at the South American Copacabana Hotel, he booked the Copa Sul for the following two nights.

Sav and Roland returned to Peter's hotel where they joined Henry at the pool. Henry was sun-bathing and listening to his MP3 player when Sav crept up and tickled his foot, which made him jump.

"We're going to the Church and I've made a booking with Marius," Henry announced excitedly.

"Okay," Peter and Sav immediately responded.

Roland was confused. "Why are you going to church on a Friday evening and who is Marius?"

"Marius is the name of a restaurant," Peter explained, "and the Church isn't exactly a real church, although it is a place where Henry gives thanks – it's a gentlemen's club."

Nearing the time of departure, Henry seemed impatient when Roland rolled up. "Where are the others?" Roland asked.

Henry's face turned sour. "They should be on their way, but they're late."

Roland checked his watch and it was only a few minutes past the scheduled meeting time, but Henry was growing impatient again. The lift door opened and Henry sprang up from the lounge, but it was a false alarm.

The other lift door opened and this time Henry remained seated, but Peter and Sav appeared. The moment Henry saw the two, he stood to attention. "Let's go," he ordered, and started marching.

They made it to the Church in good time with Henry giving a running commentary about the procedures along the way. Roland could hardly keep up.

They paid 300 reais at the door, which included a lady and use of a room for 40 minutes. They were then handed a numbered key for a locker and entered the change rooms.

"Change into a robe and flip flops," Peter instructed. "Whether you keep your underpants on is up to you."

Following Peter and Sav into a bar area, Roland was struck by a smorgasbord of beautiful, young women wearing lingerie and high heels. Henry was in his element, chatting away with two ladies and he didn't mess around as he soon took off with both of them.

Roland noticed a rather stunning creature who could easily adorn the pages of Vogue. She had large green eyes, fantastic cheek bones, a wonderful smile and a top-of-the-line body. His stare prompted her to introduce herself and they started talking.

Samantha was sitting next to Roland when she noticed his friends had all gone and she started placing a bit of pressure on him. "Your friends have gone; what are you waiting for? Don't you like me?"

"Yes, I like you, I'm just taking it easy," Roland responded.

Samantha didn't seem too impressed and she started to twitch, turn, look up and look down. Her body language clearly communicated that she was waiting for the loser to make up his mind.

The guys have gone, we've arranged to go for dinner and I don't want to be left here on my own, Roland thought. *In any case, it's not as if I'm ever going to dump this lady and try to pick up another. I don't expect an experience with Samantha will be anything special, but I might as well give her a try.*

"Okay, we can go if you like," Roland eventually said.

Samantha dragged Roland up the stairs, told him to wait and left him standing in the corridor. She came back in another garment and took him into a small room. "Take off your clothes and get on the bed," she ordered. "Move over and place yourself a little lower; give me more room."

Roland made the mistake of complimenting her great breasts. "They're silicone," she snapped back with her tone implying: *you idiot!*

Samantha was very routine, disciplined and businesslike. The mission was completed in rapid time and Roland suspected his mild erection was due to fright rather than arousal.

Roland caressed Samantha's breasts for a moment and she interrupted. "What do you think you're doing?" she asked and he was speechless.

Samantha proceeded to ask a series of questions. "Have you been to Morro do Pao de Azucar?"

Roland didn't quite catch what she asked, but did know that azucar meant sugar. It then dawned on him that she must have been asking about Sugar Loaf Mountain. He was about to answer, but he obviously ran out of time.

"Do you know Statua Cristo Redentor sobre Corcovado?" Samantha then asked.

Roland picked up on Corcovado, but couldn't make out the associated words. He sought clarification, but she interjected. "You really don't know much and you don't seem to have been to too many places; what are you doing here?"

Guessing that he failed the quiz, Roland wondered, *What am I doing here?*

"Get dressed," Samantha ordered. She edged Roland out of the room and reverted back to her pleasant persona. She gave him an air kiss, thanked him and said goodbye.

Roland had a shower and made his way into the change rooms in a slightly stunned state. Once dressed, he returned to the entrance area where the guys were recounting their respective experiences with excitement.

"How did you like your first time at the Church?" Sav asked Roland.

"Terrific," Roland replied. "I had a root Nazi."

They caught a cab directly to Marius where there were two restaurants. One was a meat restaurant and the other seafood. They entered the seafood restaurant, which was easily identifiable with its seafaring theme. They ordered beers and helped themselves to the all-you-can-eat seafood extravaganza.

After dinner, the guys took a walk along the beach to work off some of the food. However, they didn't travel too far before they caught a cab back to their respective hotels.

Roland had a solid four hours sleep and stayed in bed watching television. He then showered, had breakfast and checked out before heading to his room at the Copa Sul Hotel.

Roland then set off for the Forte de Copacabana, which was situated on a point that provided wonderful views of Copacabana Beach on one side and Ipanema Beach on the other. He took a few photographs of the views, the fort museum buildings and the canons.

As Roland returned along Copacabana Beach, he came across Peter and Henry. "I'll return to my hotel to change and come back," Roland said.

Roland joined Peter and Henry at the baracca where they were set up with deck chairs, an umbrella and a small plastic table. It was a wonderful, hot and fine Saturday afternoon and the beach was packed. He went for a swim and found the sea water cool and refreshing. He returned to his chair, dried off and relaxed, sipping on a caipiroska.

Roland got the urge to take a few photographs and once he commenced, ladies started flocking around and liberating themselves of their bikini tops. This was a surprise as it was not customary for women to go topless on the beaches in Rio. A few of the young ladies gave delightful smiles so Roland obligingly took a few snaps in their direction.

As the day wore on, Roland left the guys to freshen up and set off to experience the traditional Brazilian dish of feijoada. It was described as a black bean based, set menu meal that evolved from the slave days where they lumped together whatever food stuffs they could muster from the local produce.

After his feast, Roland met up with the guys and described his feijoada experience. They seemed uninterested, more intent on recounting their latest experiences at the Church with their usual enthusiasm.

Exhausted from their latest adventures at the Church, Henry, Sav and Peter decided to return to their hotel. Roland wasn't keen on going out alone so he also returned to his hotel.

Roland and Sav met up with Peter after breakfast bound for Ipanema Beach. As was often the case, Henry preferred to spend the day at the hotel pool.

It took less than half an hour to walk to Ipanema Beach and they settled into a spot. It was a hot Sunday afternoon and the beach was packed. Unlike Copacabana Beach that had a large presence of tourists, Ipanema Beach seemed to be more for the locals.

After a few hours on the beach, they went for a walk to the Garota de Ipanema Café – the café where the famous *Girl from Ipanema* song was inspired. They had a snack and a drink before they returned to their respective hotels.

It was Roland's last night accommodation at the Copa Sul so he enquired at Peter's hotel where he was able to book his last three nights' in Rio. He also booked the Petropolis tour for the following day.

The gang met up in the evening at the outdoor seating area of a restaurant on Copacabana Beach. There were young ladies parading and hovering around, waiting for the slightest sign of interest from the men.

Approaching midnight, the guys decided to go to the club. Roland felt ill-at-ease so he got stuck into the drinks. He had a caipirinha, followed by a caipiroska, a Cuba libre and a few beers. He didn't have much to eat that day so the alcohol went straight to his head and he was soon very happily drunk.

Peter, Sav and Henry decided to leave, but Roland wanted to stay. He was talking to a lady for some time and he thought she was nice. She asked him for a drink and, even though he wasn't interested in sleeping with her, he didn't mind buying her one. He was waiting for an order of Red Bull, but she just asked for a beer.

Roland was all over the place when an attractive, mulata lady gave him a hand. He had a good feel about her and they went for a dance, although it was more of a case of her propping him up. "I'd like to go with you," he routinely stated and they were off.

They took a taxi to a love hotel and the lady removed Roland's clothes and put him to bed. The next thing he knew he was waking up with the lady in his arms. She had her back to him and he was cuddling up to her.

The lady sensed Roland's awakening so she turned around and started to kiss and caress him. He was still in a bit of a daze and she seemed to sense this. "I need to go," he stated and she assisted him to get dressed.

As they were leaving, Roland took out his money. "How much do I owe you?" he asked.

The lady seemed reluctant to answer. "We agreed on 150 reais," she meekly replied. He gave her 200 reais as he was aware that the amount was at the lower end of the scale and he respected her honesty.

They stepped onto the street and said goodbye. As Roland started walking away, the lady called out to him. When she saw that he kept on going, she chased after him. She was going on about catching a taxi, but he tried to reassure her. "I'll be all right and I prefer to walk," he said.

"You take a cab," she insisted and she hailed one down.

The lady shoved Roland in the cab, asked him the name of his hotel and communicated to the driver where to take him. As he travelled in the taxi, he realized that he was a long distance from Copacabana, in an unfamiliar and dodgy area. *That lady was all right,* Roland thought, *and I don't even know her name.*

Arriving in his hotel room, Roland collapsed on his bed only to be revived by his wakeup call. He slowly got up, showered, packed his bags and checked out of the hotel. It was one of the rare occasions he didn't mind missing out on breakfast. He walked across to his new hotel wheeling his suitcase behind him and checked in.

Roland's room wasn't ready so he placed his bags in storage. Sav made an appearance and they waited for their tour pickup. It took over an hour to get to Petropolis, which was set in the mountains and known as the Imperial City. During the 1800s, the city was the destination for the Emperor and his family to escape the summer heat.

Sav and Roland immediately felt the cooler, mountain air as they disembarked the bus. They were taken to a chocolate factory where they enjoyed the samples. They then visited the Imperial Museum – the former summer palace – where they were given some information about Emperor Pedro II and time to explore the buildings.

There was an optional buffet lunch; however, Sav and Roland elected to do their own thing. They went for a walk about town and stumbled upon an American-style diner. The building and staff exuded character so they dropped in for a burger and a beer.

Sav and Roland rejoined the group and were taken to the Catedral Sao Pedro de Alcantara and finally to Palacio de Cristal.

Arriving back in Rio, Roland settled into his new hotel room before meeting up with the guys for dinner.

After dinner, Peter and Henry decided to go to the Church, but Sav was keen to go to the club. Roland was not too keen on either, but decided to accompany Sav.

Sav and Roland spoke to a number of ladies with Sav asking the ladies a series of questions, including their going rate. Most of them wanted well over 300 reais for times ranging from an hour to all night.

Roland noticed a fun, attractive lady behind him. They started chatting and were soon negotiating. Sav considered it appropriate to involve himself in the negotiations. "You must go with my friend for 150 reais for the night," Sav proclaimed.

"No, it's 300 reais," the lady swiftly replied.

While Sav was distracted, Roland spoke to another lady named Tina. "I'll go with you for 230 reais until six in the morning," she offered. He wondered why she chose such an odd number as 230 reais. "The 30 reais is for a taxi home," she added as if she could read his mind and he accepted.

Tina wanted to dance and she led Roland to the dance floor where they danced with a few of her girlfriends. "I'm going to the toilet and we can leave when I return," she stated.

Roland advised Sav of the arrangement and that they'd be leaving soon. "You're paying too much; don't go with her," Sav argued.

"She's quoted the lowest price of all the girls, she's one of the best looking and I like her," Roland countered.

"Let's go talk to more girls," Sav said.

"Listen; I've already made an arrangement and I'm going to stick to it," Roland asserted.

"That's okay, but just come with me to chat to a few more girls," Sav insisted and he led Roland to a group of ladies.

Tina eventually reappeared. "We're leaving," Roland told Sav.

"Let's go talk to some other women," Sav persisted.

"No," Roland said.

"Let's go talk to just one more woman," Sav begged.

"No," Roland repeated.

"Hold on a minute as I'll leave with you," Sav pleaded. "After I have just one more beer."

"Sav, we're going now!" Roland confirmed.

Tina and Roland were on their way out and Sav was in quick pursuit.

They hailed a cab, Sav got in the front passenger seat while Tina and Roland got in the back.

Sav started talking to the cab driver who must have been one of the few cab drivers in Rio who spoke fluent English. Sav and the cabbie were soon engaged in a passionate discussion about Brazilian politics. It was Lula this, democracy that. They were so immersed in their conversation the driver was virtually at a standstill in the middle of the main drag. The driver slowly and agonisingly puttered along.

They eventually arrived at the hotel, but it was the wrong hotel. Sav and the driver laughed off the mistake. "Ha ha ha, very funny, we're absolutely in stitches back here!" Roland said.

They finally made it to the correct hotel with a five minute taxi ride taking half an hour. Sav looked back at Roland. "Could you get the fare as I've got nothing less than a 50?"

"Anything else?" Roland said as he paid the fare.

Tina and Roland made it up to the room and Tina peered out the window where she noticed that Sav was still in the cab, talking with the driver. "Is Sav gay?" asked Tina.

"No," Roland replied. "Sav's not gay; he's just a little strange."

Tina and Roland only had two hours and they engaged in some physically strong and intense sex. He thought she had a fantastic figure so it wasn't too surprising for him to learn that she was training for a national body sculpturing competition.

"I have to go now as my mother is due to arrive today in Rio for a few days' holiday," Tina advised. She gave Roland her details and departed.

Roland dozed off for a couple of hours before he got up, showered and went down to breakfast. Peter and Henry then made an appearance. "I'm thinking about going to the Centro area," Peter said. Henry wasn't interested, but Roland was.

Peter and Roland caught one of the many buses that headed to the city centre and they disembarked at the markets. Roland was interested in a Brazilian soccer shirt as a gift and noticed some that looked reasonable and he asked the man the price. The man mumbled a bit, but Roland was sure he'd said 25 reais. He checked with Peter who confirmed that the man said 25 reais.

"I'll take it," said Roland and handed the man 50 reais.

The man placed the shirt in a plastic bag, which he handed to Roland with the change and a small picture of Jesus Christ.

Roland checked his change and realised the man had only given him 15 reais. "You need to give me another 10 reais," he said.

"No, that's correct; the shirt is 35 reais," replied the man.

"I thought you said 25 reais."

"The price is 35 reais."

"In that case, I don't want it," Roland declared as he returned the shirt and demanded his money back.

After some argument, the man returned Roland his money. Roland left with Peter before he stopped and told Peter to wait. He returned to the man and handed him the picture of Jesus Christ. "Here, this should be for you."

Peter and Roland walked around the Centro area and stopped off at the Candelaria Café, which was situated near the Candelaria Church. Roland had a banana juice, Peter had a beer and they both ordered the quail in olive oil.

They were seated at the next table to a strikingly attractive woman. She had natural, blonde hair and deep-blue eyes. She wore a tight-fitting blue dress that partially revealed her full, rounded breasts and accentuated her curvaceous body. She was exquisitely stylish, wearing a velvet, Parisian style beret.

Both Peter and Roland were captivated, unable to take their eyes off her. The lady noticed them and she smiled. It wasn't long before she finished her snack and her last sip of champagne. She placed a small pencil in her note pad, paid the bill then departed, giving another smile as she wiggled off.

Again, the guys couldn't keep their eyes off her and their captivation was only broken by the arrival of their quail. They both enjoyed their meal and had a coffee before making their way back to Copacabana.

In the evening, the guys went to a pub for a couple of drinks and then had dinner at the outside seating area of Don Camillo's Restaurant. As they finished off their meals, Henry presented some Cuban cigars. They spent some time to enjoy the balmy evening, puffing on the cigars and sipping their cognacs and espresso coffees. Roland was sure they were all thinking the same thing: *Life doesn't get much better than this.*

It was just after midnight when they decided to hit the club. Roland found it to be the same sad affair and considered the most fun he had at the club was by getting drunk. He was making his way to the bar when a very attractive lady approached him. She introduced herself as Barbie and made an offer of 300 reais for one hour. When she saw his scrunched up face, she immediately amended her offer. "Okay, 300 reais until 4.00 am."

Roland reflected on the offer before he replied. "You're beautiful, but I think I'll pass."

"That's fine," Barbie said. "I'll go for a walk." She gave him a peck on the cheek and left.

A little demon in Roland's head then talked to him: *Roland, this bird is stunning and she's allowed over two hours where she could give you a really good time. Go get her, man!*

Roland then followed Barbie. "Excuse me, but if it's still okay I'd like to take you up on your offer," he told her.

"Great," Barbie said and she gave him another peck on the cheek.

He remembered that he had a couple of pills left and thought he may need all the help he could get so he thought he'd pop one.

"I'm going to the banos and then I'll meet you back here; would you like a drink?" Roland asked.

"I wouldn't mind a mineral water," Barbie replied.

Roland handed over some money. "Could you also get me a beer?" he asked.

Roland went to the bathroom and when he returned he noticed Barbie standing with two drinks and a number of guys flocking around her. He wasn't sure whether he should interrupt so he held off. As soon as Barbie saw him, she called him over and the guys dispersed. "You're lucky you grabbed me when you could," Barbie said and he was thinking the same thing.

After their drink and a chat, they returned to Roland's hotel room. Barbie had shown him little affection in the club and on the way to the hotel so he didn't expect anything special, but the moment he closed the door she jumped him.

Barbie stripped off his clothes as well as her own. She was a really passionate kisser and Roland could hardly keep up with her, although the pill started to kick in. It wasn't long before this stunning 20-year-old lady was starting to slow.

Roland was highly excited and he took over. He was going strong, performing sex for an extended period in various positions, but he couldn't climax. After almost an hour he was exhausted. "I think I need a break," he admitted.

After a rest, Roland felt his erection growing again and Barbie obligingly jumped on top of him. They changed positions a couple of times and within another half an hour he eventually came. He fell back onto the bed and looked over to Barbie. She had a smile on her face, signifying that it was mission accomplished.

Barbie rested a while and gave Roland her details. "I'm going back to Brasilia today to spend some time with my young baby," she advised. "I'm still breast feeding, you know."

"You're kidding," Roland said.

"You can taste my milk if you like?"

Roland sucked on her breasts and tasted her milk. "It's very sweet, thanks Mummy." He then reflected on his words. *Let's not go there.*

Roland was so exhausted from the night before that he slept until early afternoon. Peter called and told him that they were all doing their own thing during the day, but were meeting up for dinner.

After dropping off his laundry, Roland hit the internet. He spent a couple of hours catching up with his emails before returning to the hotel to freshen up before dinner. It would be their last night together as he was leaving Rio the next day.

They met at the local Sindicato do Chopp where Henry and Sav were bragging about their earlier visit to the Church. "So how did you find your time in Brazil?" Sav asked Roland.

Roland didn't quite know how to answer so he thought about it for a while. "Well, I've done quite a bit of travel in my time, but I must admit the period I've spent with you guys has been the first time in my life I've felt like I've indulged in pure hedonism; however, I don't know whether it's entirely a good thing."

The guys frowned, confusion on their faces. "I think I know what your problem is," Henry said. "It's typical of our society. People are used to working all the time and simply don't know what else to do with their lives. They've probably never really had a good time, and even if they did, they feel guilty."

Silence ruled the group before Sav spoke up. "Well, whatever one's views, we're on holidays now and all that matters when one is on holidays is having a good time. So let's make the most of it."

Sav's statement gained unanimous approval, they toasted each other and polished off their drinks.

"So what are the plans for the evening?" Roland asked.

"I've already visited the Church so I'm going back to the hotel," said Henry.

Sav had similar sentiments so Roland turned to Peter. "I've slept most of the day so I wouldn't mind checking out the club," Peter stated.

Roland joined Peter and they took a seat outside the club. They were sipping on Campari when they noticed a couple of ladies sitting with a man and one of the ladies was giving them constant glances. Peter and Roland finished their drinks and entered the club.

It was the same atmosphere as previous nights, although there seemed to be fewer patrons on that cold and bleak Wednesday evening. Roland noticed a number of familiar ladies, and was uninspired by the scene. Nevertheless, he thought he'd make an effort to have some fun.

Roland chatted to a couple of ladies, but it didn't last long. He then noticed the attractive, blonde lady that had given Sav some grief a few nights earlier. "Give me 150 dollars and we can go and make love," she stated.

"Would that be 150 US dollars or Singapore dollars?" Roland joked.

Unimpressed, she scrunched up her face and walked off.

Noticing the lady seated outside had made an appearance, Roland approached her. They started chatting and he learned that her name was Lilly, she was with her friend and they were both working girls. "My friend is lined up with a man, but I'm available," Lilly added.

Looking around the club, Roland observed that there wasn't much happening. Peter was sitting at the bar on his own, having a drink. It was Roland's last night in Rio and he couldn't think of what else to do so he thought he may as well spend the night with Lilly. "Would you like a drink?" he asked her.

"The only drink I can have is champagne," Lilly replied.

Roland cringed as he made his way to the bar and was told that they didn't sell champagne by the glass, they only sold small bottles. "Terrific," he mumbled, "and I thought Red Bull was the most expensive drink."

Lilly and Roland hit the dance floor with Lilly's friends. "Would you like to leave?" Lilly asked.

"Okay," Roland responded.

Lilly's friend pleaded for her to stay a bit longer and after Roland took another look at her man, he suspected he knew why. He visited the bathroom, popped his last pill and said goodbye to Peter.

As soon as Lilly and Roland arrived in his hotel room, they engaged in foreplay and commenced intercourse. She seemed to be putting on an act with her moaning seeming to be unnecessarily over the top. After a period he'd had enough and he brought about a stay in proceedings.

They slept until the early morning, at which time Roland woke with a strong hard-on. He commenced foreplay and Lilly responded. She recommenced her previous antics, which he found to be a total turn off. After a period of intercourse, he was far from climaxing so he gave up.

"I really should be going now," Lilly mentioned a number of times.

"You're free to go," Roland told her, but she never did.

Eventually, Lilly slowly changed with Roland looking around the room for her clothes and handing them to her.

Lilly had put on most of her skimpy outfit when she started fooling around. Roland helped her with her shoes and tried to lead her to the door. She started rubbing up against him and dry rooting him in fun. He reciprocated a little in jest; however, all of a sudden he got an unanticipated, huge erection. He then changed direction, led her back and threw her onto the bed.

Roland stripped off Lilly's clothes and they engaged in intense sex. This time her moans seemed more genuine. He came within ten minutes and collapsed on the bed. Lilly dressed, threw a piece of paper with her details on the bed and left. As he lay on the bed he thought, *thank goodness that was my last pill!*

After a little repose, Roland rolled out of bed, had a shower and went down for breakfast. He visited reception where a distinguished, elderly man in a bow tie booked a cab for him. He returned to his room, collected his things and headed downstairs.

On the way down, Roland buzzed Peter's door bell. "Hi Peter, I'm leaving now; I'd like to thank you for everything."

"No problem, Roland, have a good trip," Peter replied.

Roland heard the bell from the elevator and positioned himself in front of the elevator door. "Goodbye and say goodbye to Henry and Sav for me."

Roland made the airport in time to check out the shops. He then headed off to board his 14:10 LA 0751 Lan Chile flight to Santiago.

Chapter 62 – Destination Patagonia

The plane arrived in Santiago and Roland wasn't impressed to learn that Australians were required to pay a reciprocal entry fee into Chile. It cost him $30US, although he felt slightly better when he discovered the fee for Americans was $100US.

Roland proceeded through immigration, collected his suitcase and went on to purchase a $5US ticket on the TRANVIP minibus for the Hotel Liberdator. The driver took an eternity to do the hotel drop-offs, and of course Roland had to be last.

After checking in, Roland slept through till morning. He went down for breakfast, grabbed a safe key from reception to store his valuables and then started on his walking tour.

Roland visited Plaza de la Constitucion and took a photo of the Palacio de la Moneda before finding a post office where he mailed a few postcards. He then trekked to Cerro Santo Lucia and was greeted at the entrance by Terraza Neptune – a beautiful courtyard with a fountain statuette and an ornate building. He took a photo before making his way up the hill.

The site was a former fortress and contained Japanese gardens. Roland took a photograph of the statue of the Virgin Mary, referred to as Santuario Immaculata Concepcion – the Sanctuary of the Immaculate Conception.

The elevated location allowed Roland to take photographs of the views of the city and surrounding areas. Unfortunately, the smog and cloud-cover limited the views out to the Andes Mountain Range, but he thought the views to be impressive nonetheless.

Continuing down Avenida O'Higgins and Avenida Providencia, Roland found an AMEX travel office and was able to change some travellers' cheques. He then walked through General Holley and some of the side streets that were clustered with bars, clubs and restaurants.

Roland purchased fruit on his way back to the hotel where he indulged his appetite then put on the television and fell asleep.

Heading off for dinner, Roland caught the bus and managed to get off at the stop close to General Holley. It was a festive atmosphere and a pretty lady in a vamp costume invited him to take a seat. He inspected the menu and decided to stay; his decision influenced more so by the pretty lady rather than the food selection.

"Is there anything special on tonight or is the atmosphere always like this?" Roland asked.

"It's Halloween," advised the waiter.

Roland checked his watch: Friday, 31st October. *Indeed Halloween.*

The streets were overtaken by the festivities. Even Freddie Kruger made an appearance when there was a fight scene staged in the street just in front of Roland's street-side dining table. Roland was really frightened at one point as Freddie almost spilled his bottle of wine.

After an entertaining dinner, Roland polished off his wine and was happily drunk. He moved on to check out a few bars and clubs where he had a few more drinks. He decided to call it quits and was about to search for a cab when he noticed that the buses were still running.

The next morning, Roland lay in bed watching television before he had breakfast and continued his walking tour. He strode along the pedestrian malls to the Plaza de Armas and took pictures of the post office, the Catedral Metropolitana and the Palacio de la Real Audencia, which housed the Museo Historico Nacionale. He also visited the National Congress, Tribunales de Justicia and the Mercado Central.

Stopping off at a supermarket, Roland placed his daypack in a locker and was assured by a guard that he would get his 100 pesos back when he retrieved his bag. He purchased water and an apple juice before returning to his hotel room where he slept through until the early evening.

Roland set off and thought he'd explore the Barrio Bellavista area, which reputedly had some good restaurants and bars. He settled on the La Palmera Restaurant and deliberated over the menu for some time. He eventually ordered eel in white wine sauce with salad and a bottle of Don Diablo white wine.

After an enjoyable dinner, Roland checked out a few of the bars; however, they all seemed uneventful so he decided to return to the hotel. On the way back, he stumbled across a nightclub. "Cuanto costa?" he instinctively asked.

"The entry costs 3,000 pesos, which includes a beer," the doorman advised.

Roland entered the seedy establishment and was escorted to a seat upstairs. "What would you like to drink?" asked the waiter.

"I'd like a beer," Roland promptly responded.

A lady appeared. "Would you like to buy me a drink?"

"Cuanto costa?" Roland instinctively replied.

"6,000 pesos," she stated.

It cost me around $8 AUS for me to enter, which included a beer, but it costs me around $15 AUS for you to have a drink? "No gracias," Roland replied.

"Buying me a drink also includes my company," the lady clarified.

"No gracias," Roland responded.

Roland gulped down his beer while he viewed two lame and uninspiring strips.

"Would you like another beer?" asked the waiter.

"No thanks," Roland replied. "I'll have the bill."

The waiter came back with a bill for 3,000 pesos. "A propina for me," the menacing looking waiter stated as Roland reached for his wallet. Roland handed over the 3,000 pesos plus a tip of 1,000 pesos in gratitude that the establishment had not ripped him off and to ensure his safe passage out.

Slowly rising the next morning, Roland had breakfast and checked out of his single room. He was advised that he would be sharing a room with a gentleman on the Patagonian tour, and went to his new room to meet his roomy, named Frank.

Roland settled in and then went in search of an internet café. The street internet cafés were full and chaotic so he used one in a shopping centre charging a premium. After dealing with his email messages in quick time he walked to the Plaza de Armas.

It was a cool and overcast Sunday morning. Roland noticed some men in uniform with long sideburns and he took a photo. The guards marched off and he heard the sound of drums approaching.

A parade burst into the square with a long line of dancers and musicians in bright, colourful, silk costumes. The parade proceeded with different musical and costume themes.

One theme was of traditional dancers and performers with some waving large, colourful flags. Another theme was of clowns and performers on stilts. There was also a small army band with soldiers wearing Spanish-style, body armour with turned up helmets.

The performers completed a couple of laps before parading out of the square. Their figures and the sound of the music diminished as they faded from view.

Roland felt peckish so he grabbed a beer and an empanada. He then took a seat on a bench in the plaza, consumed his food and contemplated what to do next. Devoid of ideas, he returned to the hotel where he spent a couple of hours talking with Frank before their group meeting.

The guide, Fred, introduced himself and then introduced the driver, Mike. Fred provided a short briefing and addressed some administrative matters before the group was given the option of having dinner at the hotel and about half of the group accepted.

The group members came from Australia, Canada, England, Ireland and Norway. There were 27 travellers, comprising five couples, 14 ladies and only two men. An extra male traveller was to join the tour later. Roland was left pondering over the numbers.

Waking first, Roland woke Frank before he went off for breakfast, taking his luggage with him. He finished breakfast in 10 minutes and was ready in time for the scheduled departure.

Mike instructed the passengers to load their bags before he allowed them to take a seat on the bus. Roland took a seat and everyone else straggled on except for Frank. Roland scooted upstairs and found Frank still in the room. Roland assisted him to the bus and the group set off.

Roland slept on the bus and was woken when they stopped at the Salto Del Laja Waterfall. Fred and Mike prepared lunch with a little help from the passengers. After lunch, they were given time to go for a walk to gain closer views of the falls and to take photos.

The group travelled through the lakes district of Chile and made it to the small resort town of Pucon situated by Lake Villarica near the foot of the Villarica Volcano. They arrived at the Hotel Del Volcan and were assigned their rooms. They hardly had time to settle in before they went for a boot fitting.

They walked to Sol y Nieve, which operated hikes up the mountain volcano. They were given important information about the hike and were fitted out with boots before they rushed to purchase their food supplies for the hike.

Roland first stopped off at an ATM for some much needed local currency before visiting the supermarket. He made his way back to the hotel and dropped off his purchases then met up with the others before they headed to a restaurant for dinner. They walked back to their hotel hoping for a good night's sleep ahead of their hike up the volcano.

Frank and Roland went down for breakfast, and as Frank elected not to do the hike, he wished Roland the best.

Roland was one of a first few to arrive at Sol y Nieve and the others arrived soon after. Collecting the boots was the easy part, trying to get fitted with the rest of the gear was a fracas. Roland stepped back while everyone else threw themselves into the merchandise as if it was a post-Christmas sale.

After the dust had settled, Roland tried to select some items from those that were left. He picked up gaiters, crampons, pants, gloves, an ice pick and sticks; however, he failed to find a suitable jacket. He had his own cap, sunglasses and sunscreen.

They took a van to the chairlift and were paired off. Roland shared a chair with Rita and they joined the rest of the group after they dismounted. They headed off in smaller groups of around half a dozen climbers guided by tour leaders.

Rita found it extremely arduous as she didn't feel very well. She was struggling and Roland tried to help her.

"I just can't do it," Rita stated as she sat down in the snow and started crying.

Roland sensed that part of the reason why she stopped was that she didn't want to be a burden to the others. He stayed with her, not knowing what to do.

The tour leader from the next group arrived. "You can rejoin the group ahead," the tour leader advised Roland. "I'll take care of Rita."

Roland continued and found the going easier once he got into a groove. The lines of climbers zigzagged up the mountain, placing their boots in the footprints in the snow of those in front of them.

They climbed 1,000 metres and finally reached the summit at around 1.00 pm. It took them almost four hours and they were all very tired. Their reward was the magnificent snow peaked mountain scenery with passing puffs of clouds.

Wanting to get a view of the volcano before he sat down to relax, Roland headed for the crater. He was warned to be careful of the fumes given off by the volcano. As he peaked over the edge, he was surprised to see that the volcano was smoking. A smile emerged on his face as he realised another lifetime first and he took a few photos to commemorate the event.

Roland found a smooth rock, sat down, drank some water and ate his queso and jamon rolls. He was curious to examine the difference in colours of the terrain and landscape between the crater and surrounding areas. He took numerous photographs before they made their way down the mountain.

The group slid down the snow capped mountain most of the way. Roland was having a ball, but became overconfident and was sliding down at speed when he lost control. He tried to use his ice pick to slow himself down, but the pick got caught in the snow and he just kept on going.

Roland eventually came to a stop with his daypack and various items strewn across the mountainside. He slowly got up and began collecting his gear, starting with his sticks, his daypack and ice pick. His cap was being blown away by the wind and he had just about given up on retrieving it when one of the guides glided across the snow, snatched it up, slid over to Roland and slapped it on his head. Before Roland had a chance to say thanks, the guide was off to aid other climbers.

Roland was exhausted by the end of the day's adventure and felt that he had earned his diploma certificate.

Returning to the hotel, Roland bumped into Frank as he was leaving in search of Indian food for dinner. As Roland had a headache, he rested on his bed and fell asleep.

At dusk, Roland went for a walk to Lake Villarica. He admired the sunset over the lake with Mount Villarica in the background. Feeling better, he wandered around town in search of something to eat, finally settling on a restaurant named Sobremesa. He then headed to Mamas y Tapas bar where he found the rest of the group and joined them for a few drinks.

Fred arranged with the locals to go to a place for salsa dancing. Kate was extremely enthusiastic as she was a keen Latin dancer. Being one of the few available guys, Roland was grabbed by Kate, then Lauren and then Lyn to have their turn for a dance. Given his exhaustive day, he was on his last legs when he announced that he was leaving. He had to endure a number of protestations before he left, finally finding peace when he made it to bed.

Frank and Roland had breakfast together. Frank then headed off to do some exploring whilst Roland hung around the room before he went to mail some postcards.

Roland proceeded on a walk to La Poza yacht harbour where he took a photo of the Villarica Volcano. He noticed a young lady sun-bathing on a bench and admired her for a short time before he decided that he'd better move on.

On his way back to the hotel, Roland stopped off at an internet café, but he couldn't log into his webmail. He got back to his hotel room, placed his belongings in order and went for a return visit to the beach.

There were only a few people on the beach and Roland bumped into two Irish ladies from the tour, Karen and Eileen. They were surprised to hear that he was going for a dip. "Even though it's fine and warm, the water's cold," said Karen.

The Irish ladies departed and Roland was left wondering whether they were having him on about the water – they *were* from Ireland. He found a spot and sun-bathed for a little while to warm up, then decided to go for a dip.

Finding the water to be tolerable, Roland waded a bit further. The deeper he went, the colder the water got, and he stopped at a sufficient depth to submerge his head and do a few strokes. "That's enough," he muttered and swam back to shore. He sun-bathed a little more then headed back to the hotel.

Roland freshened up before joining the group for dinner at the restaurant attached to the hotel. He ordered a Lama and the waiter looked at him strangely until the waiter realized that the item was Lomo – beef tenderloin – not Lama.

"Oh, I'm sorry," Roland apologised. "I'll have the Lomo then."

After dinner, the group went down to Mamas y Tapas to have a few drinks. They had a two for the price of one pisco sour special and most of them took advantage of the deal before returning to their hotel.

Chapter 63 – Glaciers that Go Bang!

Roland woke late, but still had time for a quick shower before breakfast. It was a while before the waitress noticed him in the corner; however, when she did she made sure he received his full complement of coffee, juice, bread, scones and croissants. Frank woke up on his own accord and preferred to munch on his own food.

The group departed for the Chilean border, their passports were stamped and they proceeded through immigration. It was a short drive to the Argentine border control and as the documentation was examined there seemed to be a problem. The Chileans had stamped the 5th November rather than 6th November and the group was ordered back.

Mike started up the engine when he was waved down; the Argentines had changed their mind and allowed the group to proceed. As they headed into Argentina, Roland wondered if the Argentines advised the Chileans that they were a day behind.

The group stopped off along the road for lunch and then proceeded to Bariloche, making it by mid-afternoon. They checked into their hotel within the Parque Nacional Nahuel Huapi on the shores of Lake Nahuel Huapi.

Going for a stroll, Roland dropped off his laundry then visited a bank. He observed the town and considered that it lived up to its reputation as a pretty, alpine tourist village. It had numerous shops, particularly its famed chocolate shops. The Swiss and German influence shone through the architecture of the chalets and other buildings.

Roland returned to the hotel and saw Frank. "Would you be interested in going out for dinner," Roland asked.

"Yes, but first I have to drop off some laundry," Frank advised.

At the laundry, Roland asked the owner if he could recommend a good parilla restaurant. The man recommended a restaurant, which they tracked down, but it didn't open until 8.00 pm. Frank was keen for an earlier sitting so they continued on.

They then came across the Carlos Gardel Restaurante-Parilla. "This must be destiny," Roland stated. "Not only have we found a parilla restaurant, but one in the name of the famous tango performer."

Roland ordered red wine with Frank's approval, and the waiter poured some wine to taste. Roland took a sip and produced a sour looking expression. He was far from being a wine expert, but he thought if a wine was ever off, it was this one. "I think this wine doesn't taste right," he told

Frank.

Frank, who was also a wine novice, had a taste. "I think you're right."

The waiter, who had been waiting patiently, was formally advised of their verdict. The waiter looked lost and called the manager. "Excuse me, sir," Roland said. "I'm not a wine expert, but I believe that this wine is off."

The manager took one whiff and immediately agreed. "Yes sir, this wine is definitely off. I'm sorry, but this happens to be the last bottle of its type. However, I'm prepared to provide a better quality wine for the same price," the manager offered and Roland readily accepted.

"That was a nice gesture," Roland commented.

"If he was to make a nice gesture, he could have given us the bottle for free," Frank said.

Roland was exceptionally proud of himself as he had achieved another lifetime first. "How many people can say they've returned a bottle of wine because it was off?"

Frank seemed totally disinterested with Roland's boast.

The waiter returned and proudly displayed the new bottle. Roland nodded and whirled the wine in the glass and inhaled the aroma like a true professional. He then took a sip and produced another sour looking expression. The waiter almost had a seizure. "I think it's fine," Roland finally stated.

There were only about a dozen people in the establishment that Thursday night. Roland ordered the 400 gram Lomo, being beef tenderloin, and Frank ordered the same.

An elderly man in a dinner suit and bow tie approached each of the occupied tables and had a chat with the patrons. He was delighted to learn Frank and Roland came from Australia.

"Is that man the famous Carlos Gardel?" asked Frank.

"No," Roland replied. "Not unless he's around a hundred years old and has come back from the dead."

The meals were served, and shortly thereafter the man reappeared, stood before the microphone and introduced himself. He first spoke in Spanish and then in English. The man thanked everyone for their attendance.

Frank and Roland were getting stuck into their steaks when the man made an announcement. "I'd especially like to thank our friends from Australia."

The spotlight then turned on Frank and Roland. They stopped chewing, looked at each other, looked at the man and took a bow.

The man started singing tango songs and a table of Argentine tourists who were celebrating a birthday joined in. After the performance and having finished their dinner, Frank and Roland returned to their hotel.

Going down to breakfast, Roland met a few of the other members of the group. They were planning a day outing and they invited him to join them. They visited a few of the shops at the town centre, then purchased tickets for the Cerro Otto and took the bus to the cable railway.

Roland shared a cable car with Carol and Sue – two Australians who had been working in London and were both heading back to Australia via Patagonia.

The group disembarked from the cable cars into cold and windy weather. They reassembled before heading off for a hike where they took quite a few photos of the beautiful views, including the township of Bariloche five kilometres away. They hiked around for a couple of hours before catching the cable cars and bus back to town.

After lunch, the group was splitting up and Roland gained the approval of Carol and Sue to tag along with them; they seemed happy to adopt him. The threesome shopped at some clothing stores before raiding the chocolate shops.

The group had dinner at the La Libre Restaurant where they made full use of the buffet. After they had their fill, they lifted themselves from their seats and slowly left. It was cold, wet and windy as they struggled back to the hotel.

Even after his feast of the previous evening, Roland still made an effort to have breakfast. The group boarded the bus and, due to his tardiness, Roland was relegated to the back for the drive to Perito Merino.

They moved on the next day and Roland made sure he secured a front seat. He was joined by Carrie and they talked continuously until the stop for lunch. Carrie was a recruitment consultant who was highly intelligent and perceptive. She was also a fiery female and he couldn't help but fuel her fire.

After lunch, Carrie wasn't feeling well so she swapped seats with Lauren who had been enjoying two seats to herself. The moment Lauren sat beside Roland, she started telling her life story.

Lauren was Korean who was adopted by a family from America and they migrated to Australia. She was brought up on a farm and was a music teacher. He found her story fascinating and they talked continuously until they reached their destination at El Chalten.

Roland was getting dressed when Frank arrived back from his early dinner and he seemed pretty happy. On further investigation, Roland learned Frank ate at the corner restaurant and apparently had a good time with the waitress. "I also had a couple of pisco sours," Frank confessed.

Passing the corner restaurant, Roland noted that it had a German theme and the waitress was a buxom lady wearing a traditional German dress. Roland could imagine how she could have taken Frank's fancy.

Roland continued on, passing a pizza place where most of the group was seated and he waved to them. He went further down the road and came across a restaurant where Carol, Sue, Kate and Sylvia were seated and they waved him in. They were in hysterics as he took up a chair.

"So what's up?" Roland asked. They didn't say a word and handed him a menu. He studied the menu for a few moments and when he looked up they were in further hysterics. The menu had attempted translating every dish into English; however, most of the items were lost in translation or misspelled. He looked at the name of the restaurant, which was noted as *Las Lengas* and he wondered whether this was spelled correctly.

Sue showed Roland one item in particular, which was *GARGOYLE*. "Have you asked what it is?" Roland asked.

"I tried, but I couldn't stop laughing," Carol said, still giggling.

"So what have you ordered?" Roland queried.

"Nothing yet as we haven't been able to stop laughing," said Sue.

The waiter made an appearance and he was a very pleasant and distinguished gentleman. "I find it difficult to select something from the menu," Roland said, which generated more laughter. "Could the señor recommend anything?"

The waiter recommended a local dish, which was described as a type of stew.

"Okay, I'll have that," Roland said, and everyone else ordered the same.

The meal was a casserole consisting of carrots, pumpkin, corn and osso buco. The waiter was exceptionally friendly and made continuous enquiries to ensure that all was in order. They ordered final drinks and coffees whilst complimenting the waiter on the meal before heading back to the hotel, well fed and still laughing.

There was an early morning wakeup call and the group rolled up to stow their bags on the bus where they were driven to the commencement point of their hike through the Fitz Roy National Park.

It took the group almost 1½ hours to find the lookout to Cerro Fitz Roy. The summit of the snow capped mountain was 3441 metres high and the top of the mountain glistened as it reflected the morning sun.

The view was picture-postcard perfect and they took many photographs. Frank and Roland had their photo taken as they stood either side of the main towers of the Fitz Roy range. The group made their way back in a fraction of the time it took to get to the lookout.

They had lunch before they drove on to El Calafate and checked into the Hostal del Glaciar. They found their rooms, which had bunk-bed accommodation. Frank and Roland shared their room with Roy, an English professor who had joined the tour.

The group met up at the hostel restaurant where Roland enjoyed dinner with the members of the group whose company he was growing to value: Sue, Carol, Lauren, Adele, Philip and Frank. They had a nightcap of pisco sour before heading to their bunk beds.

It was another early wakeup call and the group set off by minibus where they had an eccentric tour guide – Diego.

Diego kept the passengers entertained as he described the various wildlife and natural features of the Los Glaciares National Park with great humour. It took a few hours' drive to arrive at a point where they were handed a lunch box and commenced their nature walk.

The group was standing on rocky terrain on the bank of Lake Argentino when they heard a loud cracking sound in the distance. "In case you were wondering," said Diego, "even though we are a long way off, that noise would have been ice that had broken off the glacier."

Moments later, a noticeable wave lapped up to the bank in the otherwise still waters. Members of the group looked at each other with expressions of incredulity and they quickly made their way towards the glacier. As they were moving, another almighty crack sounded, which hurried them along.

Although they had been gaining glimpses of the natural wonder as they neared, they were wide eyed and opened mouthed as Moreno Glacier came closer into view.

Frank and Roland trekked along the man-made walkways including the Primer Balcon and Interior Balcon until they found a prime location on a wooden bench with open views in front of the glacier. It was fairly calm and quiet so Roland decided to eat his lunch before the warmth of the afternoon sun started to create more activity on the enormous sheet of moving ice. The Perito Moreno Glacier had a phenomenal average height of 60 metres and it spanned five kilometres.

Keeping one eye on the glacier, Roland quickly consumed his ham, cheese and tomato sandwich then was getting stuck into his schnitzel roll when another huge cracking and impact noise resounded. Frank and Roland quickly scanned their surroundings, but couldn't make out from where it originated. They assumed the ice fell from within the glacier and was not visible.

Roland took another bite of his roll when a large chunk of ice broke from the terminus of the glacier and crashed into the lake with an almighty bang. "Did you see that?" Roland cried.

"Wow, yeah!" Frank shouted, even though it was rare for him to show any emotion.

Cursing that he'd missed getting a photo of the spectacular event, Roland quickly finished his roll and stored away his apple and chocolate. He grabbed his camera, eye at the ready for a photograph – he was determined to get a shot of cascading ice.

Frank and Roland sat there for two hours with not much happening and even Roland's determination was starting to wane.

Roland sensed something and right before his eyes a huge block of ice started cracking, and he snapped away as the ice went hurtling down and smashed into the lake with an almighty crash, boom, bang!

When the waters calmed, Roland stood up, raised both hands high into the air and shouted: "YEAHHHHH!"

Frank cheered on, but the rest of the crowd looked at Roland as if he was a crazy man.

The group assembled later in the afternoon and went for a 45-minute boat ride with the boat nearing the glacier terminus. It was a scenic ride, although after Roland's previous glacier experience, there wasn't much more that could excite him now.

After a deep sleep, Roland was spritely as he rose the next morning. As he was one of the first on the bus, he was rewarded with a front seat. He was hoping that one of the pretty ladies on the tour would sit next to him, but Frank was uncharacteristically early and made himself comfortable next to him.

The group departed and it took about half an hour to get to the Argentine border. They crossed into Chile and arrived at Puerto Natales where they were given an hour to hunt around the town for currency and snacks.

Returning to the bus, the group set up lunch on a large triangular patch of lawn in the middle of town. After lunch, it was off for Torres Del Paine, which translated from Tehuelche Indian and Spanish to *Blue Towers*.

They arrived at their accommodation in the Parque Nacional Torres Del Paine where there were lengthy negotiations between Fred, Mike and the park officials. They eventually worked out an arrangement, which resulted in the group being split up and accommodated at different locations.

Frank, Roy and Roland ended up sharing a dome-shaped structure made out of white canvas, aluminium framing and pine flooring. They settled in before they trekked over to the toilet block to freshen up.

The group met up and went off for dinner. It was an evening of pleasant socialising before everyone retired to their respective rooms. Lyn was kind enough to lend Roland a torch so he could locate his dome accommodation in the dark of night.

Roland had a very poor night's sleep as he had to put up with the melodious cacophony of Frank and Roy's alternating snoring arias. Further, although the domes warmed up during the day they were very cold at night. Roland put on his thermals and wrapped blankets around him to keep warm.

Rising early was the only way Roland could put an end to his hardship. He had a shower, dressed, prepared his lunch and walked over to reception, which incorporated the breakfast area. He found a seat and did some reading whilst he waited for breakfast. He was in the continental breakfast group and had to wait a considerable time before he was served.

After breakfast, Roland joined Lauren and Lyn for their hike. Lauren set a cracking pace, and Lyn was having trouble keeping up so Lauren obliged by slowing down a little.

They made it to the lookout point where they witnessed magnificent views of Torres Del Paine with its enormous granite monoliths. Three main towers sprung up majestically from the snow-based mountain range. Silvery, grey rock emerged from the snow at a lower level, which met the turquoise lake down below. They took quite a few photos before they sat down for lunch and continued to admire the vista.

Roland had prepared four peanut butter sandwiches for the trek so he was able to offer one each to Lauren and Lyn. They then got involved in a snow fight where nobody won as they simultaneously called a cease fire.

They started their descent and Lyn again began to struggle. They came across a group that had decided not to go any further and was to turn back after a rest. Lyn decided to join them, which liberated Lauren to set her own pace and Roland followed.

When they arrived back, Roland learned he and his roommates had been evicted from the dome and were to be provided with alternative accommodation. After a relieving, warm shower, he was notified they'd been relocated to a dormitory room. As Frank and Roy returned from their hike he advised them of their new abode.

The group was treated to an outside buffet with an open fire, which was a sociable event with much alcohol consumed.

The next morning, the group was driven to the waterfall of Salto Grande and given 1½ hours to explore. They then boarded a catamaran and cruised for 30 minutes in cool and windy weather before stopping at Refugio & Camping Lago Pehoe where they had lunch.

Roland joined Lyn, Lauren, Carol and Sue for a hike to Grey Glacier. It lived up to the reports of being amongst the most beautiful and unspoiled scenery in the world. The mountains were spectacular, and provided the perfect backdrop of beautiful lakes, gorgeous flora, amazing fauna and stunning glaciers. They took numerous photos whilst being buffeted by gale force winds.

They returned to the refugio where they were offered snacks and drinks, which they took advantage of whilst waiting for the rest of the group. As the remaining group members rolled up, they waited in the bitter cold for the next catamaran.

Returning to the Estancia Cerro Paine, Roland had a quick shower before meeting the group for their barbeque dinner. It was a plentiful meal and they drank loads of beer and cask wine.

Roland retired to bed but tossed and turned all night. He tried to think beautiful thoughts and to meditate, but failed to sleep. Getting up was the only way to put an end to his misery.

The time to depart on their horse ride approached. They each paid the

$39US fee and were matched up with horses to suit the riders' experience and size. Lauren declared herself an expert rider and wanted the most testing horse. She was assigned a fine, black horse with spirit. Roland, on the other hand, sat back and was happy to have any of the remaining horses. He was assigned a docile, tan horse with a white face. The horse's colour explained its name of *El Bronceado*, although Roland preferred to call him Brownie.

The weather was slightly overcast and mild, which was considered good weather for that time of the year. Roland was content to follow the guide, Guido. Lauren; however, was off galloping her horse around the adjacent hills, making appearances every now and then.

They stopped at a lookout point that provided a magnificent view of the lake and a backdrop of snow capped mountains. When they returned to the hostel, they were greeted with hot chocolate.

The group went to the nearby hotel to enjoy the $35US buffet. They thoroughly enjoyed dinner, rubbing their full stomachs as they finished off their feast. After three hours, and with the aid of a few torches, they waddled back to their lodgings in the dark.

It was another restless night for Roland as Frank snored the house down. Roland was relieved it would be their last night in the bunks. He rose early and washed with cold water under dim daylight as the electricity wasn't working.

Roland skipped breakfast as he was still bloated from the buffet of the previous evening. He went for a walk and observed the staff as they prepared for work. He then packed, waited outside for the van to arrive and helped with the loading.

Chapter 64 – The Magellanes

The group changed from their van to a bus and continued on to Puerto Natales. It was midday when they set off again through the Magellanes, which was a cold, rugged and windswept area in the heart of Chilean Patagonia.

They stopped to visit a penguin colony at Seno Otway and disembarked into cold and windy weather. It wasn't far along the trail when they began to see Magellanic penguins. The penguins seemed much more comfortable in the climate compared to the visitor specie.

Carrie stayed on the bus as she wasn't feeling well, and Roland was the first to return. "How was your penguin experience?" Carrie asked.

Roland's response was succinct. "It was very cold and very smelly, but the penguins were cute."

The group reached Punta Arenas, but they could not secure accommodation for everyone at the one location so they were split into two smaller groups. Roland was in the group that was dropped off at Hostal Corpa Manzano.

Roland had a warm shower and placed his belongings in order before walking to the city centre. He entered the Plaza de Armas then walked down a couple of the side streets. He noticed a small, nondescript restaurant and decided to enter. Only one of the tables was occupied with a foursome of English-speaking tourists. He made himself comfortable at a vacant table and ordered the beef casserole with vegetables and a bottle of Santa Emilia red wine.

Roland complimented the waiter on the meal and headed off to the Bar e Cucina Restaurant where he saw the rest of the group. They were leaving as he entered, but Frank was happy to stay on for a drink.

Frank and Roland made their way back to their accommodation and, as they were staying at different locations, they said goodnight at a crossroad.

Waking up after a good night's sleep, Roland stayed comfortably in bed. When he finally rose, he went down to breakfast and sat at a vacant table in front of the television set where he was soon joined by Ethel, Sylvia and Carrie.

After breakfast, Roland prepared himself for their scheduled pickup to Zona Franca. Sue and Carol arrived from the other accommodation and expressed some concern as they walked by the bus that was parked in the street. Mike had arranged to take them to Zona Franca, but there was no sign of him. "I don't think Mike's going to turn up," Carol stated.

"Mike's probably just late," Roland suggested.

"I confirmed the time with Mike on three separate occasions," Carol said. "But you know how unreliable he can be."

After half an hour, they gave up on Mike and decided to walk. It was a fine day, although there was a cool wind blowing. It was over a three kilometre walk to Punta Arenas, which was a duty free port town, and the Zona Franca was a duty free district.

When they arrived, they bumped into others from the group who didn't seem too thrilled to see them; they'd apparently been dropped off by Mike earlier.

Roland walked around and purchased a few presents then checked out the rest of the shopping zone before he returned to the hostel for a bite to eat and then headed into town.

Strolling to Plaza de Armas Munoz Gamero, Roland walked around the square and inspected the cathedral then walked around the square once more. After much deliberation, he took a photograph of the statue of Hernando De Magallanes with the cathedral in the background.

Roland sat down in the square, enjoying a cool breeze and the warmth of the sun before heading to the port. He was fascinated by the feel of the area. *You can sense the history and a buccaneering spirit.*

Arriving back to his room, Roland soon heard a knock on the door and it was Sue. "I wanted to make sure that you didn't dine alone."

"Dining alone can be fun," Roland remarked.

"Not for two nights in a row," Sue said with a smile.

Roland sat down to dinner at a table with Sue, Carol, Lyn, Lauren, Roy and Frank. They had already ordered so Roland ordered rhea, which was described as a local animal like an ostrich.

After dinner, they moved to a taberna that was having a happy hour with the drinks at two for the price of one. Soon after they settled in, other members of the group, including Fred and Mike arrived. The newcomers said hello and found their own table. Roland was not entirely happy with their arrival, but Carol was livid.

Roland finished off several drinks before he decided to return to the hostel. "I'll go with you," Lauren stated.

As they walked along, Lauren and Roland had a pleasant chat and experienced a few quiet moments. They came to the crossroad at the point where they were to part ways. He was tempted to kiss her; however, he simply wished her goodnight.

Chapter 65 – The End of the World

The cocktails and beer worked a treat to assist Roland to sleep. He woke early and prepared in ample time ahead of departure. The bus collected those from his hostel before picking up the rest of the gang.

It took a couple of hours to travel to the ferry port and Roland slept most of the way. It was cold and wet so the group waited for the ferry in the cafeteria whilst sipping hot chocolate. The bus was driven on the ferry and the group followed.

It took 25 minutes to cross the Strait of Magellan, and another couple of hours on the bus to the Chilean immigration station where their passports were stamped – everyone double checking to ensure they stamped the correct date.

"Gee, the 18 NOV 03 looks like 19 NOV 03. I wonder whether this means we'll have to wait a day before we can travel through," Roland joked.

Mike completely missed the attempted humour. "Let me see your passport," he demanded.

Roland had put up with Mike for the whole trip, but even his usual patience was wearing thin. "Don't worry about it," Roland said, but Mike kept on. "You don't need to look at my passport," Roland suggested. "Just look at your own passport as the guy used the same stamp."

Mike heeded the advice and looked at his passport. Roland waited for Mike's usual barrage of criticism and torment, but he was amazed with Mike's reaction. "Oh, I see what you mean, the 18 really does look like a 19; sorry about that."

Apparently the ink on Mike's passport did not show up as well and the number 18 actually looked like the number 19.

The group took respite from the cold and rain during lunch, then proceeded to the Argentine side of the border crossing. Fred collected the passports and entered the immigration office. It took an hour to process, but the group was cleared to go.

Roland fell asleep again; however, Carol woke him to declare that it was snowing. *Snowing in Tierra del Fuego?* Roland thought. *How ironic that it's snowing in the Land of Fire.*

The story behind the Land of Fire was that the land got its name from Ferdinand Magellan who, on passing the archipelago, spotted a number of fires burning along the coastline.

The group arrived at Ushuaia and settled into their rooms at the Hotel

Cabo de Hornos. They then headed to the Dublin Pub where they assembled for a meeting and ordered pizzas and beers.

After dinner, Roland went for a walk and came across a few bars with a show. He walked into one, paid five pesos for a beer and sat down. "Do you want sex?" queried a lady.

"No gracias," Roland replied and he looked to the stage.

Another lady approached and she spoke English, although the extent of the conversation didn't require much fluency. "Do you want fuckie?" she asked.

"I'm not interested, but I am curious about the cost," Roland replied.

She was happy to explain. "A lady is 150 pesos for one hour and it is 30 pesos to buy a lady a drink."

Roland thanked her, finished his five pesos drink and left.

After having breakfast, Roland set off and checked out a few stores before visiting the former prison, now Maritime Museum, where he spent a couple of hours exploring the buildings and inspecting the exhibits.

Roland then visited the End of the World Museum where he spent a couple of hours admiring the objects that had been preserved from the expeditions, shipwrecks and first settlements. He valued his End of the World stamp they printed on his passport and he didn't have to worry about them printing the correct number as the stamp didn't include a date.

The group made their way to the port, which was the closest port to Antarctica and from where most of the Antarctica expeditions and tours departed. As the boat set off, Roland took a photo of the Ushuaia township with the snow capped mountain range dominating the background.

Roland shared a booth with Lyn, Lauren, Carrie, Sylvia and Ethel. They stayed inside to shelter from the outdoor cold and wind. Each time there was an attraction to view they would run out, take a photo and rush back to their warm booth. They took numerous photos including the lighthouse, the sea lions, the penguins, the seals and Beagle Channel.

Making it back to town, Roland observed the shops that had just reopened after the workers' midday siesta. The daylight spanned around 17 hours that time of the year. Roland stopped on a street corner, turned 360 degrees to take in the scene and reflected. *Even with the cold, the wind and the rain, I'm grateful that I'm at the End of the World.*

Fred gave a small talk about the Tierra del Fuego National Park before the group freshened up for dinner. Roland shared a table with Carrie, Lyn, Lauren, Roy and Frank. They had an enjoyable time, although the loud people on the tour, seated at another table, seemed determined to ensure they remained the loudest. The group went to the Dublin bar for a few drinks before retreating to their beds.

The next morning, the group was taken to Tierra del Fuego National Park. Roland joined Frank, Carol and Sue to explore the area. They decided to go on the smaller walks with the first being the beaver trail.

Frank and Roland were walking along the trail when they arrived at a crossroad and came face-to-face with a fox. The fox was only ten or so metres away and they stood eyeing each other off. They admired the beautiful creature with its full length, fluffy tail.

The fox seemed to come to the conclusion that the objects in its way were not going to move so it backtracked. Roland was so captivated by the encounter he didn't even think to take a photo.

Frank and Roland ventured into a café. Roland was examining the postcards when he came across an image of a fox with the same appearance and positioning as the fox he'd just witnessed. He purchased the postcard as it was an image he was sure would remind him of his real-life experience.

The group caught the minibus to town and later met for dinner. They enjoyed a buffet salad and parilla before heading to a pub, keen to celebrate their last night at the End of the World.

Most of the group was up and dancing, but Roland was feeling tired and opted to sit back, relax and drink. Lauren asked Roland to dance a couple of times and his reasons for not dancing didn't seem to satisfy her. He eventually agreed to dance with her later.

It was getting late in the night and most of the group were leaving when Lauren reminded Roland about his promise to dance. The moment they started dancing, some unusual music started playing so they just stood and swayed in each other's arms. The rest of the group had now left and the couple began kissing.

After a while, they decided to go back to the hotel with thoughts of spending the night together. As they returned, they noticed Sue and Carol standing outside. "The hotel door is locked," Sue explained "We've rung the door bell and we're still waiting for it to open."

Eventually the door opened. Carol and Sue made their way up the stairs to their room as they looked back and giggled. "Do you have any spare rooms?" Roland asked the receptionist.

"Sorry we are full," the receptionist responded.

"We could try another hotel," Lauren suggested.

They went to another hotel and it was also full. It was the same story at three other hotels and they surrendered to the fate that it was not meant to be. On the way back to their hotel, they noticed the Nautica Bar still open. "You are free to stay as long as you like," stated the barman.

They noticed another couple sitting down together. Lauren pulled up a large chair, Roland sat down and she sat on his lap. They stayed there for the rest of the night, caressing and kissing each other as they watched the sunrise over the harbour.

In the early morning, they returned to their respective rooms at the hotel. Roland struggled out of bed after an hour's shut eye. He was tired and had a sore throat. He showered and went down for breakfast. Lauren failed to make an appearance.

Roland returned to his room, packed and went downstairs for the departure. It was a significant juncture of the tour as some of the passengers were flying to Buenos Aires and the others were making their way to Buenos Aires overland. Roland was flying and Lauren was going overland.

It was approaching the time of departure and the full group was present for the goodbyes, except for Lauren. Roland understood her not turning up, but as they were about to leave, Lauren appeared and they said goodbye.

Chapter 66 – Señor Tango, I Presume

The group members who were flying to Buenos Aires were driven to the airport where they checked in their luggage. Fred made sure everything was in order then said goodbye. They did not see Mike, and assumed he stayed on the bus.

Roland took a seat alongside Kate on the plane and she seemed to be in a bad mood. The mere mention of Mike or Fred made her even more annoyed. Roland was well aware Mike was a pain and Fred wasn't the best tour guide in the world, but he wasn't sure why she was so angry with them.

"Fred didn't book the Señor Tango Show," Kate blurted out.

Roland was surprised as Kate had mentioned it to Fred a number of times over the duration of the tour and he consistently replied that he would arrange it and not to worry.

They arrived in Buenos Aires, collected their luggage and waited for their transfer to the hotel. A lady appeared and introduced herself as Acacia, their tour guide. They were briskly escorted on the bus and driven to the hotel. On the way, Kate was just about to raise the matter of the tango show when Acacia brought it up.

"The moment it was communicated to me that the group wanted to see the Señor Tango Show I made enquiries, but they could not accommodate the group. This is not surprising as it is the most popular show and bookings need to be made well in advance."

Kate and Roland looked at each other and he was sure they shared the same thought. *Bloody Fred.*

"I made a booking for another show for tonight, so those of you who wish to attend, please raise your hand," Acacia said and everyone raised their hand.

On arrival at the hotel, the group was allocated their room keys and given an hour before they were asked to front for a city tour.

The group was ready on time and Acacia led them to the bus. The organisation was lively and Roland moved quickly to walk alongside Acacia. They visited the area of San Telmo – the hub of art and tango. They then visited La Boca where they were given 45 minutes to roam the streets.

Roland took a photo of the multi-coloured houses constructed from various materials, mainly timber and corrugated iron. He also took a picture of a model of Eva Peron standing on a balcony.

They were then driven along the Puerto Madero and on to Parque 3 de

Febrero and El Rosedal where they enjoyed a lovely walk through the rose garden, the parklands and around the magnificent lakes.

The group arrived back at the hotel and had an hour to prepare before the Esquina Carlos Gardel Tango Show. They were ready just ahead of their scheduled departure time, but after waiting half an hour they enquired at reception. "We have these show pickups all the time and they are invariably late," assured a receptionist. However, when another half hour elapsed even the receptionists were concerned and they made a few calls.

The bus arrived 1½ hours late and the group was rushed along. Arriving at the venue, they were hurriedly seated at the grand theatre where it was apparent most of the audience had almost finished their meals. The group was pressed to place their orders and there was panic to serve them. They were seated in a prominent position just in front of the stage, which meant that they had to look up in order to view the show.

Roland got stuck into his meal and glanced up intermittently at the performance. He considered the situation to be less than ideal, but accepted it for what it was. He particularly liked the music, partly because he didn't have to look up to enjoy it and partly because of the Bohemian style. It seemed chaotic at times, but always seemed to come together in a masterly fashion at the end.

The show rounded out its finale and it was synchronised with Roland's own finale – he downed his last scoop of tiramisu and took his last sip of coffee, tahh rahhhhhm!

"I thought the show was good," Kate commented, although Roland detected a tinge of regret in her voice.

Roland had a reasonable night's sleep, which was his last night sharing a room with Frank and Roy. They woke to the news that England had beaten Australia in the Rugby World Cup.

Sitting at breakfast, Roland was joined by Kate and Sylvia with Carrie and Frank joining soon after. Carrie was due to leave that day so they said goodbye.

Roland set off for a walk and as he was passing reception he enquired about the Señor Tango Show. "What are the chances of booking three tickets for the show tonight?" he casually asked.

"It would be extremely difficult to get tickets for tonight's show," the receptionist stated. "However, I know someone and it is not impossible. I would need a prepayment to confirm any booking and I can let you know later today."

Roland walked the stretch of the Florida pedestrian mall to the Plaza de Mayo where he stopped to admire the cathedral and Casa Rosada. He walked along the docks of Puerto Madero and continued along Lavalle pedestrian mall where he checked out a few of the leather shops for a leather jacket. Nothing really appealed and he was getting similar frustrations as he had in Istanbul years earlier.

Continuing along Avenida 9 de Julio, Roland took a photo of the wide thoroughfare featuring the obelisk before making his way back to his hotel. "Excuse me, sir," the receptionist called out.

When Roland turned, the receptionist was waving three tickets. Roland thanked the receptionist then gave him a tip. "You have just made a young lady very happy," he said with a grin.

There was a note slipped under the door of Roland's hotel room from Kate and Sylvia that advised they were meeting for dinner and then going to a salsa place if he wanted to join them.

Roland went to Kate's room, knocked on the door and Sylvia answered. "I might be interested in joining you for dinner, but I wanted to know more of the details," he said.

"Kate knows more about it," Sylvia advised and she allowed him in.

Kate was resting in bed. "So what are your plans for tonight?" Roland asked her.

"We haven't actually decided on a restaurant, but we can find some place in the centre," said Kate nonchalantly. "We're also going to a place for salsa music and dancing."

"That doesn't sound too appealing, particularly as it's Saturday night and your last night in Buenos Aires," Roland said.

"Well, do you have any better ideas?" Kate asked.

Roland pulled the tickets from his pocket and placed them on the bed. "What do you think about this place?" he asked.

Kate and Sylvia peered down at the tickets and they started screaming and hugging Roland.

Roland broke up the group hug. "Hurry up, it's past seven o'clock and we have to be ready for pickup at eight…or whatever time the pickup actually arrives!"

Kate, Sylvia and Roland were at reception bang on 8.00 pm. They were excited as well as nervous. It was getting late and they started to worry. They were about to enquire at reception when their pickup arrived.

It was a very long drive to the Señor Tango Show so Roland thought he would set the scene by asking about the origins of tango. Kate was enthusiastic to explain.

"The tango is important from the perspective of its origins and history. The music and dance evolved from the immigrants to Argentina. The tango was performed by prostitutes working in bordellos who used the dance to attract customers for business. Argentina also provided the cultural setting for the tango, with the macho male's domination they sought to exert over women."

Arriving at the venue, they were escorted upstairs to a table away from the balcony. Three other people that shared the bus ride were seated opposite. There was a buzz in the theatre and the excitement was building.

They ordered their meals and were promptly served beer and wine. The first course was an antipasto. The second course was a choice between an enormous cut of beef or a decent piece of chicken. On seeing his brontosaurus steak, Roland pulled out his camera. "I've got to get a shot of this," he said.

Roland took a few shots of the ladies with their food and drink. He also took a photo of a mural of Carlos Gardel. "Give me your camera," Sylvia stated and she took a shot of Roland holding a wine glass, looking out from the balcony in a robust posture – chest out, shoulders back.

After dessert, the sound of the audience seemed to build. The moment the show was about to start, the crowd on the top level swarmed the balconies.

Roland was not impressed with the situation so he waved over the waiter who served them. He pointed to the crowd and shrugged his shoulders. The waiter immediately reacted by placing his two hands up in a stopping motion and zipped off.

The waiter soon returned and motioned for them to follow him. They were led around to the other side where the waiter cleared the way and placed them in a prime balcony position overlooking the stage.

Kate and Sylvia were thrilled and Roland was most impressed. He tipped the waiter what he thought to be the modest amount of 20 pesos. The waiter served the ladies another glass of white wine and Roland another beer, followed by red wine.

The show was an extravaganza and Roland almost gained as much pleasure seeing the delight on the faces of Kate and Sylvia as he did the show.

The waiter regularly replenished their drinks during the course of the performance. "I may have tipped the waiter too much," Roland suggested. "I'm going to be drunk before the finale."

Roland thoroughly enjoyed the show, but more importantly to him, the ladies thought the show was perfect.

Roland woke up after a deep sleep and was slightly hung over. He had a shower then went to breakfast where he met up with Sue, Carol and Frank. They were going on a couple of excursions and invited Roland to join them.

It was overcast and drizzling so they took a taxi to Plaza Dorrego where they strolled around the flea market before moving on to Plaza Mayo and Teatro Colon. They then headed for Recoleta and the cemetery.

They entered the cemetery intent to view the monument of Eva Peron. It was a Sunday and there were many people so it took some time to pass by the Duarte family monument. Roland took a couple of photos and spent the time to read the plaques.

Returning to the hotel, the group decided to go to the nearby Galerias

Pacifico shopping complex where they dined at the food court. Roland did a few rounds before settling for a beef rump steak with salad and a beer. While they were enjoying their meal, they were entertained by tango singing and dancing. They headed back to the hotel where Roland watched some television before going to sleep.

Chapter 67 – Home for Good?

Roland woke a number of times throughout the night, but stayed in bed until he got up to have a shower and went to breakfast. He sat at a table on his own before he was delighted to have Carol and Sue join him.

As Carol and Sue were leaving for Australia, Roland thanked them for their company on the tour and they bid goodbye. He returned to his room and placed his belongings in order, ahead of his departure the next day.

Roland bumped into Frank at the front foyer of the hotel. Unbeknown to the group, Frank was also leaving and he wanted to leave quietly. "Thanks for being a great roomie and I wish you well," Roland said.

"Thanks to you too," Frank said. "I hope to catch up with you in Melbourne one day."

Embarking on a walk, Roland returned to the Plaza Dorrego area where he visited some leather shops. There was a jacket he liked; however, it required an alteration and he wasn't comfortable with the idea so he didn't buy it. Instead, he purchased several leather belts as gifts.

It was Roland's last night in Buenos Aires and he had dinner alone. He then set off to check out the nightlife. He cabbed it to Recoleta and found it curious there were a number of gentlemen's clubs in close proximity to the cemetery and he stopped at one of them.

"It costs 20 pesos to enter, which includes two drinks," the doorman advised.

Entering the establishment, Roland was served his first beer and a lady explained the system to him. "You may choose any available lady and can buy her a drink. If you wish to take a lady, you will have to buy her two drinks. Each drink for the lady costs 30 pesos and you will then have to negotiate the price for the lady with her."

Roland considered this to be reasonably clear and thanked the lady for the information. He continued drinking and was waiting for the strip show to commence when he was approached by a slim lady with blonde hair and blue eyes, named Lara.

Lara chatted to Roland for a little while, but when he indicated that he wasn't interested she soon let him be. He finished his second drink and concluded that the strip show wasn't going to happen so he left.

Roland checked out a couple of other clubs, but they were either very seedy or quiet. It appeared the only place with any life was the club he originally attended so he returned.

The doorman gave Roland a strange look as if he appeared familiar, but he couldn't place him. Roland just smiled, purchased his entry again, walked in and ordered a beer.

Roland moved around and found a spot he felt more comfortable. He then caught Lara's eye, she smiled and eventually approached him again. Lara asked if he would buy her a drink and he agreed.

They talked for some time and Roland found her to be a nice person, although her life seemed to be a complete mess. Lara finished her drink and looked at him. "I'm reluctant to buy you another drink as you may get the idea that I want you to go with me," he stated and she laughed.

They talked some more and negotiated an arrangement. Roland was ready to depart; however, Lara reminded him that he needed to buy her another drink. When she finally finished her second drink, they went back to his hotel.

Lara was very affectionate and she loved to kiss. Roland thought she was a great kisser even though, being a smoker, it was like kissing an ashtray. They had sex and rested for a while. "Do you mind if I smoke?" Lara asked.

Roland nodded: *What difference would it make?*

Having great difficulty trying to get some sleep in the single bed with Lara, Roland was restless and was at a loss to know what to do. After a little while he started foreplay and they had sex for a second time. Lara then settled into sleep again.

Lara departed and Roland stayed in bed until he realised that there was only ten minutes left for breakfast. He had a quick shower and rushed to the restaurant to find that most of the good stuff had been taken away so he settled for fruit juice, a croissant and a ghastly cup of hot chocolate.

Returning to his room, Roland packed his bags and went down to reception to check out. He stowed his suitcase then went off for a final walk.

Roland passed a couple of leather shops and noticed the jacket he'd seen the day before that needed adjustment. He entered the shop and tried it on. Even though it was the same styled jacket and the same size, it somehow fit him perfectly. He looked it over and over; *could this be it, after so many years?* He then looked over to the saleslady. "I think I'll take it."

Deciding on an early dinner, Roland entered La Estancia Restaurant that had an impressive parilla displayed in the front window and he had the Especiale Bife and a large beer.

Roland returned to the hotel to collect his bag then caught a cab to the airport and checked in for his flight. He took a seat and pulled out his diary. He peered down at the itinerary section and his eyes fixated on that day's note. *25/11/2003 - Return on Aerolineas Argentinas flight AR1182 at 23:59.*

The plane touched down in Auckland and there was a stay of around an hour before flying on to Sydney. The plane touched down at Sydney Airport to a round of applause. Roland went through the last-chance duty free and purchased some smokes for friends and booze for himself. He then transferred to the domestic terminal where he waited a couple of hours.

Boarding his 12:00 Qantas flight QF431 to Melbourne, Roland was cognisant that it was the last leg of his travels. Touchdown in Melbourne was at 13:30 on Thursday, 27th November 2003. He grabbed a cab to his home, dropped off his luggage and proceeded to his father's place. He rang the door bell, but there was no answer. He rang the bell again. Still there was no answer.

Roland then considered the possibilities. *It's 2.30 pm on a Thursday, Dad would have finished lunch at 12.30 pm. It's too early to prepare for dinner and it's not a scheduled time slot for television. He wouldn't be working in the garden; he does the gardening in the morning. He must be hanging up the laundry in the backyard.*

Jumping over the side gate, Roland walked into the backyard where John was hanging clothes on the line. "Hi Dad, how are they hanging?"

Roland spent most of the rest of the week with John before he returned to work the following Monday.

Peter had already returned to work. "The guys enjoyed your company and they wanted to know whether you'd be interested in a trip to Thailand next year."

"I'm not planning to travel overseas anymore," Roland said.

"Never mind," Peter remarked. "You've probably already visited the places we're planning to go."

"So where exactly are you planning to go?" Roland queried.

"We plan to go to Bangkok, Phuket and Kho Samui," Peter advised.

"I've been to Bangkok, but I haven't been to those other places," Roland admitted. "In fact, I haven't been to any of the beaches in Thailand."

"The Thai beaches are supposed to be really good, but I guess it doesn't matter if you're not travelling overseas anymore," Peter said.

Roland reflected for a short time then looked to Peter. "So when exactly are you planning to go?"

THE END ?